It All Falls Down

Books by Denise Grover Swank

Rose Gardner Investigations
Family Jewels
For the Birds
Hell in a Handbasket
Up Shute Creek
Come Rain or Shine
It All Falls Down

Neely Kate Mystery
Trailer Trash
In High Cotton
Dirty Money

Magnolia Steele Mystery
Center Stage
Act Two
Call Back
Curtain Call

The Wedding Pact Series
The Substitute
The Player
The Gambler
The Valentine (short story)

Asheville Brewing
Any Luck at All
Better Luck Next Time
Getting Lucky
Bad Luck Club

Discover Denise's other books at
denisegroverswank.com

It all Falls Down

Rose Gardner Investigations #7

Denise Grover Swank

This book is a work of fiction. References to real people, events, establishments, organizations, or locations are intended only to provide a sense of authenticity, and are used fictitiously. All other characters, and all incidents and dialogue, are drawn from the author's imagination and are not to be construed as real.

Copyright 2021 by Denise Grover Swank

Cover art and design: Bookfly Cover Design
Model photographer: With Magic Photography
Developmental Editor: Angela Polidoro
All rights reserved.

Chapter One

"Your turn," I said, reaching out blindly for Joe in the darkness. My hand connected with his elbow, and I gave him a shove as the baby's wails grew louder.

He tugged the sheet over his head, but I still heard his muffled response. "I got up last time."

Had he? I was so sleep deprived I couldn't be sure, but baby Hope didn't appreciate our debate and cried even louder.

"I'm so tired I think I might be brain dead," I groaned as I rolled out of bed and stumbled across the hall to the nursery. Hope had worked herself up to a decibel level that would have been fitting for a fire alarm. My dog, Muffy, was giving me an anxious glare from her new bed next to the crib. The day we brought Hope home from the hospital Muffy had appointed herself my daughter's guardian, and she rarely left her side.

"It's okay. Momma's here," I said as I reached into the crib and scooped Hope up. "What's wrong? Are you missin' us, sweet girl? You just ate."

Her response was to cry louder. Muffy got out of her bed and gave me a look that begged me to do something.

"Okay. Okay," I said, soothing them both as I cuddled Hope close to my chest. I sat in the rocking chair and lifted my pajama T-shirt so I could nurse her. She latched on immediately and settled down, putting Muffy at ease. My little dog went back to her bed and resumed her guard post.

Hope nursed for less than five minutes before she dozed off. I was so tired, I leaned the back of my head against the high back of the rocking chair as I fought to stay awake. Between the two of us, Joe and I had been up at least five times tonight—thank God she took bottled breast milk from Joe—but this had become a pattern for the past several nights. Nurse for a few minutes, then fall asleep and wake up soon afterward, wanting to nurse again. We'd moved her from the bassinet next to our bed to her crib in the nursery in the hopes it would help—Joe had to wake up at a specific time for work, and it always roused her, plus he occasionally got work calls or alerts in the middle of the night—but it hadn't helped.

My head knew she needed to learn to put herself back to sleep, but my heart couldn't handle letting her cry. Thankfully—or not—Joe felt the same way. There was no question about Muffy's opinion on the matter.

I must have fallen asleep, because the next thing I knew, Joe was leaning in front of me, his hand on my arm.

"Rose, come to bed," he whispered.

Hope was in the crook of my arm, fast asleep.

"She's just gonna wake up again," I said, so tired I was close to tears. "Maybe I should stay in here."

"Bring her to bed with us."

"Back in the bassinet, you mean?"

He cradled my upper arm and gently pulled me out of the rocking chair. "It'll be more of the same if you put her in there. Let her sleep in the bed tonight. It's obvious she wants us. She barely takes any milk from either of us before dozing off. Just bring her to bed so we all can get some sleep."

"But the experts—"

"Screw the experts," he whispered, wrapping an arm around my back and leading me toward the door. "We need sleep, and I refuse to let her cry, thinkin' her parents won't be there when she needs them."

I couldn't argue with that, so I didn't. I felt exactly the same way. Instead, I let him help me into bed. I was scared we would roll over and smother her, so I carefully laid her on the middle of the bed, and Joe put two narrow throw pillows on either side of her.

Muffy hopped up onto the bed, using the bench at the end as a springboard, and curled up into a ball.

Hope started to fuss now that she wasn't pressed against my body, so Joe lay down on his side facing her. He rested his head on his pillow and placed a hand on her chest. "Daddy's here, Hope," he cooed softly. "You're safe."

At his touch, her whimpering stopped.

I lay down on my side, facing him in the semi-darkness. My heart melted into a puddle of goo as I saw him looking down at her. His gaze lifted to mine, and I could barely make out his soft smile. "Get some sleep. I've got this."

And he did. He'd been with me every step of the way over the last six weeks. He'd taken a week of vacation on top of his two-week parental leave so he could help with her nightly feedings and make sure I napped during the day. He'd gone with me to her doctor checkups, helped keep her mountain of laundry maintained, taken turns cooking and cleaning, and insisted I leave the house from time to time so I got a break. I had no idea how I would have managed without him.

He'd been back to work for nearly three weeks, and I'd missed him being around so much that I'd started back to work part-time at the landscaping business I co-owned, bringing Hope with me. My business partner, Bruce Wayne, was trying to stay on top of things, but March through June was our busiest time, which meant we were plenty behind. Especially since I wasn't the only one being pulled in different directions. Neely Kate, my best friend and the third full-time employee in the landscaping business, had just gotten married a matter of weeks ago. Before long, she'd have her own newborn baby—she and Jed were adopting, and their baby's birth mama was over a week overdue. Babies didn't stay in the womb forever, though, so it was a matter of days, not weeks. I figured it was best to try to catch up while we could.

The dark and the quiet lulled me back to sleep, and I was deep under by the time a ringing phone jolted me to wakefulness.

"Simmons," Joe answered quietly in the dark, and I felt the bed shift as he got up and left the room.

Hope whimpered again, so I placed a hand on her stomach. She settled immediately, letting me catch a snippet from Joe's conversation.

"When was he found?" he asked, then said, "Uh-huh."

His voice was stiff, and given the way he'd answered the phone and the dark sky beyond the curtains, I knew this was an official call. Something bad had happened in Fenton County, and Chief Deputy Joe Simmons was being called into action.

My heart sank. Other than the usual burglaries and minor assaults, the crime world had been relatively quiet since my niece and nephew's kidnapping and Hope's birth.

Six weeks ago, a prepper family—the Collards—had kidnapped the kids for the Hardshaw Group, a crime syndicate from Dallas that was trying to get a foothold in Fenton County. Mike had done some work for them, and they'd felt a powerful interest in keeping him quiet. We still weren't sure what role he'd played for them and why, let alone for how long, but he'd wanted access to the county courthouse. Vera Pullman, the woman who'd brought me to my niece and nephew—at gunpoint—had told me as much. Mike had gone into hiding after the kids were taken, but he'd reemerged as soon as I found them and marched himself to the state police to tell his side of the story.

I'd gone into labor while helping the kids escape, and Hope had been born in the woods with the help of Tim Dermot, a former nurse and present crime boss. After her traumatic birth, we'd both been admitted to the hospital to recover, and Ashley and Mikey had gone to stay with Mike's parents. Two days later, they'd disappeared again. According to Mike's parents, they were with him, and he was in protective custody. Joe had tried to get more details from the state police, but they were tight-lipped, only assuring him that Mike and the kids were safe. No one would tell us anything.

There wasn't a thing I could do about it, but I knew my sister was likely rolling over in her grave. She'd wanted me to get custody of her kids, which was an impossible request given their father very much wanted them and—until their kidnapping—had been a great father. She'd left me a flash drive in her will, something that would supposedly change everything, but I still didn't know what was on it, because the sealed manila envelope that held it had been stolen from her attorney's safe.

I might never see Violet's kids again. The thought was even more painful because I wanted Hope to know them—and for them to know her.

Joe slipped back into the room, his phone in his hand.

"What's goin' on?" I asked softly.

His glance dropped to Hope as he walked around the end of the bed. "I have to go to a crime scene," he said, stopping next to me.

"A murder?" I wasn't out of line for asking. Not much else would drag him out before the sun rose.

He grimaced. "They found a body." But he didn't admit it was a murder, which meant they were still keeping it under wraps.

"Do you think it has anything to do with James or the Collards?"

While the sheriff's department had arrested Gerard Collard and two of his sons after a standoff, his son Brox, a man who had helped me on more than one occasion, was missing, and I had a hard time believing he'd been part of their scheme. But Gerard must have a lot of money and/or assets, because he and his sons had posted bail. Then again, I knew he'd been dealing in arms.

And Hope's biological father, James Malcolm, had been supplying them.

Joe hesitated, then said, "It's too soon to tell."

My chest tightened, and I sat up, struggling to draw a breath. "Joe, please be careful."

He sat down on the edge of the bed, wrapping his arms around me and holding me close. "I will," he whispered in my ear. "I have too much to lose."

"But James…"

"Skeeter Malcolm is many things, but stupid isn't one of them. He's not gonna kill me."

"But my vision—"

He pulled back slightly. "Have another."

I sucked in a breath.

"Have another," he said, cupping the side of my face.

I was scared to try again. I'd had the first vision the day Hope was born…and twice since. Both repeat visions had shown me the same thing: Joe's murder by James.

Joe pressed a soft kiss to my lips. "Knowledge is power."

James had told me the same thing what seemed like a lifetime ago. No matter who said it, there was truth in the statement. I nodded. "Okay."

Leaning my face into his palm, I reached up and covered his hand with mine, then closed my eyes. *Does James shoot Joe?*

The vision was immediate. James stood about six feet in front of me, his brown eyes full of hate. "You thought you could take what was mine, Simmons?"

"You could never deserve them, Malcolm," I snarled in Joe's voice.

"Maybe not, but neither do you." Then James pulled the trigger, hitting me square in the chest. A white-hot heat spread through my body, and I fell to the ground.

The vision faded, and I found myself staring into Joe's worried eyes, my heart pounding so hard I was surprised it didn't burst out of my chest. "He's gonna kill you."

He gave me a tight smile. "No. He's not. Did you see where we were this time?"

I shook my head as tears stung my eyes. "No. It was dark, so it must have been night, but I couldn't tell if you were outside."

"I have no intention of forcing a confrontation with Skeeter Malcolm, inside or out. We'll figure out how to stop it, so try not to worry." He gave me a lingering kiss, then stood. "I need to get dressed and head out."

"Okay."

He made quick work of shaving and putting on his uniform. "You gonna head into the office today?"

"Just for a few hours. Bruce Wayne's doin' the best he can, but he's overwhelmed. His specialty is overseeing installments, not makin' designs and meetin' with clients."

His gaze shifted to Hope.

"We'll be careful," I said. "I'll lock the office door."

"Okay…" I could tell he wanted to tell me to stay home, but he bit his tongue and trusted me to use my best judgment. He knew I'd never knowingly put our baby in danger. "Check in with me today."

"And you let me know when you have something you can share."

"Deal."

He leaned over and kissed Hope on the forehead. Then he stood, gave me another kiss, and walked out the door.

Chapter Two

I couldn't go back to sleep after Joe left. I was too worried about him and what he was investigating. So I moved Hope to her bassinet, shocked when she didn't wake up, and coerced Muffy to come downstairs and go out to pee. Muffy shot out the back door quickly enough that no one would have guessed she'd been hit by a car a month and a half earlier. It was as if having a new purpose—guarding Hope—had given her a burst of energy. As soon as she did her business, she ran back inside and back up the stairs to the bedroom.

Deciding to take advantage of the quiet, I grabbed my laptop and headed back upstairs and into the small sunroom off my bedroom, which I'd turned into an office so I could be close to Hope while she slept. Being in there made me happy, because so many of the people I loved had worked together to make it special. Joe had made me a desk from an old wooden door he'd found at an auction, and Neely Kate had found a pretty blue rug that popped against the crisp white walls. Bruce Wayne had brought me an ergonomic office chair, and Maeve, who'd been managing the nursery since Violet's death, had brought in several decor pieces from the shop. We'd hung some curtains and added a chair, and other than the nursery, it had become my favorite part of the house.

The sun began to rise, and the trees behind the barn at the back of my property were suffused with a soft pink glow. It was a beautiful sunrise, but I struggled to enjoy it. My vision of Joe haunted me, and I had a bad feeling the crime scene he was investigating might be the start of something ominous.

I tried to work on a backyard redesign based on the measurements and photos Bruce Wayne had taken during his consultation with the clients, but I was too distracted to focus. I needed to know what was going on, and I knew someone who might be able to tell me.

I got up and peered through the open door to my room to check on Hope. She was still sleeping, and Muffy had resumed her place on the bed. Then I sat in my office chair and tapped out a text to Tim Dermot.

Would you like a home-cooked breakfast and a chance to see your goddaughter?

It was around six, so I didn't expect an answer for at least another hour or so, but he responded right away.

Will there be three at breakfast or four?

He was asking if Joe would be there.

I wasn't surprised. Dermot was a big player in the criminal world, although I was still unsure exactly what he did, and I preferred to keep it that way. Plausible deniability and all. But Dermot had helped me out of more than one difficult situation, including delivering Hope under extremely harrowing conditions. I owed the man my life. Joe recognized that fact, but he was still the chief deputy sheriff, so I tried not to put him in awkward situations.

Two until Hope wakes up, which will likely be sooner than later.

Give me an hour. I'm dealing with a situation.

A situation. Did it involve whatever crime had driven Joe out of the house before dawn?

Okay. See you then.

Work was impossible, so I headed into Hope's room to grab her laundry basket. Although we'd moved the monitor set up to her bedroom, I wasn't concerned about hearing her once she woke up. She had a set of lungs on her that could be heard throughout the house. I carted her laundry downstairs to the basement and put a load in the washing machine. Just as I was heading back upstairs, I paused. Something didn't feel right, but I couldn't pinpoint what it was. It was like something was out of place.

I glanced around the unfinished space, trying to figure out what was making me uneasy, and I realized that some of the boxes along the far wall looked like they'd been moved around. When I'd inherited the house, I'd also inherited boxes of photos and keepsakes that had been stored in the house for decades. Joe and I had been going through them, trying to determine what to keep and what to toss out. It must have been from the last time he was down here.

Feeling more at ease, I headed back upstairs to figure out what to make for breakfast. I got the impression Dermot didn't cook for himself, so I tried to spoil him on the rare occasions when he ate with me. I decided on waffles, bacon, and fried eggs, and of course, a pot of coffee. I'd started the bacon frying, made the waffle fixings, and set the iron to heating when I heard a soft knock at the back door.

I hurried over and opened the door when I saw Dermot on the stoop. "Something smells good," he said as he walked inside.

"It's the bacon. Coffee's in the pot."

Dark semi-circles hung under his eyes, and he gave me a weary smile. "I could drink a gallon."

"I think I'm more rested than you, which is saying something," I said wryly. "Especially since Hope has decided sleep is for losers."

He released a laugh and headed to the coffee pot. "I remember those days." There was plenty of longing in his tone.

Before Hope was born, Dermot had told me that he'd had a wife and children, but he hadn't said what had become of them, and I hadn't asked.

"You want to get to business right away or stick to pleasantries for now?" he asked as he poured coffee into a mug I'd left on the counter.

I spread batter into the waffle iron and closed it. "I say we get the business out of the way, then we can do pleasantries when Hope wakes up."

"Okay," he said, taking a sip of his coffee, then turning around and leaning his butt against the counter. "I take it Joe isn't here is because he's dealing with the murder south of town."

"So it was a murder?" I asked. "He only told me they found a body."

One side of his mouth quirked up. "A bullet to the back of the head is usually due to murder."

A chill ran down my back. "Anyone I might know?"

"It was one of Malcolm's men, but someone he brought on after the two of you split. I doubt you'd know him."

I nodded.

James "Skeeter" Malcolm was the king of the crime world in Fenton County, Arkansas. He had a long criminal career, but he'd bought his crown a year and a half ago with my reluctant help. I'd seen his murder in a vision. It had happened at the auction for the top dog position in the Fenton County underworld, and rather than skip the event, he'd insisted I come with him. Since I was dating the assistant district attorney at the time, I'd needed a disguise—a sexy black dress, heels, and a hat with a thick veil to hide my face.

And so the Lady in Black was born.

I'd donned that hat and veil for several months, using my visions to help James figure out who was trying to sabotage him. Although I was helping James, I wasn't doing it for him; in exchange, he'd agreed to protect my then-boyfriend, Mason (unbeknownst to Mason). But a funny thing happened over those months—James and I had become friends, and we'd stayed friends even after Mason broke up with me, and I (temporarily, it turned out) retired my hat and veil. We continued to be friends for several months, meeting once a week behind the abandoned Sinclair gas station on the west side of town. That was how I discovered something most people didn't realize about the man most of the county feared. James Malcolm—Skeeter to everyone else—had a good heart.

I hadn't meant to give him mine.

Our fling had begun with clandestine meetings that were dangerous and seductive and exciting. We would meet at his secret house in the woods south of town and play a beautiful game of pretend. Because James had made it very clear he had no interest in marriage or a family, and I had always dreamed of having both. We weren't supposed to fall in love, only we had, and it had made everything more complicated.

Then I got pregnant, despite having been careful with birth control, and everything fell apart. He'd given me an ultimatum: him or the baby, but it hadn't been a choice at all. He'd made his decision the moment he uttered those words.

He'd told me that if I aligned myself with the criminals who were joining forces to keep the Hardshaw Group out of the county, we would be enemies.

So that had been his choice too. Because from what I'd learned, Hardshaw had infiltrated other counties like a disease, bringing in hard drugs and harder people. Having Hardshaw in Fenton County wouldn't be good for anyone other than the few people it enriched, and I had no intention of allowing them to destroy my home. *Hope's* home.

"Any idea who did it?"

"If I had to guess, Denny Carmichael." He took a sip of his coffee, then added, "I doubt he did it personally. Probably had a goon do it."

"Do you think Denny is about to make a play for James' position?"

"Hard to say. It could be that Carmichael found Malcolm's guy snoopin' around on his property and decided to teach him a lesson. Could be things are escalating. Carmichael is none too pleased with Malcolm's involvement with Hardshaw. Maybe he's acting on that. Especially in light of the news that Hardshaw kidnapped the kids."

I nodded as I took the last of the bacon out of the skillet and cracked a couple of eggs into the pan. The waffle iron beeped, and I took the first one out, pouring batter for a second.

"You know you can't tell Simmons any of this, right?" he asked in a nonchalant tone, but there was an edge to his voice.

"I know. What we discuss is purely confidential. Always has been. Always will be."

He gave me a tight smile. I suspected he understood how hard it was for me to keep secrets from Joe. My life had been full of secrets, and I wanted to be done with them. But I also knew sharing certain things would cause more harm than good.

"Where do you think we stand with Hardshaw's presence in the county?" I asked.

"Two months ago, I would have said they didn't have much of one," he said with a sigh. "Seemed like they'd retreated with their tail between their legs. But their connection to Sonder Tech makes me think they never fully left. Are they lying low, trying to sneak in under the radar? Or are they cleaning up loose ends before they leave town for good? Given their recent troubles with the FBI in Dallas, I suspect it's the latter. Especially with your brother-in-law turning himself in to the state police."

Sonder Tech had come to town last fall to open up shop in Henryetta, which seemed strange since most legitimate businesses were hanging shutters and leaving town. But we'd figured out they were tied to Hardshaw, even if the manager hadn't realized it.

"Which leaves James vulnerable," I said. "Hence the murder of one of his men."

He shrugged. "Maybe. Maybe not."

"But if you had to lean one way or the other…?" I gave him an expectant look.

"I'd say Malcolm best be watching his back."

My blood turned icy with fear. I'd made my choice, and I didn't regret it, but I still didn't want anything to happen to James.

"Have you heard from him since he reached out before Hope's birth?" Dermot asked.

"No." James had told me he didn't want anything to do with the baby, yet he'd refused to sign papers abdicating his claim to paternity...until recently. On the day of Hope's birth, James had told me he'd sign the papers on two conditions. One, that I stop inquiring about the evidence stolen from Violet's attorney's office, and two, that I spend forty-eight hours with him before I gave birth, with no contact with anyone until our time was up.

That hadn't come to pass, for obvious reasons, and I hadn't heard from him since then. I had no idea what he'd intended, although Dermot had voiced his suspicions. None of them good.

"Did you find out if he'd tried to hire a midwife?" I asked.

He shook his head. "No. But he could have been planning to take you to Louisiana."

"Kidnapping me across state lines?" I asked, dubious.

"It wouldn't have been kidnapping. You would have been gone 'willingly,' but it's all a moot point. It didn't happen. Still, it's worrying that we don't know why he wanted that time with you."

I just nodded, because he was right, and I'd devoted plenty of worrying to it.

The waffle iron alarm went off again, and I pulled it out and put it on a plate. I added eggs and bacon to each, then brought them back to the table with some utensils.

Glancing around, he said, "Where's Muffy? I'm surprised she's not after the bacon."

I released a laugh. "She's abandoned me for the baby. She's her guard dog now."

He grinned at that, an approving grin, then asked, "How's it goin' with the horses? Any trouble with Margi?"

I'd dated Margi's brother, Levi, briefly, what felt like a million years ago. So I'd understood why she'd been standoffish with me in the beginning, only she'd changed her tune on a dime after learning I had an unused horse barn and pasture. Then she'd treated me like her new best friend, not backing off until I agreed to board her rescue horses.

"No," I said. "I rarely see her. She has a teenage girl come out to tend to them in the morning, and a woman in her thirties in the afternoons. Margi only comes out when one of them can't make it."

He gave a nod, then asked me if I'd been working, frowning when I admitted I had been putting in a few hours a day for the past couple of weeks. He told me that Hope's birth had been traumatic and I needed to give myself time to heal, but I waved away his concerns, assuring him I was just fine.

I'd eaten half my breakfast when I heard Hope's cries.

Dermot's eyes lit up, and I released a laugh. "I'll go get her."

Muffy was standing at the edge of my bed, sending me an anxious look when I walked into the room. I scooped Hope up and took her into her room to change her diaper. She stopped crying as she stared up at me.

"Good morning, sweet baby," I cooed. "Are you ready to see Uncle Dermot?"

She released a gurgling sound that I took for a yes.

When I finished, I picked her up and carried her downstairs with Muffy in tow.

"Look who's up," I said as we walked into the kitchen.

Dermot broke into a huge smile, and it struck me that I'd never seen him look so happy.

"Want to hold her?"

"Of course."

He reached for her, then cradled her in his arms.

He'd come to see her twice since her birth. The first time Joe had insisted on being there so he could thank Dermot for saving both of our lives. They'd traded handshakes, Dermot had assured him it had been his pleasure, and Joe had taken off. I knew it was hard for him to have Dermot around. Dermot was a criminal, the very thing he was trying to clean out of the county, and now he felt beholden to him.

I took advantage of Hope being distracted and finished my breakfast, then picked up our empty plates and took them to the sink. Muffy watched Hope vigilantly, but I convinced her to eat her food even though someone other than Mommy or Daddy was holding her charge.

Dermot talked to Hope about the weather, the horses, and her personal guard dog.

He'd held her for nearly ten minutes before she remembered she hadn't had a full meal in many hours and started to wail.

Dermot laughed and stood. "I think this is the part where you take over. Thanks for breakfast and time with Hope."

"Of course, Dermot," I said, getting up too. "You have a standing invitation as far as I'm concerned."

"Thanks," he said again with a soft smile, but there was no denying the pain in his eyes. Once again, I wondered what had happened to his family. But he didn't give me time to ask, even if I'd been inclined. He placed Hope in my arms and walked out the back door.

Chapter Three

It took me an hour and a half to get us packed and ready to leave the house. Although I could work at home, I wanted a change of scenery, for both of us, and the office was more conducive to getting work done. Hope would likely go down for another nap soon, and hopefully, I could draw up a couple of plans.

Downtown Henryetta was busy, with nearly every parking space full, but I managed to get a space close to the coffee shop and its taunting aromas, wrestle the car seat carrier out of the truck, and get me, Muffy, and Hope inside the office with less stress than the last several times I'd tried this.

The office was locked up, which meant Neely Kate was probably out on a consult, so I let us in, then locked us in. I'd already brought Hope here half a dozen times, but I took her out of her car seat and showed her around.

"Here's Aunt Neely Kate's desk. She's out on a job right now, but she's about to get a baby of her own. That means you'll get a new cousin, and your aunt will be off work for a couple of months." Or at least I hoped she planned on coming back. Neely Kate wanted a baby more than anything—with the exception of Jed—and I suspected she wasn't going to waste a minute of it. Which meant she might decide to stay home for the foreseeable future, not that I could blame her. Part of me wanted to hole up with Hope out at the farm, but for one thing, I was half-owner of the business, which meant I couldn't just quit. And two, if I were honest, I was bored and lonely out there with only a newborn who spent most of her time pooping and crying and sleeping. I loved being Hope's mother more than anything in the world, but the business was part of me too, and I wanted to hold on to it.

I'd taken her to the back of the office, telling her that Mommy had once locked herself in the bathroom to hide from bad guys, when I heard a knock on the front door. Muffy, who was at my feet, let out a low growl. I jumped, startling Hope, who released a tiny whimper. Bouncing her in my arms, I carefully crept out of the shadows and peeked at the door to see who was knocking, relieved when I saw it was Mason.

He was cupping the side of his face and peering through the glass, and I lifted a hand in acknowledgment as I made my way to the door. When I unlocked and opened it, Muffy raced to the doorframe and jumped up, planting her front paws on Mason's legs.

"Mason. This is a surprise."

"I hope I'm not intruding," he said, his gaze firmly on my daughter, who was staring up at him with a blank expression. He reached down and picked up Muffy, stroking the back of her head. "I saw your truck parked in front of the coffee shop and thought I'd drop by for a quick chat if you have time."

A quick chat meant his visit likely had another purpose than to just say hello. Was he here to talk to me about the murder Joe was currently working?

"Yes," I said after a second-long delay. I took a step back. "Of course. Sorry. You're dealing with a woman with an extreme case of sleep deprivation."

He gave a forced chuckle as he walked into the office then set Muffy onto the floor. I shut the door behind him and locked it.

He watched my movements and nodded. "You're playing it safe. That's good."

"Is something goin' on that I should know about?" I asked with my heart in my throat.

"Actually," he said, shuffling his feet and sticking a hand in his pocket before locking gazes with me. "I was hoping *you* could tell *me*."

"Is this about the case Joe is workin' south of town?"

"Yes. Do you know anything?"

"Seems like Joe would be a better source of information," I said with my free hand on my hip.

"One would think," he said, his gaze back on Hope, a soft smile on his lips. "But over the past year, I've found you often know more than both of us combined."

I could have taken offense that he was here for information, but he and I had reached a kind of truce. He'd accepted my involvement in the criminal world, such as it was, and he'd shared useful information on a couple of occasions.

"Would you like to hold her?" I asked.

His eyes widened in surprise. "Oh…"

"She's not as fragile as she looks," I said, leading him to the client table. "Why don't you have a seat and take her? It'll give me a chance to get my computer booted up."

"Okay…" He headed over to the table and took a seat, then looked up at me expectantly.

"Just keep her head up a little," I said as I grabbed a small towel out of her diaper bag. "It's been a bit since she last ate, but she's prone to spitting up. I don't want you getting it on your shirt."

He smiled. "I think I can handle a little spit-up."

"Famous last words," I said, grinning as I placed her in his crooked arm. Muffy, realizing someone else was holding her charge, plopped at Mason's feet.

Mason looked nervous as he took her, shifting his arm up so her head was higher. It felt a little strange seeing them together, if only because I'd wondered, before going to that auction with James, whether I might be pregnant with Mason's baby. If everything had unfolded differently, she might have been our baby. The look in his eyes said he knew it.

"She's so light," he commented.

"She weighed nearly ten pounds at her last checkup."

He shifted her again, a brief flash of fear in his eyes as he did so. "She's absolutely beautiful, Rose."

"I think so," I said with pride in my voice. "Some people would think I'm biased, but I know beautiful when I see it."

He laughed. "In this instance, I have to agree with you." He lifted his gaze to me. "I hear you had a rough delivery."

"Understatement of the century," I said as I sat in the chair in front of my desk and reached behind my computer to turn it on.

"I also heard that Tim Dermot delivered her."

I paused, wondering what he was fishing for, then said, "You heard correctly."

"Did he help you find the kids?"

"I'm sure you read the police report, and I can assure you it was an accurate portrayal of what happened."

"How did Dermot know you were there?" When I hesitated, he added, "What we discuss here this morning is between the two of us."

Which meant he was hoping for an exchange of information, not just to ask me questions. "Vera Pullman reached out to me, telling me she knew where to find the kids, but she'd only show me if I came alone. Joe was busy investigatin' the murders of Calista and her boyfriend, and I didn't want to put Jed in a bad situation, so I contacted Dermot."

"You have other friends in the sheriff's department," he said in a neutral tone. "You could have called them."

"I have fewer than you might think," I said, "but in this case, I didn't necessarily want to follow the rules." I gave him a challenging look.

"You risked Hope's life, Rose," he said in a pleading tone. "You both could have died, and not just because you delivered her in the woods, breech."

He wasn't saying anything I hadn't already thought a thousand times over. If Dermot hadn't been there, I would have been shot by Carey Collard before I even delivered, and Ashley and Mikey might have been killed too.

"Vera came to the nursery a couple of months before," I said, "and she seemed like she was in trouble. She knew I was the Lady in Black, but she took off before she could tell me what she needed. I figured she wanted to meet me alone because she was scared someone would see her talking to me. I had absolutely no idea she was dangerous. I thought I was meeting a scared woman who needed help and could tell me where to find my niece and nephew."

He glanced down at Hope, who was staring up at him, but her eyelids were drooping, which suggested that nap was coming soon after all.

"I'm not here to cast judgment," he said, keeping his gaze on my baby's face. "I'm here because of the murdered man found early this morning."

"I don't know anything about that," I said, turning my chair to face him. "Joe wouldn't even tell me it was a murder. Only that they'd found a body."

Technically true, even if Dermot had told me more.

"I can tell you it was definitely murder. He was shot at close range in the back of the head."

I shuddered, and I noticed that Mason held Hope a little tighter.

"I swear to you, Mason, the first I heard of it was this morning, when Joe told me he was headed to a crime scene."

"You're misunderstanding my intentions," he said, lifting his gaze. "I'm not here to ask you questions. I'm here to give you some information."

My brow shot up. "Oh."

He hesitated, then said, "The man found murdered was Rufus Wilson. We know he was working for Malcolm. He moved here from Oklahoma this past summer, and we're fairly certain he had ties to Hardshaw."

I swallowed hard. Dermot hadn't known that part, although it made sense given the man's connection to James.

"Rufus had an interesting skill set." Mason held my gaze. "Four years ago, he was arrested for breaking into a safe in Oklahoma."

I gasped. "Do you think he broke into the safe at Violet's attorney's office?"

"Honestly? Yeah, I do."

My heart constricted. "Does Joe know about this?"

"I can't say with certainty, but I wouldn't be surprised if he does. Malcolm was the obvious suspect in the break-in, and Rufus' arrival in Fenton County fits the timeline."

Joe knew how much I wanted to find the flash drive. Hurt bubbled up at the thought that he'd learned something this important and kept it from me, which was irrational given it had only been a few hours, but I told myself that Joe was bound by the law to keep from sharing confidential police matters. Mason was too, but for some reason, the man whose entire life had been defined by the rules was breaking them—again—with me.

"Did Denny Carmichael kill Rufus Wilson?"

His eyes narrowed. "What makes you ask that?"

"Carmichael threatened the manager at Sonder Tech right around the time the kids were kidnapped, but Stewart swore he didn't know anything about Hardshaw."

He nodded. "I spoke to Stewart Adams and believed his story. I think poisoning the azalea bushes was a warning to Calista Johnson and her boyfriend, Patrick Nestle, to leave town. I'm 99.9% sure Denny Carmichael killed them—or had his henchmen do it—I just can't prove it, and neither can Joe. So Carmichael's walking around a free man, and he's still killing people, as evidenced by the body found this morning."

I'd gone by Sonder Tech to investigate the poisoned plants and had one of the most memorable—and embarrassing—visions ever. It had indicated Calista and her boyfriend were connected to Hardshaw in some way, and sure enough, she and her boyfriend turned up dead a day later. "Carmichael hates Hardshaw, and he knows James Malcolm is working with them. It stands to reason he would kill Rufus Wilson. Not only was the guy part of Hardshaw, but he also worked for James."

He studied me for a moment, then nodded. "I suspect you're right."

A new thought hit me. "Do you think Carmichael killed him because he wants what was in the safe?"

He cocked his head. "How many people knew what was in that safe?" Mason knew Violet's attorney's safe had been robbed, but we'd tried to keep the details quiet.

I shook my head. "I don't know. I haven't heard much discussion about it in the criminal world, but I've always suspected James stole the flash drive. After Mike went to the state police, I realized Violet must have dug up dirt on Hardshaw through him. James found out and took it. The real question is how he knew."

"That part probably isn't important. What *is* important is Rufus' girlfriend, Roberta Hanover."

"Why? Do you think Carmichael's goin' after her next?"

"I don't know, but I wouldn't be surprised, especially if Denny was after something Rufus had. I had a discussion with her last fall after she was arrested for shoplifting. I used the opportunity to question her about her boyfriend. She never shared anything, but I got the impression that he didn't keep her in the dark as much as she would have liked me to believe." His gaze held mine. "If her boyfriend broke into that safe, I wouldn't be surprised if she knows a thing or two about it."

I took a moment to absorb that, my gaze falling to Hope, who was snuggled up against Mason like she'd known him all her life. I ripped my gaze away from her, forcing my mind back to our discussion. "So if

Carmichael killed Rufus Wilson because of the safe, you think he might go after her next?"

"Honestly, I don't know. For all I know, Carmichael killed Wilson just because he was breathing. Or maybe he did it just to push Malcolm's buttons. There's been a war brewing between them for some time now. Maybe Carmichael decided it was finally time to set it in motion."

I pushed out a breath. I knew about the brewing war. I'd had visions of it, and in them, I'd stood on Denny Carmichael's side. I still couldn't believe that would ever happen. Denny and I might agree about Hardshaw, but it was the only thing we did agree on. I wanted nothing to do with his turf war with James…and yet Carmichael had saved my life the previous August and told me I owed him a favor. I'd always suspected he'd call it in when I least wanted him to.

"Do you think Roberta's in trouble?" I asked quietly. "Gut reaction."

"Yeah," he said. "I do."

My stomach twisted. "Why are you telling me this?"

"Because I think she might be the only chance you have of finding out what was in that safe. I'm definitely not suggesting you go talk to her in person." He paused and seemed to choose his words carefully. "But I suspect you might know people who could intervene on your behalf."

Dermot. Jed. Either one of them would help. Dermot seemed the better choice, but what if this was a trap? The last time I'd asked him to step in and help me, he'd been shot. His men attacked and killed. I wouldn't walk him into a different kind of ambush. "If you think she's in trouble, why don't you or Joe offer her protection?"

"Because she's not going to talk to the authorities. I doubt she trusts anyone at this point, and likely with just cause. We wouldn't get anything out of it."

My back stiffened. "So you'll only protect her if you get something out of it."

"We have a budget, Rose," he said with an exhausted sigh, "and it's not an option. Joe and I have to justify every expense, and we can't be doling out money to protect a woman who not only refuses to help us, but doesn't want our intervention in the first place."

"Yeah," I said, glancing down at my lap. "I guess you're right."

"I understand your frustration, trust me. That's part of the reason I'm here. I'm bound by rules and laws, but you…"

"Are not."

"Actually," he said, "you are. Which means you'll need to be *very* careful. I'm sure there will be eyes on her, and it won't just be criminals watching, if you understand my meaning."

Roberta Hanover was under surveillance. They might not be protecting her, but they were watching to see what she did next.

"Is her phone tapped?"

"Not by the county or state."

"I notice you left out federal and local."

"Local is a non-issue," he scoffed.

"How likely is federal?"

"If there was any surveillance, it was probably on his phone, not hers. But there might be something in their house. So if someone wanted to call her, they'd be wise to wait until she's not home."

"Any idea if she has a job?"

"She works at the convenience store at Maple and Hugo Drive. The Stop-N-Go. I hear she works the day shift."

He gave me a sad smile as he said it—a look I recognized all too well. He hated that he was feeding me information that would drag me back into this mess, but here he was, doing it anyway.

"Do you expect me to report back what I find?"

"Only if you think it's necessary," he said softly, lowering his gaze to my now-sleeping daughter.

That surprised me, and I wondered if he was being truthful, but Mason had never lied to me before. I couldn't see him starting now.

Nor did I believe he was trying to ambush me. Especially since I had Hope.

"If I get the opportunity to talk to Ms. Hanover, or get someone else to do it in my proxy, I'll tell you if I learn anything you really need to know."

His gaze lifted. "Thank you." He drew in a breath, then said, "I dropped by to see your daughter. We never discussed state or county business."

I nodded, and said emphatically, "Of course."

"You can't share this with anyone."

Which included Joe. That gave me pause, but if this helped me find that flash drive—or what was on it—didn't I need to take the opportunity? Joe had his own secrets from the sheriff's department. I had Lady in Black secrets. I could hang this situation under *her* hat, even if I'd vowed I was done with secrets. "I understand."

He nodded, then slowly got to his feet. "I need to be getting back to the courthouse. Thanks for letting me see Hope."

"Of course. I've always hoped we could be friends. Despite everything." I stood to take Hope, smiling as I looked down at her sleeping face. "Looks like you have the magic touch. Let's put her in the cradle."

Mason gently laid her down in the bed in the back of the office. Hope stirred slightly and fell back asleep, releasing a contented sigh. It was a peaceful moment, and Mason gave me a look of longing. I didn't think it was for me so much as for the life we'd planned once upon a time.

"You should date," I said softly. "Fall in love. Have babies of your own. You deserve all of that, Mason. You deserve to be happy."

He slowly shook his head.

I knew he was haunted by demons. By his sister's murder. By nearly beating to death the man who'd killed her. By my transformation into the Lady in Black. In spite of everything that had passed between us and the hurt we'd caused each other, I hoped he'd find a way to release all of it. I hoped he'd find a way to be happy too.

He headed for the door, then turned back to me. "Be careful, Rose. You have a whole lot more at stake now."

Which was the very reason I had to act on what he'd told me.

Hope would never be safe as long as there was a monster on the loose.

Chapter Four

As soon as I locked the door behind Mason, I sat down at my desk and tried to figure out how to best handle the situation. Would it freak her out if Jed or Dermot intercepted her? I suspected it would, especially if she thought there were men out to kill or abduct her. We needed to take a softer approach.

A voice in my head reminded me that I'd tried the softer approach with Vera, and it had badly misfired, but I'd met Vera in a secluded place. If I talked to Roberta in public, it should be safe. Besides, if she were dangerous, I doubted Mason would have told me about her in the first place. Sure, he'd suggested I use a proxy to contact her, but he knew me well enough to anticipate I might go myself.

Maybe I was making excuses for myself, but I hadn't heard anything about my niece and nephew in weeks. It felt like they were being pulled farther out of reach with every passing day, and I was feeling plenty desperate.

The bell on the door jingled, and I looked up to see Neely Kate walking in. She was wearing jean shorts, a bedazzled RBW Landscaping T-shirt, and a sparkly headband. A large diamond ring glittered on her left ring finger. Although the engagement ring had been there for a while now, I often caught her glancing at it with a big smile on her face. She and Jed were still very much in the honeymoon stage.

"Where's my favorite girl?" she demanded as she closed the door behind her, her face beaming with excitement.

"I'd love to think you're talkin' about me," I said with a cheesy grin, "but we both know I've been usurped. She's sleeping in the back, but you're first in line to hold her when she wakes up."

"I better be. I haven't seen her in two days." She glanced toward the door. "Did I see Mason leaving when I pulled up?"

"He saw my truck out front and dropped in to see Hope."

Neely Kate sat down at her desk. "And how'd that go?"

"Better than I would have expected." I took a deep breath. "Did you hear about the murder south of town?"

Her smile fell. "No."

"I talked to Dermot this morning. I found out it was one of James' men—Rufus Wilson." I leaned forward. "Neely Kate, he had experience opening safes, and he came to town around the time Violet died."

"Dermot told you all that?" she asked incredulously.

I made a face. "The source of my information isn't important. What's important is his girlfriend might actually know what was in the safe."

Her eyes widened. "Do you know who she is?"

"Her name's Roberta Hanover, and she works at the Stop-N-Go on Maple and Hugo."

She studied me for a moment. "Dermot didn't tell you any of that."

My breath caught in my throat. "Why would you say that?"

"Because Mason just came strolling out of here, and I doubt he just came by to see Hope. *He* told you all of that."

My blood ran cold. "Neely Kate, you can't tell anyone."

"I won't."

"I meant it, not anyone," I said emphatically. "Not even Jed."

She rolled her chair across the wooden floor toward me and took both of my hands in hers. "Rose, Mason's the one who told me that

Ronnie was already married when he stood at the altar at our wedding, and it was all just a sham. He could have gotten fired for that, but he did it to save me more heartache. I'd never tell anyone that you got information from him. Your secret is safe with me."

I nodded as relief washed through me. "Thank you."

"My next question," she said as she rolled her chair back a couple of feet, "is what you plan to do about it."

"If Denny Carmichael killed Rufus Wilson because of the safe, he might be after Roberta next. I considered asking Jed or Dermot to go talk to her, but I don't think she'd talk to a man, especially not one connected to the underworld. It'll go better if I talk to her, or you and me if you decide to come."

Neely Kate held up her hands. "Whoa. Denny Carmichael killed him?"

I told her what Mason and I had discussed, and she sat back in her chair, her gaze on the wall behind me as she took it all in.

"Do you really think it's safe for you to talk to her if Carmichael's involved?"

"I don't know,' I said, my stomach balling with anxiety. "But I feel like I have to try. I owe it to Violet. I owe it to her kids."

They were the last living part of her in this world. It wasn't that I wanted to take them from Mike—I just wanted to be allowed to be part of their lives.

Neely Kate was quiet for a moment, her lips pressed together, then she lifted her gaze to mine. "Okay. I think you're right. I'm in."

"You don't have to do this with me, Neely Kate," I insisted. "This is my problem, not yours."

A blaze of anger filled her eyes. "Your problems are my problems, and my problems are yours."

She was still angry I'd left her out of the loop when I went to talk to Vera. "For the millionth time, I'm sorry."

But I wasn't. Vera had shot everyone with me. What if she'd killed Neely Kate? I never would have forgiven myself.

She pressed her lips more tightly together. "Whatever. Don't you dare leave me out of this."

"But your adoption—" If either of them was caught doing something illegal, or even close, it might put a halt to the process. I could never forgive myself if that happened.

"You let me worry about that. Besides, you're an actual mother to a baby. You need to be way more careful than me."

"Neely Kate, you're every bit as much of a momma as I am," I insisted. "You're just waiting for your little girl to be born."

"You're right," she said evenly. "I am a momma to three babies up in heaven, but I'm starting to think I'll never be a mother again."

She'd never held those three babies. She'd never even made it past her second trimester with the last two before she'd miscarried. She wanted to be a mother so badly, but I could see she was starting to lose faith in the process. Even though the birth momma of her baby had made it very clear she intended to go through with the adoption, Neely Kate had seemed to take the late delivery as a sign. She didn't feel comfortable letting herself believe it would happen.

"It's gonna happen, Neely Kate," I said quietly. "I just don't want to be the reason motherhood gets snatched from you."

"How dangerous will it be for us to just to talk to a woman while paying for gas at the Stop-N-Go?" Neely Kate shrugged, and a sly grin cracked her mouth. "Of course, with us, everything is dangerous."

I lifted my shoulder in a half-hearted shrug. "True…"

"We'll share the danger," she said, her chin held high. "Because that's what best friends do." She glanced back at the cradle. "But as much as it pains me to say so, I don't think Hope should be comin' along."

She had a point. "Maybe we should drop her off with Maeve," I said.

"I think that's a great idea, and Maeve will be excited to spend time with her. So what's our plan?"

"Go by the convenience store and pay for gas, just like you said. When I'm payin', I'll try to convince her that the Lady in Black is offering her protection."

Neely Kate's eyes widened. "You're offering her protection? What exactly do you plan to do?"

I pushed out a sigh, because truth be told, I hadn't planned on it until that very moment. But if Roberta needed protection, I didn't plan on leaving her high and dry. And I definitely didn't want her to get hurt on account of talking to us. That had happened before, and the guilt still weighed on my soul.

"One problem at a time, Neely Kate. If she agrees, we'll figure out where to stash her."

"She can't stay with you," she said. "Not with Joe there."

I nodded. "Agreed."

"She can stay with us," she said, giving me a haughty glare that challenged me to disagree.

"What if the social worker shows up?" I said. "You know they can make impromptu, drop-in visits."

"Then Roberta can stay upstairs, out of sight." She released a short laugh. "They don't snoop in every closet. The social worker would just stick to the bottom floor, ask a few questions, and leave."

Roberta might be more willing to stay with them because Jed had willingly left James' employment. Then again, the connection might make her too uncomfortable.

"We'll table that for now," I said. "We don't know anything about her yet. I don't know if she came here from Oklahoma with Rufus, or if he picked her up at James' pool hall."

The color drained from Neely Kate's face at the mention of Oklahoma. "Where in Oklahoma?"

Neely Kate had lived in Ardmore with her mother, who'd dumped her on her grandmother's doorstep when she turned twelve, and she'd gone back looking for her after graduating high school in Fenton

County. The only thing she'd found was a life of pain and misery. It was no wonder the mere mention of the state could throw her for a loop.

"I don't know," I said, "but Mason thinks Rufus had ties to Hardshaw before he came here."

She nodded. "Okay. I guess the best way to find out is to talk to her."

"You sure?"

"Of course I'm sure. I'm tired of everyone treatin' me like a baby."

Leave it to Neely Kate to think we were spoiling her after all she'd been through. Not only was the adoption running behind schedule, but her grandmother had suffered a heart attack. Granny Rivers had still been in the hospital, recovering from surgery, at the time of her wedding. I'd seen a vision of Neely Kate's wedding before the fact, so I'd known she and Jed were sad without knowing why. They'd been mourning her grandmother's absence, thank goodness, not anything more permanent.

"We love you, Neely Kate," I insisted. "But everyone needs a shoulder to lean on. You've been through a lot."

"Granny's gonna be fine," she said, then added, "Well, as long as she cuts back on the hot wings, and yeah, I was sad she couldn't make it to the wedding, but at least she got to watch it on her iPad."

Neely Kate had wanted her granny, who'd practically raised her, to walk her down the aisle, but of course that had been out of the question. She and Jed had considered postponing the wedding, especially since it had been put together on such short notice, but Granny Rivers had had a conniption at the very suggestion.

"If two people were ever destined to be together, it's you and that fine man," she'd told Neely Kate, "so get that fool idea about canceling out of your head."

So Witt, who'd always been more of a brother than a cousin, had done it instead. I knew Joe would have been happy to walk her down the aisle, but they'd only just discovered they were half-siblings a little over a year ago. Neely Kate and Witt had history, and lots of it, something that had been made abundantly clear in his wedding toast. He'd had a few too many beers and then launched into a story about finding Neely Kate skinny dipping in the cow pond with his best friend—now *ex*-best friend—back in high school. Jed had needed to hold Neely Kate back from snatching him bald.

"I'm fine," Neely Kate insisted with more force. "So don't you go getting any crazy ideas about leaving me out of this."

I started to respond when Hope released a frustrated grunt.

Neely Kate's eyes lit up. "My niece is waking up."

I lifted a brow. "That could have been a pooping grunt."

She shrugged. "Gotta take the good with the bad."

"Yeah," I said, feeling a wash of misgivings.

I was terrified I was about to drop us into a whole mess of bad.

Neely Kate changed what was indeed a blowout diaper before handing Hope to me so she could nurse.

"You're not going to call Jed and let him know what we're about to do?" I asked once Hope was latched on.

"No," she said gravely. "In this instance, the fewer people who know, the better."

Sadly, I had to agree.

When I finished nursing, I handed Hope to Neely Kate. My best friend's face lit up, and I once again questioned why God had blessed me with a beautiful baby girl, an unexpected surprise, while Neely Kate had been cursed with infertility. It wasn't fair, but many things in life weren't. Like Roberta being hung out to dry because her boyfriend had been mixed up with something.

"It occurs to me," I said, hating to break up Neely Kate's bonding time, but Roberta's life could be in danger, "there's a strong likelihood that Roberta won't be at work today. Her boyfriend was just murdered. She probably either called in or left after she found out."

"*If* she knows," Neely Kate said, staring at my daughter in a way that made my heart gush. "And if she's not there, whoever is may be able to help us find her."

Hope had a firm grasp on her finger as she stared back, her mouth twitching before lifting into a smile.

"She's smiling!" Neely Kate said, excitement in her voice, then swung her gaze to me. "She's actually smiling!"

"She just started doing that yesterday," I said. "I teased Joe it was gas, but he swore he could tell the difference."

"She's gonna be a daddy's girl through and through," Neely Kate said with wonder in her voice. "How would you feel about that?"

I gave her a reassuring smile. "I'd be fine with it. No, *better* than fine. I'm ecstatic. All I've ever wanted is to have a family with a man who'll love our children the way I always wanted to be loved as a child. And Joe feels the same way. Our babies will never doubt we love them. Ever."

Her eyes widened. "Babies. Plural?"

"Oh!" I lifted my hands in surrender. "No, no, no, no. I'm not pregnant."

She laughed. "I didn't think you were. It's only been six weeks. You haven't gotten the all-clear for sex. I'm sure it's perfectly fine, but I know Joe's been waiting until the doctor gives you her stamp of approval." Her eyes filled with mischief. "When is that appointment, by the way?"

My cheeks grew hot. "The day after tomorrow."

She got to her feet, holding Hope on her shoulder while she continued to pat her back. "We need to get this Roberta situation cleared up so you two can have a romantic evening to consummate your relationship. In fact," she said, getting excited, "I think Jed and I should keep Hope overnight so you two can be uninterrupted."

I laughed. "And what if your baby girl is home by then? The two of them will be up all hours, especially since Hope has given up sleeping for longer than a couple of hours at a time. The last few nights have been torture."

"Not my sweet baby niece," Neely Kate said as she carried her to the car seat. "She's an angel."

Hope belched, and pasty white spit-up covered Neely Kate's shoulder.

I couldn't help laughing. "Not so much an angel now."

"Hush your mouth," Neely Kate teased. "She's perfect." She set her in the seat, and I moved over to fasten all the straps while Neely Kate went to the bathroom to clean her shirt.

"But if you're suggestin' there will be more babies..." Neely Kate said through the open door as she turned the water on. "That means you see something more permanent with Joe."

I knew Neely Kate worried that I was settling for Joe simply because he'd asked to be Hope's father, but I knew from the bottom of my heart that this was what I wanted. Every day, Joe proved that I'd made the right decision. Every day, I fell more in love with him. "I want forever with Joe."

But I wasn't sure she heard me, because she walked out of the bathroom with a damp spot on her shoulder and her phone clutched in her hand. Her face was several shades paler than when she'd walked into the restroom.

Muffy jumped to her feet and moved closer to Hope.

"Neely Kate, honey," I said, trying not to panic. I had no idea what had just happened, but whatever it was had clearly shaken her to the core. "What is it? Is your granny okay?"

She held up her phone, and I saw Kate's name at the top of a page of texts. At the bottom, Kate had sent: *Don't you worry, sister dearest. I'll make sure you're happy. No matter what it takes.*

I glanced up at Neely Kate in horror.

And just like that, we had two problems.

Chapter Five

"Were all of those from today?" I asked, trying not to panic now even though this was definitely panic worthy. "We need to call Jed."

"No," she said, still pale but looking less shell-shocked. "She only sent that last one, and we're not telling Jed yet. Once he knows, he'll get all super protective and keep me under his thumb. We have work to do."

"Neely Kate…"

"No." Her response was firm.

It was her decision, ultimately, but I still felt responsible.

"Wipe that guilty look off your face," she said. "This has nothing to do with you."

"I just really think you should tell Jed."

"And I will tell him. *After* we find Roberta. Besides, what's he going to do? We have no idea what Kate's up to this time."

"Then let's not waste any time finding Roberta," I said, and picked up the car seat. "Come on, Muff. You and Hope get to see Nana Maeve."

Neely Kate locked up the office and followed me to the truck. I got Hope's car seat clicked in, and Muffy hopped up and sat on the bench seat next to Hope.

"Muffy really has become her guard dog, hasn't she?" Neely Kate asked as I started the truck.

"You have no idea."

We rode to the nursery in silence. I wanted to talk about Kate, to offer Neely Kate some reassurance that her sister wouldn't do anything *too* crazy, but the thing was, Kate was clinically insane. Anything was possible with her.

There were several cars in the nursery's parking lot, and a wave of guilt swept through me. The last thing Maeve needed right now was to babysit Hope, but I didn't dare take her with us. It would hopefully be an hour, max.

I got Hope's seat out of the backseat and slung the diaper bag over my shoulder. Muffy hopped out and followed. Neely Kate stayed outside, looking over the inventory of plants. In her will, Violet had left my best friend a third of the ownership of the nursery (the other two-thirds belonged to Joe and me). I knew that Neely Kate would love to split her time between the nursery and the landscaping company, but my maternity leave had forced her to cover my absence.

Maeve was ringing up a customer when we walked in. Her face lit up as soon as she saw us. She handed the customer her receipt, then hurried around the counter to greet us.

"There's my sweet baby." She bent over the car seat and smiled. "Did you come to see Nana Maeve?"

"She'd like to stay with you for a bit," I said hesitantly. "But I'm worried you're too busy to deal with her."

"Nonsense. I'm never too busy for my favorite girl." She glanced up at me. "I thought your doctor's appointment was the day after tomorrow."

"It is, but Neely Kate and I have an errand to run. It might be better if Hope and Muffy don't tag along."

Maeve stilled, then stood upright. "Does this have anything to do with the man they found murdered this morning?"

"I didn't know the word had gotten out."

She held my gaze. "I'll take that as a yes." She took a deep breath, still studying me. "You have so much more to think about now, Rose. Are you sure you want to do this?"

This was the first time she'd ever lectured me about my extracurricular activities. In fact, a year ago, she'd gone as far as to condone them. But she'd also had a feeling that what I was doing would save Mason.

"Maeve, I don't take this lightly."

"But you could have died going after Ashley and Mikey. What if something happens to you this time? What about Hope?"

"I'm doin' this for Violet," I said quietly. I understood her concerns. Shoot, I shared them, but I still needed to go through with this. I couldn't very well tell her that her son was the one who'd sent me on this task. "And I'm doin' it for Hope too. We're not gettin' mixed up in anythin' dangerous. We just need to talk to a woman. Then I'll come back and collect Hope and Muffy, and they'll be out of your hair."

Hurt filled her eyes. "You know this isn't about me being inconvenienced."

"I know, Maeve," I said with a weary sigh. "And I'm sorry I can't tell you more, but trust me when I say I wouldn't willingly walk into danger."

She studied me for a moment, then nodded. "I do."

Holding the car seat with one hand, I wrapped my free arm around her back. "Thank you."

"Rose," she said softly, "I love you like you're my own flesh and blood daughter."

Tears burning in my eyes, I said, "I'm just grateful you chose to keep me in your life."

I knew how rare that was. After a breakup, you usually lost not only the other person, but also their family and friends. Maeve, though…she'd always been there for me. I knew she'd be there for Hope too.

Her eyes turned glassy, and her chin wobbled. "Go. Run your errand. Hope can help me run the cash register."

I smiled a little, then launched into an account of Hope's nap and eating schedule, finishing with, "And in case I'm not back before she gets hungry, there's a bottle and a small package of formula in the bag. She's not crazy about it, but she'll take it if she's hungry enough."

"We'll be fine," she said. "You go. And if I get busy and she gets fussy, I'll just bring out her swing."

I'd left one at both the nursery and the landscaping office.

"Okay." I handed the car seat to Maeve, surprised by how reluctant I was to let her go. Of course, I'd rarely left her with anyone other than Joe. I trusted Maeve, though, and knew Hope would be safe.

I leaned over the seat, soaking in the sight of my daughter's face. She stared up at me, and her mouth lifted into a smile that made her eyes sparkle.

"She's smiling!" Maeve exclaimed.

"I love you, Hope," I whispered, my voice tight. "I'll do everything in my power to protect you." I placed a lingering kiss on her forehead, then stood upright. "Thank you, Maeve."

Worry covered her face, and I was sure she heard what I'd said to my daughter, but I didn't have time to offer her reassurances. I needed to find Roberta and put all of this to rest.

I turned around and left without saying goodbye. Neely Kate saw me come out and joined me in the truck.

"You okay?" she asked.

"No," I said. "But I will be when we find Roberta."

"Just keep in mind that she might not know anything," Neely Kate said. "Or she might just refuse to talk to us."

I started to back out of the parking space. "I guess there's only one way to find out."

The Stop-N-Go had several cars at the gas pumps and a few more in the parking spaces. I pulled up to a pump and turned off the engine.

"I'll head inside and get a drink," Neely Kate said. "Get the lay of the land. You come in when you're finished."

We both got out, and as I pumped the gas, I watched Neely Kate head toward the entrance. It looked like a normal weekday morning at any convenience store, although that meant nothing.

Once the tank was full, I grabbed my purse and headed inside. Neely Kate was by the fountain drink station, filling a cup with ice.

"Find anything?" I asked.

She shot me a dazed look. "She's here."

"Who?" I whisper-shouted. "Roberta?" I resisted the urge to turn around and look.

She nodded as she moved the cup to the Coke dispenser and began filling it. "She's working the register."

I took a breath. "Do you think she knows?" But how could she not? Maeve had heard about a murder, which suggested it was public news, or becoming that way, and based on what Mason had said, Roberta and Rufus had been serious about each other.

"Yeah. Her eyes are puffy and bloodshot, and her nose is red as though she's been crying."

"Why on earth is she still here?" I asked. "Why didn't she go home?"

Neely Kate shot me a dark look. "Maybe her boss wouldn't let her go, and she needs the job. If she's workin' here, she's not makin' much, and who knows how much her boyfriend was bringin' in. Even if he was makin' good money, that income source is gone, so now she needs this job more than ever."

Her outrage felt a bit too personal, but now didn't seem like the best time to bring it up.

"Okay," I said slowly. "You make some very good points. And," I added, so I didn't look totally judgmental, "maybe she thinks there's nothing she can do. Maybe she'd rather keep busy than go home and stare at his spot on the bed."

Neely Kate's gaze held mine. "Or maybe she's here because it's a public place and safer than being alone at home."

She had a point there.

"Okay," Neely Kate said, sliding over to the counter and grabbing a lid. "There's no one at the counter. Let's head over."

She plucked a straw out of the holder and marched up to the counter, leaving me to follow.

There was only one woman at the counter. She looked young—in her early twenties—and had short dark hair pulled back into a stubby ponytail at the base of her neck. Her blue polo shirt had a Stop-N-Go logo on the chest, right below a name tag that said, *Bobby*.

Neely Kate put her drink on the counter. "When did y'all restart the bottomless drink promotion?"

"It started last week," Bobby said, punching buttons on her cash register. She didn't glance up as she slapped a sticker on the cup and said, "That sticker lets you get refills for the rest of the day. That'll be a dollar and ten cents."

Neely Kate put a couple of dollar bills on the counter and slid them over, then glanced back at me.

"Bobby," I said softly. "You don't know me, but I heard about Rufus, and I wanted to extend my sympathies."

Her head jerked up. Fear covered her face, but anger drove it out. "How do you know about Rufus?"

I held my hands up in surrender. "I'm not here to hurt you, Bobby, but I'm worried someone else will."

"No shit," she muttered as two streams of tears slid down her cheeks. "I know they're comin' for me."

"Who?" Neely Kate asked. "Denny Carmichael?"

"He's not the only one," she said, her body starting to shake. "Skeeter Malcolm's comin' for me too."

Chapter Six

"You think Skeeter Malcolm is after you?" I asked in shock. "Didn't Rufus work for him?"

Bobby shook her head, panic filling her eyes. "I shouldn't have said that. Forget I said that."

"It's okay," I said gently. "I'm a friend. I want to help you."

"Why would you want to help me?" she asked, anger in her voice. "You don't even know me."

"Because that's what I do." I glanced around, noticing no one except a man scratching his crotch as he studied the selection of Slim Jims in the snack aisle. "I'm the Lady in Black."

Her eyes grew huge. It was obvious she knew exactly who I was and what it meant. "Why would you help me?" she whispered, her gaze shifting from me to Neely Kate, then back again.

"I already told you," I said. "I help people. People come to me when they're stuck in impossible situations, and I try to find them a way out."

"She's very good," Neely Kate said.

"I've heard of you," Bobby said. "You used to work for Skeeter."

I started to correct her and say we'd partnered together, but it felt like semantics. "I have a foot in the criminal world, and I've negotiated truces between warring factions."

She snorted. "Then why haven't you negotiated one with Malcolm and Carmichael?"

She had a point. "Because neither party is interested in a truce."

"You've got that right," she scoffed. "They both want total dominion."

"You're in danger," I said. "And I want to help you."

"Out of the kindness of your heart," Bobby said with a sneer.

This would only work if I was honest with her. "I think you might have information that will be useful to me."

Disgust filled her eyes. "I knew it. There's always strings attached."

"That's not entirely true," I said, lowering my voice as a woman walked through the door holding a preschool-aged boy's hand. "You fell onto my radar because of your boyfriend, but I'll help you whether you know anything or not."

"Why?" Bobby demanded. "And even if I buy the good Samaritan act, what do you plan on doin' for me?"

"I can offer you protection," I said. "And a place to hide."

She glanced from me to Neely Kate again. "I think I'll take my chances."

I couldn't force her to talk to me.

"Okay," I said, pulling a business card out of my purse. I placed it on the counter and pushed it toward her. "My name is Rose Gardner, and my cell phone number is on the card. Call if you need me, and I'll find a way to get to you."

She stared at the card so hard I expected it to burst into flames, then picked it up and tossed it into the trash can behind her. "I don't need your help. Now, get the hell out of my store."

"You're making a mistake," Neely Kate said, leaning forward. "We can help you."

Bobby's eyes narrowed. "You have three seconds to get out before I call the cops."

"That's not necessary," I said, then reached for her hand and forced a vision, asking, *Will Bobby be okay?*

Everything went black, and I found myself at my front door, staring at the fake dogwood wreath Joe had gotten me for Mother's Day. Then the door swung open, and vision Bobby was face to face with me.

"Hey, Bobby," Vision Rose said. "I'm glad you called. Come on in. You're safe here."

The vision faded, and I found myself standing face to face with an irate woman, blurting out, "You're gonna be okay." I wrapped my hand around Neely Kate's arm. "We'll go."

As soon as we walked out, Neely Kate asked, "Did you have a vision?"

"I asked if she'd be okay, and I saw myself letting her into the farmhouse."

"Well, that's a relief." I continued to drag Neely Kate across the parking lot, but she stopped in her tracks. "Hey. I didn't get my change."

I tugged her arm, forcing her to continue walking. "I'll buy you lunch to make up for it."

"That's okay," Neely Kate said, taking a sip of her drink. "I'll make up for it in refills."

"That's thirty-two ounces of diabetes in a cup," I said. "Why on earth would you need a refill?"

"A girl can use options."

We got into the truck, and my gaze was drawn to a car parked at the end of the strip. A man sat in the front seat, making no move to get out. "That car was here when we pulled up."

"So?" she asked, then took a sip of her drink before putting it into the cup holder.

"So, he's just sitting there. Doing nothing." I turned to Neely Kate. "He's watching her."

She sat upright and leaned forward. "Oh my stars and garters. I think you're right."

I grabbed my phone out of my purse. Opening the camera app, I took a photo, then zoomed in to get a closer look at the guy.

"Do you recognize him?" I asked, snapping a couple of pictures.

"No, but you'd have a better chance of knowing him than me."

"If he's James' guy, then not so much," I said. "I hear all the old guys are gone."

"He could be with Carmichael. If he killed Rufus for information about the safe, it stands to reason he'd go after Bobby, even if she's more scared of Skeeter," she said.

"I feel like we should warn her," I said. "But she came to me in my vision. I don't think I should mess with anything. If I go to her again, it might piss her off enough that she doesn't come."

"Agreed," Neely Kate said. "Besides, that guy saw us goin' in and comin' out. If we go back in, it'll draw more attention to us, and whoever sent him might put it together that it's us. Shoot," she said, motioning to her window. "The name of the landscaping company is on the side of the truck."

"And if there were any doubt, you're wearing the name on your bedazzled shirt," I said. "But he hasn't so much as glanced at us. Don't you think he'd be checkin' us out too if he thought we were involved in this?"

"I don't know, but I *do* think it's time to take this to Jed."

"Agreed." I started the truck, then headed toward Jed's mechanic shop.

"You don't want to pick up Hope first?" Neely Kate asked, sounding confused.

"Not yet. Let's talk to Jed first." Hope was a baby. She wouldn't understand what we were discussing, but I was reluctant to have her around any of this mess...even if it was quickly becoming obvious this wasn't going away any time soon.

We rode in silence for a few blocks, both lost in thought, before Neely Kate asked, "Do you think this has anything to do with Kate?"

Her question caught me by surprise. "The murder?"

"We know she was workin' to double-cross Hardshaw," she said. "She told me so during our road trip. And then there's the timin'…"

Kate held Hardshaw partially to blame for the murder of her fiancé, and last summer, she'd kidnapped Neely Kate and taken her on a road trip to help her understand the workings of the group. Or so she had claimed. I'd pointed out that Kate could have just told her everything she'd shown her. Drugging Neely Kate and dragging her around Texas and Oklahoma hadn't been necessary. It had been an attempt to Stockholm Syndrome Neely Kate into loving her. To cinch the deal, the warped sister bonding trip had culminated with Kate handing Ronnie over like a cat offering a mouse to its owner.

To be fair, we did think Kate was responsible for Hardshaw's recent hiatus. She'd handed over some dirty money to Neely Kate—money with the fingerprints of Anthony Carson Roberts, one of the Hardshaw Three, all over them. We didn't know what had happened with it, possibly nothing, but at least they'd backed off for a while. Or maybe they'd only made it seem like they were backing off.

"Rufus likely worked for Hardshaw," I said. "So it's not outside the realm of possibility. Let's just talk to Jed, okay?"

We didn't waste time getting out of the truck once I pulled into the parking lot of Carlisle Rivers Auto Shop. The garage doors were closed, so we headed into the office waiting room and went through the garage's side door.

Jed was leaning over the engine of a car, but he glanced up at us, as though Neely Kate's presence drew his attention. A smile spread across his face at the sight of her, but a frown quickly replaced it.

He walked over and kissed her, then said, "While I'm not going to complain about an opportunity to see you, I take it this isn't a casual visit."

"No," I said. "We have something to tell you."

Nodding, he glanced over at the other two men working in the adjacent bays, a nineteen-year-old boy named Marshall, and Neely Kate's cousin Witt.

Witt looked up and did a double-take when he saw Neely Kate and me. Jed motioned for him to come over.

"Let's discuss this in the breakroom," Jed said, leading the way.

Once the four of us were inside, Jed shut the door. "Does this have anything to do with the murder of Malcolm's man?"

"Partially," Neely Kate said. "We found out that he was arrested a few years ago for cracking open a safe in Oklahoma. And he started working for Skeeter around the time of Violet's death."

Jed put his hands on his hips. "And how did you come by this information?"

"That part's not relevant," Neely Kate said. "The real question is who killed Rufus? Was it Skeeter because the guy betrayed him somehow?"

"Or was it Denny Carmichael?" I said. "Shootin' the first volley in their war?"

Jed pushed out a long sigh.

"There's a third option," I said, then gave Neely Kate a pointed look.

"And what's that?" Witt asked, his body tense.

Neely Kate slipped her phone out of her shorts pocket and swiped on the screen. "I got a text from Kate." She handed Jed the phone.

"Psycho Kate?" Witt asked, taking a step back.

"Yeah," Neely Kate said.

"No offense," Witt said, "but your daddy's side of the family makes the Rivers family reunions look tame."

I'd been to a mini family reunion where there'd been barbecued squirrel and two cases of moonshine, which had ended with one of Neely Kate's cousins accusing her fifty-year-old aunt of sleeping with her husband, so that was saying something. But he had a point.

Neely Kate gave him a pointed look. "Just goes to show that you can't pick your family."

"Just for that, I won't walk you down the aisle at your next wedding," Witt grumbled good-naturedly.

"There won't be a next wedding," Jed grunted, handing Neely Kate back her phone. "This complicates things."

"Agreed," I said. "We went to talk to Rufus' girlfriend."

"You did *what?*" Jed asked.

"Guess that explains why you don't have Hope with you," Witt said.

Jed's eyes darkened. "Where is she?"

He was nearly as protective of her as Joe was. "She's with Maeve at the nursery. I didn't think it was a good idea to take her with us when we talked to Bobby."

"I presume Bobby is Rufus' girlfriend," Witt said.

"She works at the Stop-N-Go, and I needed gas," I said.

"And I got a fountain drink," Neely Kate said. "Did you know they reinstituted their bottomless cup program?"

"What were you doin' gettin' a fountain drink?" Witt asked. "You said you were givin' up Coke because it's bad for you."

"I had a moment of weakness, okay?" Neely Kate said in a huff. "And I think we have more important things to discuss than the fact I fell off the no-Coke bandwagon in less than thirty-six hours."

Which explained why I'd had no idea she'd given up soft drinks.

"Agreed," Jed said in a deep voice that let us know he intended to get down to business. "Did you talk to her?"

"Yeah," I said. "She thinks James is after her."

"So she believes Skeeter killed her boyfriend?" he asked.

"She didn't say. I told her I was the Lady in Black and offered her protection, but she was suspicious of my intentions."

"Why would you offer her protection?" Jed said, giving me a dark look.

"Maybe because it's the right thing to do, Jed Carlisle," Neely Kate said in defiance, her hands on her hips.

"While that may be true," Jed said, "I sincerely doubt either one of you heard about Rufus Wilson's murder and immediately thought, 'Hey, we should find his significant other and go offer her help.'"

"Okay," I said. "After I heard about Rufus' ability with safes, it made me wonder if Carmichael killed him because he wanted whatever was on my sister's flash drive. If so, he might go after Bobby too, in case she knows."

Jed shook his head. "I still feel like we've skipped a few steps between you hearing about Wilson's murder and going to talk to his girlfriend."

"The female mind is a mysterious thing," Neely Kate said, her chin lifted. "You've said so plenty of times yourself."

Jed opened his mouth to say something, then promptly closed it.

"Okay," Witt said, crossing his arms over his chest. "Let's say Carmichael killed this guy because he wanted to find out what was in the safe, and then let's say he thinks the guy's girlfriend knows too. What good is that going to do him? He still doesn't have the flash drive. I think we all know who probably does."

"We don't know anything," I said. "Which is why we need to talk to Bobby. Oh, and there's one other thing."

Jed and Witt gave me questioning looks.

"I'm pretty sure someone is watchin' her." I took my phone out of my purse and pulled up my photos. "Do either of you know this guy?"

Jed took the phone, scowling as he swiped the screen to go through them, then handed the phone to Witt.

"That's a cute photo of Hope," Witt said with a grin. "She's gettin' so big."

"Those aren't the photos you should be lookin' at," Jed growled. "I don't recognize him. Did you happen to get the license plate number?"

"Sure did," Neely Kate said, then tapped into her phone.

"Arkansas plate?"

"Yep."

"I'll run it and see what comes back."

Witt handed my phone to me. "Don't know him either."

"He could be Skeeter's guy," Jed said. "I don't know most of his new people. Maybe we should ask Dermot to put a tail on the girl."

"Rose had a vision," Neely Kate said. "And Bobby came to her."

Jed's scowl deepened. "I don't like the sound of that." He hesitated, then said, "But all of these theories could be wrong, especially in light of some information that came my way last night."

"Jed Carlisle," Neely Kate growled. "You came across important information and didn't think to share it with me?"

"I got it after you went to bed," he said. "And you were so beautiful when we woke up this morning, everything else became much less important."

While there was a lot of truth behind his words, I knew some of it was bullshit. But if Neely Kate detected it, she didn't let on.

"What did you find out?" I asked, slightly peeved he hadn't mentioned it right off the bat.

"There's a big drug deal goin' down this week. A South American shipment is coming in."

"Is James part of this?" Although he'd told me he didn't have a hand in selling serious drugs, I'd since learned it was a lie.

"He's the one who set it up," Jed said in disgust. "He's the go-between for the South American cartel and Hardshaw. It's been in the works for months."

"How did you get this information, Jed?" Neely Kate demanded.

"Maybe the same place you got your information about Rufus Wilson's girlfriend," he retorted.

I highly doubted that.

She propped her hands on her hips and shifted her weight to the side. "You're seriously not gonna tell me?"

Witt and I both took a step back.

"You're not tellin' me where you got your information," he snapped.

I didn't want to be the cause of a major disagreement. "Actually—"

Witt cast me a glance before turning to Jed. "Did you find out about the drug deal from Rufus Wilson? If so, maybe Malcolm found out and killed him."

"No," Jed barked. "But it would have made things a hell of a lot easier if I had. At least we'd know why he was murdered."

"Do you have any details about the deal?" I asked. "Time? Location?"

"No. They haven't pinned it down yet, but my source says they're waiting until the last minute before they name a location and a time and date."

"Does Joe know?" I asked, barely stopping myself from asking if Mason knew too.

"No," Jed said. "And we need to keep it that way."

"Why?" I demanded. "They need to be stopped."

He hesitated, then said, "Hardshaw's coverin' all their bases. Word has it they've got a foot in the door at the sheriff's department."

I shook my head. "No. Joe would know. He took great pains to make sure any corruption was rooted out after he took over for the previous corrupt chief deputy."

"Rose, we both know all sorts of people have sources in the department, and rumor has it the sheriff might even be one of them. Hardshaw and Skeeter will put the hard sell on the department to keep their nose out of it or else." He gave me a dark look. "Do you really think Joe's gonna leave it be?"

My stomach flip-flopped. "No."

"Hardshaw will go out of their way to make sure the sheriff's department doesn't intervene. Which means they'll be sure to eliminate any chance of that happenin'. Do you catch my drift?"

I felt like I was going to be sick. "I want to have a vision."

"Good idea," he said, holding out his hand, palm up.

I took his hand and squeezed my eyes shut. First, I asked, *When and where is the Hardshaw meeting?* But all I saw was the gray haze that suggested the future was too unsettled to be seen. So I switched gears. *What will happen if I tell Joe about the meeting?*

The vision instantly took hold, and I found myself holding someone who was sobbing into my chest.

"It's gonna be okay, Rose," I said in Jed's deep voice. "We'll help you through this."

Vision Rose pulled back and looked up at me with red, swollen eyes. "Joe's dead. How can anything be okay? We never should have involved the sheriff's department."

The next instant, the image shifted, and I was myself again, staring up at Jed instead of the other way around. "Joe's dead."

Neely Kate gasped.

"What was the question?" Jed asked.

My hand began to shake, so I snatched it back. "What would happen if I told Joe about the meeting. I told you it was a mistake to involve the sheriff's department."

"So we agree to keep it from him?" he asked.

I nodded. Had Joe died by James' hand like in my other visions? If I kept this from him, did that mean he'd be safe?

"If we're not tellin' the sheriff's department," Witt said, "what do we plan on doin' with this information?"

"Nothin'," Jed said. "We'll let them march on in, do their deal, then leave."

The three of us all started talking at once.

"What the hell?" Witt demanded.

"You can't be serious?" I shouted.

"You are *so* not gettin' any tonight," Neely Kate growled.

Witt shot her a look of disgust and shuddered. "TMI, NK."

"Jed," I pleaded. "Have you at least told Dermot?"

"No. I haven't decided what to do with it yet."

"But—"

Jed's gaze darkened. "Let's say I tell Dermot. What then? We're all gonna go in with our shotguns and bust up Hardshaw and a group from a South American drug cartel, all of them armed to the teeth with automatic weapons? It'll turn into a bloodbath."

"That's not necessarily true," Witt countered. "Not if we ambush them."

"Which will take plannin' and trainin'," Jed said. "Even if we could get the factions together, we'd still lose because we can't agree on anything. We discovered that last fall when we tried holding our meetin's. Then throw in the not knowing the location…" He shook his head. "It'll never work."

My stomach churned as I thought about my visions of Denny Carmichael. In them, I'd always been on his side. Was this why? "Carmichael will do it."

All eyes turned to me.

"Last summer, I had visions of me helping Denny, and at the time, I was sure we were fighting James. I couldn't conceive it at the time, but now…"

Jed studied me, then said, "It doesn't matter. We don't have a location, and by the time we get it—*if* we get it—it will be too late."

"No," I said, an idea coming to me. "I know how to get it."

"I don't like the look on your face," Witt said.

"Neither do I," Neely Kate said.

"How do you propose getting it?" Jed asked in a neutral tone.

"I'll force a vision."

"And who are you gonna force a vision of?" Neely Kate asked. "Jed? Me?"

"No," I said. "I need to go straight to the source." I swallowed my fear, but it lodged in my throat, cuttin' off my air so I had to force out, "I need to go see James."

Chapter Seven

That caused quite an uproar, all three of them arguing with me at once, although it wasn't much of an argument since I just stood there and waited for them to settle down.

When they finally realized I wasn't arguing back, they stopped shouting, one by one.

The door opened, and Marshall popped his head in, bewilderment on his face. "What's goin' on in here?"

No one said anything, and then Neely Kate gushed, "We're rehearsing for community theater auditions for *Newsies*."

He narrowed his eyes. "Huh. I thought they were gonna perform *Hello, Dolly!* this season."

How on earth did he know that?

His gaze swept the room, it paused on me, and he smiled. "Hey, Miss Rose."

"Hi, Marshall. How have you been?"

"Not too bad," he said, giving the scowling Jed a double-take. "Lookin' at buyin' a dirt bike."

"You don't say," I said. "As someone who played a part in previously savin' your life, I feel it would be remiss of me if I didn't tell you that dirt bikes are dangerous," I said the *saving his life* part staring directly at Jed, reminding him that I was no shrinking violet. I'd mixed with plenty of dangerous elements in the past.

Of course, things were different now. I was a mother. But as a mother, I wanted more for Hope. I wanted her to grow up on my birth mother's farm, feeling safe and loved, and if this drug deal went through, it would only be the first of many. Our county would become like the others that had been poisoned and tainted by Hardshaw's presence.

Marshall, who finally seemed to realize what he'd walked into, shot another look at his bosses, then said, "I think I better get back to work."

"Yeah," Jed grunted, still glaring at me. "That's a good idea."

Still, Marshall hesitated and turned to me. "Everything okay, Miss Rose?"

I gave him a warm smile, touched that he was willing to risk his boss's wrath for me. "It's a simple misunderstanding that I hope to clear up."

"Okay," he said, clearly still hesitant to leave me in the lion's den. "I'm good."

"Okay," he said again, then headed back out and closed the door.

"You have to know this is an idiotic idea," Jed grunted.

"I've had worse," I said. "We all have."

"This isn't Fenton County bullshit, Rose," Jed said. "This is big time. You get messed up in this, there's no coming back. You'll no longer be playing at being a criminal, you'll be one."

"So why can't we tell Joe?" I asked, my hand on my hip. "Why can't we let the proper authorities handle this one?"

"Because they can't stop it," he said. "Without a location, they can't do a goddamn thing."

"Which is why I need to get one for them," I insisted.

Neely Kate gave me a look of disbelief. "So let's say we agree to this crazy idea. How are you gonna approach him?"

I frowned. "I haven't worked that part out yet."

We all stood in silence for a few moments.

"After it settles in a bit," Witt said, "it's not a terrible idea."

Jed and Neely Kate turned identical looks of outrage on him.

"She has a point," Witt said, his hands out at his sides. "And she has access no one else does. He'll meet with her willingly."

"Skeeter isn't the man he was a year ago," Jed said, the pain of loss bleeding through his words. "He's harder. Meaner. Our friendship means nothing to him. He might have a sliver of affection left for you, Rose, but I wouldn't count on that saving you, and I mean that in the very literal sense. If he figures out you have a mind to betray him, you run the very real risk that he would kill you." He gave me a sharp look. "Don't forget that your visions always end with you sayin' what you saw."

A shiver ran down my back. "I'll figure somethin' out." But I didn't know how to engineer a meeting, let alone come up with a believable excuse for whatever I might blurt out. Last time I saw him, I'd snuck into his secret house, using the garage door opener he'd given me, but I was sure he'd changed the code by now. And I couldn't just march into the pool hall. Not without a good excuse. That left our meeting place behind Sinclair's, but I had no way to get him a message to meet me. He'd changed all his phone numbers. There was Carter, James' lawyer, but I didn't trust him anymore as a go-between.

Jed held up his hands. "Let's just hold off on this for now. Witt's right. Your idea has merit, but it's dangerous. Joe would never agree to it, even if he knew the stakes, and what about Hope?"

"Obviously, she can't come with me." I wanted James as far away from her as possible, especially since Dermot had suspected the only reason James wanted me for forty-eight hours before her birth was because he'd hoped to steal her and use her as leverage. Although I still wasn't sure I believed that, I wasn't taking chances where she was concerned. I pushed out a breath. "We can't wait too long before we make a decision."

No one said anything. It felt like a suffocating blanket was being wrapped around us. We'd hoped Hardshaw was gone, but they'd never left—and now they were bringing another dangerous enemy to the table. "Maybe we should take this information to Denny Carmichael."

"And what do you think he's going to do with it?" Jed asked. "He's not going to kick them out of town. He's only going to kick Skeeter out of his chair at the table and replace him."

I wasn't so sure about that. Carmichael genuinely hated the idea of Hardshaw moving in, and he made his own drugs. I couldn't see him wanting some South American cartel replacing him. At the same time, my vision aside, Denny Carmichael wasn't someone I wanted as an ally. He was a bully and a brute. A murderer. A man who hurt people for the enjoyment of it.

"We're forgetting something else," I said. "We can't ignore the timing of Kate's message to Neely Kate. It doesn't feel like a coincidence that she sent it right before the big deal. She said she would make sure Neely Kate was happy, no matter what it takes." I held my best friend's gaze. "We all know she hates Hardshaw, and she knows they tried to hurt you. What if she's got something planned for the deal?"

Jed released a few expletives and started to pace.

"Maybe Neely Kate should text her back," I said. "In fact, as unstable as Kate is, she might be pissed that Neely Kate hasn't responded yet."

Jed stopped pacing and turned to Neely Kate. "How long ago did she send that message?"

"About an hour or so."

Jed gave a sharp nod. "Text her back. Something noncommittal like you're already happy."

Neely Kate shot me a glance, and I lifted my shoulders into a small shrug. "Anything you send her is risky, but that makes the most sense."

She nodded, then bent over her phone, tapped out the message, and pressed send. "Okay," she said, glancing up. "Let's see how long it takes her to answer."

Less than five seconds, it turned out.

Neely Kate's phone made a whooshing sound, and her eyes widened as she glanced down at it. "She already responded."

"Well?" Witt asked. "What did she say?"

"She said 'but you don't have everything you want.'" Fear covered her face as she lifted her gaze to Jed's. "Is she talkin' about our adoption?"

There was another whoosh, and she checked the screen again. "She said, 'there's danger afoot, but not to worry, NK. Your big sis has things in hand.'"

"Definitely the drug deal," Witt said.

"Sounds like it," Jed agreed. "We might be better off lettin' her do her thing."

I snorted. "Remember that time we let her do her thing, and she kidnapped Mason, killed Hilary, and bombed a building?"

"To be fair," Neely Kate said, "we didn't *let* her do any of that."

I shot her an exasperated glare.

"Okay, you have a point," she conceded. "But she's crazy with a capital C, and the smart kind. If anyone can pull this off, she can. But that means we need to stay far, *far* away from it."

While part of me wanted to agree, I wasn't sure letting Kate handle this was the best plan. "The drug deal aside," I said, "I still need to find out if Bobby knows what was on that flash drive."

I had a sudden spark of memory of a couple of years ago, being hunted by Daniel Crocker for a flash drive I didn't have, for information I didn't possess, and felt a pang of sympathy for Bobby. Even if she knew more than I had, she didn't deserve to feel hunted.

"Do you want us to try to convince her?" Witt asked.

"No," I said, running a hand over my head as a wave of exhaustion overtook me. "I had a vision of her coming to me, so I guess I just wait, but it's not easy." And I still didn't know what to do with her once she came.

"So all of this is brewing around us, and we're doin' nothin'?" Witt asked in disgust.

"You got a better plan?" Jed asked.

Witt's shoulders slumped. "No."

"Okay," Jed said. "We need to get back to work." He walked over to Neely Kate, pulled her into an embrace, and whispered something into her ear. The moment looked so intimate, I turned to walk out, leaving them to their privacy. Witt was already out the door, and I followed him, surprised when he didn't go into the garage, instead beckoning me to follow him into the waiting room.

"Are you content to keep this from Dermot?" he asked quietly, his gaze on the doorway behind me.

I frowned, worried where this conversation was headed, yet not willing to nip it in the bud. "No."

He turned slightly so we were eye to eye. "*You* are Lady. Jed was your muscle. Remember that."

I gasped. "You're suggestin' that I take charge and put a stop to this?"

"Someone needs to. Jed's not thinking logically, Rose. His judgment is clouded. He's worried he'll screw up their adoption."

"It's a legitimate concern."

"Of course it is," he said, "and maybe that's what Kate meant when she said she'd take care of things so NK will be happy. Maybe she's intervenin' to keep Neely Kate and Jed's hands clean." His eyes darkened. "But I'm willing to get filthy dirty. I want to make those bastards pay." He cocked his head. "Tell me you aren't willing to wallow in it too. Your suggestion about going to see Malcolm proves it."

My stomach twisted. What we were discussing was betrayal.

"Rose...Dermot, Carmichael, you could unite them to kick these bastards out of the county once and for all. While they respect Jed, they follow *you*. And you know damn well everyone will be better off if you lead the charge than if you leave it to Carmichael. That man's rotten to the core. He can't be allowed to lead."

"Jed would never go for this."

"You saw what would happen if you tell Joe," he countered. "We can't bring this to the sheriff's department, but that doesn't mean we can't do anything."

"Let me try another vision," I said, reaching for his arm. When he didn't pull away or protest, I closed my eyes. I wanted to test if I saw the same thing about Joe, but I decided to see if I could get information about the meeting first. After I was plunged into the same gray haze, I asked what would happen if I told Joe about the Hardshaw meeting.

Suddenly, I was standing in front of a casket, staring down at Joe's face. I jerked myself out of the vision and started crying as I said, "Joe's dead."

"Shit," he grunted, half turning from me. "We really can't tell him, Rose."

"No," I said. "I have to protect him."

"Which brings us back to Dermot. And no, Jed won't agree with roping him in, which is why we can't tell him yet."

I tried to pull myself together, but seeing Joe's lifeless body had rocked me to my core. Witt was right. There was no way in hell I could tell Joe, but that didn't mean I couldn't warn Dermot.

A fire filled Witt's eyes. "You won't have Jed as your muscle, but you have me."

I gasped. This was Witt, who was rarely serious about anything, but then again, that wasn't fair or true. He'd done a lot of growing up over the past year. This wasn't the same man-child I'd met back then. This was a man who wanted to protect his county, who wanted to protect his family, and would risk everything to do it.

"Think about it, okay?" he said. "We'll talk later."

Everything in me screamed to tell him no, but a fire burned within me too. There was nothing that would convince me to sit back and let Hardshaw lay claim to the tattered soul of Fenton County in the hopes that Kate would take care of the problem for us. Kate was untrustworthy and psychotic. Literally.

But if I acted behind Jed's back…

Betrayal always started with a tiny step, but that one step could easily turn into a deep, gouging channel that could never be filled, never be repaired.

Tell him no.

Hope's face filled my vision. She was so tiny, so innocent. I wanted nothing more than to protect her, but wouldn't it be best for her in the long term if this deal didn't go through? If Hardshaw didn't take our home from us and poison it?

I'd spent the first twenty-four years of my life waiting for something to happen to me. But Witt wasn't the only one who'd grown up—I had too, and I was no longer content to let fate make my decisions. I was taking charge of my own destiny.

I lifted my gaze to Witt's, fully aware of the path I was choosing, and said, "Okay."

Chapter Eight

Witt had already gone back to the garage, and I was out standing next to the truck when Neely Kate finally came out, her eyes red from crying.

"You ready to go back to the office?" I asked.

She nodded but didn't say anything as she got into the truck.

I started the engine and turned to face her. "Talk to me, Neely Kate."

"I'm scared," she said, looking over at me, fresh tears tracking down her cheeks.

"Kate's scary as hell," I said. "And then everything else goin' on…I'm scared too."

"Jed wants to go away for a few days. Until all of this dies down…or until the baby's born."

That caught me by surprise. "Oh."

"I told him I'd think about it." She gave me a pleading look. "You could come with us. You and Hope."

"What would I tell Joe?" I asked.

Her face fell. "I'm not sure. Promise me you won't tell him the truth, okay?" Her voice rose in panic. "I can't lose him, Rose."

I grabbed her hand. "I won't. I can't lose him either." The image of Joe in a casket popped into my head, and I fought the urge to cry. "I can't live without him."

"So you'll think of something else to tell him," she said. "And we'll get far away from here."

"Let me think about it, okay?" I asked, already knowing my answer.

"Okay."

We drove in silence for a bit before Neely Kate asked in a hopeful tone, "Do you want to get lunch before we pick up Hope?"

While I would have loved to get lunch with her, I really needed to see my daughter and reassure myself that she was safe. But it wasn't just that…guilt coursed through my blood because I knew I couldn't let this go, even if that was exactly what Jed was asking me to do. I struggled to meet Neely Kate's eyes.

"Rain check?" I asked. "I think I'm going to get Hope and head home."

"Yeah," she said, trying to cover her hurt. "Of course."

I reached over and grabbed her hand again, squeezing so hard I was sure it hurt, yet she didn't pull away. "I love you, Neely Kate. Your sister's right. You deserve to be happy."

"But at what cost?" she whispered. "Runnin' off like a scared nitwit."

"You're not a nitwit," I insisted. "And sometimes runnin' is the best course of action."

"But you don't intend to run, do you?" she asked quietly, pulling her hand away.

"No," I admitted.

She was quiet until I pulled up in front of the office. I put the truck in park, but she didn't reach for the door handle. "You're not gonna go do something crazy like head over to the pool hall, are you?"

I smiled. "No, Neely Kate. I promise, my plan is to get Hope and go home."

"But you're not rulin' it out."

"Honestly, I'm not rulin' *anything* out."

Staring out the windshield, she shook her head. "We should stay."

"Why?" I asked. "What purpose would it serve? If you stay, you run the risk of losin' your baby and any hope of adoptin' future babies. You'd be foolish to get involved in this."

She turned to me in surprise.

"You want a baby, Neely Kate," I said emphatically, "and there is absolutely nothin' wrong with doin' everything possible to make that happen." Tilting my head, I gave her a sly grin. "Within reason, of course."

She released a bitter laugh. "Of course."

"So if makin' sure you're nowhere close to what's about to go down is what helps achieve that goal, then that's what you need to do." I leaned closer. "And make sure you have a water-tight alibi."

She laughed again, this time more genuine. "I love you, Rose, and I love Jed too. So I don't say this lightly." She met my gaze and held it. "You do whatever you need to do."

I stared at her for a moment, wondering if I understood her correctly.

"Yeah," she said with a sad smile. "You know what I'm talkin' about." Sucking in a breath, she sat up straighter. "I'm gonna take Jed up on his offer. I think we should go away. Get out of your hair."

Tears filled my eyes. "Jed will never forgive me."

She shook her head, her eyes full of tears too. "Haven't you learned anything from me? It's far better to ask for forgiveness than permission." She squeezed me again. "We all need to find a way to weather this storm. Whether it's hunker down or stand up and fight. Don't let anyone make that decision for you. Not even Jed." A tear slipped down her cheek.

Seeing her tears was what broke me. I started to cry.

"Oh, honey," she said, cupping my cheek with her free hand. "It's all gonna be okay in the end."

"You don't know that," I said, trying to catch my breath. "Maybe this is all the happy ending I get."

Her gaze held mine. "Maybe it is. Maybe it's mine too, but that doesn't mean I'm not going to keep fightin' for more. You should too."

I nodded and pulled my hand from hers, wiping my cheeks with my fingertips. "Where will you go?"

"Jed said something about goin' to the ocean. I've always wanted to see it."

The wistfulness in her voice broke my heart. "Then you should."

She stared into my eyes for a long moment again, then turned and got out of the car without so much as saying goodbye. I sat there watching her, though, unable to leave, and when she reached the office door, she turned and lifted her hand in a wave.

I lifted my hand too.

She blew me a kiss, then went inside.

I backed out of my parking spot, fighting my emotions while trying to figure out what to do next. I needed to meet with Dermot. I needed to figure out how to see James.

James.

What I was about to do could get him killed. I was not okay with that, but I wasn't sure what else to do other than maybe try to reason with him one more time.

I'd driven away from the square toward the nursery, but I turned the truck around and drove back, parking around the corner from Carter Hale's law office. Even though I didn't like or respect Carter, he was my best option for getting a message to James. I doubted he'd put me in touch with him, but he might agree to pass along a message. I'd tell James to meet me in our old spot behind the abandoned Sinclair station. He could pick the time. I'd figure out what to do with Hope later.

I walked into Carter's office, and a young blond woman peered up at me from the assistant's desk. She looked to be in her early twenties and wore a tight white shirt with a very low neckline. The fine sheen of glitter on the rise of her breasts suggested the shirt had been chosen for that feature.

I didn't recognize her, but then Carter seemed to have a revolving door of assistants lately, and their professionalism deteriorated with each new employee.

She eyed me up and down and seemed to find me wanting. Then again, I never seemed to pass muster with *anyone's* assistant. "Do you have an appointment?" she asked in a haughty tone. She was trying to be condescending, but it came out like she was a little girl playing dress-up.

"How long have you worked here?" I asked.

She lifted her chin and looked down her nose. "Long enough."

I shook my head, wanting to tell her that she was more than her breasts, but I only had so much fight in me. Not that she'd likely listen anyway. "Is Carter here?"

Her gaze darted to the hall, then back to me. "You can only see him if you have an appointment."

I took that as a yes.

"Is he with someone now?"

Her eyes widened with panic. "I'm not supposed to talk about it."

My heart skipped a beat. While I didn't know all of Carter's clients, I only knew of one so notorious.

I started down the hall.

"You can't go down there!" she shouted after me, but I kept marching.

"Stop!" she shouted as she ran after me.

When I reached the door to Carter's office, I didn't hesitate, throwing it open to reveal the shocked faces of Carter and the very man I was looking for.

Carter was behind his desk, and James was in one of the guest chairs. The lawyer, usually so slick and polished, stared at me in open shock, but James had a gun pointed right at me. He'd always been a man of action, so I shouldn't have been surprised when I heard the report of a single gunshot.

Chapter Nine

"Rose!" Carter shouted and jumped up from his desk.

I was surprised I was still standing, but then I'd heard it took a moment for your body to register that it had been shot. I'd been grazed with a bullet before, though, and it had hurt like hell. Why wasn't I hurting now? I glanced down at my torso but didn't see any blood.

Carter's new assistant was screaming in my ear by the time Carter reached me, but suddenly James was in the doorway too, pushing Carter out of the way and turning a deadly glare on the assistant. "Shut the fuck up."

To my surprise, she did, but then she scampered to the front office in a way that suggested Carter was going to have to find himself yet another assistant, and James grabbed my arm and dragged me inside the office. His glare shifted to his attorney. "Leave."

"This is *his* office," I said, outraged. "You can't tell him to do that." But even as I said it, I knew it was a ridiculous statement. James *owned* Carter Hale, and if he said jump, Carter would run off to find the highest bridge. He'd be grumbling as he did it, but he'd be no less dead.

Carter turned to face his client. "Try not to kill her. I don't want to explain the bloodstains." He said it flippantly, like he was joking, but there was an edge to it—like maybe he thought it needed to be said. To be fair, James *had* just shot at me.

When Carter left and shut the door behind him, James dragged me to the desk. Shoving Carter's things aside—dimly, I noticed papers, a pencil cup, a stapler—he lifted me under my arms and set me on the desk.

"You can't manhandle me, James," I protested, but I was in too much shock to try to resist.

He shot me a dark look that stole my breath. "I could have killed you." His gaze dropped to my feet and worked its way up my legs.

"What in Sam Hill are you doin'?" I demanded.

"I'm makin' goddamn sure I didn't shoot you," he said with a snarl.

"I'm fine," I said, finally coming to my senses and pushing him away as I slid off the desk. I walked to the center of the room and drew in a deep breath as the reality of the situation sank in. "You shot at me!"

"I didn't know it was *you* until the last instant, when I pulled to the side!" he shouted. "What the hell were you thinkin', slamming your way into his office unannounced? The assistant was told not to let anyone back."

"Oh, I don't know," I said, starting to pace. "Usually when you walk into someone's office unannounced, the worst you'll find is someone in a compromising situation. I didn't expect to be shot!"

"I didn't shoot you! I missed!"

"Is that supposed to make me feel better?" I demanded. My legs started to feel wobbly at the thought of what a close call it had been.

He was by me in an instant, taking my arm and guiding me back to the sofa, his touch more gentle this time. He sat on the coffee table in front of me, and I realized his hand was shaking. I stared at it for a couple of seconds before I lifted my gaze to his with a questioning look.

"You just scared the shit out of me," he said. "Give me a second."

We both sat there, our breathing rapid as we tried to calm down.

"Well, I guess that answers one of my many questions," I said dryly.

"Which one is that?" he grunted.

"Whether you want me dead."

He lifted a hand to my cheek, his eyes softer than I'd seen them in a year. This was the man I'd gotten to know, not the monster who had taken his place, and it cut me to the bone to see a glimmer of him. "If I'd wanted you dead, Rose, you would have been dead long ago."

It was true. He'd had plenty of opportunity.

"Why are you at Carter Hale's office?" he asked, his hand still cupping my face.

"Because I wanted to see you," I whispered.

Something flickered in his eyes, but then his shutters were back, and he dropped his hand. "Well, you're seein' me now, so what do you want?"

Tears stung my eyes. "I don't want to play this game anymore."

"What game?" he demanded.

"The game where you lie to me and keep secrets."

Some of his hardness faded. "I've never lied to you, Rose."

That wasn't true, but I wouldn't win his cooperation by saying so. So instead, I said, "But you sure have kept plenty of secrets."

He got up and moved to the center of the room. "Why did you want to see me?"

I hadn't put a plan together, other than forcing a vision, but being honest felt good, so I decided I'd do some more of it. I stood, remaining in front of the sofa. It was time for truth. "What's your endgame?"

He slowly turned to face me.

"Why are you workin' with Hardshaw?" I pressed. "Do you want money? Power? Do you want to move on to something bigger and better than the king of Fenton County? Have they offered you a position in Dallas?"

"That is none of your fucking business," he snapped, but it lacked heat.

"Last fall, you told me that this was all for me, which means I have a right to know. So what was your plan?"

He started to say something, then stopped and turned his back on me. "I learned long ago never to trust anyone. My father beat that lesson into me. Literally. Then J.R. turned on me."

"Jed didn't," I said. "I didn't."

"Really?" he demanded, then spun around, the monster back and firmly settled on his face. "Jed chose you over me, and we both know it."

He was right. The irony that I was now betraying Jed by acting without his knowledge wasn't lost on me.

"*I* didn't betray you."

"The hell you didn't," he sneered, walking toward Carter's desk. "You chose that baby over me. That was a choice."

"A baby doesn't have to be an either-or situation, James. You could have had us both."

"No," he snapped. "I can't, because I don't want it."

"Our baby is a she, not an it." I hesitated, then asked, "Did you really want me to get an abortion?"

"The God's honest truth?" he asked, his brow lifted.

"That's why I'm here. I want the truth."

"Yeah," he ground out through gritted teeth. He looked feral. "I wanted that baby good and gone."

I sucked in a breath. Part of me had always hoped it had been his way of protecting me. Protecting us. But that had all been a pretty lie I'd told myself, and I was done with pretty lies. "You obviously don't want her," I said evenly, trying to keep the pain out of my voice. "So why won't you sign the paternity papers and be free of her?"

"Because I'm not stupid. I'm savin' it for a rainy day. This is twice you've come to me wantin' something. You showed up at my house in April because you thought I knew where your niece and nephew were being held, and I'm not stupid enough to think you don't have a reason for being here now. Someday I'll be able to use those papers to get what

I want." He grinned, but there was nothing friendly in it. "Plus, it's drivin' you crazy knowin' I won't sign 'em. There's a certain satisfaction to that."

"So you'll use our daughter as a ploy?" I asked in disbelief. Somehow, in spite of everyone (myself included) telling me that he intended to do just that, I hadn't fully let myself believe it. But that was another pretty little lie in a long line of them.

"I'll use *your kid* as leverage."

I stared at him in horror. How badly did he want to hurt me?

He took a moment, then asked, "What made you show up at Hale's office so damn gung-ho to see me?"

I drew a breath. Was there any hope of reaching him? Was he too far gone? I had to at least try. "I'm here because I know one of your men was killed today, and I wouldn't be surprised if Denny Carmichael or his men were the ones who pulled the trigger. I have a bad, bad feeling that things are about to get ugly. I wanted to reason with you one last time." I walked around the coffee table and stood a few feet away from him. "Please stop this before it's too late. This town will be destroyed, and you will get killed."

He snorted. "Is that supposed to stop me? Come on, Lady, you can do better than that."

"James, you've replaced every single man who was loyal to you with paid mercenaries. You may be building your ivory tower, but you're sittin' up there all alone. Can't you see what you're doin'?"

"I've got a pretty good view of what I'm doin'—I'm loading up those offshore accounts so they're nice and plump. And yeah, I'm alone, but I've spent most of my damn life alone." He gave me a withering look. "I might have said I was doing it *for* you, but don't let your ego get carried away. You were just part of the plan. The idea was to make a huge profit, then go off somewhere and make a new life. I figured I'd bring you with me. But I realized you'd never go for it, and then you chose that damn baby over me."

"So you're not workin' for the FBI?"

He laughed, but it was bitter. "Still tryin' to make me into a damn saint."

I stared at him hard. "I know you sent Vera to take me to the kids. And I also know you killed her for puttin' me in danger."

His mouth parted in shock, then he quickly recovered. "Where'd you come up with that?" A slow smile spread across his face. "You're just fishin'."

"I had a vision of her, James," I said, my voice breaking. "I saw you interrogating her outside, in the dark. She was supposed to take me to the kids and make sure I got them out safely. You were pissed she left us there, so you shot her in the head." My chin trembled. "I saw it."

He looked shocked, then said, "As I've mentioned, I'm no saint, no matter how much you try to paint me as one. Maybe it's better that you saw the truth firsthand."

"So you knew where those kids were when I came to you, and you sent me away. What difference did it make whether the information came from you or Vera?"

He ran his hand over his head. For a brief moment, he looked lost, almost as if he wanted to find his way out but didn't know how, but he quickly recovered. "You said it yourself. It's all a game."

"Why was Vera following me? Why not just have her tell me straight away?"

"Because I wanted to keep tabs on you," he said matter-of-factly. "I was hoping you'd lead me to Mike."

"And what does Mike have to do with any of this?" I cocked my head slightly. "I know he was supposed to get Mark Erickson, the man who was killed, because he needed an electrician who had access to restricted areas in the courthouse."

He started to say something, but he cut it off with a shit-eating grin that suggested he was king of the world and he could take what he wanted, when he wanted it, consequences be damned.

"You always were too curious for your own good." He moved closer and made a slow circle around me with a leer in his eyes. "You know, I could take you with me and lock you in my room at the house. I could keep you as my distraction."

My mouth went dry, and my heartbeat sped up. "You wouldn't dare."

"No one knows where it is. They'd never think to look for you there."

"Jed would."

He released a bitter laugh. "I can handle him."

"What about Hope?"

"What about her?" he asked bitterly. "Let Simmons keep her since he's so damn hot on raisin' my kid."

Disgust rushed through me. He lifted a hand to my face, and I slapped it away, taking a big step back. "What *happened* to you?"

He held his hands out at his sides. "You're lookin' at a little bit of nature and a whole lot of nurture."

"Why did you want me for forty-eight hours before I had Hope?"

He laughed again. "It sure as hell wasn't to seduce you."

"Is that what this is?" I snapped. "A seduction?"

He reached for me, pulling me to his chest. His hand grabbed my hair at the base of my neck, forcing my head back to look up at him. There was nothing loving or seductive in his touch. "I can take what I want and not feel an ounce of guilt."

"You liar," I said through gritted teeth.

The side of his mouth lifted in amusement. "You think I can't take what I want?"

"Oh, I know you can, but you told me once that you never condoned rape."

He pulled me closer, and I felt his arousal pressing against my belly. "I've changed, Lady."

"Why did you want me for forty-eight hours?"

His grin spread, but a malicious look filled his eyes. "I'll tell you everything you want to know and more, but you have to screw me right now. This is a one-time offer." His brow lifted. "What do you say? I know you want it."

I stared up at him in horror. "Your offer would make me no better than a prostitute."

He lifted his shoulders slightly in a shrug. "If it makes you feel any better, I'll make sure it's good." His mouth dropped to my exposed neck, and he nipped slightly. "Damn good."

Before, his touch had me weak in the knees, but now it just made me sick.

I lifted my foot and scraped the heel of my shoe down the inside of his leg, then stomped on his foot hard, wishing the heel were a stiletto instead of a block. Then I lifted my forearm and brought it down hard on the arm holding my hair. He released me, taking some of my hair with him.

I backed up several feet, panting. "Stay the hell away from me."

He grinned, but it lacked any humor or warmth. "*There's* my hellcat come out to play."

"Is this some damn game to you?" I demanded in disbelief. What was I asking? Of course it was. Hadn't we just established that? He was in his own version of *Game of Thrones*, and I was one of the many disposable women in his life. I'd just fooled myself into thinking I was different.

No, that wasn't true. I knew I'd meant something to him once. Until I no longer fit. Until I asked for more than he wanted to give. Until I became inconvenient.

"I'm done, James," I said, sounding as weary as I felt. "Let the chips fall where they may. I'm done."

"I wish that were true, Lady," he said, sounding weary himself. Then he stomped out of the office, and as I watched him leave, I realized the extent of my failure.

I hadn't forced a vision.

Chapter Ten

I didn't waste any time getting out of there. The bullet lodged into the drywall in the hall was a sharp reminder that I'd nearly left Hope without a mother.

Carter was sitting in one of the chairs in his waiting room, his elbow on the armchair. He'd been staring out the window, but his gaze swung to me as I walked down the hall.

His assistant wasn't at her desk. "Where's your new hire?"

"Gone," he said dryly, confirming my suspicion. "Thanks to you and your little stunt."

"Maybe you'll put a little more thought into who you employ," I said. "Your taste seems to be deteriorating along with your boss's."

He started to say something, then stopped. A grin lit up his face, but it didn't quite reach his eyes. "We all seem to be on the same runaway locomotive, so what difference does it make?"

Did Carter see this as a one-way trip to prison or worse, death?

"A piece of advice," he said slowly, getting to his feet. "Go home. Stay home. Stay the hell away from Skeeter Malcolm. If you leave him alone, he'll leave you alone. I'll make sure of it."

"What's he doin', Carter?" I asked, equal parts angry and worried about James, although I had no idea why I should care after what had just happened. "Why do you look like you're about to face a firing squad?"

He released a sharp laugh. "I warn you to stay away, and you ask more questions." He inhaled deeply, then pushed it out as he shook his head. "Like I said, we're all on the same damn runaway train." He started down the hall to his office, then glanced back over his shoulder. "I hope I see you at the next station, but if I don't." He gave me a two-finger salute then walked away.

Did Carter know about the drug deal? I considered following him to his office so I could force a vision, but I doubted it would show me much. We needed a location, and the likelihood of Carter being present at the transaction was slim to none.

I'd have to find out another way.

But as I walked to my truck, I wondered if Carter was right. Maybe we *were* all aboard an out-of-control train, about to slam into a brick wall.

What did I really hope to achieve?

I was pensive and subdued when I reached the nursery, and Maeve gave me a worried look. "Is everything okay, Rose?"

"Yeah," I said with a dismissive wave, then gave her a believable excuse that would ease her concern. It also happened to be true. "I just have a headache."

"Maybe you're doing too much too soon," she said, her brow creased with worry. Based on our talk earlier, I had a feeling she wasn't just referring to my work at the office.

"That's probably it." I glanced around the store, feeling anxious. "Where's my sweet baby?"

"She's in the swing. We set it up close to the window in the back. She seems to like looking outside, and Anna and I take turns talking to her. And Muffy's with her, of course. She rarely let's Hope out of her sight."

I hurried back there and found Hope in the swing, rocking by the window while Anna sat next to her, talking to her in a soothing undertone.

Muffy lay under the swing, her chin on her outstretched front legs. When she saw me, her tail starting wagging and she raced toward me, her gait only a bit wobbly, and jumped up on my legs.

I scooped her up and held her close, scratching behind her ears and on the side of her neck. "You're a good dog, Muff," I whispered as I buried my face into her neck.

Anna looked up and noticed me. "Oh, hey, Rose. You're back already."

The disappointment in her voice was reassuring. Maeve and Anna worked for the nursery—it wasn't their job to babysit my daughter, so I was relieved they both seemed to enjoy it so much.

"How has she been?"

"A dream," Anna said with a wistful look in her eyes. Apparently, Neely Kate wasn't the only woman in town with baby fever.

I walked around the swing, nearly floored with relief when I saw Hope strapped into the seat. Her gaze was focused on Anna's face.

"When are you and Bruce Wayne gonna have a baby of your own?" I asked as I squatted and released the buckle of the straps holding Hope in.

A grin spread across her face as Maeve joined us. "Well, actually..."

"Are you tryin'?" I blurted out in excitement.

Her grimace suggested she wasn't sure how much she wanted to share, but the grin was back a moment later. "Not only did we try, we succeeded."

Maeve clapped her hands in excitement. "Another baby."

"That's the best news I've heard all day," I said. "When are you due?"

"It's still early yet," she said. "We were going to wait to tell everyone, but it's hard to keep something so wonderful to yourself for long."

"Trust me. I understand," I said. "Bruce Wayne will be an amazing father."

"Hey," she said in mock outrage. "What about me?"

I waved a hand, then lifted Hope out of the swing. "Please. You being an incredible mother is a given. But people tend to dismiss Bruce Wayne."

"You didn't," she said quietly.

"No," I said, matching her tone. "And neither did you. He's a good man, and he'll make a great father."

"I know. But don't tell him I told you, okay? I think he wants to be the one to tell you."

"Don't worry," I said. "We'll keep your secret."

What would happen to other people in the community if this drug deal went down? Would Bruce Wayne and Anna have to leave town? I hated to think of it, not just for myself, since it would be a huge loss for the landscaping business, but because he'd have to start over if he moved somewhere else.

"When did she last eat?" I asked, the heaviness in my breasts reminding me it had been a while.

"She hasn't since you left her, but we changed her diaper about ten minutes ago," Maeve said. "She's been awake the entire time."

"So a feeding and a nap are in our future," I said with a brightness I didn't feel.

"Maybe you can get a nap too," Maeve said, looking worried. "You seem exhausted."

I nodded. "Sounds like a good plan."

Hope was quiet most of the drive back out to the farm, but she started to wail about five minutes out. When we got out of the truck, I sat in a chair on the porch to nurse her, Muffy at my feet.

It was early June, typically hot and humid in southern Arkansas, but the temperature was mild, and the breeze felt good. It felt like there was a storm of locusts in my head, but I tried to focus on the baby in my arms, taking in her sweet chubby cheeks, her dark hair, and balled fists. I ran a fingertip down her arm, marveling at the softness of her skin. God had given me an incredible gift. James' derision of her didn't diminish that, but it still made my heart ache. It also reinforced my decision to name Joe as her father. He would never turn his back on her. He would sooner die than let harm come her way. *That* was love. Joe was the father I wanted for her, especially if things went wrong over the next few days.

I heard a car coming down the short, tree-lined drive, relieved when I saw Joe's sheriff's sedan heading toward the house. He parked and got out, walking toward us. He was wearing his uniform, and the sun hit his brown hair, bringing out the copper highlights. He looked so much like the man I'd met two years ago, only he was different, humbled and more mature. Trouble had come for him from all sides, but it had taught him what was important in life, and it wasn't money or power. It was love. It was family.

"Hey," he said, hurrying up the steps with worry-filled eyes. "What's wrong?"

I realized I'd been crying and offered him a weak smile. "Long morning, but that's not why I'm emotional." My voice broke. "I'm just so grateful to have you, Joe."

"Hey," he said, taking Hope from me, and I realized she had fallen asleep.

I adjusted my bra and shirt before standing.

He pulled me into an embrace, holding me to the side. "What's really wrong, darlin'?" he whispered into my ear.

The tears kept coming, and he leaned back to take in my face. "I'm gonna put Hope down, then we'll talk, okay?" he said.

I nodded. "Have you had lunch?"

"Not yet, but—"

"I'm starvin'," I said, forcing a smile. "I'll make us something to eat." And hopefully, get myself under control.

"Okay." But he didn't sound convinced as I walked past him into the house.

Muffy followed him upstairs as I headed into the kitchen, trying to figure out what to tell him as I also searched for what to make for lunch. We had some leftover baked chicken in the fridge, so I pulled that out along with a jar of mayonnaise and dijon mustard to make chicken salad. I started chopping onions and celery, still trying to figure out what to say. I really, really didn't want to keep secrets from him, but I also couldn't give away other people's confidences, especially if it implicated them in any way.

I was mixing everything together in a bowl when he entered the kitchen with the monitor in hand. "Sorry I took so long," he said as he set it on the counter. "She woke up, so I rocked her back to sleep."

I gave him a wobbly smile. "You're such a good daddy."

Worry creased his forehead. "We've already established that fact," he teased, although no spark of humor lit his eyes, "so let's move on to the unknowns, like what has you so upset."

I carried the bowl of chicken salad to the table, then walked over to the cabinet to get some plates. "Can you get the bread?"

"Rose," he said, pulling me to a stop. "Let me just hold you first."

I wrapped my arms around his back and pressed my face to his chest.

He rubbed my back and placed a kiss on top of my head, squeezing me tighter.

"I love you, Joe. I'm so very grateful for you."

"Yeah," he said softly into my ear. "We've established that too. What happened?"

I lifted my hand to cup his cheek and leaned back to look up into his warm brown eyes.

He stared back with a mixture of wonder and concern. Stretching up, I pressed my mouth to his and kissed him. It started out soft, simple, but a powerful need for him rushed through my veins, and I kissed him harder.

His arm tightened around me, pulling me closer as he kissed me back with pent-up frustration. We'd been together for a month and a half, but we had yet to consummate our new relationship.

I needed more of him. I needed to feel his bare skin next to mine, so I tugged at his button-down shirt, untucking it from his pants, then skimmed my hand up his chest.

He sucked in a breath and followed suit, pulling my T-shirt over my head and pressing kisses to my neck and down to my breasts.

But then he froze and stood upright, his breath coming in heavy pants. "As much as I want this—want *you*—we need to wait until the doctor says it's okay."

"Neely Kate says it's probably fine," I said, reaching for the buttons on his shirt.

His hand covered mine, stilling my fingers. "I'll be sure to send a donation to the imaginary medical school Neely Kate graduated from. Now tell me what's goin' on?"

I stared up at him again. If I survived this, would I lose him like I'd lost Mason? Joe was more understanding of my place in the criminal world, but if I actually tried to forestall the drug deal by rounding up the other criminals in the county…that was huge, and I couldn't see him letting me go through with it.

"Let's sit," I said, curling my fingers around his hand.

"That bad, huh?"

Reaching up to grab both sides of his face, I kissed him again, this time softer and more reassuring. "We can get through anything, Joe."

He didn't look all that reassured as he picked up my shirt from the floor and handed it to me. I pulled it over my head as he grabbed the loaf of bread and a bag of chips, snagging two plates before he joined me at the table.

After he set the bread out on the plates, I started to fix the sandwiches.

"I know a lot of the things you learn on the job are confidential," I said slowly. "That there are aspects you can't tell me." I glanced up at him. "I respect that, and it makes me think more highly of you that you take your vows seriously, especially the ones you've made to Hope and me."

I could see the questions swirling in his mind. The uncertainty of where this was heading.

"But we both know I have a persona in this county."

Dread filled his eyes, and his breath quickened. "What happened?"

"Joe," I reached across the table and grabbed his hand, holding on tightly for fear he'd pull away from me. "Something big is happenin' this week. Do you know anything about it?"

He hesitated, then said, "We've caught some chatter, but none of it points to a definite time or date. We don't even know that it will happen this week."

"Do you know what's supposed to happen?"

He inhaled, then pushed out a breath. "No. Not really."

"You do know, don't you? You're just not supposed to tell me."

Guilt filled his eyes. "You know I can't share details like that."

"I know," I assured him, squeezing his hand. "A year or so ago, I would have been upset by your answer, but I've grown up. I understand."

"Where is this headed, Rose? Has someone in the criminal world reached out to you?"

"This is where it gets tricky," I said, looking at him earnestly and hanging onto his hand for dear life. "I may not have sworn an oath to the county or the sheriff's department, but I've made an oath of my own to the citizens of the county, and I've garnered respect from some of the criminally minded individuals who reside here."

His shoulders sank. "Someone *has* reached out, and you don't want to tell me."

"Remember when I first found out I was pregnant? I went to those meetings as the Lady in Black because I wanted to keep Hardshaw out of town badly enough to take the risk. I wanted it for Hope's safety...for the county. And remember how you turned your back and didn't ask questions?" I took a breath. "Why did you do that?"

"Because I love you. I never stopped, even when I tried to convince myself otherwise." He paused, looking at me. "I've grown up too. We both know you're not the naïve woman I met on my front porch two years ago. You told me that before my father died, and you were right. You've grown and changed and seen things I can't even imagine, all of them makin' you the woman you are now. I can't control you, Rose, but I also don't want to, because *I trust you*," he said emphatically. "I trust you to do what you think is right and fair, and not to take unnecessary chances." He lifted his free hand to my face. "Because your insistence on helping people is one of the things I love about you, and I'd be a fool to try and change it."

I covered his hand on my face with my own. "Do you still trust me?"

"What you're askin' me is hard, Rose. So damn hard," he said, conflict raging in his eyes. "You're askin' me to let you associate with known criminals, to put yourself in physical danger and at the risk of arrest and prosecution. It was hard before, but I had no right to ask you to stop. No claim to demand you listen to me."

"And you do now?" I gasped, my disappointment ready to bubble over.

"No. I made a vow to love you and protect you, but I also made a vow to myself that I would never box you in. That I would let you have the freedom you need to be the woman I love." A sad smile twisted the corners of his lips. "If I caged you, you'd come to resent me, and I never want to live in a world without you by my side. Which makes this even harder." He swallowed. "I run the risk of losin' you anyway."

"Oh, Joe..."

"But what about Hope, Rose? What if you leave her without a mother?"

"Then I'll know she has the best father I could ever hope to give her," I said, my voice breaking. Because there was a risk what we were doing could kill me, but I knew for a fact that telling Joe would lead me straight to that coffin I'd seen earlier. I couldn't risk it. I *wouldn't* risk it.

"Rose." Keeping his hand on my cheek, he wove the tips of his fingers into my hair.

"Something big is happenin', Joe. Something that could change this county for the worse for a long, long time."

"Then tell me," he insisted. "Give me the details, and let me and the deputies with actual badges take care of it."

"It's not that simple."

"Then we'll make it simple," he insisted.

I gave him a sad smile. "You and I both know that's not how the world works." When he didn't respond, I said, "I don't take this lightly. I've struggled with it all day. I've considered takin' Hope and leavin' town until everything blows over. You should know that's exactly what Jed and Neely Kate are doin'."

Alarm covered his face, and he pulled his hand away. "What the hell is goin' on that would send them packin' and not you?"

I wasn't sure what to tell him. "Their baby is going to be born any day now," I finally said. "They can't risk any stench stickin' to them. I think it's a good decision for them to steer clear of this."

"But you don't intend to." His voice was flat.

"I have skills that no one else can replicate. I have the means to prevent this from blowing up, Joe."

He sat up straight, his back stiff. "Your visions."

"My visions." I tilted my head. "If I can save a lot of lives and a lot of heartache, don't I have the responsibility to do so?"

"But what about your responsibility to Hope?" he pleaded. "To me?"

"I don't know, Joe. Why do you think I'm struggling so?" My throat tightened. "What would you do? You're sworn to protect the citizens of this county. What would you do if you had the ability to save people? Possibly save the county? Would you risk your life?"

He slowly shook his head, his eyes glassy. "That's not fair, Rose."

"It's perfectly fair," I insisted softly. "What would you do?"

He glanced away, toward the back windows, then instantly sat up, his body tense. "Did Madison leave the barn door open?"

Madison was the teenage girl who showed up once or twice a day to take care of Margi's horses.

"No," I said, staring at the window facing the barn behind the house. "I'm positive she closed it. Muffy was sniffing around out there before we headed to town."

He got to his feet. "Stay here." Before I could respond, he strode to the back door and went outside.

"To heck with waitin'," I muttered to myself. I usually used Muffy as a sounding board to reason things out, but she was currently protecting my daughter. So I put our uneaten lunches in the fridge and headed out the door too. To my relief, Joe didn't tell me to turn back, thus avoiding an unnecessary argument.

An open barn door didn't mean that something nefarious had happened. It could have meant anything.

But I knew in my heart that it wasn't nothing.

Joe got to the edge of the barn door, shooting me a frown, then motioned for me to move behind him and stay close to the wall.

Given my lack of a weapon, it seemed like a reasonable request.

Joe called out, "If someone is in there, make your presence known."

We were greeted with silence.

"Maybe I was wrong," I whispered. "Maybe Madison did leave it open."

Joe didn't respond, instead glancing around the barn, his gaze pausing on a patch of dirt a few feet from the doors. "Did Margi have anyone workin' on the barn today?"

"Not that I know of. Why?" I asked, moving over to him.

He pointed to the ground. "That's definitely a fresh tire print."

Sure enough, there were deep grooves in the foot-wide patch of dirt in the grass.

He stood upright. "Maybe you should go back to the house."

"Do you think there's anyone in the barn?" But I realized it was a foolish question even as I asked it. Neither one of us would be walking around in front of the barn if he thought there was someone dangerous inside.

"No."

"Then I'm stickin' with you, Joe," I said, looking up at him. "So let's go check it out. But hurry, because I forgot the baby monitor."

He paused, glancing toward the house. "Muffy's a pretty good monitor, and she's quiet, so I think we're good for the moment."

Taking my hand, he led me to the side of the barn again, then crept up to the edge of the door, peering through a crack.

"Shit."

"What?" I moved up next him, and peered around the door.

Margi had put in four horse stalls on the barn's left side, but the walls were ruined in the back of the stable, and a huge pile of dirt covered the floor.

"Don't go in," Joe grunted. "Let's walk around back."

We walked around the back of the barn, and Joe pulled his keys out of his pocket to use on the lock Margi had installed after revamping the barn. Using the end of his still-untucked shirt, he grabbed the handle and pulled the door open.

I gasped again as we stared at a hole the length and width of the last stable. It was at least six feet deep.

"What just happened here?" I asked in shock and confusion.

"That's what I'd like to know."

Chapter Eleven

"Seriously, Joe," I said, scanning the hole. "Why would someone do this?"

"They were obviously diggin' something up. Something big."

"What would fit in a hole that big?" Even as I said it, it dawned on me that the hole was plenty big enough to fit a body. It wouldn't be the first one. Neely Kate had found a buried body out there with James once, over a year ago, but he'd taken care of it. I had to admit I was still worried about the possibility there was DNA evidence linked to the murdered man.

A glance at Joe suggested he was thinking along the same lines, but neither of us seemed eager to voice our fear.

"Were they watchin' the house?" he asked, his voice sounding strangled. His gaze swung to mine. "Did they purposely plan this for when you left the house? And what would have happened if you'd come home early? What if you and Hope had been here?" His voice broke.

I wrapped my arms around his neck and held him close. His arms tightened around me. "Don't be thinkin' the what-ifs, Joe. They'll only drive you crazy."

"I could have lost you, Rose. I could have lost you both."

I grabbed his face with both hands and stared up into his eyes. "But you didn't. We're both here. I suspect they were watching and came after we left."

Fear filled his eyes. "They probably needed hours to do this."

I held his gaze and gave him a half-smile. "Then it's a good thing I was gone for hours."

"But if you'd come home, you might not have thought anything about a truck bein' here," he said. "You might have thought it was one of Margi's many workers."

"If it didn't look suspicious, I might have ignored it, especially if Hope was fussy," I said. "But if I'd been uncomfortable, I would have turned around and left." I paused. "I would never knowingly put Hope in danger. You have to know that."

His face softened. "I've never once questioned that."

His answer was a balm to my own fears. I took a breath. "Of course, you should be speculating about why they chose this time or how long it took, but no more freakin' out over what-ifs. It steals the energy you need to put into finding who did this. Besides, we have surveillance cameras on the barn. Maybe we'll get lucky, and whoever did this will be on tape."

He nodded, then gave me a gentle kiss. "You're right, and it's time for me to do my job."

He sent me into the house to check on Hope while he called the sheriff's department, requesting deputies to start an investigation. I used the opportunity to call Neely Kate and tell her what we'd discovered.

"I'm comin' over," she said.

"I thought you were leavin' town."

"I'll be right there."

Which didn't answer my question, but I didn't push her.

Amazingly, Hope slept through the arrival of four sheriff cars (a couple of which showed up with sirens blaring), the forensic team, and Neely Kate.

When she arrived, she walked into the house without knocking and found me in the kitchen as I watched the mess from the back windows.

She gave me a hug as soon as she saw me. "I guess our big goodbye earlier was just for practice."

I laughed. "We had it pretty perfect, so maybe we'll just say 'ditto,' next time."

She laughed too, then sobered. "Why in the blazes would someone go diggin' in your barn?"

"It's obvious something was hidden out there, and by someone other than us. The most obvious suspect is Margi. She had complete access, and we never would have been the wiser."

Joe must have seen Neely Kate's car pull in because he was making his way to the house.

"What on earth would she have buried?" Neely Kate asked.

I shook my head. "I have *no* idea. It was big enough to be a body, but if so, I can't think why someone else would want to dig it up."

She made a face as if to say she'd beg to differ, and it occurred to me that Neely Kate and Jed *had* dug up a body—the body of the man she'd killed in self-defense, Pearce Manchester—in order to dispose of evidence. "You never know." Then she added, "You have to admit that she's always been on the suspicious side."

She had a point.

Joe walked in through the back door and headed straight for Neely Kate, pulling her into a tight hug.

"What's that for?" she asked, her voice muffled.

"Can't I hug my little sister?" he asked, but he held her for a few moments longer before letting her go. "I'm surprised to see you. Rose told me you and Jed are leavin' town for a while."

She swung a panicked look my way.

"He doesn't know all the details, and we were in the middle of a discussion about it when he noticed the barn door was ajar."

She cast an anxious look at her brother.

He reached out and squeezed her shoulder. "We're fine, Neely Kate. It was a very civil and thoughtful conversation."

Her mouth dropped open, and I could see she was wondering what, exactly, we had discussed.

Joe turned his attention to me. "I think it goes without sayin' that you two need to stay away from the barn while we're workin' the crime scene. We don't know much yet, but it looks like there might have been some boxes buried down there."

"Not a body?" I asked.

"No," Joe said with relief in his eyes. "No body."

"So what was in the boxes?" Neely Kate asked.

He hesitated, then said, "It's all speculation, but based on the indentations left behind in the hole and everything that's goin' on in the county right now, we suspect they stored weapons down there."

"Weapons?" I asked in shock. "Why would they bury weapons in our barn?"

"Who would think to look there?" he asked with a small shrug. "We don't have any way of knowing how long they've been stored down there. We're tryin' to track Margi down, and so far, we haven't had any luck."

My stomach churned. "Why would Margi, of all people, be burying guns in our barn?"

His face went blank, and he seemed to choose his words carefully. "I take it that you are genuinely shocked by this and aren't withholding information?"

I nodded my head vigorously. "I had no idea that anything was buried out there, let alone what Margi might be up to. Other than seeing her at Levi's office and around town, the only dealin's I've had with her are in regard to the horses. I swear to you, Joe. I don't know anything."

He closed the short distance between us and gave me a light kiss on my lips. "Thank you."

"Do you think she's workin' for Hardshaw?" I asked.

"The timin' sure is right," Neely Kate said. "I wouldn't be all that surprised if it were true."

I felt sick. While Margi wasn't my favorite person, she'd grown on me, and I'd genuinely believed in her mission to save the horses. "What about Levi?"

"I've got a deputy headed out to his practice." He cast a glance at the ceiling. "Hope still sleepin'?"

"Yeah." I patted the monitor, which I'd tucked into my pocket.

He shook his head with a wry grin. "Do you think that means we're in for another night of torture?"

I released a laugh. "I sure as Pete hope not, but I was actually thinkin' about checkin' on her soon. She's only been down for about an hour, but if we make sure she's good and tired, maybe she'll sleep more tonight."

"There's my smart…" His voice trailed off, and I could see he was struggling to define what we were to each other. I'd had the same thought. Girlfriend seemed lacking since we were living together and raising a child together, but partner felt too business-like.

I pressed another kiss to his lips. "I love you."

His smile looked slightly forced. I wasn't sure what was bothering him at that particular moment, but we sure had plenty of issues to provide him just cause.

"I've considered relocating us for the night," he said. "But I think they got what they came for and aren't comin' back." He searched my face. "Unless you think we should pack up and go somewhere else."

"No," I said quietly, unsure how to handle this subtle, indirect Joe. "I don't think we need to go."

He nodded. "Okay. That's why I came in—to give you an update and ask if you wanted to stay somewhere else." His gaze dropped to his empty plate on the table. "And maybe grab a sandwich. I'm still starving."

"I put the chicken salad in the fridge," I said, walking over to it. "Let me get your sandwich."

I got it out and handed it to him, wrapped in a paper towel. He gave me another kiss, then looked deep into my eyes. "To answer your previous question: I would do anything in my power to protect you and Hope," he said quietly. "I understand and support your need to do the same. All I ask is that you do everything you can to stay safe and in one piece. Can you promise me that?"

Biting my lower lip, I gave him a slight nod as tears stung my eyes. "Yeah. I promise. I have too much to lose."

"Then that's all I can ask." He gave me another quick kiss before spinning around and walking out the door.

"What just happened?" Neely Kate asked, watching him, slack-jawed.

"Joe just gave me permission to do whatever I think is necessary to protect my family and the county, no questions asked."

"Okay," she said, "what have you done with my brother?"

I laughed softly, but I was still in awe of what he'd just said.

"So…" she said, turning to me with excitement in her eyes. "What do we do first?"

"We?" I asked. "You're to have no part in this, Neely Kate," I said in a stern tone. "You and Jed are leavin' town so you don't get involved in this mess."

She propped a hand on her hip and gave me plenty of attitude. "Well, I haven't left yet, have I? I'll help until we leave."

"I highly doubt Jed would approve."

Her brow shot up. "We might be married, but that man doesn't own me."

"Neely Kate," I said with a sigh. I started to remind her that he was looking out for her best interests, but I saw that Joe had stopped midstride on his way back to the barn and pulled out his phone.

He talked for about ten seconds before heading back to the house, his phone still pressed to his ear. He hung up while he stood at the bottom step of the back door, then let himself into the house.

"Is everything okay?" I asked as soon as he walked back in. I knew it wasn't, but I hated to speculate.

"I just got a call," he said with a heavy sigh as he started to rub the back of his neck. "Word about Margi."

"Well, don't keep us in suspense," Neely Kate prodded.

But even before he said it, I knew he had bad news.

Joe's gaze lifted to mine. "Margi was found dead, and Levi Romano is missin'."

Chapter Twelve

"Oh my word," I said, feeling lightheaded. I couldn't believe it. I'd just seen her two days ago.

Fear had returned to Joe's eyes, and I knew he was playing the what-if game again, only his scenarios had all turned more violent.

"What happened?" Neely Kate asked.

Joe gave her a grim look. "A deputy found her in her home."

"How'd she die?" Neely Kate asked.

"I can't release that yet, and even if I could, I wouldn't have anything to tell you since we don't know yet."

So it likely wasn't something obvious like a gunshot wound. Then a new thought hit me.

"Does Randy know?" Randy Miller, a sheriff's deputy who'd helped me plenty in the past, had dated Margi for a few months, but last I'd heard, they'd broken up about a month ago.

Joe made a face. "Yeah."

"Is he okay?" Neely Kate asked.

"I don't know," Joe said, "but he's definitely not working on her murder investigation."

That made sense, but I wondered how Randy was handling it. It was hard for me to accept she was gone, and we'd barely known each other. They'd gone out for months.

We all stood in stunned silence for several moments before I jerked my gaze to Joe. "You said Levi is missin'?"

"He never showed up to work this morning. His assistant thought maybe he was out on an emergency call and forgot to tell her, but he still hasn't shown up, and his phone goes straight to voicemail."

"Do you think Levi might have killed his sister and run off?" Neely Kate asked.

"Neely Kate!" I admonished. "That's *Levi* you're talkin' about. The man who saved Muffy's life."

She met my gaze. "Sometimes you don't know what people are capable of. And he might have done it in a fit of rage."

"I've never seen Levi enraged," I said.

"Just because you haven't seen it, doesn't mean it hasn't happened," Neely Kate countered.

She was right, but it seemed far more likely Margi had been mixed up in something bad. Her attitude toward me had always seemed a bit strange, and it probably wasn't a coincidence she'd arrived in town right about the time Hardshaw had gotten serious about wiggling into town.

"At the moment," Joe said in a slightly louder than usual voice, "anything is possible, but it's all speculation at this stage. So we'll investigate everything until the clues start pointin' us in the right direction."

"Did you get anything from the surveillance tapes?" I asked.

"There's nothin' on them."

"What?" I asked. "How can that be?"

"Someone knew they were there because they covered the lenses from the side. We got nothin'."

I knew nothing good would come of pinning too much hope on the cameras. And now we knew a deep level of forethought had been put into the action.

Joe cast a glance out the back window. "I need to go check on things out there and make a call to the DA."

"Okay," I said, watching him head back outside. I lowered into a chair, feeling sick. "I can't believe Margi's dead."

"I might not have liked her much," Neely Kate muttered, "but I would never have wished her dead." She made a face. "I'm gonna go to the bathroom and then call Jed and let him know what's goin' on."

"Good idea." I had a couple of texts of my own to send.

As soon as she was out of sight, I grabbed my phone and pulled up Mason's number.

Have you heard about Margi Romano?

I was just sending off a check-in text to Randy when my phone rang with a call from Mason.

"What do you know?" he asked.

That gave me pause. Were they trying to keep her murder under wraps?

I cast a glance at the powder room, where Neely Kate had gone, then headed for the stairs. I'd likely share what I found out with her, but I didn't want to risk her overhearing something that Mason wanted me to keep to myself. She'd already guessed he was my source earlier.

"Have you heard about my barn?" I asked, stalling as I came up with a plan. I suspected he'd confirm information I already had, but he probably wouldn't freely drop anything else into my lap. Not like this morning.

"It would have been impossible not to," he said in a flat tone. "Joe wasn't quiet about calling for help."

"You think he should have been?" I asked with a frown. I headed up to my room and shut the door behind me. I could see everything going on around the barn from the sunroom.

He paused, then sounded guarded. "So you're calling about the break-in at your barn?"

"That's *one* of the reasons," I said. "And it was more than a break-in. They dug a huge hole out there sometime after I headed to town this morning. Not a quick or easy task."

"Do you know who was responsible?" Mason asked. "You don't have to give me a direct answer. A hint will suffice."

"No, but I suspect someone bigger like Hardshaw," I said. "Especially with everything goin' down this week But now that I think about it, it could also have been Carmichael. We already suspect he killed Rufus Wilson, so it's not outside the realm of possibility that he knew what Margi had buried out there and forced her to tell him the location before he killed her."

"Wait. Margi Romano is *dead?*" he asked in surprise.

I sat on the edge of my desk. "I thought you knew that was why I texted."

Mason released a string of expletives under his breath.

"What do you know about Margi's ties to my barn?" I asked.

"I know she's keeping horses out there," he said. "And that she did some construction on your barn."

"Were you watchin' my barn or Margi?" I asked in a blunt tone.

He was silent for several seconds. "You haven't been under surveillance since around the time of the grand jury."

Not exactly an answer as to whether the state had been watching Margi. Especially since she'd started her construction around the same time as the grand jury last October.

While I was peeved I'd been under surveillance, I wasn't exactly surprised by it. They'd tried to get information from me about the murder of two Sugar Branch policemen. Denny had killed them, saving me, but the police thought James was behind it. They'd hoped to nail him to the wall with my information.

"Why were you watchin' Margi?" I pressed.

"I never said we were. You're speculating."

Time to take a different tactic. "Why would she have hidden boxes of guns in my barn?"

"How did you know they were guns?" he asked, his voice cold.

Score one for me. Sure, Joe had told me as much, but Mason had just confirmed it. "I have my ways. The real question is who stole them and to what purpose."

"Did you find out from Roberta Hanover?"

I found it interesting that he thought she might know. Did he think James was involved? I knew he'd been selling arms to the Collards, but he'd had a falling out with them last year...before Margi started working on the barn.

"No, I haven't found out anything from her yet," I admitted.

He was silent for a moment. "I've got to go," he said. "It's been an interesting chat. If you harvested anything from this conversation, I hope that our confidentiality agreement remains intact."

"Always."

"Thank you." Then he hung up.

"No," I whispered as I watched a deputy string crime tape around my barn, "thank *you*."

Now what to do with this information?

I heard whimpers on the monitor, still tucked in my pocket, so I turned it off and headed to Hope's nursery. She was still half asleep, her hands fisted as she waved them around and kicked her feet, trying to free herself from the blanket burrito Joe must have made when he put her down. Muffy was in her room, watching me.

"Good afternoon, Sweet Hope," I cooed. "Are you ready to get up and see all of the commotion goin' on?"

Her response was to let out a tiny wail of anger.

"I know," I said in a soft voice. "You're upset that you missed out on all the excitement. You're just like your momma. Aunt Neely Kate is here, and so is Daddy. He's busy workin', but when he finds out you're up, I'm sure he'll come in and tell you good afternoon."

I unwrapped her as I spoke, then grabbed a diaper from the stack next to the bed and made quick work of changing her. She had to be hungry again, because she was crying in outrage by the time I carried her downstairs, Muffy following on my heels.

Neely Kate was standing in the living room with an anxious look.

"Do you look that way because you can't stand to hear your niece cry or because you got some bad news from Jed?" I asked as I made my way to the sofa. I got settled, then lifted my shirt to nurse Hope.

"Both, I guess," Neely Kate said as she sat down beside me. Muffy jumped up onto the sofa between us, resting her head on Neely Kate, who began to absently rub behind her ear.

"Well," I said, my back tensing. "Spit it out."

"Jed wants us to meet with Dermot."

"Okay," I said. "I'm all for that, and I'm sure I can get away. But who's gonna be at this meeting? I need to know if I'm bringin' Hope."

"I think it's safe to bring her. It's just you and me, Jed, Witt, and Dermot."

"Dermot's not bringin' any men?"

Muffy moved her head, and Neely Kate stopped petting her. "Jed told him that you'd likely have the baby since Joe's workin'."

"A safe bet now that he has two murder investigations and the barn robbery."

She nodded. "I guess Dermot has heard rumors he wants to discuss."

I pushed out a sigh. "Well, that's good, right?"

"Yeah." But the way she was wringing her hands in her lap didn't suggest good news.

"Why are you so pent up?" I asked, narrowing my eyes. Something told me it was more than worry that she and Jed wouldn't be able to get away now. "I mean, I know a lot's goin' on, but you've handled worse than this while singin' 'Whistle While You Work.'"

Her head jutted back in outrage. "I've never sung that song in my life."

"Okay, so maybe while you were paintin' your nails would be a better analogy."

She nodded her acceptance and forgiveness for suggesting such a thing. I made a mental note to find out why she found that so offensive later.

"What's goin' on, Neely Kate?"

"Jed heard something else." She shook her head. "Something unrelated to the mess with your barn and Margi."

"What is it? Are you worried about going away while all of this is happenin', because I still think it's a good idea."

She let out a bitter laugh. "Oh, we're not goin' anywhere. Kate has made sure of that."

I involuntarily sucked in a breath, and Hope stopped nursing to look up at me. "Sorry, sweet baby," I said, stroking her tiny arm with my fingertip. "Momma was just surprised is all."

She stared at me with huge eyes, then seemed to accept my answer and resumed nursing.

"What happened with Kate?" I asked as I grabbed a pillow to prop under Hope's body.

Neely Kate reached over and helped me situate it. "We think she tried to make contact with our baby's birth mother."

"What?" I practically shouted, disturbing Hope again. Startled, she began to wail.

I bounced her in my arm. "Momma's so sorry, sweet baby. I didn't mean to scare you."

"Maybe we should talk about this later," Neely Kate said over Hope's crying, guilt filling her eyes.

"No," I said, trying to guide the baby to latch back on. "Now that the shock has worn off, I promise not to overreact again, although to be fair, it wasn't really an overreaction."

"True, but you're nursing your baby," she said, worrying her hands. "We can talk about this later."

As if Hope wanted to convince Neely Kate to heed my suggestion, she stopped crying and latched on again.

"My baby doesn't take precedence over yours, Neely Kate," I insisted in a hushed tone. "What did Kate do?"

"Well, Jed found out through a mutual friend that a strange woman approached her last night at the Dairy Bar where she works down in Sugar Branch. The woman ordered an ice cream cone but then hung around, asking personal questions until the manager made her leave."

"What kind of personal questions?"

"What she planned to do with her life now that she had graduated. If her family had any history of mental illness or alcoholism or drug abuse."

"What?" I whisper-shouted.

Neely Kate grimaced and glanced down at Hope, who didn't seem disturbed. "I know. It could just be some random weirdo, but the timing feels too coincidental."

"Did the woman say anything direct about the baby?"

She shook her head. "No. She asked our birth mother where she was going to college and whether she could afford it."

"And did the birth mother answer her questions?" I felt weird calling her 'birth mother,' but Neely Kate and Jed had said they had sworn to protect her privacy and thus refused to tell me or anyone else her name.

"I think she answered a few of the innocuous ones, like that she's going to LSU and doesn't know what she's going to major in, and then got weirded out by the rest. That's when the manager stepped in." Tears filled her eyes. "Her brother—the one who told Jed that she was putting her baby up for adoption—was the one who told Jed. He thought it was weird and wondered if it had anything to do with Skeeter. But the woman had short dark hair. In a bob. She was medium height and looked like she was in her mid to late twenties."

I pressed my lips together. "What do you think she was up to?"

"I don't know," Neely Kate said, "But we're definitely not leaving town until *she* does. It's just… How did Kate find out who she is? We haven't even told you and Joe. Only our attorney knows."

"I don't know," I said with a worried sigh. "How does Kate find out anything? Could she have tapped your phone or hacked your computer?"

"I don't know. I haven't seen her since last summer."

"We both know that doesn't mean she hasn't dropped in for a visit and forgotten to say hello."

"True." She looked down at her hands, still worrying them, then glanced up at me with panic in her eyes. "What if Kate tries to hurt the baby?"

"I know it's a legitimate concern," I said. "Kate is criminally insane, but she also has a weird devotion to you. She takes her big sister role seriously."

"I know, but she has a weird and dangerous way of proving her affection," Neely Kate grumbled.

She had a point. Kate had done some horrible things to Neely Kate in the past, all because Kate had a warped idea of what people did to and for the people they loved. "Still," I said, "she knows how much you want a baby. Shoot, she killed Stella and Branson because she held them responsible for making you sterile. She's not going to take that baby away from you." It occurred to me that I wasn't just trying to convince her—I was hoping to convince myself too. Kate might mean well where Neely Kate was concerned, but she didn't always think logically. "Maybe that was her way of screening the birth mother."

"Screen her for what?"

"Her approval?" I asked, my brow lifted.

Neely Kate bit her lip. "What if she didn't pass?"

"How could she *not* pass? She's super smart, and you said she comes from a loving family. She's not a drug addict and doesn't even drink." I leaned closer. "And we both know that Kate didn't need her in-person interview to find out any of that. She knew every bit of it and more before she walked up to the counter."

"So why talk to her at all?"

"It's Kate," I reminded her. "I think she's still trying to prove she's worthy of bein' your big sister. Maybe she knew it would get back to you and Jed, and in her weird, warped way, she thought it would prove to you that she has your best interests in mind."

Her eyes widened. "She's dangerous."

"She is," I agreed. "I'm not implying that I trust her. I'm only telling you what I think her reasoning is."

Nodding, she pushed out a sigh and sat back on the cushions.

I switched Hope to the other side, then glanced over at Neely Kate. "Why don't you call the baby Daisy?"

She glanced up at the ceiling. "Because she's not mine yet."

My heart skipped a beat. "Do you think the birth mother will change her mind? Because I know you passed your home study."

"I don't want to get my hopes up," she said quietly. "I don't want to jinx it."

I could have told her everything would be okay, but I couldn't guarantee that. Not with everything else going on. "I get it. But I sure hope you're holding her next week."

She gave me a soft smile. "Me too."

Why was I worried that was never going to happen?

Chapter Thirteen

I needed to focus on what was in my control. "So when and where are we meeting Jed and Dermot?"

"He said he'd let us know, but he's hoping for sooner rather than later."

"Good," I said. "I want to do this while Joe's busy with the barn and the murder investigations."

"I don't think it will be long. Jed's anxious to get Dermot's perspective."

"I am too." Hope lost interest in nursing and stared up at me, a smile lighting up her eyes. I smiled back, my heart bursting with love.

I picked her up and rested her on my shoulder, patting her back. "I'll burp her, and then she's all yours."

Neely Kate sat up and reached for her. "I'll burp her."

I laughed. "Deal, but fair warning, she's been spitting up a lot more lately. You got hit earlier."

"I'll take my chances again," she said as she placed Hope on her shoulder and began to speak in a higher pitch. "Aunt Neely Kate can deal with more spit-up, can't I, Hope?"

Hope's answer was a loud belch.

"You might want to grab a towel off the coffee table," I said as I got up and headed to the kitchen. "Come on, Muff. Hope's safe with Neely Kate, and you need to go outside." It was true, but I also wanted to check on the horses. The commotion likely had them spooked. It was doubtful they'd be able to stay in the barn tonight, which meant I needed to figure out what to do with them, especially since Margi wouldn't be around to make arrangements anymore.

It hit me again. Margi was dead. Someone had *killed* her.

What had she been messed up in? Had she dated Randy to get information about what the sheriff department knew? Who was she affiliated with? Hardshaw? The Collards?

Both?

I grabbed two apples from the fruit bowl, then clipped Muffy's leash to her collar, just in case she decided to take off for the barn. My phone buzzed in my back pocket, and while Muffy sniffed the bushes and peed, I set the apples down on the back steps and took it out.

Dermot had sent a text. *Things are progressing. We need to chat again.*

My heart skipped a beat. Was he talking about my barn and Margi, or did he have other information?

NK said Jed was setting up a meeting.

He responded immediately. *In 30 minutes at Carlisle's garage.*

I shot a glance over at Joe, who was standing on the perimeter of the crime scene tape. As though he sensed I was watching, he turned to look at me, and even from this distance, I could feel his love and concern.

It would take fifteen minutes to get there, and I still needed to pack up Hope's things, but I had to talk to Joe first.

I grabbed the apples, then led Muffy toward the edge of the field where the horses were kept during the day. In the beginning, they'd had a smaller corral, but then Margi had asked permission to fence a larger area so they'd have room to roam. All expenses paid.

Why hadn't I questioned where all the money was coming from? Although I'd been wary of her in the beginning, I'd dismissed my own concerns…and Joe's. Had she and Randy broken up because he'd become suspicious too?

The horses seemed skittish—and so did the deputies in the barn. They kept shooting me looks, so I headed toward the field, turning about halfway between the house and the barn, to make everyone more comfortable.

Buttercup wandered over first, not that I was surprised. She'd been the first horse to arrive on the farm and had taken to me right away. I rubbed her nose. "It's a crazy day, isn't it, Buttercup? But you're okay. I'll figure out what to do with you tonight."

"I already called Madison," Joe said as he moved in next to me. "She says she knows someone who can take them in tonight."

I gave him a grateful smile. "Thanks." One less thing to worry about.

"Of course I asked her whether she'd noticed anything this morning. She said everything was in its place, and she closed the barn door but didn't lock it. She feels terrible."

"Shoot," I said, glancing over at Ninja, the second horse we sheltered. He was still about twenty feet away, watching me cautiously. "Half the time *I* don't lock it."

"I assured her that it didn't matter if the doors were locked or not; they were gettin' in one way or the other."

I nodded, rubbing Buttercup's nose with one hand and holding Muffy's leash with the other, but my dog tugged on the leash to show me she didn't approve of being restrained.

"Why's Muffy on a leash?" Joe asked.

"I was worried she'd run into the barn. You know I worry about letting her off-leash after what happened."

For a few days, I'd been terrified we'd lost her. Without Levi, we probably would have…and now he was missing.

Joe took the leash from me and bent down next to her. "Are you gonna be a good girl, Muff?"

She responded by licking his nose.

He laughed. "I'll take that as a yes." He unhooked her and held her gaze. "I need you to stay here with your momma and me, okay?"

Muffy licked his nose again, then wandered a few feet away from us but stayed next to the fence.

"Did you tell Madison that Margi was murdered?" I asked as he stood upright.

"No. We're still keepin' that under wraps."

Quiet enough that even Mason didn't know. "Do you have any suspects?" I asked, holding up the other apple so that Ninja could see it.

"It's too early to be namin' anyone," Joe said, "and even if I had anyone in mind, I wouldn't be at liberty to tell you."

A year ago, I might have been pissed at that—especially since Mason, of all people, had been more forthcoming—but the last thing I wanted to do was get Joe in trouble. He took enough risks being with me. But that didn't mean I couldn't feed information to him. "Do you want to know my thoughts?"

His brow lifted in surprise. "Always."

"In my mind, there are two possible suspects. One is Hardshaw. Margi showed up in town around the same time they did. What if they gave her the guns, and she hid them so the weapons would be ready when they wanted to make their big move?"

"I have a similar suspicion," he said. "And the other?"

Ninja moved up next to Buttercup, and I handed him the apple before glancing over at Joe. "Denny Carmichael. He's my number one suspect for Rufus Wilson's murder as well."

His eyes narrowed. "Wilson's name hasn't been released yet."

I leaned closer and lowered my voice. "Why do you think we were havin' that conversation earlier?"

He frowned.

"Joe, the sooner you accept that I know things, the easier this will all be."

"I don't have a problem with you knowin' things," he said without heat. "It's how you came by the information that has me worried."

I pressed a kiss to his lips. "I need you to trust me, Joe."

He studied me for several long seconds, then asked, "Why do you think Carmichael's responsible for Rufus?"

"This remains between the two of us?" I asked.

"Of course," he said, wrapping an arm around my back and tugging me to him.

"I know Rufus worked for James." I held up a hand. "Don't ask me how I know."

His lips pinched together, but he didn't look pissed.

"I think Carmichael killed him to start a war." I wasn't ready to tell him about Rufus' background with safe opening. Joe had enough on his plate, and I still suspected Bobby was more likely to talk to me than someone official. I wasn't willing to take chances, not when my ability to see Violet's kids again was on the line.

He frowned. "A war between Carmichael and Malcolm, or Carmichael and Hardshaw?"

"If I had to guess, Hardshaw, which includes or included James. And if Carmichael's plannin' for a war, he's gonna need weapons."

"The guns in the barn."

I hesitated, then said, "Let's just say you're on the right track suspectin' guns." Maybe his intelligence and Mason's had come from the same source, but if not, the validation might help.

He gave me a wary look.

"Again, don't ask me how I know, and I'm not one hundred percent certain, but I'd bet good money on it."

"So where did Margi get the guns?" he asked.

"That I don't know. But again, we have our two main players. Hardshaw and Carmichael. They're behind this, one way or another."

He released me and ran a hand over his head.

"Of course there's someone else around who is interested in weapons and pissed as hell," I said, lifting my brow. "The Collards."

"How would the Collards connect with Margi?" he asked. "They don't even have any animals other than chickens."

"I don't know, and even if I did, I can't give you everything." I gave him a teasing grin, but in truth, I had given him everything, or near enough. The information about Rufus was all I'd held back.

He lifted a hand to my cheek and brushed a strand of hair behind my ear. "You're pretty good at this sleuthin' stuff."

I smiled. "I learned from the best." I rested a hand on his shoulder. "Remember when I was investigating the murder Bruce Wayne was on trial for? You told me not to presume someone was guilty without lookin' at the clues." I leaned closer. "So while those are all working theories, I wouldn't hang my hat on any of them without evidence."

Pride filled his eyes. "Smart woman." But his gaze quickly turned inquisitive, worried. "You've spent some time thinkin' this through."

"I've got to think about *something* while I'm nursin' our daughter."

"Are you plannin' to act on these cases?" he asked carefully.

"They're on my radar," I said. "I'm workin' on a couple of somethings."

He studied me.

"I want to be as honest with you as I can, Joe. I truly believe we can work this out, but you have to trust me."

He sucked in a breath, then glanced back to the barn. I knew I was asking a lot of him, but he'd also come a long way. Finally, he turned to face me, wearing a serious expression. "I trust you, Rose. And to answer the question you asked earlier." He wrapped his arms around me again and pulled me flush to his body. "If I had the power to help you or Hope or the citizens of Fenton County, I would do so. I'm not sure anything could stop me. I wouldn't be much of a man if I tried to prevent you from doing the same." But even as he said the words, I could see that it cost him. He'd love nothing more than to lock me up in the house to keep me safe, but he respected me too much to consider it.

"Thank you," I whispered. "I love you."

"I love you too," he said in a husky tone. "When's your doctor's appointment again?"

I laughed. "It's the day after tomorrow. And you already know that."

"Just checkin'," he teased. He gave me a soft, lingering kiss.

I wrapped my arms around his neck, not caring what the deputies saw or thought. "There's one more thing you need to know." I paused. "Kate texted Neely Kate this morning, and they think she reached out to Jed and Neely Kate's birth mother."

He dropped his arms and took a step back. "*What?*"

"Shh..." I murmured with an upturned brow. "You can't tell anyone, Joe."

He started to say something but cut himself off.

"We're agreed?" When he didn't answer, I said, "Are you going to keep this to yourself?"

"It depends on what you tell me."

I slowly shook my head. "Then I can't tell you anything else. In fact, I shouldn't have mentioned it at all. It's not my information to give."

"Don't you see that you're puttin' me in a difficult position here?" he asked. "Both as the chief deputy sheriff and her brother?"

"Yes, Joe," I said softly. "I *can* see, but Neely Kate doesn't seem to be in any danger, and the birth mother is safe and doesn't appear to be any the wiser. There's really nothing for you to do, and you know Neely Kate will be furious with both of us if you intervene without being asked. You need to focus your resources on Margi and the break-in."

He remained quiet for several seconds, then said, "About that...I need to head over to Margi's house, and I don't feel comfortable leavin' you and Hope here."

I forced a grin. "Even with all these deputies milling around?"

He shrugged. "It's not a logical fear."

"Well...I was just about to run an errand with Neely Kate," I said.

His brow lifted. "An errand?"

"I'm gonna go hang out with Neely Kate and Jed. Neely Kate's feeling a little freaked out about Kate, part of her reason for possibly leavin' town—and she'll feel better with Jed around."

He glanced toward the house. "Maybe I should talk to her before I go."

"As long as you don't interrogate her."

He gave me a long look. "Okay. But I'm telling her I know Kate sent her a text and contacted the birth mother. I'm not pretendin' I don't."

"That's fair," I said. The horses had wandered off and seemed fairly content, and I'd talked to Joe. I'd set out what I'd hoped to accomplish. "I need to get goin'."

He reached out and took my hand, squeezing tight. "We're good, right?"

"Joe," I said, my voice breaking. "We're better than good. We're damn near perfect."

He pulled me to him, wrapping me up in his strong arms as he buried his face into my hair. "Something feels off," he whispered, "like I'm about to lose everything."

I considered forcing another vision to see if anything had changed after my encounter with James that morning, but I always felt unsettled after witnessing Joe's death—and now I'd had two totally different visions of his demise. It would only make both of us feel worse. It was easier to dismiss the vision when everything was going well, but things were quickly turning to crap, and suddenly it felt all too real.

"You're not losin' me," I said through the sudden lump in my throat, "and you're not losin' Hope. In fact," I said, leaning back slightly so I could see his face, "I was thinkin' maybe we could make our family more official."

"What do you mean?" he asked, looking confused. "I'm already on Hope's birth certificate, and I don't want you going anywhere near Malcolm to get him to sign those paternity papers."

Little did he know...

I smiled up at him despite my guilt over not telling him about my encounter with James, which would only piss him off. I needed him to focus on Margi's death and who'd dug up our barn. And what I was about to propose. Literally.

"Not that," I said. "Something more sentimental."

He still looked confused.

I laughed. "I'm askin' you to marry me, Joe. I want to be able to call you my husband, not just my boyfriend, which feels incredibly lacking."

He stared at me with a blank look. "You're askin' me to marry you?"

"Well, don't act like you'd rather lick the bottom of my boots after I've helped Madison clean the horse barn."

A huge smile spread over his face. "It's not that, it's..." He swallowed and suddenly looked unsure of himself. "Rose, I bought an engagement ring three days after Hope was born."

"You did?" My chest filled with butterflies, a feeling that reminded me of when Joe and I had first gotten to know each other, and he was Joe McAllister, my mysterious next-door neighbor.

"Yeah. I love you and Hope, and I love our home and this farm, even when there's trouble in the barn...*and* everywhere else."

He gestured to it, and I wondered if now was a bad time to tell him there had been so much more trouble out in that barn than he knew about.

He took a breath. "What I'm tryin' to say is..." His eyes filled with warmth and heat. "I've spent my whole life lookin' for a place where I fit. Where I belong. You're it, Rose. It's you. You're my home."

Tears filled my eyes. "Joe..."

"I've known it since I helped you paint your livin' room to cover the blood from your mother's murder. I tried to let you go, because when I was finally able to pull my head out of my ass, I realized that while you fit me, I didn't fit you. You needed someone worthy of your love, so I became a better man. And I confess, I gave up on you a few times. And when you and Mason broke up...I didn't make a move because I knew I wasn't worthy of you yet."

"Oh, Joe," I said, closing the distance between us and cupping his cheek. "Don't say that."

"No," he said. "It's true. I had a lot of soul searchin' to do, and I know I'm not perfect, but—"

I covered his lips with my fingertips. "I'm not perfect either. Far from it. We'll just work on it together."

He laughed, his eyes shining with unshed tears. "I was planning on proposing to you when I thought you were ready."

"So I beat you to it," I said, then pierced him with my gaze. "We're never gonna be a normal couple, you know. We're always gonna do things backward. Maybe you want something else."

"No, Rose. As long as I have you and Hope, that's all I want or need." He pulled me close again, staring down at my face. "I love you, Rose Anne Gardner. It will make me the happiest man in the world to be your husband."

I laughed. "I feel like I should be on bended knee, puttin' a ring on your finger."

He laughed too. "The only ring I want is the one you'll put on my finger at our weddin'. But I need to give you yours."

My mood turned somber. "I want to wait."

Pain and confusion filled his eyes. "Why?"

"Because the moment you put that ring on my finger, I want to make plans for our weddin', and we both have other things to deal with right now." Plus, it could put Joe in danger. What if James saw me wearing Joe's ring, and that was what pushed him over the edge to shoot him?

Joe nodded, and relief filtered through me. "So you want a weddin'?"

"Of course I want a weddin', but not a big one. Something small, with just our close friends and family. Like Neely Kate and Jed's."

He smiled. "I like the sound of that."

"Then we're in agreement?" I asked. "No ring yet, and a small wedding soon after this mess is wrapped up?"

"That sounds perfect to me."

"Good." I gave him another quick kiss, but his arms held me close, and his mouth claimed mine in a slow, seductive kiss that made my toes curl. Heat filled me that had nothing to do with the rising temperatures. I wanted this man in every way.

"Wow," I said when he lifted his head. "If I'd known you'd kiss me like that, I would have asked you to marry me long ago."

He leaned back his head and laughed, a merry sound I felt all the way down to my marrow. I wanted more of that.

I'd finally found happiness and a family of my own. Now it was time to protect it.

Chapter Fourteen

Neely Kate had already started restocking Hope's diaper bag. "Did you pack some extra clothes and diapers?" I asked.

"There were eight diapers left, so I only grabbed a couple. Surely that's enough."

"I'll just go grab a few more," I said as I headed for the door to the living room. "Who knows if I'll need to go somewhere else and how long I'll be gone."

She started to protest, but I ignored her and went up to Hope's room to gather what I needed, then went into my room and opened my underwear drawer to get my gun and ammunition. I quickly changed into a sundress with pockets so I could attach my thigh holster and strapped in my gun. There was no reason to believe I'd be facing danger—I wouldn't be bringing Hope otherwise—but that didn't mean I shouldn't be fully prepared to defend myself. The dress would make it harder to nurse Hope, but safety took precedence here. My pepper spray was already in my purse. When I headed back down the stairs, I could hear Neely Kate's and Joe's voices coming from the kitchen.

The first words that registered were Neely Kate's: "I'm gonna kill Rose."

"She's worried," Joe said. "And so am I. But I'm going to trust Jed has things in hand."

I reached the doorway, watching them as they stood next to the table. Joe was holding Hope, her back to his chest, her booty on his forearm while his other arm crossed over her chest and held her in place. He was swaying from side to side, although I was sure he wasn't aware he was doing it.

My heart burst with love, but my attention quickly shifted to Neely Kate. Neither of them seemed to be aware of my presence, and she nodded. "He does."

"Then that's all I need to know for now," he said. "Just remember I'm here for you, Neely Kate. As your big brother or as a law enforcement officer for the county. I can be one or both. Whatever you need me to be."

"I love you, Joe," she said, her voice breaking.

"I love you too." He pulled her into a sideways hug so as to not crush Hope. "Our dad was pretty shitty, but at least that whole mess ended with me finding you."

She released a laugh as she pulled away, then finally caught sight of me standing in the doorway.

"I didn't mean to interrupt," I said.

"We got it worked out," Joe said, his gaze dropping to my bare legs—not in a sexy kind of way, but like he was wondering what I was up to.

"No thanks to you," Neely Kate said, but it lacked the sting of real anger.

"Kate's his sister too," I said. "He'd tell you if he heard from her, *wouldn't* you, Joe?" I pinned my gaze on him.

"Yeah," he said. "Sure."

Neely Kate propped a hand on her hip. "That didn't sound very convincin'."

"Don't hurt him," I teased as I crossed the room toward him and wrapped an arm around his back. "Not after he just agreed to marry me."

"*What?*" she squealed.

Hope startled and started to cry.

Joe turned her around and cradled her to his chest. "There, there, Hope. Your aunt does that a lot, so the sooner you get used to it the better."

"You asked *him* to marry *you?*" Neely Kate asked, incredulous.

"Yeah," Joe said with a huge grin. "She asked me out by the horse pasture, right next to a huge pile of poo. I turned her down and told her I was holding out for something social media worthy."

I burst out laughing, and Neely Kate looked like she wanted to hit him. "You liar, and you better be thankin' your lucky stars you're holdin' my favorite niece or you'd be pummeled."

Joe laughed. "Why do you think I'm holdin' her? I'm no fool."

It was total bull. He'd had no idea I was going to tell her.

"I can't believe you asked *him*," she said, shaking her head.

"Turns out he was waiting to ask me," I said. "He claims he bought a ring three days after Hope was born."

She waved her hand as she rolled her eyes. "*Please.* I'm not surprised. He would have asked you to marry him last summer if he'd thought he stood a chance." She glanced at the clock on the wall. "But we need to go if we're gonna make our meetin'."

I cringed as Joe turned to me with a lifted brow. "*Meetin'?* I thought you were just goin' to their house."

"Oops," Neely Kate said, then scooped Hope out of Joe's arms. "I'm gonna get Hope strapped into her car seat."

She quickly headed to the living room.

"I'm doin' what needs to be done, Joe," I said softly. "And I was truthful when I said I was going to hang out with Jed and Neely Kate."

"And does that meetin' have anything to do with you changing your clothes?"

"Yeah, but I'm fine. I promise. It's just a precaution."

He nodded, but he still didn't look happy. "I'm headin' into town, but I'm only a phone call away."

"Me too," I said, making a production of picking up my phone from the table and slipping it into my pocket.

He started to head out the back door, only to stop a few steps in, turning back to face me. "Please tell me you have your gun strapped to your leg."

"I do."

"Good," he grunted, reaching for the doorknob. "If you pull that thing out of its holster, shoot to kill." Then he walked out the back door.

Neely Kate was strapping Hope into her seat while Muffy sat on the sofa and supervised. My friend glanced up at me. "Did you really ask Joe to marry you? Not the other way around?"

I laughed. "I already told you I did. No joke. It just feels so right with him, and somehow it seemed more fitting for me to suggest it first, you know?"

"Yeah," she said with a smile. "I do. But out by the horse pasture?"

"Mason asked me at Jaspers, and look how that turned out," I said. "It wouldn't matter if we had an Instagram-worthy proposal or got engaged wearing coveralls. What's important is that we love each other. Besides you, he's my best friend, and he makes me happy. There's something about knowing the man in your life is there when you need him—whether it's facing danger or moving the baby's clothes from the washer to the dryer, you know?"

"Yeah," she said with a soft smile. "I do."

"Good," I said. "Now that *that's* settled, let's head over to the garage. We're already late. But I think we should each take our own vehicle."

Because Neely Kate and Jed had made it clear they wanted to sit this out, and there was a chance I could figure out another safe errand that would yield information about the deal.

Neely Kate didn't look pleased with my suggestion. I knew she had plenty of questions, but she pressed her lips together, and we locked up the house and set the alarm. Since I didn't know where we would be heading or what we'd be doing after the meeting with Dermot, I left Muffy at home, much to her disappointment.

Hope made grunts and soft coos during the drive, but she didn't fall asleep, and no smells drifted up to the front seat to alert me to a desperate need for a diaper change. Neely Kate beat me to the garage by about twenty seconds, and wasted no time grabbing the car seat and lugging it inside. I grabbed the diaper bag and followed her in.

Jed, Dermot, and Witt were already sitting in the breakroom—Jed and Dermot in chairs at the table, Witt on the couch.

"Sorry we're late," I said, setting the bag down on the floor next to the sofa. Neely Kate got Hope out of her seat and handed her to Jed, who held her as if she were made of glass.

"I just got here myself," Dermot said, leaning back in his chair.

I plopped onto the sofa next to Witt. "Quite a few things have happened since we last talked this mornin'."

"You were never one to let grass grow under your feet," Dermot said.

I made a face. "In this instance, very little of what happened today was of my own doin'. As you've probably heard, someone dug a huge hole in my barn. Two different sources have suggested the perpetrators were diggin' up at least one box of guns. Have any of you heard any whispers about buried weapons?"

Witt and Jed were quiet, but Dermot shifted his weight.

That was unusual. Dermot usually told me things straight out. That was one of the things I admired most about him.

"What is it?" I asked him, holding his gaze.

"I've heard rumors that there were two boxes of stolen weapons in the county somewhere, but no one knew where they were hidden."

"Why haven't *I* heard anything about it?" Jed asked, cradling Hope in the crook of his arm.

"Because it's the kind of thing guys shoot the shit about while drinkin'," Dermot said. "You don't associate with that crowd anymore."

"Where did the story originate?" Jed asked.

"It was all rumors. No mention about who had them or even if they were for sale. No one even knows where the rumor came from."

"That makes no sense," Witt said. "What would be the purpose of talkin' about it?"

"I don't know," Dermot said. "I didn't really ask questions. Everyone knows the Collards have been amassing guns for years. I figured it had to do with them, and they were gearin' up for some kind of standoff with law enforcement. Normally, they just keep to themselves, but after I killed Carey, I started payin' closer attention. I'm worried they'll be out for revenge."

"A justified concern," Jed said. "Now that they're out on bail, I've been worried they might go after Rose."

"It's a safe assumption Margi put them there, given how much she pushed me to renovate the barn, but how did she get the guns?" I asked, not wanting to dwell on the Collards' intentions toward me.

Dermot swung his gaze to me. "Good question. Her name was never mentioned."

"So we don't know anything?" I asked.

"It might *not* have been Margi," Neely Kate said.

We all turned to face her.

"It could have been the construction guys," Neely Kate said. "Maybe she didn't know anything about it. I mean, we know Hardshaw was using Mike because he had his own construction company."

"And we still don't know what they were scheming," I said, deep in thought. "Vera said that Mike approached her boyfriend because Hardshaw needed an electrician with access to a restricted area at the courthouse." I turned to Dermot. "Did you ever figure out what they were up to?"

"No. We looked at upcomin' cases and anyone of note comin' to the courthouse, thinkin' they might be after plantin' a bomb, but nothing popped up on our radar. We're just as clueless now as we were six weeks ago."

"And anyone who knew anything is dead," Jed added.

"Or in witness protection," Neely Kate added, which made me think again of Ashley and Mikey. Were they okay? Did they think I'd abandoned them? Pain sliced into me.

"Violet left me something important in that safe," I said, getting frustrated. "And I'm beginning to suspect that Denny Carmichael knows of its existence. Especially since he was the one who killed so many people connected to Mike." Because Vera's boyfriend had directly worked for my brother-in-law, and Mike had also done work for Sonder Tech.

"Whatever it is, it's more than just a simple piece of information," Jed said. "Otherwise, he would have gotten it from any of the three people he murdered." He glanced in my direction. "I don't suppose you've heard anything from Roberta Hanover?"

"No." I was considering reaching out to her again, but the vision had shown me that she would come to me.

"Who's Roberta?" Dermot asked.

"Rufus Wilson's girlfriend," I said.

"We got information that Rufus has experience cracking safes," Neely Kate said, then held up her hand. "And, no. We're not tellin' how we got that information."

Dermot nodded. "You think she might know something?"

"There's a chance," I said. "Neely Kate and I dropped by the Stop-N-Go at the corner of Maple and Hugo to talk to her. That's where she works. She seemed pretty scared. There was someone in a parked car when we got there, and he was still there when we left. We're pretty sure he was watching her."

"Jed?" Neely Kate asked, turning to him. "Did you find out anything from the license plate number I gave you?"

Jed made a face. "Stolen car from Texarkana."

Dermot shot Jed a hard look. "Texarkana is on the way from Dallas."

"You think Hardshaw is watchin' her?" Neely Kate asked.

"It makes sense," Witt said, watching Jed bounce Hope in his arms. "I'm just surprised they didn't skip straight to snatching her."

"How important do you think this woman is?" Dermot asked me.

"I don't know," I said, "but there's a chance she knows something about what Violet was storing in her attorney's safe, and I'm starting to think it's really important."

Dermot's mouth pressed into a tight line. "Maybe I should send a couple of guys to pick her up."

I shook my head. "While I'm worried about her safety, if we're heavy-handed, she won't talk. I need her to trust me. I had a vision of her coming to me. On her own terms."

"She might not make it long enough to show up at your front door," Dermot said. "I'll at least send someone to keep tabs on her."

"Don't freak her out, Dermot," I said. "She'll run."

"My guy will be subtle," Dermot said as he pulled out his phone. "Not even the Hardshaw guy will know he's there. But Rose, if she knows something, we need to find out what it is, and the sooner the better."

He was right. The contents of that manila envelope were even more important than I'd thought.

"We need to find Margi and make her talk," Witt said.

"Hasn't Jed told you?" Neely Kate said. "Margi's dead. The sheriff deputies found her in her house when they went to question her." She took a deep breath. "But that's not all. Her brother is missing. He didn't show up to the clinic this morning."

"Levi Romano?" Witt asked in shock.

"Yeah."

"Is the vet part of this mess?" Jed asked.

"That's a very good question," Dermot said. "We're surrounded by more very good questions than we need."

"Here's another," I said. "Where does Carmichael fit into all of this? I can't help thinking they were either his guns in the first place or he heard the rumors and traced them back to the source."

"Either is plausible," Jed said. "What does Joe think?"

"He won't say."

"Rose," Witt groaned.

I spun to face him. "It's too early in the investigation, and besides, he and I have reached an understanding that some things can't be shared."

"You're kiddin'," Witt said.

"I told him I suspected Denny Carmichael might be responsible for it all—Rufus Wilson, the guns, Margi. All of it. I offered no proof, just my gut reaction."

Everyone was silent for a few moments, and the only sounds were Hope's happy coos as Jed swayed her from side to side.

"I'll do some diggin'," Dermot said. "Because while I think Carmichael has his hands in this, I'm not ruling out the Collards."

"Have you heard anything about Brox?" I asked. "Last I heard, he was still missing."

There was a note of concern in my voice, and Dermot shot me a surprised look.

"It's just that he's helped me on two occasions. I have trouble believing he would be part of this."

"He wasn't arrested," Neely Kate said. "Just his dad and two brothers."

"And his other brother is dead," Witt added.

But where was Brox? Had he run off to avoid retribution from his own family?

Dermot's phone vibrated. He checked the screen, then got up. "Gotta go. I'll let you know if I find out anything. Y'all do the same."

Jed nodded, and I said, "Yeah."

Dermot gave a short wave and walked out.

"Well," I said, picking up the diaper bag. "I think we've covered everything."

"What are you planning to do now?" Jed asked.

"Hope's almost out of diapers, and I think things are about to get crazy. I should probably go buy some."

"Do you really think that's a good idea right now?" Witt asked.

"The world may be spinning out of control, yet my daughter still pees and poops," I said sarcastically.

"Witt can get them," Jed said, but Witt gave him a look of terror, as if he might get a girl pregnant by buying diapers.

"No need for that," I said. "I'll be fine." I patted the outside of my left leg.

"You have your gun," Jed said solemnly.

"Someone dug up my barn, and I'm expecting Bobby Hanover to show up at my doorstep at any moment. I want to be prepared if someone comes after me and my family." But it occurred to me that my vision had shown Bobby at my front door. Which would be a moot point if I wasn't home. Still, my yard was swarming with deputies. I couldn't see her risking that.

"Do you want to leave Hope with me?" Neely Kate asked hopefully. "I can take her to my house, and then you can come back and hang out."

"Actually, Neely Kate," Jed said, "with Kate millin' around, I think you and Hope should stay here until I finish with the car I'm workin' on. It should take another hour or so."

I gasped. "We didn't tell Dermot about Kate."

Jed's mouth twisted to the side. "I'd like to keep it from him until we know what she's up to."

Neely Kate hung her head slightly, and I realized she and Jed had had this discussion at some point. "Now, we all know she's here to cause trouble. He deserves to know."

"Kate is a family matter," Jed said.

"I'm not buyin' that for a hot minute," I said, getting pissed. "Just this morning we discussed how her arrival can't be a coincidence."

"Nevertheless," Jed said.

Neely Kate didn't say anything; she was still hanging her head as though she couldn't bear to meet my eyes.

What was going on here? Then it hit me.

"She texted again."

Neely Kate's chin finally lifted, her eyes wide.

"What did she say?"

She took a breath, then said with a shaky voice, "She said her appearance in Fenton County was a family matter and that our birth mother was lovely."

"It was a threat, Rose," Jed said. "And yes, it was vague, but that doesn't change the intention behind it."

"This isn't like you, Jed," I said insistently. "You don't hide from danger. You stand up to it and shout in its face."

"Yeah," he said, rubbing the back of his neck. "That was when it was just me. I'd do *anything* to protect my family."

Which meant they could be used against him. That scared me more than I liked.

I stared at him for a long second. "So what do you think her end game is?"

"I don't know," he admitted, "but it won't change a thing if Dermot knows she's around."

"I disagree," I said with a lifted chin. "We all know she intends to interfere, *but*—" I took a breath, wondering if this was a huge mistake, "—I'm willing to keep this from him for *now*. However, if I feel like something has changed, I'm tellin' him."

Jed nodded.

"But I have one condition," I added. "If she texts again, you have to tell me. No secrets."

He hesitated, then nodded again.

"Neely Kate?"

When she looked up, there were tears streaming down her face, and she was clinging to Hope. "I can't lose my baby, Rose."

"I know," I whispered. But I suddenly didn't feel comfortable leaving Hope with them. Not if Kate was playing her games…and they were playing them with her.

"I think I'll just take Hope home and ask Joe to pick up diapers on the way home," I said, forcing a smile as I lifted Hope from Neely Kate's arms.

She nodded, still crying, but neither of them said anything as I placed Hope in her car seat and buckled her in.

"No," Witt blurted out. For a moment, I wasn't sure what he was objecting to, and maybe he wasn't so sure either, but he added, "I *am* going to get you those diapers, Rose," shooting a furious look at Jed. Then he walked out of the room.

I wasn't long in following him, and as I carried Hope out to the truck, I couldn't help thinking that we might win this war but destroy each other doing it.

Chapter Fifteen

A couple of minutes after I pulled out of the parking lot, I got a call from Dr. Newton's office.

"Hey, Rose," Loretta, the receptionist, said. "I'm just callin' to inform you that Dr. Newton has to go out of town tomorrow, so we're gonna have to cancel your appointment."

"What?" I groaned. "When can you reschedule me?"

"Not until the week after next," Loretta said. Then she added, "*Unless* you can make it here by four."

I glanced at the clock on my dashboard. It was 3:45. Heart racing, I said, "It's gonna be close, but I can make it. Is it okay if I have my baby with me?" Did I risk turning around and leaving her with Neely Kate?

"Don't you worry about that," Loretta said. "New mommas bring their babies in all the time. If she gets fussy while Dr. Newton's doin' your exam, then we'll hold her until you're done."

We made it just in time. Hope was an angel, but the staff insisted on holding her anyway. Dr. Newton declared me healed and healthy, and we discussed my birth control options. I told her Joe and I had already discussed it, and he'd said he would cover it. Literally.

I thought about stopping at Walmart for diapers on the way home—Witt had said he'd pick some up, but I couldn't tell if he'd meant it literally or if he'd just said it as a statement against Jed's attitude—but I was suddenly anxious to get home. Because Bobby might show up, and I needed to be there if she did. And I was suddenly anxious to see Joe. The doctor had given me the all-clear, and if Joe came home at a decent time, we could finally celebrate our engagement the way we both wanted to.

The deputies were still at the barn when I got back, but they looked to be packing up. I let Muffy out front on her leash and carried Hope in her car seat. She was starting to get restless, and I didn't need a vision to see another nursing session and nap were in our immediate future. I stepped into the shade of the oak tree and lingered there for a moment, Muffy tugging on the lead I'd wrapped around my wrist, to text Joe.

Hope and I are back at the house and safe. See you soon?

He didn't immediately respond, so I knew he had to be tied up with official business.

After I put her down for her nap, I set the monitor on my desk in the sunroom and tried to get some work done. The county was falling apart, but my business would soon be in shambles if I didn't start making the designs Bruce Wayne needed to install the plants.

But there was crime scene tape strung around my barn and at least eight deputies still inside. The horses were skittish in the field, and the woman who'd brought them here was dead.

Who was I kidding? I wouldn't be getting any work done.

I started to Google "Hardshaw Group" and even James' name, although nothing came up that I hadn't seen already the last time I'd tried. Next, I Googled Rufus Wilson and found several results that mentioned his arrest for breaking into a safe in Oklahoma City. The article said he was originally from Dallas, where he was suspected of more break-ins, although he'd never been charged due to lack of evidence. In Oklahoma, he'd plea bargained down to less than a year of jail time. There was nothing on him after that.

Next, I searched for Roberta Hanover. There was an article in the *Henryetta Gazette* mentioning a shoplifting charge last fall. The only other thing I found was her name mentioned in a list of graduating seniors from Fenton County High School four years ago.

So she was a local girl, which meant she'd met Rufus after he came to town. Where would they have met? At a bar?

There were only a couple of bars that catered to the rougher crowd—The Wagon Wheel and One-Eyed Joes—and I had half a mind to drop by one of them tonight, but I cast a glance at the wall connecting the sunroom to my daughter's nursery. A year ago, that might have been an option. Now it was out of the question.

Hope started to stir, so I went to her room, scooped her up, and headed downstairs. The deputies had all left, although the crime scene tape was still up. It was late enough I could start dinner, although I had no idea when Joe would be home. I decided on a pasta salad—something he wouldn't have to heat up when he got home. I filled a pot of water to boil and carried Hope back outside so we could check on the horses.

Muffy took off running once we were out of the house, enjoying the freedom of her yard again. Both horses came up to us, and I told Hope all about them even though I'd told her multiple times. She seemed fascinated by them, and they needed some attention. I was about to text Madison and ask her when her friend was picking them up when a car turned onto my driveaway, heading toward the house.

I froze. There was no way we'd make it back to the house in time to hide, and I was considering taking Hope behind the barn when I realized it was Witt's car.

I headed toward the house and met him in front. He stood at the base of the steps holding a package of diapers.

"I told you I was going to do it. Size one," he said with a grin. "I even asked the sales lady at Walmart to make sure it was right."

Groaning, I walked over to him and pulled him into a sideways hug. "I'm sorry I was such a witch earlier."

He laughed. "You were right. If I hadn't asked for help, I probably would have brought back a package of adult diapers."

"Liar," I said, pushing Hope toward him as I grabbed the package.

He took her with her butt resting on one hand, her head on the other while he held her at arm's length. "What am I supposed to do with this?"

I laughed. "You *hold* her."

"You better take her back," he said, still holding her with his outstretched arms. He looked like a half-hearted reenactment of Mufasa presenting Simba to his kingdom in *The Lion King*. "I'm gonna drop her."

"You are if you keep holding her like that," I said, resisting the urge to rescue her. I'd made up my mind that a village was going to raise my daughter, so if anything ever happened to me, she would never lack love and affection. Witt included. "Hold her closer. Against your chest."

He pulled her closer but still looked awkward. "Like this?"

Shaking my head, I grinned and said, "Close enough. You won't break her, and it'll get more natural the more you do it."

"If I had known I was gonna have to hold a baby, I wouldn't have come over," he teased.

"Why *did* you come over?" I asked, balancing the diaper package on my hip.

His smile faded. "I figured Joe was still workin', and I didn't like the idea of you and Hope bein' out here by yourself."

"You came to stay with us?"

He squirmed, unable to look me in the eye. "I wasn't doin' anything else."

"Have you eaten?" I asked. "I have a pot of water on that has likely boiled half away, but I was plannin' on makin' a pasta salad. I can cook some chicken breasts too."

A hungry look filled his eyes. "I don't want you to go to any trouble…"

"How good are you at grillin'?"

"No one's complained yet," he said with a grin.

"No one would have complained if you'd never cooked on one before."

He laughed, starting to look more comfortable with my baby. "I've grilled. Are you sayin' I have to earn my supper?"

"I'm sayin' it will be a team effort."

"Sounds good to me."

We went inside, and I set the diaper package on the bottom step before heading into the kitchen. Sure enough, half the water was gone, so I filled the pot with more before heading out back to start the grill Joe had brought with him when he moved in.

When I came back in, Witt was sitting in a chair with Hope lying down on his legs, staring up at him. He was smiling back, but his smile was a bit nervous.

"That's Uncle Witt," I told her as I walked by. "You're gonna have *so much* fun with him."

He stared up at me in surprise.

"You better be okay with that title," I said, pointing a wooden spoon at him. "Don't forget I've seen you with Ashely and Mikey. I expect you to play with Hope too."

He grinned from ear to ear. "Deal." He held his finger close to her hand and she immediately grasped it. "She's got a good grip."

"That she does," I said as I pulled a package of chicken out of the fridge.

"I know Neely Kate and Jed seem pretty self-centered right now," he said, his cheeks flushing. I could see how hard it was for him to talk about her like this.

"I know it looks that way," I said. "But Neely Kate is scared, which makes Jed scared and anxious. She can't handle the thought of losing another baby. I understand, trust me."

"I feel like Jed's leavin' you hangin'," Witt said, looking down at my daughter. "He's always had your back, and now he doesn't."

"That's understandable too. He has his own family to worry about now." I hesitated. "But it's not your responsibility, Witt."

He glanced up at me. "It takes a village, remember? You said that the other day when we were with Jed and NK. I'm not gonna sit on my ass while someone shows up to take you out and little Hope with you."

I shuddered, then said, "You're not supposed to have a gun. Not after your prison time." He'd served a few years for armed robbery back when he was barely an adult, but he'd left all that behind and now co-owned the garage with Jed.

"I'll take my chances, Rose." Then, in a quieter voice, he said, "Have you heard from Carly?"

Neely Kate and I had found Carly stranded next to a broken-down car on the side of the road last August. At the time, Neely Kate and I were living together, and we'd taken her in and given her a job at the nursery. Turned out her father was Randall Blakely, one of the three heads of the Hardshaw Group. She'd gone on the run after learning her father and fiancé had been scheming to murder her. We all would have preferred for her to stay forever, but Hardshaw and her father would have found her in Henryetta. So we'd sent her away with a new hair color and style and a new identity.

We had no idea where she was holed up, but Jed had set up secure email accounts on both ends so we could communicate. We heard from her occasionally, but much less than we had in the beginning.

"Not since April."

He nodded, but didn't say anything.

"I know you liked her," I said softly. "I'm sorry."

He shrugged. "Whatever. She's gone." But his glib dismissal had a sharp edge. Despite all of their good-natured bickering—or likely because of it—I suspected he'd started to have feelings for her. I knew he resented that he hadn't had a chance to say goodbye.

After a few seconds, he smiled at Hope. "You make pretty cute babies, Rose. You gonna pop out any more?"

I laughed. "After her nightmare delivery, it's probably too soon to ask me *that* question, but yeah, I hope to have one or two more. I guess we'll have to see how many Joe wants."

His brow shot to his forehead as he tilted his face up to look at me. "So you're really gonna do it?"

"By *do it* do you mean get married? Yeah, as soon as this mess is cleaned up we're gettin' married. And if you mean babies, I'd like to wait at least a year before I do that to my body again." Then, to see him blush, I added, "And if you mean do it, as in sex, yes, I got the all-clear this afternoon, and I plan on havin' wild sex tonight."

His face flushed. "TMI, Rose."

I laughed, surprised that I could feel happy and hopeful despite the chaos unfurling around us.

We finished dinner companionably, Witt handling the chicken while I made the salad, and when everything was ready, I put Hope in her bouncy seat at the far end of the table. We had just sat down to eat when the doorbell rang.

Witt and I looked at each other with wide eyes.

"You expectin' anyone?" he asked as he set down his fork, the laidback version of him gone.

I placed my napkin on the table. "No."

He slowly pulled a gun out of a holster on his ankle.

"Witt," I whisper-shouted. "You're not supposed to be carryin'."

"And I'm not supposed to eat greasy cheeseburgers and french fries, yet I still do." He stood up. "Let me see who's at the door."

"Hold up," I said, remembering my vision about Bobby. Wasn't that one of the reasons I'd come right home in the first place? "If it's not a bad guy or a deputy, you might scare them off."

"Fine," he said. "We'll peek through the window."

But the visitor was standing out of our line of sight. There wasn't a car out front either.

The doorbell rang again.

"Maybe it's a ghost," he teased, but his body was tense.

"Not funny," I said. "I'm gonna open it. I had a vision that Roberta Hanover came to see me. I opened the front door and came face to face with myself. I bet it's her."

"Okay," he said, but he didn't look convinced. Instead, he stood to the side, his gun drawn and ready.

I grabbed the doorknob and swung the door open, ready to welcome her in, only it wasn't Roberta Hanover at my front door. It was Denny Carmichael.

"Hello, Lady," he said with a smarmy smile. "Long time no see. Why don't you invite me in?"

Chapter Sixteen

I stared at him in shock, but Witt was quicker on his feet, pushing himself between me and the threshold.

"Get the hell out of here," he said in a menacing voice that sounded totally unlike the perpetually laidback guy I knew.

Carmichael chuckled. "You think you scare me, *boy*? Do you even know how to use that thing?"

I was terrified Witt would shoot him just to prove he could, so I gave him a small push to the side. "What do you want, Carmichael?"

His grin lit up his eyes, but there was nothing friendly about it. "You owe me, Lady, and your payment is now due."

Muffy released a low, threatening growl in the kitchen as Hope let out a mewl of discontent.

Carmichael perked up, and glee filled his eyes. "That your kid?"

Witt's body tensed, and then a new terror washed through me. I spun on my heels and ran for the kitchen, swallowing a sob when I saw a man I'd met the previous summer offering my daughter a grubby finger to hold, a shotgun in his other hand. Clyde.

Muffy was under the table, looking like she was about to attack his leg.

"Get away from my daughter," I said in a shaky voice.

"You don't sound so high and mighty now," Clyde said with an evil grin. The previous summer, Carmichael had sent him to bring me to Carmichael's property for a chat with his boss. I'd been kidnapped—no if, ands, or buts about it—and I'd snatched his gun and held it on Carmichael. I had no idea what he would have done if I hadn't gotten the upper hand, but I was fairly certain I was about to find out.

"Are you gonna invite me in?" Carmichael called out from the front, his snide tone holding plenty of bite. He still stood at the opening of my front door.

"Let him in, Witt," I said, finally getting control of myself. I might be terrified, but Hope's life depended on how I handled this, which meant I needed to pull it together.

Witt followed Carmichael into the kitchen as I rushed over to my daughter and slapped Clyde's hand away. "Don't you touch my daughter," I said through gritted teeth.

Muffy released a sharp bark to back me up.

"That's no way to talk to your guests," Carmichael said, meandering around the kitchen. "Quite a homey place you have here."

Muffy's growl deepened, and I worried she'd launch herself at him. Carmichael and his buddy wouldn't think twice about shooting her. "Muffy," I snapped.

She quieted, looking hurt by my reprimand.

Part of me wanted to snatch Hope out of her seat and hold her close, but the rest wanted both hands free in case I needed to reach for my gun. She was likely safer in her seat.

Witt, who also seemed concerned for Hope's safety, moved over to stand in front of her, providing cover should either of them try to shoot her.

"Enough with the theatrics, Denny Carmichael," I said. "I never took you to be interested in drama."

"Well," he said, grabbing the big spoon in the pasta salad bowl on the table and scooping out a big bite. He shoved about half of it into his mouth, then said through a mouthful of food, "Maybe I'm doing it to please you. I always thought *you* liked drama, with your costumes and all."

The hat and veil I'd worn in my early days as the Lady in Black. "I gave that up over a year ago when my identity became known, and you know it. If you want to have a chat, get on with it. You're interrupting our dinner."

His gaze jerked to mine, and a hard look filled his eyes. "Where's your boyfriend?"

"That's none of your damn business," I said, taking a step toward him since Witt was covering Hope. "You can't just show up at my house, barge in, threaten my daughter, and expect me to jump."

He dropped the spoon on the table. It hit with a clatter that echoed eerily throughout the room. "It seems like threatenin' your daughter is exactly what gets you to jump," he said with a sly grin.

"I don't work that way, and you damn well know it."

"So we should just shoot your daughter then?" he asked, his brow raised in a quizzical look.

"You'd be stupid to try it," I said, trying to hide my terror with a no-nonsense attitude. "First of all, you hurt my daughter, and I guaran-damn-tee you that I will *never* help you with *anything*." Hands clenched at my sides, I steeled my back and held his gaze with a dark look of my own. "My daughter is off limits or I will *end you*, Denny Carmichael."

We had a staring match for several seconds before he broke eye contact and turned to his man. "Stand down."

I had no idea what Clyde's reaction was, because I didn't dare take my gaze off Carmichael. "Did he stand down, Witt?"

"I'd prefer him to head out the back door and off your property," Witt said, his voice gravelly, "but yeah, he stood down."

"Now what the hell do you want with me, Carmichael?" I demanded.

"I need to know when and where Malcolm is havin' his big meetin'."

I lifted my chin. "Sorry to break it to you, but I don't work with Malcolm anymore. Not since I discovered he was workin' with Hardshaw. I thought we'd established that in our meetings last fall."

He pointed a finger at me. "Now *that* is still common ground for us to stand upon. Our mutual distaste for Hardshaw." When I didn't say anything, he said, "Don't you agree?"

"At the moment, I'm trying to get past the fact you barged into my house and threatened my daughter's life. If you've learned nothing about me over the last year, you should know by now that if you want to talk to me, you will treat me with respect."

He laughed. "Yeah, you're big on respect, but you gotta give it to earn it."

"Then I'm not sure why we're havin' this conversation," I said in a haughty tone. "Because you haven't shown me one iota of respect since you showed up at my front door."

He held out his hand and turned it palm up. "Touché." He resumed his jaunt around the room, stopping at the back windows to look out at the barn. Behind Hope. Witt still stood watch, but Carmichael could easily draw his gun and shoot my daughter through the back of her seat.

Everything in me screamed to grab her and run, but my gut told me that I needed to stand up to this man. He'd only respect me if I was strong, and I needed that respect if I had any hope of getting us out of this alive.

"Did you store guns in my barn?" I asked.

He laughed, still looking out the window. "You think I'm gonna admit it if I did?"

"Why not? You seem pretty cocky about your accomplishments."

He turned to face me, leveling me with a menacing glare. "You don't know a damn thing about my accomplishments."

"I find it hard to believe a proud man such as yourself would keep them hidden," I said. "You seem more like the braggin' type."

"A time to plant and a time to harvest," he said, then added with a mocking grin, "Ecclesiastes 3:2. I've been plantin' my seeds, and it's about time to harvest, just like the Good Book says."

Witt released a short bark. "I never took you for a God-fearin' man, Carmichael."

He grinned wider. "I'm more of an Old Testament kind of guy. You know, an eye for an eye." He winked at me. "That's more my speed."

"I have a motto of my own." I held his gaze for a second. "Don't count your chickens before they've hatched."

Chuckling, he resumed his walk around the large kitchen, moving to the back door and peering out the window at the still-hot grill. Then his gaze shifted to the security keypad next to the back door, and he stared at it for several tense seconds before he swung his head around to face me. "You think this is gonna protect you this far out of town?" he asked, sounding amused.

"I can usually hold off trouble until help arrives."

He reached behind his back and pulled out his gun, aiming it at my head.

Muffy resumed growling.

"You think so?" Carmichael asked, cocking his head with a gleeful look in his eyes. "How about I trip the alarm, and we see how long you can hold me off?"

"Get the hell out of my house, Denny Carmichael," I said, my hands balled into fists at my sides. My left hand brushed against the gun strapped to my thigh, but there was no way I could get it out without getting me, Witt, or Hope shot.

He motioned with his free hand. "Seems like you're in no position to be negotiatin'."

"Then you obviously haven't been listenin'," I said. "Threatenin' me, my child, or *anyone* I care about will only make me *not* help you. You yourself said we share a common goal—to stop Hardshaw. Seems to me you should have led with that."

"You *will* help me, Rose Gardner," he spat out, his face reddening with anger.

"Maybe I will," I admitted, "because I suspect you and me workin' as a united front could be strong enough to force them out of this county for good, but unfortunately for you, it's not gonna happen tonight." I took a step toward him. "If you wish to try again tomorrow, and you approach me in a respectful manner, then I'll be willing to listen. If not, we'll be permanently finished."

"I could just shoot you and be done with it," he sneered.

"You could," I admitted, "but then you wouldn't get what you came for. So put your damn gun away, or I'll refuse to help you tomorrow too."

He continued to glare at me, teeth gritted, then lowered his gun as he lifted his shoulders into a lazy shrug. "I tried to make it easier on you, Lady. I came to *you*. Next time you're gonna have to come to *me*."

I nodded slightly. "But I'm not comin' alone. I'll be bringing someone with me."

He snorted in amusement, then said, "You bringin' your boyfriend? The chief deputy sheriff?" He motioned to Witt. "I wouldn't bring this guy. He's worthless."

Carmichael's buddy snickered.

Witt released a low growl to match Muffy's, and Carmichael laughed. "Tomorrow morning. Nine sharp. I presume you remember how to get to my place."

"I do," I forced out, pissed as hell at how he was talking to Witt.

Carmichael turned and headed for the front door, his buddy trailing behind him.

"Stay with Hope," I said to Witt, pulling my gun from my thigh strap and trailing them to the front door.

Carmichael stopped and glanced over his shoulder at me, chuckling when he saw my gun. "That verse was only part of Ecclesiastes 3:2," he said with a cocky grin. "The first part is 'A time to be born, a time to die.' We're all gonna be buried in the ground at some point, Lady. Some of us much sooner than nature intended." He jutted his head forward with a dark gaze that barely contained the cruelty spilling out of him. "Do not underestimate me." Then he headed down the steps, Clyde a few steps in front of him.

I held up my gun, aiming for his back. My finger was on the trigger, and everything in me screamed to shoot. He was a madman capable of horrible things, and I had the power to end that.

The only thing that stopped me was because shooting him in the back would be murder, plain and simple. There would be no justifying that. I really did think his forces and mine could send Hardshaw packing, but I was beginning to have serious doubts that a collaboration would work. The man was a murdering sociopath. How could I agree to work with someone who'd just threatened to murder my six-week-old daughter? Even if we did work together, and we managed to push Hardshaw out of the county for good, where would that leave us?

Carmichael and his man strode toward the drive that led to the highway, and I realized they'd parked on the highway to give themselves the element of surprise.

As soon as they were out of sight, I slipped my gun back in its holster and reached for my phone, calling the one person I trusted to help me with all of this. As soon as he answered, I steeled my back so I wouldn't break down. "Dermot, I hope you're free tomorrow because we have an appointment with Denny Carmichael at nine a.m."

Chapter Seventeen

"*Say what?*"

"Carmichael and his buddy just paid me a visit." Instinct screamed for me to go to Hope and hold her close, but I knew the minute she was in my arms, I'd fall to pieces. I needed to take care of business first.

"Were you alone?" he demanded, sounding panicked.

"Witt was with me, but Denny's man snuck in through the back door and threatened Hope while she was in her bouncy seat."

"That son of a bitch," he growled. "I'm gonna kill the bastard myself."

"I think Witt's first in line for that task," I said. "I'm pretty sure he's gonna feel responsible for this."

"What happened?"

I told him everything, and he was silent for a long moment before he said, "If Witt had shot Carmichael on the porch, Hope would be dead right now. So you make sure he knows that."

A burning lump filled my throat, and I pushed out, "I will." I couldn't let myself dwell on that scenario.

"I take it all the deputies are gone."

"Yeah."

"Okay, I'm gonna send some men to watch the property and make sure no one's goin' in who shouldn't be there."

"How will they know who shouldn't be here?"

"Please," he said as though I'd asked why water was wet. "I'll swing by to pick you up at eight thirty tomorrow morning, but the next question is who do you trust to watch Hope?"

"I don't know."

"I thought for certain you'd say Carlisle and Neely Kate, and then the real dilemma would be how to keep them from going with us."

"Yeah, well," I said, then took a deep breath. "They have their own baby issues goin' on."

He was silent for a moment as though processing what I wasn't saying. "What about the woman who runs the nursery? Deveraux's mother?"

I hadn't explicitly mentioned Maeve to him, so the comment surprised me...or maybe it didn't. I just wasn't sure what to make of it. "She *can* and *will* watch her, but Maeve can't protect her."

"I'll take care of that part," he said. "So how about we meet at the nursery at eight forty?"

"Yeah," I said, wondering how he planned to take care of it, but I trusted him with our lives. "Okay."

"Rose?" he said. "One more thing." He paused. "Roberta Hanover is missing."

"*What?*"

"When I sent my guys to the convenience store to check on her, she was gone. Her car was still in the lot, but her co-worker said she'd left several hours earlier. He said someone else had come in askin' about her. A guy. He drove the white sedan that was parked in the lot most of the day."

"The guy who had been watchin' her. She must have slipped out the back. At least we know he and the people he works for don't have her. She's hiding."

"Well, let's hope she reaches out to you soon," Dermot said. "Let me know if she does."

"I will, and Dermot?"

"Yeah?"

"Thank you."

"My pleasure, Lady." Then he hung up.

Scanning the drive to the highway, I took a deep breath, preparing myself to face Witt. This wasn't going to be pretty.

He was in the kitchen, cradling Hope to his chest and looking like he was near tears. His face fell the moment he saw me. "Rose," he said, his voice breaking. "I'm so sorry."

I knew Witt well enough to know coddling wouldn't do any good. Instead, I lifted my chin and said with plenty of attitude, "What the hell for?"

His eyes widened. "I let you down. They almost…Hope…"

I gave him a stern gaze. "You didn't let me down. You did everything you could have done."

"If I'd just shot him on the porch—"

"Carmichael's goon would have killed Hope."

He started to protest, but I gave a slight shake of my head. "No. You *know* he would have, and Dermot just said the same thing. If she'd been killed because you up and shot Carmichael, *then* how would you feel?"

His chin trembled. "I left her alone in the kitchen when I followed you to the door. They could have killed her." He held her tighter.

A wave of fear made me lightheaded, but I took another breath, waiting for it to pass. "Yes," I said, trying to sound strong, but I was closer to falling apart than I would have liked. "But they didn't. Mistakes were made. I was too lax. Too trusting of my damn vision. I should have been more careful. I should have locked the back door too."

Witt glanced down at Hope, then kissed the top of her head and handed her to me. "I swear to you, Rose, I will never let her get that close to danger again."

I nodded, not trusting my voice. My knees felt weak, and I held her so tight I worried I was smothering her, but she snuggled into me, looking sleepy. Tears burned my eyes, but I didn't want to fall apart in front of Witt. "I'm gonna take her upstairs and change her diaper. You can eat if you like."

"I've lost my appetite," he grunted, staring at the bowl of pasta salad, a few pieces of macaroni scattered on the table.

"Throw it out. We won't be eating anything that man touched." My voice broke, and I hurried for the stairs.

I didn't stop until I reached her room. Then I sat down in the rocking chair, holding her close, and let my tears fall, quickly giving way to loud sobs. A small part of me worried that Witt could hear me, but now that I'd started, I couldn't stop. Hope was my entire world. I'd die if anything happened to her.

She started to cry, and I realized I was scaring her, so I forced myself to settle down, pulling the neckline of my dress down to let her nurse. I tried to stop thinking of all the horrible things that could have happened to her. Had I done enough to protect her? Had I spent too much time trying to one-up Denny?

I switched sides and gave her a weak smile. "I love you so much, Hope Violet Simmons. I don't have much other than you and your daddy. The farm and my businesses. But those things have meaning. Worth. This is our home, and I need to make sure you're safe here. The only way to do that is to risk my life. I don't want to die. Even if you have plenty of people to care for you, I don't want you to be motherless. My own birth mother died when I was about your age, and every day I wish I'd known her." I gasped, the truthfulness of the statement hitting me full force.

My birth mother had been murdered under the guise of a car accident when I was less than two months old. Had she held me like this? Tried to pour as much love into me as physically possible? She'd been dealing with corruption at the plant where she worked, trying to expose it and make things right. Had she felt people breathing down her neck? Had she worried I'd be caught in the crossfire?

But Hope was oblivious to my inner thoughts. She continued to nurse, staring up at me with soulful eyes that seemed to take in the world.

"I don't want to leave you motherless, but know that your daddy loves you *so much*," I said through fresh tears. "I couldn't have picked a better daddy for you in all the world."

Better than Dora had chosen for me. My father had taken me after Dora's death. We'd stayed with Aunt Bessie and Uncle Earl for a while, but my father had gone back to his wife, and I'd been raised by the woman I called Momma. A woman who'd always hated me because of my mother. Because of my visions. Because Dora's death had broken my father, so much so he hadn't been my protector. He'd become an accomplice to my mother's abuse.

Was that why I was making sure everyone who came into contact with Hope loved her and felt a responsibility to make sure she was taken care of? So if I died and Joe fell apart, there would be a huge safety net to catch her?

Was that why Violet had been so adamant about me getting custody of her kids? Had she worried that Mike would devolve into the same spiral of hopelessness that had consumed our father? That the safety and well-being of her kids would be threatened?

I needed to find out what was in that safe. I needed to make sure that Ashley and Mikey were safe. It was the only thing I could still do for my sister.

I needed to talk to Joe about the what-ifs in case something happened to me, but deep in my heart, I knew I had nothing to fear. Joe would mourn me, but he wouldn't shirk his responsibility to Hope. He loved her too much. He loved *me* too much.

I took a breath. "If something happens to me, your daddy will make sure you are loved. That you know you matter." I started to cry again, then gave her my finger to hold as she looked up at me. "You will never feel unloved or unwanted. You will never feel lacking. You will *always* know how precious you are, and God forbid, if you are cursed with my visions, you will never, ever be made to feel like a freak. Your daddy will make sure you know how special you are."

"Hey," Joe said softly from the doorway, still wearing his deputy sheriff uniform. "What's goin' on?"

I looked up at him, and fresh tears pooled in my eyes. "Joe."

Hope stopped nursing and turned her head at the sound of Joe's voice.

He came to us and pulled me to a standing position before wrapping his arms around me, sandwiching Hope between us.

"I'm so glad you're home," I said, my voice breaking. I had to tell him what had just happened. He needed to know so he could play a part in protecting our daughter, but what could I tell him? I'd been frustrated by the wall between us before, but now I wanted to rip it down with a bulldozer. If he knew, though…he'd do something that might get him killed. Or Hope killed. And then the drug deal would happen anyway, and we wouldn't be the only ones to suffer for it.

Without a word, he led me to our bedroom and took Hope as he gently pushed me to sit on the bed.

"Rose, what's goin' on?" he repeated gently.

"I'm just bein' silly," I murmured, the excuse spilling out. "My hormones are all out of whack." Even as I said the words, I hated myself for lying to him. Maybe I should leave Hope with him and go somewhere else until everything died down. Lord knew he'd do a much better job of protecting her than I had.

"Why's Witt downstairs lookin' like someone kicked him in the shins?"

I glanced up at him and said nothing.

"I take it he has guard duty? Is he unhappy with the assignment?"

"No," I said, refusing to let him think badly of Witt. "He's just having a moment."

"A moment."

"Yeah."

"Why are you up here tellin' Hope how wonderful I am? I mean, it's true, of course, but still." He gave me a cocky grin, but it looked forced. Even now, he was trying to make me feel better.

"Because I can never tell her that enough, Joe."

He turned serious.

"If something happens to me…" I began.

"What's gonna happen to you?"

"If something happens to me," I repeated with more force, "you have to promise me that you will make sure the woman you eventually marry will be kind to Hope."

"Well, first of all," he said, sitting on the bed next to me. "There's only one woman I plan on ever marryin', and that's you."

"But someday…"

"I would sooner cut off my foot before I'd let anyone hurt our daughter, either physically or emotionally."

"Thank you," I whispered.

He clasped my hand, twining our fingers. "Rose, what's goin' on? Let me help you."

I turned to look up at him, giving him a watery smile. "You said something similar to me after Momma was murdered. I was sittin' on her bed lookin' at old photos, and you found me cryin'. You begged me to let you help." I took a breath. "But you had an ulterior motive. You were workin' undercover tryin' to get information out of me."

Hurt filled his eyes. "Is that what you think I'm doin' now? Tryin' to weasel information out of you for my investigation?"

I shook my head. "No. The opposite. Now you're goin' out of your way to make sure I know you have my best interests in mind."

"I did back then too, you know," he said quietly. "I knew you were in trouble, and I was desperate to help you." The corners of his mouth lifted into a soft smile. "Just like I'm desperate to help you now."

"I know."

He laid our daughter in the bassinet, and Muffy hopped onto the mattress next to it, curling up as close to her as possible. Hope's eyes were so heavy, it was almost comical, and the sight of them lying down so close to each other was achingly sweet.

I had so much to lose.

He turned sideways on the edge of the bed to face me. "Do you have any idea how scared I am right now?" he asked, his voice sounding strangled.

"I'm sorry. I want to tell you what's goin' on. To reassure you." I squeezed his hand. "There's so much I want to tell you, but people have confided in me only because I've given them my word I won't tell anyone they've spoken to me. I *will* tell you, as your future wife to her soon-to-be husband, that something big is about to go down. Big and incredibly dangerous. Whether it happens or not could affect the future of the county for a very long time."

He searched my face. "And you think you can stop it?" A year ago, he would have asked in disbelief, as though I were delusional. Now he was asking as though weighing the risk against the consequences.

"I'm not naïve enough to think I'm that special," I said with a derisive laugh. "But I've spent a year and a half earning a reputation in the underworld, and like it or not, I still have it. People come to me."

"As a mediator?" he asked.

I nodded, searching his face. "Sometimes I really wish I could share more with you. I'd like your insight into situations, and I hate that we have secrets, but I can't forget there's a line separating us."

"Between law enforcement and the criminal world."

"I'm not a criminal, Joe," I insisted.

He lifted his hand to cup my cheek. "I know," he said with a weak smile, but then it fell. "What you're about to do is dangerous?"

I nodded. "I'd say no to this, but I can't."

"Who's protecting you?" he asked, his voice tight.

"Tomorrow morning? Dermot."

"What about Jed?" he asked, ignoring my comment about tomorrow.

"No. He and Neely Kate are worried about Kate hanging around. They're holin' up at home, hopin' to ride out the storm."

"That's not Jed's style," he said in disbelief, "not to mention he's always been protective of you."

"They're scared they're gonna lose their baby," I said. "He has his own family to think about."

His mouth parted in surprise, and he lowered his hand to his lap, staring at me for a second before his face began to harden.

"Please don't pull away from me, Joe," I pleaded. "I need you more than I've ever needed you before. Please try to understand."

He studied me, his face devoid of emotion. "If I weren't in law enforcement, would you tell me things?"

Would I? Last year, no. He would have thought me incapable of navigating these dark, deep waters, but now? He'd known I was doing something dangerous last fall and winter, even if I hadn't shared any specifics. And while he'd been worried and scared, he hadn't interfered. Would it be different now?

"That depends," I said slowly. "Like I said, I wouldn't be able to tell you everything. I protect my sources, but I do have meetings with Jed, Dermot, and Witt about how to handle things."

And I had to protect him too. If I told him about the meeting, he would feel duty-bound to do something about it. He would tell his boss, and if his boss or someone else in the department was a source for Hardshaw, then Joe's fate would be sealed.

"And you give them more information than you share with me?" he asked, his voice still neutral, but I could see a storm brewing in his eyes.

"Yes," I admitted. "I wish I could share everything I know with you, but I can't. It's to protect you too."

"Because of my job?"

I nodded tightly, because it was true, and we both knew it.

He glanced to the side, his body rigid, and I wondered if this was it. If yet another relationship had been destroyed by the Lady in Black.

He got off the bed and headed toward the door, and I was sure he was walking away from me, from Hope and our life together, but he stopped at his dresser and reached for the badge on his uniform. He turned back to face me, then unhooked it, placing it on the dresser.

I got off the bed. "What are you doin'?"

Next, he removed the weapon holstered at his waist and placed it next to the badge.

"What are you doin, Joe?"

He lifted his hand to the buttons on his uniform shirt, slowly unfastening them, his gaze boring into mine with a heat that felt scorching. "I just quit. I'll turn in my resignation within the next half hour."

Panic swirled through my head. "You can't do that."

"I sat on that bed, asking you who was goin' to protect you, all the while dyin' inside because *I* want to be the one to protect you, Rose. *Me.*"

I shook my head, "Joe…"

"Even Jed is circlin' the wagons, protectin' his family, and I'm supposed to stand back and let Dermot protect you. *Again*," he spat in self-loathing. "You would think bein' the damn chief deputy sheriff would be enough."

"I'm sorry," I said, choking back a sob. I glanced at Hope, worried we were disturbing her, but she was fast asleep. My gaze shot back to Joe, who was staring at me with fire in his eyes.

"Don't you *ever* apologize for being who you are. Not to me. Not to anyone." Something subtle between us shifted, and everything felt charged.

A fire swept through my blood, and my breathing hitched. "You can't quit your job, Joe. You love it. The sheriff's department needs you. The *county* needs you."

But I flashed to my visions again. Maybe quitting was the safest route for him. Telling him about the meeting had led to his death because he worked for the sheriff's department. If he didn't...

He took a step toward me, his voice low. "It's just a damn job, Rose. You and Hope are more important."

But I knew it was more than a job to him. He liked keeping people safe. "If you quit, what will you do?"

"I don't know," he said, his dark, possessive gaze pinned on me. "And right now, I don't care." He closed the distance between us, grabbing the back of my head in a tight hold and pulling me flush to his body, then said fiercely, "I want you, Rose." His voice was husky with need. "Every last part of you. Tomorrow feels like a decade away."

"I went to the doctor today," I said, my fingers shaking as I reached for the remaining buttons on his shirt. "They had to change Dr. Newton's schedule."

Surprise filled his eyes.

"I'm good. I'm healed." I grabbed his cheeks with both hands. "And you have no idea how much I want every last part of you too."

His mouth covered mine, hungry with need, and I matched him, tugging off his shirt while his lips claimed mine.

His free hand cupped my bottom and then slid down my leg, hiking the fabric of my dress higher as he went until his hand brushed the holster strapped to my thigh. He lifted his head, his gaze dipping to my legs before lifting to my eyes.

My breath hitched at the raw hunger I saw in them.

His touch on my leg lightened, his fingers skimming the skin up and down my inner thigh.

A wave of lust rushed through me as he traced his way up to the crotch of my panties, then back down my leg.

I released a low moan.

"Do you have any idea how incredibly sexy it is that you can protect yourself?" he said in a low voice as he turned me and pushed me backward until my back was to the wall by the dresser. He dropped to his knees and spread my legs wide, then hooked my left calf over his shoulder. He swept the hem of my dress higher up my thigh, over my holster, as he pressed kisses to my inner thigh.

I shivered, placing my hands on his shoulders, needing to touch him more than I needed support.

He nimbly unhooked my holster and reached up to place it on the dresser. His gaze lifted to mine again. Dark and hungry. Possessive. "But I'm taking over your bodyguard position. You are *mine* to protect."

Another wave of heat washed through me, making my knees weak.

He kissed the red mark on my thigh where the holster had been, moving higher until he reached the edge of my panties.

My breath came in short bursts as I watched him, the anticipation of what he was about to do setting my body on fire.

He lifted my leg off his shoulder in a slow, deliberate movement, placing it so that I was standing with my legs spread. The hem of my dress fell.

"Take off your dress," he said in a husky tone, looking up at me from his knees.

Without a word, I reached down and pulled the dress over my head, and let it drop to the floor.

His gaze swept over my body with hungry need, and I realized I wasn't embarrassed by the stretch marks and loose skin that hadn't been there the last time we'd slept together before. I had more weight on my hips, and my beige nursing bra and faded navy blue panties could in no way be called lingerie, but he made me feel like the most beautiful woman in the world.

His fingers hooked on the top of my panties, and he slowly slid them over my hips and then my legs, lifting my feet one at a time until I was free of them.

Starting at my ankle, his mouth and tongue trailed up my leg, stopping at my core. I leaned my head against the wall, closing my eyes as a white hot fire shot through me.

He grabbed my leg and hooked it over his shoulder again, giving him better access.

I dug my hands in his hair, holding on while he pushed me higher and higher.

"Joe," I moaned. "I need you. *Now.*"

He kissed his way up my stomach, pushing my leg off his shoulder as he got to his feet.

I grabbed his face, kissing him hard as his hands reached behind me to unfasten my bra and toss it aside.

I wanted him naked and against me. I wanted him inside me, and there was too much fabric between us. I dropped my hands and fumbled with his belt, but he impatiently brushed my hands away and undid it himself, pushing his pants and underwear to his feet, then taking a step back from me to slide off his shoes, socks, and pants, until he stood naked in front of me.

I sucked in a breath, pressing my back to the wall as I took him in. While my body had gotten softer, his had gotten harder, and his muscles were more defined than I remembered them. Nostalgia washed through me, and I thought about the last time we'd made love. It had been filled with desperation and the sense of imminent loss, but this…this was filled with the promise of forever.

"I had tomorrow night all planned out," Joe walked to his dresser and opened the top drawer. "Candlelight. Flowers. Seduction."

"This is seduction, Joe," I said breathlessly. "Those other things would be nice, but I need this too. I'm not the good girl you remember."

He pulled out a box of condoms and broke the sealed lid. "Good. Because I want you here against this wall."

A jolt of heat shot straight to my core.

He pulled out a foil wrapper and tossed the box into the still-open drawer. A predatory smile spread across his face as he closed the distance between us.

I reached between us and took him in my hand.

He released an agonized groan, then ripped the wrapper and pushed my hand away as he quickly slid it on.

He stared down at me with hooded eyes, his chest rising and falling. "Are you sure you don't want to wait until it's more romantic?"

"No." I grabbed the back of his neck and pulled his mouth to mine.

His hands found my breasts, his thumbs brushing over my nipples. A wave of need washed through me as the ache between my legs grew.

"Joe. *Please*." It came out as a whine, but I didn't care. I needed him. I'd needed him for months, and the need had only grown stronger.

He grabbed my butt and lifted me as he pressed me against the wall, holding me up as he slowly entered me, the sensation so intense my legs might have buckled if he hadn't been supporting my weight.

"Are you okay?" he grunted, his face buried in the crook of my neck.

I wrapped my legs around his waist. "You better not stop now."

That released something inside him, and he drove into me hard and wild. I met him every step of the way, pleading for more as the pressure built and climbed, sure I would shatter. But he pushed me higher and higher, to a height so dizzying I was sure I would die. My arms and legs were wrapped around him, so the only things holding me up were the wall and Joe, and then the wall was gone as he struggled to get deeper, and I fell apart, crying out his name over and over, and then he was right behind me. Holding me just as tightly as I was holding him, and I knew that from this moment forward, I wasn't on my own.

Joe would be with me every step of the way.

Chapter Eighteen

When my senses returned, I realized that Joe had moved us into the bathroom and partially closed the door. I was amazed that he'd had the presence of mind to do so.

We got dressed, me back in my dress and Joe in shorts and a T-shirt. We left Hope sleeping in her bassinet and went downstairs to face a red-faced Witt.

"Are you plannin' on stickin' around tonight?" Witt asked Joe.

"I won't be leavin' Rose's side," Joe said.

Witt gave him a questioning look.

"I'm heading into my office to write up my resignation and email it to the sheriff, the county, and send out a press release. Effective immediately."

Witt's mouth dropped open. "Say what?"

"It's my understanding that Rose has backup in dangerous situations," Joe said, his tone gruff and unyielding. "Jed. Dermot. You."

Witt gave me a bewildered look, and I nodded. "Uh…yeah," he stammered, still caught off guard. "Jed was her bodyguard when she was workin' for Skeeter, but Dermot's been takin' over his job more and more. When she needs big guns, I go too."

163

"I'll be joinin' whoever is assigned to protect her from here on out," Joe said. "Tell whoever needs to be told." Then he went into his office and shut the door.

Witt's mouth still hung open. "What just happened?"

"Joe has joined our side."

"Do you think that's really a good idea?" he asked, incredulous.

"From what standpoint?" I asked. "From the fact that he's no longer keepin' the county safe? No, it's a great loss. Or are you asking whether it's safe for him to show up as my bodyguard? I'm not sure about that either, but he doesn't want to trust other people to protect me. He wants to be more proactive."

He made a face. "Dermot's not gonna like it, and how are guys like Denny Carmichael gonna react when he shows up? They're bound to know who he is, and there's a good chance they'll kill him, thinkin' he's there to spy."

"I suspect that's why he's sending it to the newspaper. To sell it."

Witt shot a glance toward the closed office door and lowered his voice. "Do you think he's really quittin'? Is this just a ploy to find out what you know?"

I could have gotten pissed at him for asking, but I understood why he might think that. In the past, Joe had acted in the way he saw best, without considering he might be wrong. But I'd seen the fierce protectiveness in his eyes earlier. He hadn't been pretending. "It's not. He's terrified something's gonna happen to me, and I don't think he could live with himself if he wasn't there doin' everything he could to protect me." I cast a glance to the door. Plus, he knew if he lied to me, we would be over. He wouldn't risk it.

Joe was being truthful. I was betting my life on it.

He came out of the office twenty minutes later, looking less certain than he had when he'd gone in. I got up from the sofa, where I'd been anxiously waiting, and went to him. Wrapping my arms around him and burying my face into his chest, I whispered, "I'm sorry."

"I'm not," he said gruffly.

"What excuse did you give him for quittin' so abruptly?"

"I said I felt targeted because of my position and that it felt unsafe for my family. But the official statement will be that my priorities have changed and the hours are too demanding for a man who wants to spend time with his family."

I nodded.

"And now that I'm officially no longer an officer of the law, it's time to tell me everything you can."

Witt's brow rose. "I think I should be goin'."

Joe moved out of my embrace and extended his hand to Witt. "Thank you for everything you've done to protect Rose and Hope. I'm not sure I can ever repay you."

Witt made a face, refusing to take Joe's hand. "You might want to wait until you hear what happened when Carmichael paid Rose a visit about a half hour before you got home before you go thankin' me."

My chest tightened. "Witt."

He gave me a hasty hug, then headed out the front door.

Joe stared at me in disbelief. "Denny Carmichael was here? Did he come in the house?" His voice pitched with anxiety.

"When you say you want to know everything…"

"Was he here or not?"

I took a deep breath. "I think you're gonna need a beer or two to listen to all of this. I know I definitely need a glass of wine." I headed into the kitchen, calling over my shoulder, "Dr. Newton said it was safe to have a glass every so often."

Joe followed me into the kitchen and headed straight for the security box and turned it on. "Was Denny Carmichael in our house or not, Rose?"

I opened the fridge and grabbed a bottle of beer for Joe, then scanned the shelves. "Damn it. I haven't had alcohol since last summer. Why would I think I'd have some in there now?"

Joe set his beer on the table, then headed to the basement. I considered following him and asking him what he was doing, but I needed to start trusting him, just like he needed to trust me. I only hoped he caught up to speed quickly enough.

When he emerged from the doorway, he was holding a bottle of champagne, but he still looked grim. "I was saving this for tomorrow night."

"To seduce me?" I asked with a half-smile.

"I will spend the rest of my life seducing you, Rose," he said with an intensity in his eyes I wasn't used to seeing. "I will never take you or us for granted." He grabbed two juice glasses and set them on the table, still carrying the champagne bottle. Then he opened it with a loud pop and poured it into the glasses. "We don't have champagne flutes," he said as he picked up both glasses, handing one to me.

"We don't seem like champagne flute kind of people," I teased, but then I realized Joe used to be a champagne flute kind of person. His parents had been very well off and flaunted it. "But maybe you want to be…again."

He held his glass in his hand. "I've never felt more me than when I'm with *you,* Rose. You know I hated that life."

"I had to be sure," I said softly.

He lifted his glass and gave me an adoring smile, even though I could see the worry in his eyes. "To my beautiful wife-to-be and our many years together."

I touched my glass to his and held it there. "And to my incredible soon-to-be husband. No more secrets."

Joe drained his glass, but I took a sip and made a face. "Maybe I'm not a champagne person either."

Joe released a hearty laugh and pulled me into a hug. "Noted."

I gazed up at him, still in awe we had reached this place. "I love you, Joe."

He gave me a soft, lingering kiss. "I love you too. Now quit stalling and tell me about Denny Carmichael."

"I think I need to start at the beginning." But which beginning? How far back did I go? For Joe to be part of this, he needed to be fully aware of what he was getting mixed up in. It wasn't lost on me that maybe this should have occurred to me before he quit his job. I looked up at him, stricken as what he'd done hit home. "You quit your job. You love your job."

It suddenly hit me that perhaps this was what led to James murdering Joe—that it might have nothing to do with the sheriff's department at all. Should I have had a vision before he gave his notice? Would whatever I saw—good or bad—have made him change his mind? Not likely.

"It's just a job, and I love you more," he said without any sign of regret.

I loved him too, but what was I willing to give up for him?

My privacy. My secrets. I still ran the risk of sending him running, but he deserved to know the woman he was marrying.

"You know a lot of this already," I said, my voice a little hoarse from nerves, "but I'm going to tell you everything, right from the beginning, so you'll know the whole story."

Because he deserved to know, and because I had to believe it would make him safer now that he'd left his job.

I started with the bank robbery a year and a half ago, when a huge cash deposit for the nursery had been stolen. Mason would have needed to cash in his retirement plan to help me, so I'd gone to see Skeeter Malcolm to trade information: my knowledge about his competition in the auction (gleaned from visions) for his retrieval of my money. It had all unfurled from there. Because I'd seen James die in my visions, many times, just like I now kept seeing Joe die.

Joe listened, asking questions from time to time, asking if I'd been scared at the auction.

"Terrified," I said. "Especially when you raided the barn. But James and Jed whisked me out through a hidden tunnel and got me out safely. I made it home, and the next day the cash was on my front porch. He kept his word. I thought I was done."

"How'd you get dragged back in?"

I told him about the slide into working with James rather than being compelled by him. How it had begun with threats and then become a mutually beneficial arrangement. How we'd worked together to bring down Joe's father, J.R. Simmons, who had been the source of so much tumult in our county.

"That's what led to my father's arrest that February," he said, sounding subdued. I had a feeling I knew why.

Before that meeting, I had been kidnapped. James and Jed had saved me, but in order to keep me safe, they'd insisted on a ruse that made everyone think I was dead. Joe hadn't handled it well.

"I wanted to tell you that I was okay, Joe, but James wouldn't let me. He took my phone and kept me holed up in a cabin until it was time to go meet your father."

"So he forced you to go through with the meetin'?" he asked, his body shaking with rage.

"No." I took his hand and led him to the living room, then tugged him down to the sofa. I straddled him, looking him in the eyes as I held his face between my hands. "I willingly and eagerly went to that meeting to get your father to confess. James and I didn't agree on how to handle what happened before the meetin', but I was fully on board with the rest."

He leaned his forehead against mine and closed his eyes, wrapping his arms loosely around me. "I wanted to die when I thought you were dead."

"I know," I whispered. "I'm *so* sorry."

We sat like that for several seconds before he opened his eyes.

"They had planned to kill Mason too," I said. "And it took near hysterics to get James to bring him to the cabin to protect him. He did, but he warned me that Mason would learn what I'd been doing and never forgive me."

"And he ended your engagement," Joe said in a flat tone.

I released a quick, mirthless laugh. "Our very short engagement. James was right. When Mason found out about my secret identity, he couldn't handle it. After Kate's big showdown and your father's death, he broke up with me and went back to Little Rock."

"But he came back that summer."

"Not of his own volition," I said with a wry smile. "He didn't want to be here. He was chosen because of his history in Fenton County, so he decided to make the most of it. He decided to go after the man who he held responsible for breaking us up. Skeeter Malcolm." I sighed. "By the time Mason left town, James and I had a mutual respect for each other. He saw me as a strong, capable woman."

"While I saw you as a fragile flower that needed protectin'," he said.

I didn't respond because we both knew it was true. "Mason left me. Violet was sick and went to Texas. I had Neely Kate, but the both of you were lost in your own demons after findin' out you were siblings, and I...I was lost, Joe. I was broken, and I needed a friend. James was that friend."

"He took advantage of you," he said in the first judgmental tone he'd used since I'd started telling my story.

"No," I said evenly. "We were just friends. We met every Tuesday night in secret at our usual meetin' spot. No one knew what we were doin', not even Neely Kate or Jed. He'd tell me about his difficulties tryin' to rein in the lawlessness in the county, while I told him my pathetic stories about my job and how scared I was about Violet. This went on from February until June. And then Neely Kate agreed to find Homer Dyer's stupid necklace. We thought it was a nothin' case, but that necklace was coveted by several men in the criminal world, and a war nearly broke out over it. Neely Kate and I got our hands on it, and we declared a parley between James and Buck Reynolds and Kip Wagner."

"You did *what?*" he asked.

I gave him another wry smile. "That was how I started being seen as a neutral party. People started comin' to me for help, and I'd give it when I could. I was like an impartial judge, but not all criminals saw me that way, and James felt responsible for dragging me into it in the first place. Still, he respected my strength and had Jed teach me and Neely Kate how to shoot and defend ourselves, and by mid-summer, I realized I liked him as more than a friend." I didn't want to tell him the next part, but he needed to understand that I wasn't a victim in all of this. I had been a very active participant.

The emotion in his eyes shuttered, but then he said, "Go on. I can handle it."

I gave him a sad smile and brushed his cheek with my thumb as I held his gaze. I prayed he *could* handle it. The last thing I wanted to do was hurt him, but he had to understand. "I forced myself on him, Joe. He told me from the start that we wanted different things, and stupid me thought that we could have a fling and I could walk away. But then I fell in love with him, and I thought he felt the same way. I've since realized that we were living in a make-believe bubble. Then Denny Carmichael dragged me to his property last August, insistin' I do for him what I'd done for James. I told him to forget it, but I had several visions of him. Carmichael was making a stand against James, and I was part of it. I didn't want to believe it, but then I discovered that James was the one who'd bought the police down in Sugar Branch. They attacked me in the parking lot of that bar, just like I told you. James and I had just had a huge fight, but I called him anyway, asking him to come help me."

"You called me too," Joe said, his voice tight. "I came."

I pressed my hand harder into his cheek. "I called you first, Joe."

He covered my hand with his.

"But I was in immediate danger, and I knew you wouldn't reach me in time. James was closer." I paused. "But he didn't come. He sent Denny Carmichael instead. Denny killed those officers, but then he told me I owed him, and one day he'd collect." I shrugged. "Today, he came to collect."

"Carmichael and Malcolm are enemies, even I know that. Why on earth would he send Carmichael to save you? He could have just as easily have killed you. In fact," he said, getting more agitated, "I can't believe he didn't."

"No," I said. "Carmichael used it as an opportunity to get his hooks into me, and James handed me to him on a silver platter."

"Did you ask him why he did it?"

"Yeah, but he was his usual evasive self. He had a reason, but he couldn't tell me. Then he said we couldn't see each other anymore, and we didn't. Not until I went to his pool hall in October to tell him I was pregnant. His first reaction was to tell me in no uncertain terms to get an abortion."

Joe was silent.

"Around that time, Jed put together that James was working with Hardshaw. And we started those meetin's tryin' to unite the rest of the underworld against James. Dermot told them to follow the Lady in Black."

He didn't say anything.

"Those meetin's were short-lived," I said. "The different factions were worse than bickering children, and then Mason warned me that word was getting around that I was involved with some secret meetings with criminals. Since the meetings themselves were worthless, Dermot, Jed, and I agreed to disband them."

"Mason?" he asked in surprise.

I laughed. "You'd be surprised."

His hands tightened around me. "One of your sources?"

"No comment."

He kissed me, soft and tenderly, but I deepened the kiss, still holding his face between my hands.

"I love you, Joe," I whispered. "You have no idea how happy I am that I can share this with you."

His phone vibrated in his pocket. He shifted his hips, and I rolled off of his lap so he could pull it out. He checked the screen, then turned it off. "The sheriff," he said as he reached forward to set it down on the coffee table.

"Shouldn't you answer that? I'm sure they have questions. Your resignation was pretty sudden."

"It can wait," he said, turning on the sofa to face me. "This is more important." He caressed my cheek. "How long have you been carryin' this load alone?"

Tears sprang to my eyes. "What?"

"I know there is so much more that you're not tellin' me. So much more that you've dealt with. You've got Mason and others as secret sources, and all while you were juggling Malcolm." He paused. "I'm presuming you didn't tell him everything."

I shook my head. "I didn't."

"Have you shared everything with Neely Kate?"

"No."

He gave me a soft smile. "From here on out, you're not shouldering this alone. And don't worry about me tryin' to take over. I'm here as your rock, your protector, your support." His grin turned cheesy. "You're the queen, Rose, and I'm the knight who does your bidding. I will never try to usurp your power, because it would be pointless." He picked up my hand and placed our palms together, linking our fingers. "Where you go, I go. Just tell me what you need."

I kissed him, relief and gratitude stealing my breath. "Thank you."

He leaned back and held my gaze. "Now tell me why Denny Carmichael was in our house and why I shouldn't hunt him down and kill him."

I sucked in a breath. I couldn't tell if he was being literal or metaphorical. "That was a sudden change of sides."

His eyes darkened. "I'm doin' this to protect you and Hope, Rose."

That was what I was afraid of. I had another flash of my vision, of James looking Joe in the eyes and pulling the trigger. I couldn't stop the pool of dread from rising inside me. What if their face-off was at the Hardshaw meeting?

"I need to have another vision," I said, squeezing his hand. But I didn't wait for his approval or acknowledgment—I just closed my eyes and asked, *Will Joe die if I tell him about the Hardshaw meeting?*

Gray murkiness engulfed me, so I shifted the phrasing—*Where will Joe be when the meeting happens?* This time I was in a car, sitting in the passenger seat and pounding the dashboard of a car with my palm. "Make this thing go faster. We have to get to her before it's too late!"

I opened my eyes and stared into his. "You have to get to me."

It wasn't exactly a reprieve, but I hadn't seen his death either. Instead, he seemed to be racing to prevent mine.

I could live with that for now.

Chapter Nineteen

"What did you see?"

"I didn't see you murdered this time, so maybe this changed things."

His eyes brightened just as my stomach released a loud growl.

"When was the last time you ate?" Joe shook his head as he got up and tugged me off the sofa. "Never mind. We need to feed you. You're still eating for two."

Holding my hand, he led me into the kitchen, then pushed me to sit in a chair while he grabbed the chicken and some leftover vegetables out of the fridge.

"There's something you should know," I said, watching him. "It's one of the things I told you I was working on." Despite the vision I'd just had, I was still scared to tell him, but if he was in my inner circle, he needed to know.

"Okay."

"There's a big meetin' this week…between Hardshaw and a South American drug cartel, and it's takin' place somewhere here in Fenton County."

"Shit." He stopped dishing the veggies onto two plates and turned to face me. "Just when I think you can't surprise me anymore, you come up with that. How do you know about this? *I* didn't even know that. I only knew something was coming."

"I didn't think you did," I said, my guilt sweeping in. "And you know I can't tell you where the info came from. It was given to me second or third hand, but it's reliable."

He placed a plate in the microwave. "I don't think I'm out of line askin' why you told me the other things this afternoon, but not this."

"The number one reason was because I saw you dead in visions with Jed and Witt, and your death was a result of me telling you about the meeting. So I kept it to myself until I could sort things out." I gave him a pleading look. "I hadn't ruled out tellin' you, because I thought it was important for you to know, but after my visions, I decided it would cause harm for absolutely no purpose since I had no real information to give you. I still don't know the time or place, not even the date. Just that it's supposed to be this week."

His lips pressed together, but he remained silent as he turned the microwave on. "You're right. Without more information, all I would have been able to do was put out a few feelers and hope we got some information." But he still didn't look happy, not that I blamed him. "And if you thought tellin' me instigated my death, I'm even more understandin' of you withholdin' it from me."

"But we can't ignore that there's still dirty people in the sheriff's department. There are too many leaks. You could have been killed from within your own department, Joe."

His eyes hardened.

"There's something else," I said carefully. "James is facilitatin' the meetin'."

He nodded slowly. "I guess I'm not surprised."

"Denny Carmichael doesn't want Hardshaw here in Fenton County either, so I wouldn't be surprised if he caught wind of the meeting and captured Rufus Wilson in an attempt to find out the when and where."

Joe rested his butt against the kitchen counter and gave me a pensive look. "That makes sense."

"I'm guessing he also knew Rufus was responsible for the safe break-in. Someone was trailing Rufus' girlfriend this morning. We think it was Hardshaw, but it could have been Carmichael. She was worried about him and also about James. The question is whether Carmichael found out about the safe before or after he captured Rufus. Was he tortured?"

"You know I can't tell you…" His voice trailed off. "Just because I no longer work for the Fenton County Sheriff's Department doesn't mean I can leak all their secrets."

"Okay," I said, shifting my position in the chair. "So tell me this: is it *possible* that he was tortured?"

He hesitated, then said slowly, "No comment."

It wasn't a no, so I'd take it as a yes.

I sat upright. "So what if Carmichael didn't know about the safe before he got his hands on Rufus, and he found out while he was tryin' to get other information out of him? Otherwise Carmichael would have gone after Rufus earlier, right?"

"Yeah," he said. The microwave dinged, and he grabbed a fork. He set the plate and fork in front of me, then put the other plate in the microwave. "That's a logical presumption."

"Someone suggested to me that Rufus' girlfriend might know a thing or two about what was in the safe, so Neely Kate and I went to talk to Bobby—Roberta Hanover—at the Stop-N-Go. She was anxious and scared, so I gave her my card and told her to come see me if she wanted help." I held up a hand. "And before you ask, no, Hope was nowhere near the situation. She was with Maeve and Anna."

"Rose," he said tenderly. "I know you would *never* do anything to put Hope in danger." He started to walk over to the microwave, then stopped and turned back to face me. "You have Lady in Black business cards?"

I laughed. "No. RBW cards with my cell phone number."

He scowled. "You shouldn't be usin' your personal cell phone. You need a burner. Something harder to trace. I'll get you one tomorrow."

I stared at him in surprise.

"What?" he said. "I can't believe Jed or Dermot didn't think of it sooner."

"I don't usually text incriminating things on my phone."

"They can link numbers, Rose. Guilty by association. You need a prepaid burner. And if you're handin' out cards, I'll work on that too."

"What?"

"No more legit business cards bein' handed out to people of questionable character."

"Hey," I protested. "Not all of them are questionable."

His brow shot up as he gave me a pointed look. "Plain white card with the number. Or maybe they should be black." He took the plate out of the microwave and sat down across from me at the table. "The number will periodically change, depending on use." He nodded to my plate. "Eat."

I narrowed my eyes. "What are you doin'?"

He picked up his fork and stabbed several vegetables with the tines, then held my gaze. "I'm doin' my job, Rose. Protectin' you." He waved his fork in a slow arc. "Every single person before me has had their own agenda. Sure, Jed was guardin' you, but worked for Malcolm for most of that time, then he was with Neely Kate and she became his priority. Dermot saved Hope's life and yours, probably on more than one occasion, but he works for himself. You need someone who's one hundred percent behind you." He shook his head and stuffed the vegetables in his mouth. "Hell, I can't believe I never questioned this before. Now, tell me why Carmichael was here tonight."

I put my fork down, suddenly losing my appetite. Although I'd told him so much tonight, this revelation was somehow the hardest. Voice shaking, I told him about Denny's visit, leaving out nothing.

I ended with a shaky, "Carmichael could have killed our daughter, Joe."

"But he didn't. She's asleep upstairs with Muffy watchin' over her. Now tell me what he wanted."

He was far too calm about this.

"He said I owed him for what happened in Sugar Branch, and he was there to collect. There was a lot of posturing, mostly on my part to get him to behave, but I told him that I'd end him if he hurt Hope, and I meant it. I refused to discuss his request tonight since he'd treated me so disrespectfully, and after some threats of his own, he told me to come to his property at nine tomorrow morning. I told him I'd be bringing backup. Then he left."

"Respect. You mentioned that before."

I drew a deep breath. "I've demanded it from every person I've come across since entering this world. It's all I have for protection. I've refused to deal with anyone who treats me disrespectfully, James included, unless they change their tune. Carmichael showed up actin' like he had the upper hand, and I had to put him in his place."

His face paled. "He could have killed you, Rose."

"If I hadn't demanded respect, he would have thought I was weak. He doesn't suffer the weak to live." I paused, meeting his eyes. "Do you think tonight was the first time I've stared down the barrel of a gun? I've pretty much told you otherwise."

His jaw set. "He pulled a gun on you tonight?"

"Not when he first showed up. He was weaponless at that point, even if Clyde had a shotgun. But if I let Carmichael get away with actin' the way he did, I knew I'd lose any hope of controlling the situation. I can't be his puppet, Joe. I have to face him as his equal. He's a dangerous man, and he thinks I owe him a favor."

He nodded slowly, still looking terrified.

"But I put Hope at risk," I said, my voice breaking again. "It could have all gone wrong."

He got up and walked around to me, pulling me out of my seat and into his arms. "But it didn't. She's fine, and you *are* meeting Carmichael as his equal because of it." He held me closer. "Yeah, it could have gone horribly wrong, but it didn't."

"She's in danger, Joe. It's not safe for her to be around me."

"No," he said, tucking my head beneath his chin. "Between the two of us, we'll keep her safe."

"But if it gets too dangerous, we need to send her away," I said, forcing the words past the lump in my throat.

"If Jed's gonna sit this out, then maybe the safest place for Hope would be with him and Neely Kate."

I shook my head. "Not with Kate around. I don't trust her."

"Kate." He frowned. "If there's a big Hardshaw deal going down this week, then that has to be why she's here."

"But she won't miss the opportunity to torment Neely Kate at the same time."

"My sister has always been a great multitasker," he said wryly.

"We can send her to Aunt Bessie."

Pushing out a loud sigh, he led me out of the kitchen. "Come on. Let's sit in the living room while we sort this out."

We sat down on the sofa, Joe settling me in his lap. "My aunt's is far enough away that Hope would be safe." I glanced back at him, looking him in the eye. "But if we send her away, I want you to go with her. I want you here with me, obviously, but at least I'm capable of protectin' myself. Hope is defenseless."

He met my gaze unflinchingly. "We'll cross that bridge when we come to it. The more immediate concern is who is going to watch her tomorrow when we pay a visit to Carmichael."

"I want to leave her with Maeve at the nursery, which reminds me. I need to send her a text lettin' her know."

Joe frowned. "Maeve can't protect Hope, Rose."

"No, but Dermot's men will. He told me to meet him at the nursery and he'll have his men ready."

He pondered it for a moment. "Like they did when Vera snatched you? Fat lot of good that did you."

"I think they underestimated Vera."

Then again, we all had. Were we doing it again?

His brow shot up. "You think?" His expression turned hard. "They can guard from the outside, but I want Witt inside the nursery with Hope."

"He won't want to do it," I said. "He feels like he failed her tonight."

He leaned over and kissed me. "Which is exactly why I want him guarding our daughter. He won't let it happen again."

Chapter Twenty

Turning off his phone hadn't been the best way for Joe to handle his resignation. The sheriff and DA had shown up at our doorstep at around nine thirty, and after Joe introduced me and Hope (who had woken) as his fiancée and daughter, he took them into his office and shut the door.

I took the opportunity to check my own phone. Madison had sent a text that the horses had been picked up and would be taken care of until we figured out what to do with them. Maeve sent a text to both Joe and me saying she was sorry she'd missed his call and would love to watch Hope tomorrow. But it was the text from Neely Kate that tripped my heart.

Witt told us what happened. Please don't let anything happen to Joe, Rose.

I could have been offended, but I knew she was scared. I was too.
I won't. I swear.

They'd been in there a good fifteen minutes, half of which included plenty of shouting, mostly from the sheriff, when Randy Miller showed up at the front door. He didn't say anything, just stood there looking forlorn. Something told me this was his way of replying to my check-in text earlier. I had Hope in my arms, but I pulled him into a sideways hug and then immediately led him back to the kitchen.

"Are you hungry?" I asked, latching on to the one thing I could do to help him besides listening. "Thirsty?"

"Uh..." He stared at me as though he wasn't sure.

"Did you have anything for dinner?"

He paused again, then shook his head. "No."

"You sit down, and I'll get you something."

I considered asking him to hold Hope, but he looked so out of it that I worried he'd forget he was holding her and drop her. Muffy whined as his feet, and he absently picked her up and set her on his lap, stroking her head. At least if he dropped her, she'd likely land on her feet.

Holding Hope in one arm, I found a container of leftover spaghetti and meatballs in the fridge and dumped what was left onto a plate, then put it into the microwave.

"I was so sorry to hear about Margi," I said as I grabbed a glass and filled it with ice. "It all came as a complete surprise."

"I just can't believe it," he said, dry-eyed but sounding like he was in the middle of a nightmare.

"I can't either," I said, pouring him a glass of sweet tea and setting it in front of him. "I'm still in shock."

He turned his gaze to me. "Do you think she knew about something being buried in your barn?"

I took a seat next to him and set Hope on my lap, her back to me. "Honestly, Randy, I don't know. I'll admit that I got some strange vibes from her in the beginning, but ultimately I figured she just had an abrasive personality and, like she said, lacked some social skills." I cringed. "Sorry, Randy. The last thing I need to be doin' is besmirching your ex-girlfriend the day she was killed."

He shook his head. "I know she rubbed people the wrong way sometimes. Hell, she did with me too in the beginning. But after you got to know her, you could see the softer side of her."

"She was very good with the horses," I said. "It was obvious she had a passion for them."

"They were her life. She said she'd learned you couldn't count on people, but animals were always loyal to the people who treated them right."

I tilted my head. "I thought she was close to her brother."

He gave me an odd look, like he wanted to contradict me, then said, "I think she was talkin' about her old boyfriends. She never wanted to talk about her past." He wrapped his hand around his tea glass but didn't pick it up. "Most of her stories were from her childhood, before she left high school."

"If you don't mind me askin'," I said, "why did you break up?"

"*She* broke up with *me*," he said, "but I could see there was more she wasn't tellin' me."

"And everything had been goin' okay until that point?"

"I thought so," he said mournfully, staring at the glass in his hand. "We'd been together since last summer. I'll admit we were movin' slow, but I was okay with that. When we broke up, we were seein' each other five or six days a week and spendin' the night together most of 'em. But she always wanted to stay at my place. Never hers."

My brow pinched together. "That seems odd. Did she say why?"

"She claimed my place was nicer, which wasn't a lie. But the week before she broke up with me, she started gettin' phone calls that she refused to answer. She got upset when I asked about them."

"Do you have any idea who was calling her?"

"No." He hung his head. "But I wrote a few of the numbers down when she went to the bathroom and left her phone unlocked." He glanced up. "I looked them up, of course. They were burner phones."

"Maybe they were people reportin' abused horses," I said. "And they didn't want to be traced." I knew it was unlikely, especially given everything else I knew, but he looked so heartbroken I needed to give him some hope that Margi hadn't been on the wrong side of the law.

He snorted. "I asked her why she was gettin' calls from untraceable numbers. She freaked out, asking me if I'd called any of them. I told her no, I'd just looked them up, but the way she reacted... I took her phone and pulled up one of the numbers and started to call it. She became hysterical and took it from me. That's when she broke up with me. She said she couldn't be with someone who didn't respect her privacy. I told her that I was scared for her. That I was worried she was in trouble and wanted to help her, but that only seemed to upset her more. She threatened to call 911 if I didn't leave." He shook his head. His eyes were dry, but he still looked grief stricken. "So I left."

I reached out and covered his hand on the table. "I'm so sorry."

"I tried to make up with her. I'm not ashamed to say I begged, but she said it was for the best. That she loved me, but I'd be better off with a woman who was meek and mild and didn't have a past."

I shook my head in confusion. "A past. What did she mean by that?"

He reached into his jeans pocket and pulled out a folded and worn piece of paper, which he slid across the table to me.

I opened it, squeezing Hope to my chest as I pried it open, surprised to see a rap sheet for a Margi Kindred.

Glancing up with narrowed eyes, I said, "Her name was Margi Romano."

"No," he said. "She was Margi Kindred. And she's not Levi's sister. She's his cousin."

"This doesn't make any sense." I scanned the sheet, surprised by the multiple arrests. Drug possession. Possession with intent to sell. Burglary. Shoplifting. They had all taken place in Oklahoma. "Randy. What is this?"

"Margi fell in with the wrong crowd in Oklahoma. Got probation but then she was arrested for possession with intent to sell, and it wasn't lookin' good. Then it was dropped out of the blue. She didn't even have to plead it down."

I cocked my head. "Did she tell you about any of this?"

"No. I went to Levi last week and asked him what was going on with her. He didn't want to talk about it, but I told him that I loved her. That I was worried and desperate for a way to help. He must have realized I meant it, because he admitted to being worried too. Then he told me about her arrests. I looked them up as soon as I left his house."

"Why the name change and the lie about being his sister?"

"When she found out he was moving here, she asked if she could come too. Said she wanted to start over and leave her old crowd behind. He was hesitant, but she'd been off drugs for over a year by then. She'd gotten a job workin' with horses, and she said it fulfilled something in her. They'd been close when they were younger, so he agreed. Since she planned on changing her name, he suggested she use Romano and pose as his sister. They didn't know anyone here, and he figured it would offer her some degree of protection. Everything went okay for a little while, but soon after she came to town, she had some money to buy a barn, and he had no idea where it came from. She told him someone had donated it. And then months later, she had money to fix up your barn. When he asked her about that, she told him her previous benefactor had donated again."

"Did Levi believe it?"

"He said he wanted to. He loved Margi, and he'd hoped she was turnin' her life around. But now...not so much. He thinks those phone calls were from her contacts in Oklahoma and that they were the ones who gave her money."

My breath froze in my chest. "*Randy.*" We both knew who she'd been talking to.

Tears filled his eyes and he choked out, "I know. Hardshaw's all over Oklahoma. I think she came here to hide, and they found her."

"Or," I said gently, "she came here to do their biddin'." And maybe get inside information by dating a sheriff's deputy, but his pain was too raw for me to throw any salt into his wound.

He shook his head. "I need your help, Rose. I love her." He made a choking sound, then said, "I loved her. Someone murdered her and I don't trust the sheriff's department to find out who really did it. Especially since Joe just quit. You have a way of knowing things, of finding killers. Please say you'll help me."

I squeezed his hand harder. "Of course, Randy. I'll find out who did this. I promise you." It was only after I said it that I realized I shouldn't have made a promise like that, one I didn't know if I could keep, but his eyes flooded with gratitude, and I couldn't take it back.

"Thank you," he mouthed as he released a soft sob.

Suddenly male voices came from the living room, and I realized Joe's meeting had finally ended. Panic washed over Randy's face. "I was hoping not to see them. I already answered a bunch of questions, and..." He looked like he was about to fall into a million pieces.

"No one will bother you here," I said as I got out of my chair and turned Hope around, her chest to mine. "I'll make sure of it." I moved into the doorway and blocked the entrance to the kitchen.

The sheriff and the DA stood in the middle of the living room, still trying to convince Joe to change his mind, but I noticed the sheriff was holding Joe's gun and badge.

"Is someone pressuring you to do this?" asked the DA, a man who looked to be in his fifties. Mason's old boss had left, and tonight was the first time I'd met his replacement.

"For the umpteenth time," Joe groaned. "No one has pressured me into anything. I came to this decision of my own volition. The destruction of our barn has put things in perspective." He moved toward the front door. "Now, I appreciate your concerns, and I'm flattered by your attempts at persuasion, but I've made up my mind. Rose and Hope are the most important things in my life, and this is what's best for our family."

The sheriff shot me a hateful glare. "You did this."

My mouth dropped open in shock.

"*Sheriff*," Joe said, just this side of a shout, "you have overstayed your welcome. Now if you would kindly be on your way." He jerked the front door open, and a bright spotlight shone through it.

"Chief Deputy Simmons," someone shouted from outside, and it sounded like Barry Whitlow, the self-appointed news source for Fenton County. He was a nineteen-year-old crusader who posted "news" on his YouTube channel. He mostly got things wrong, but people seemed to love it, and he had about five thousand subscribers. I couldn't help wondering if Joe had invited Barry to come ask for a statement. It was the fastest way to spread information. Even faster than the *Henryetta Gazette*. "Can you give us a statement in regards to your sudden departure?"

Joe gave the sheriff and DA a grim look. "I would prefer to make this look amicable. We can do that together right now."

The two men walked out onto the porch, and Joe swung the door partially shut behind them. "Stay inside, okay?" he said, turning to me. "This will be less of a circus if you and Hope aren't involved."

"Yeah. Whatever you want." I walked toward him and pushed the door all the way shut, Hope giving a little mewl as if to say she agreed. "Are you sure, Joe? Are you really sure? Because you don't need to do this for me. You have me, no matter what you choose."

"I've never been more certain of anything in my life." Then he kissed me on the lips and walked out the door.

I moved to the side window and peered out of a gap in the curtain as Joe stood at the top of the steps.

"Chief Deputy!" Barry called out. Someone behind him held a camera, and a third person hoisted up a large spotlight. Looked like Barry had staff now. Cables ran from the light to a white van behind them with *Barry Whitlow Action News* painted on the side. "Were you forced to resign?"

Joe let out a hearty laugh. "No, definitely not. And it's not Chief Deputy anymore. It's just plain old Joe Simmons. I resigned of my own free will. In fact, the sheriff and the DA dropped by to try to talk me out of it, but after our discussion, they both recognize that my decision wasn't hasty or coerced. You see, six weeks ago, I became a father to a beautiful baby girl, and my priorities have changed."

"Chief Deputy," a woman called out. "I mean Joe."

The few people in front of the porch laughed, including Joe.

"I'm Philippa Black from the *Henryetta Gazette*," the woman continued. I wasn't surprised she was here. Rumor had it the paper was tired of being out-scooped by Barry. Even if he was mostly wrong. "Does your decision have anything to do with the invasion of your barn?"

"I'd be lying if I said it didn't have something to do with it, but it was the last straw in Rose and I making our decision. As for what I plan to do now, I have several options. I'm part owner in the Gardner Sisters Nursery, or I might work in Rose's landscaping business." He paused, then said jovially, "Whatever I'll be doin', you can be certain that my wife-to-be will be in charge."

I had no doubt that message was intended for any criminal elements that might be listening, but it did set my mind turning. Would either of those things be satisfying to Joe? I didn't intend for his bodyguard position to be a long-term arrangement. With any luck at all, this would be the last time I interfered with the Fenton County underworld. What would he do when everything settled down?

"Thank you all for your interest," Joe said, "but I'd appreciate it if you got on with your evening. We have a newborn daughter we'd like to put to bed, and all the commotion will likely keep her up." Then he gave a wave and turned and walked inside.

As soon as he closed the door, he gave me a grim smile. "Was that subtle enough for the people you deal with?"

"I hope this was the right thing to do, Joe."

"It was." He reached for Hope and cradled her in the crook of his arm. "Are you about ready to go to sleep, baby girl? Daddy wants to do all kinds of naughty things with Mommy."

"Joe!" I protested with a laugh. "You can't tell her things like that."

"She's too young to understand." He leaned closer and placed a kiss on my neck. "Tell me you don't want to do naughty things."

"I do," I whispered, "but Randy Miller's sittin' at our kitchen table."

His smile fell. "Oh, shit."

"He asked me to find out who killed Margi. He doesn't trust the sheriff's department."

"What did you tell him?"

"That I'd do it, of course. But I think he needs to talk to you, Joe. He really needs a friend right now." I took Hope from him and led him into the kitchen. Randy hadn't moved, but his glass of tea was half gone. "Randy, Joe's done with his meeting and would like to talk to you."

"Hey," Joe said, walking over to him. "I'm really sorry, Randy."

Randy stood, and Joe enveloped him in a hug.

"I'm gonna let you two talk," I said. "But Joe, try to make sure he eats something. There's a plate of spaghetti in the microwave."

I brought Hope upstairs to start her bedtime routine. She was half-asleep by the time I put her in her crib, and I hoped she'd sleep for more than a few hours this time. My mind was turning the whole time, thinking of Joe and what he'd done for us. Of Randy and his grief. Of Denny Carmichael and the lives he'd ruined.

I'd just gotten ready for bed, wearing a simple short nightgown with spaghetti straps and no panties underneath, when Joe came in and shut the door.

"How's Randy?" I asked, sitting on the edge of the bed.

"A mess," he said, coming over to sit by me. He checked the monitor, smiling at the sight of Hope in her crib. "I tried to get him to stay the night, but he turned me down. At least I convinced him to wait until Barry's crew left. He was tryin' to get interviews out of the sheriff and the DA." He kissed my temple. "And I got him to eat half the spaghetti."

"Good," I said with a smile. I took his hand. "I want to have a vision of tomorrow. Facing Carmichael. I should have done it earlier, but I want to see what happens."

"You know they don't always come true."

"Well, it would be foolish not to be prepared." I closed my eyes and concentrated on the meeting in the morning. *Will Carmichael hurt Joe?*

I was plunged into a murky vision. At first I thought we were meeting Carmichael at night, but then I realized the vision itself was hazy. I was facing Carmichael and several of his men in front of what was unmistakably Carmichael's compound. Dermot was next to me, and Vision Rose stood in front of us, her feet in a defensive stance. Carmichael's full attention was on me.

"What the hell is this, Simmons?" he shouted, looking furious. "You think you can just show up and then take whatever we say back to your boss?"

"I quit the department," I said in Joe's voice. "I know you've got no reason to trust me, but I'm here as Lady's guard. Nothin' more. Nothin' less."

Carmichael turned to Vision Rose. "I ain't sayin' shit in front of him."

"I was crooked," Joe said. "I covered things up in the sheriff's department. I fabricated evidence to get Rose arrested. I hid evidence to protect my father. I serve my own best interests, always have and always will. It just so happens that our interests overlap in this case. So take it or leave it, but it would be to your advantage to take it." He slowly slipped his hand into his front jeans pocket and withdrew a flash drive. "Information the sheriff's department has on you and every major player in the county, especially Skeeter Malcolm."

Carmichael's scorn shifted to interest. "Go on."

But the vision slipped away, and I found myself staring up into Joe's face. "You're gonna give him information about every player in the county."

He studied me for a moment. "Did it work?"

"The vision ended, but he seemed interested."

He nodded. "Good."

"You were already considerin' it?" I asked in surprise.

"I have to give him something, Rose. I'd already started compiling a list while I was working on my letter of resignation, and then I texted Jed and asked him to supply me with more information, especially on Malcolm. He said he would work on it tonight and email me in the morning." He gave me a pointed look. "I'm not stupid enough to think I can just waltz into his compound."

"Is the information real?"

"With Jed's touches, it should be convincing enough that he'll buy it. I suspect a good portion of it will be fabrications based on truth."

"So Jed knows you quit?"

He grinned. "His response was 'welcome to the dark side.'"

I grinned too, then turned serious. "Are you sure you want to do this?"

He pulled me to him, kissing me softly but with building heat. "Very," he breathed against my lips.

I reached up and wrapped my hand around the back of his head, and held him in place. "I hate to start bossing you around already, but I don't know how long your daughter's gonna sleep, and I'm exhausted."

"We don't have to do this tonight, Rose. We can wait until tomorrow."

I pushed him back onto the bed and grinned. "Not a chance."

Chapter Twenty-One

Hope slept until around three. Joe got up, changed her diaper, then brought her to me so I could nurse in bed. She nursed longer than the previous two nights but fell asleep.

Joe and I exchanged a look, and a silent communication passed between us. Neither of us wanted to let her go just now. Joe arranged her in the middle of the bed, once more placing small pillows around her. We both lay on our sides, facing each other, and he reached across Hope toward me. I took his hand, and he linked our fingers and offered me a smile. "I love you, Rose."

"I love you too."

I fell asleep, our fingers still linked, and when I woke up around seven thirty, Joe and Hope weren't in bed. I sat upright in a moment of pure panic, but the bedroom door was partially open, and I could faintly hear Joe's voice coming from downstairs. Based on the tone of his voice, he was either talking to Hope or Muffy, possibly both.

I got up and headed downstairs, finding them in the kitchen. Hope was in her bouncy seat on the table with an empty bottle next to her, while Joe stood in front of the stove, frying bacon. Muffy sat on the floor under the table, giving the skillet a longing look.

"What's goin' on down here?" I asked. "I woke up and found myself all alone."

Joe grinned, but I could see he was anxious. "Hope and I decided to have a little father-daughter bonding time, and after she had her breakfast, I decided to make sure you had yours."

"Thanks."

"Maeve called."

"Oh?"

"She heard about me quittin'. She's worried. I think she knows there's more goin' on than meets the eye."

I gave him a grim smile. "She's a very intuitive woman. Is she still okay with watchin' Hope?"

"Even more so. And she was relieved to hear that Witt would be hangin' out with 'em."

We spent the next hour trying to pretend like our life was normal, and Joe and I were just ordinary parents who were taking their daughter to the sitter on their way to work.

After I showered, I put on a navy blue sundress and attached my thigh holster, my stomach in knots. I stayed with Hope downstairs while Joe showered and changed. When he descended the stairs, he was wearing jeans, a fitted black T-shirt, and a shoulder harness with his pistol strapped to his chest.

"Is it wrong to say you look incredibly sexy?" I asked, my stomach fluttering with more than nerves.

He grinned, but it looked forced. "If I'd known this was what it took to turn you on, I would have quit the force ages ago."

I got to my feet. "Joe…"

He shook his head. "Let's take my car. It's less conspicuous than your truck."

"Agreed. Do you have the flash drive?"

He patted his pocket. "Jed came through, and I downloaded it while I was feeding Hope. Let's go."

"I want to have another vision first."

"Okay." He reached for my hand and laced our fingers. "Go for it. Of this morning?"

"That's probably a good idea," I said, "but I was thinking about something else." I paused. While I'd been waiting, I'd realized that Joe was definitely part of this now. Which meant he'd likely be involved in the meeting in some way. It might be possible to get more information from him. "I want to see if I can determine the time or location of the drug deal."

"Good idea." He squeezed my hand, then waited.

Closing my eyes again, I concentrated on the question—*When and where is the meeting with Hardshaw and the drug cartel?* I slid into the familiar gray haze, so I shifted it to another pressing concern—*Will Joe get hurt at this meeting with Carmichael?*

I had a vision of Joe sitting in a car, and Dermot saying, "That went better than expected."

I opened my eyes and said, "It goes better than expected."

His face lit up. "You got the time and place?"

"No, that question didn't reveal anything, so I asked if you got hurt during the meeting today, and the vision was of you and Dermot in the front seat of a car. He said it went better than expected."

"Well, that's one less thing to worry about, right?"

"Well, yeah…" But I didn't *feel* less worried. Maybe it was because I'd seen Clyde holding a gun on our baby just last night, or because I was well aware Joe had given up his career to be here with me. Either way, I was wound up.

"Come on," he said. "We're gonna be late."

We put Hope in her car seat, Muffy immediately curling up beneath it, and headed to town, dread growing like a mushroom in my chest. I still hadn't warned Dermot, although I suspected Witt had. He knew everything, and Joe had convinced him to be Hope's bodyguard while we were gone. I didn't delude myself into thinking he'd be pleased, but I was mostly worried about Carmichael's reaction, especially after his snide comment about bringing Joe. While Carmichael had shown interest in Joe's offer, I hadn't seen anything indicating whether he'd accept it.

Dermot was already in the parking lot, leaning against his car, and Joe pulled into the spot next to him. He didn't look surprised to see Joe. Joe glanced his direction without acknowledging him, then got Hope's car seat and diaper bag out of the back. Muffy hopped out with him.

"Is Witt here?" he asked Dermot.

Dermot nodded once toward the building. "Inside."

Joe nodded back, then turned to me. "I'll take Hope and Muffy in and make sure everything is situated."

I wasn't sure what that meant, but I didn't question him. He took Hope's safety very seriously. I just took a long moment to say goodbye to them both, studying Hope's eyes as I told her I loved her.

As soon as Joe entered the nursery, Dermot's face morphed with outrage. "Have you lost your fuckin' mind?"

"Maybe," I conceded. "But Joe presented a convincing argument as to why he should be part of this."

"You're smarter than this," Dermot said through gritted teeth. He shifted his weight and leaned closer. "Carmichael's gonna chew him up one side and down the other, and then, just for fun, he's likely to shoot him. There's no way he'll incriminate himself in front of the *ex*-chief deputy sheriff."

I propped my hands on my hips. "Are you about finished?"

He didn't respond, which I took as a yes.

"Glad to see you think I'll let a man run roughshod over me," I said, seething.

Some of his outrage faded. "That's not what I meant, and you know it."

My brow shot up. "Oh? Because that's exactly what it sounds like to me." I understood why he was concerned, though, and nothing good would come of sowing more discord between us. Carmichael was likely to pick up on it and use it against us. "I realize the risks, but like I said, Joe makes a convincing argument for being part of my protection detail, and we've already thought out Carmichael's reaction. Joe will appease him by providin' information the sheriff's department has on James and other players in the county."

His brow shot up. "He would freely give that to Carmichael?"

"Jed helped create most of it, so it should be convincin'."

"There's no guarantee it will work, Rose."

"Which is why I forced a vision to see if it would. Carmichael was interested. It'll work."

He shot a dark look toward the building. "I don't like it."

"Because Joe was law enforcement less than twelve hours ago?"

"Among other things."

I felt Joe walk up behind me. He pulled a pair of sunglasses from his T-shirt pocket and put them on. "Is there a problem here?"

Dermot's look grew darker. "Your sudden about-face will be nothin' but a distraction that will put Lady's and everyone else's lives in danger."

Joe's back stiffened, but his voice was absent of anger as he said, "Everyone around her has an agenda that involves something or someone other than Rose. I am the only person in this who is one hundred percent behind her."

Dermot turned murderous. "Are you insinuatin' I don't take her safety seriously? I've put a lot on the line to stand with her."

"No," Joe said calmly. "I know you take her safety seriously or we wouldn't be havin' this discussion. But you have your own empire to run. Jed has Neely Kate and their baby. Your men have families and worries of their own." Joe paused. "Rose and Hope are my entire world. I will stop at nothing to protect them. Surely you can see the advantage of havin' someone with that amount of dedication on her detail."

Dermot's expression softened. "It could just as easily be turned against you. They could hurt her to make you talk, thinkin' you know something."

Joe gave a slow nod. "I know. But it's a risk for you too. I can't believe you would stand by and let someone hurt or torture her. Not after savin' her and Hope out in that field."

Dermot pushed out a sigh and turned to face the road. "He'll use your relationship against you. He'll taunt and goad you to get a reaction." He turned to face Joe, his voice hardening. "You can *not* respond. Do you understand? No matter what the man says, no matter how disgusting or vile, you are to remain emotionless and calm. You are a fuckin' robot with absolutely no emotions. Can you handle that?"

"I've been undercover. I know how to play a part."

Dermot didn't look convinced, not that I was either. "When it involves the woman you love? You can just stand there impassively if he starts talking about screwin' her in the most vile ways? You can pretend it doesn't bother you? Because *he* will try to get a reaction out of you, and he'll keep pushin' until you snap."

I couldn't help but think of Daniel Crocker, and how Joe and I had been in the exact situation he'd described. But that wasn't going to happen now. I wouldn't allow it. I shook my head firmly. "I wouldn't let Carmichael get away with that nonsense, whether Joe was there or not."

"Agreed," Dermot said, then shot Joe a pointed look, "but does Simmons know that?"

Joe tilted his head.

"Lady calls the shots," Dermot said. "You do as she says, no questions asked. We are backup and bodyguards. I only speak when necessary, and let's not forget I bring my own contingent, while you, as you pointed out, bring nothing."

I nearly pushed back on Dermot's statement, but he had a point.

"Understood," Joe said.

"Do you?" Dermot countered. "I'm not so sure." He turned to me. "And you, are you prepared to go against his wishes? Or will you go along with what he wants to protect his masculine pride?"

I narrowed my gaze, my anger reigniting. "I stood up to James Malcolm on more than one occasion and held my ground. I can do the same with Joe."

Dermot scowled. "We need to go, but I'm givin' you one last chance to change your mind about this."

Resisting the urge to shoot a glance at Joe, I said, "I've already made my decision."

"Then let's go," Dermot said, reaching for his door. "Simmons, you ride shotgun. Lady rides in back."

Dermot and I got into his car, but Joe hung back and popped the trunk of his car. He grabbed out a shotgun, then shut the lid and climbed into the passenger seat.

When had he loaded *that* into his car?

Dermot pulled out of the parking space, and I glanced back at the nursery. Maeve stood in the window, holding Hope as we pulled away. Witt stood to one side with a grave expression. I wasn't sure if it was from concern over our safety, the responsibility of guarding Hope, or both, but the sight filled me with dread.

No one spoke until we were out of the city limits, then Dermot glanced in his rearview mirror and asked, "How do you plan for this to go?"

"I want to make sure he is plannin' on behavin', and if not, we leave."

"That will be twice you talked to him without findin' out what he wants. You sure you want to do that?"

"Yeah," I said, trying to settle my nerves. "I can't let him think he's one-uppin' me, especially not *now*. He made it very clear he wants help taking down Hardshaw. The timing can't be a coincidence. In fact, I'd bet good money that he killed Rufus Wilson for the time and location of the meeting, only it didn't work, and he came to me because he failed. He thinks I owe him a favor, which apparently he's been hoarding like the guy with the ring in *Lord of the Rings*, and apparently, this is important enough for him to use it. Couple that with the fact he thinks

I know things, I bet ten to one he expects me to get him the date, time, and location of the drug deal."

Dermot was silent for a few moments. "Yeah. I think you're right."

"But there's more. Remember my vision of him from last year? I thought I was a reluctant participant in his stand-off with James. After our gatherings in the fall, I wondered if I actually would work with him. He's dangerous, but we have a common goal—evict Hardshaw from the county. I don't trust him one bit, though, and he seems to be getting bolder by the day. Hitchin' our wagon to his would likely be a suicidal move. Especially since he'll likely expect us to go along with *him*."

"Shit," Dermot groaned.

"Subtle shift of power, but it would position him to be the king of the castle once Hardshaw and James are run out of town. That wouldn't do any of us any good."

"Is that how you see this endin'?" Dermot asked, glancing in the mirror again. "James leavin' town?"

"I don't see him bein' able to stay."

"Exactly," Dermot said, "but I don't see him runnin'. He's fought for his dominion, and I don't see him leavin' willingly."

I had a sudden flash of James from those visions I kept having. *You thought you could take what was mine, Simmons.*

"Unless he had bigger plans," I said in an undertone, glancing out the side window. "Maybe Hardshaw's offered him a position workin' with them." I resisted the urge to tell him I'd asked James that very thing the day before. But one, I hadn't told Joe about my visit to Carter Hale's office, and I didn't want him finding out like this, and two, James hadn't answered me. It was speculation at this point.

"I can't see him takin' orders from someone," Dermot said.

"Isn't that what he's doin' now?" I asked. "Takin' orders from Hardshaw?"

"Yes and no. He's takin' orders, but it's still his men he's orderin' around. Still his domain. Once he moves on, he's just another cog in the wheel. I can't see him bein' happy with somethin' like that, but you know him better. What do you think?"

I turned to face him in the mirror, once more resisting the urge to shoot a glance at Joe. Was this discussion about James upsetting him? For his sake, I was tempted to drop it, but I understood. There was too much on the line for us not to explore every possibility.

"I don't know what to think. He's not the man I knew a year ago. That man genuinely cared about the innocent people in this county. He was workin' on a deal to bring in a small factory to provide jobs. The legal businesses he owned in this county made more than his illegal ventures, but he worried Carmichael would fill the vacuum left by his absence." I took a breath. "*That* man wouldn't be doin' any of this. He'd be protectin' his people, the ones he employs and the ones who don't even know he exists. I don't know him anymore," I said, my sadness seeping in. "The man operatin' now is capable of anything."

This would be James' downfall, and no matter what he'd become, it still broke my heart. Still…I had my own conscience to follow, which meant clearing my head and getting ready to meet a madman who had his own agenda. "When we get done with this meetin', you need to contact the people who pledged allegiance to us last fall. We have to circle our own wagons and let Carmichael know that if he wants to join forces, he'll be workin' with us. Not the other way around."

"We haven't reached out in a couple of months," Dermot said. "The others might have fallen in line with Carmichael."

"Then we need to contact them and find out," I said, shorter than I'd intended.

"Agreed."

I could see the entrance to Carmichael's property ahead, and I took in a deep breath and held it, trying to settle my nerves.

Joe turned back to look at me, my reflection visible in the lenses of his sunglasses. "You okay?"

"Yeah. Fine." Except I wasn't sure that was true. Facing Carmichael had always unnerved me, and now I had more on the line. Joe was with me.

"You up to killin' a man today?" Dermot asked him. "Because that's what this job entails. Bein' ready to pull the trigger with no hesitation."

"I'm fully aware of what this job entails," Joe said without a hint of confrontation.

"You ready to take on a pile of shit, Lady?" Dermot asked, glancing in the mirror again. "Because you'll have two strikes against you the moment you step out of the car." He jerked his gaze to the digital display on the dashboard, which read 9:02.

I felt like I was going to throw up. "I can handle it," I said, making sure my gun was easily accessible on my thigh. Dermot pulled over on the edge of the newly poured gravel drive and turned off the engine.

Carmichael walked out of his ramshackle house, several men streaming out behind him.

"Have your shotgun ready," Dermot said, keeping his gaze on Carmichael and his men as he unfastened his seatbelt. "Pointed to the ground but with a round in the chamber."

"Already done," Joe said, his body stiff.

"Well, all righty then," Dermot said, opening his car door. "It's show time."

Chapter Twenty-Two

Dermot and Joe got out of the car simultaneously, with me a second behind. They walked to the front of the car and stopped, waiting for me to take my place in front of them. I forced my hands to hang naturally at my sides instead of balling them into sweaty fists.

Carmichael came to a stop about ten feet away, his four men fanning out around him. All were armed, but none held their weapons on us, which I considered a win. They were the same men I'd seen in my visions of Joe, so at least that part had come true.

He did a double-take when he saw Joe. "I didn't think you'd take my suggestion that you bring your boyfriend as a challenge."

Here we go.

I lifted my chin. "I'm not here to catch up on our private lives, although from what I hear, you don't have much of one. I guess that saves us some time, which means we can get right to business."

"How's that little one of yours?" Carmichael asked with a toothy grin. "Hope, isn't it? Such a cute little thing. I've always been fascinated with babies. So fragile."

I shot him a dark look and slowly shook my head as I swallowed my terror. I wasn't playing this game. "Obviously you're a slow learner,

Mr. Carmichael, so you let me know when you're ready to do business. But don't call me until you're actually ready." I paused. "I'm a firm believer in three strikes, and you're out, and this is your second strike. Gentlemen." I turned around to walk back to the car.

Dermot and Joe were stone-faced, waiting for me to walk past them.

"Wait," Carmichael called out. "Don't be so touchy."

I paused and turned at the waist to face him. "You have a lot to learn about manners and hospitality, Mr. Carmichael. I suggest you brush up on it before we meet again."

"We'll be doin' our business now," he growled.

His men lifted their guns, pointing them at me, and Dermot and Joe responded by aiming theirs at Carmichael a half second later.

My heart began to race.

Don't back down, Rose. You can't.

I turned around to face him. "Are you *really* a stupid man, Mr. Carmichael, or do you just put that out there so people will underestimate you?"

He clenched his fists at his sides as his face reddened. He took one step closer. "What the fuck did you just say to me?"

"I'm sure you heard me quite clearly, but here's the thing—you *need* me. That's the only reason you left my house yesterday and proposed this meetin' today. You need me. You're trying to fluff out your feathers like a damn peacock and make yourself look like the important one, because God forbid you admit you need the help of a woman. You *hate* the fact that you can't boss me around like everyone else around you, yet here we are."

He looked like he would strangle me if he could get away with it. I had to make sure he knew he couldn't.

"Nevertheless, you're forgettin' one *very* important fact, Mr. Carmichael." I paused and cocked my head. "*I* don't need *you*."

He shot me daggers of hate.

I held out a hand. "Now I was walkin' away and you called me back, which means I'm actually countin' *this* as a potential strike number three, so I suggest you think *very carefully* about everything you say from here on out, because I *will* leave, and that will be the end of our discussion."

"If that's the case," he said, in a tight voice, "what's to stop me from killin' you now?"

"Well, that's a very good question," I said, thinking on the fly. Why hadn't I reasoned this out beforehand? What could he possibly want other than the information about Hardshaw's meeting? Then it hit me. "What stops you is the insurance I purchased this morning." I gave him a wry grin. "I have Roberta Hanover under my protection, and she'll be lost to you if any of us are harmed in any way."

His body tensed, then he grinned. "Now, where did you find her?" he asked in a happy-go-lucky tone.

"Don't you worry about that," I said dismissively. "I'd be more concerned about what she's told me."

He froze. "Does she have proof?"

Of what? What in the world was on that flash drive?

"Of course," I bluffed. "But we're not here to discuss my acquaintance. We're here to talk about why you need me."

He turned to the side, and I could practically see the wheels turning in his head. After a couple of seconds, he said, "I ain't talkin' in front of him." He flung a finger toward Joe.

Honestly, I was surprised it had taken him so long to fully address the subject of Joe.

"I take it you're concerned about his prior connection to the sheriff's department."

"*Prior*," Carmichael spat out. "Hell, the ink is so fresh on his resignation letter, you could sniff it and get high."

"I guess gettin' high is your area of expertise," I said, "but I can assure you that Joe truly did quit, and as a sign of good faith, he brought you a gift." I nodded my head slightly toward Joe without moving my gaze off Carmichael. "Joe."

This wasn't going like it had in my vision, but I wasn't going to panic.

Joe moved up a step, nearly beside me. "I know you've got no reason to trust me, but I'm here as Lady's guard. Nothin' more. Nothin' less." Then the scene from my vision played out in front of me, word for word the same as it had been. I only hoped that meant everything would go well for us.

Joe drew out the flash drive. "Information the sheriff's department has on you and every major player in the county, especially Skeeter Malcolm."

Carmichael squinted at Joe. "Why would you give me this?"

Joe took several steps closer and tossed it to Carmichael. "As Lady said, a sign of good faith."

Carmichael easily caught it and looked it over, then he handed it to one of the guys behind him. "Look it over and let me know what you find."

"On it," the guy said as he snatched it out of his boss's hand and disappeared into the house.

"Let me make one thing clear," I said in a no-nonsense tone. "This is a one-time offer of good faith."

Carmichael looked irritated but remained silent while we stood around waiting for his man to check the information. Less than a minute later, the guy came out, looking elated.

"It's legit. He brought information about Malcolm buyin' those cops in Sugar Branch."

Carmichael still looked dubious. "Is the sheriff department about to move on Malcolm?"

"They're bidin' their time, waitin' for something big to go down," Joe said. "But they're clueless about the meetin' this week."

Carmichael's brow shot up. "Then how do *you* know about it?"

"He knows the same way you do," Dermot grunted, obviously annoyed that Joe had become the distraction he'd predicted.

I shifted my weight and propped my hands on my hips. "I'm a busy woman, Carmichael, so how about we cut to the chase? What do you want?"

"You know what I want," he grunted. "The time and the place of that meetin'."

"What makes you think I have it when poor Rufus Wilson couldn't tell you even after you tortured him?"

"You find that out from your ex-deputy?" He grinned. "I guess you *do* have your hands in all the pies." He looked like he wanted to go on, but in a moment of rare self-control, he didn't.

"We both know I gather information, but this is something I don't have."

"Come on, Lady," Carmichael cajoled. "Last fall you were all for the county unitin' together to throw off the tyranny of Hardshaw. Can't you see the benefit of joinin' me now?"

"I assure you, Mr. Carmichael, that if I had the information, I would be sharing it with the members of *the coalition* we formed last fall, so we could come up with a strategy to stop Hardshaw together." Then I decided to go out on a limb. "But for you, this isn't just about pushing Hardshaw out of the county. It's a power grab, and you have two things you didn't have the last time around. Two things that you think will give you the upper hand."

He put his hands on his hips as an amused grin spread across his face. "Go on. What might those be?"

"One," I said, holding up my index finger. "You are now in possession of high-power weapons. We all know a South American drug cartel isn't going to show up with pistols and shotguns, and you caught wind that there were two cases of weapons hidden in the county. You killed Margi Romano to find their location."

It was partly bluster. There was still a chance Hardshaw had killed her, but Denny Carmichael had been on a killing spree, and I had a gut feeling.

A smug smile spread over his face. "I'm sure you can see that if I admitted to stealing the stash on your property or murderin' a woman to find its location, it could be seen as a confession, so I'll have to plead the fifth."

My rage and horror began to build, but I made myself shut it off. I couldn't react, or he'd take advantage of my weakness. "Kudos to you," I said dryly. "That must feel like quite the coup."

"We both know Hardshaw's not gonna be happy to lose 'em, and there was a certain satisfaction knowin' I'd snatched them out from underneath you too." Evil flickered in his eyes. "That's not the only thing I'd like underneath you."

My brow shot up. "*Really?* I hope that little remark was worth it, because we're done." I took two backward steps, then turned around to close the distance to the back door, Joe moving to the side to cover me.

"We're not done," Carmichael shouted.

I didn't answer as I opened the car door.

"I want that time and place!" he shouted, his face turning red.

I started to get in and stopped. "Then perhaps you should be thinkin' of something to offer *me*, Mr. Carmichael. When you have something you think I'll be interested in, give me a call. We both know you have my number." I paused, then added, "But be forewarned, I won't be entertaining any more drop-in visits." I got in the car and shut the door, and Dermot and Joe didn't waste time following suit.

Dermot turned the car in a wide circle and drove away, casting a glance in his rearview mirror. None of us said a word until we drove off Carmichael's property and determined we weren't being followed.

"That went better than expected," Dermot said, grudgingly.

I didn't respond. All I could see was Margi's face in my mind. Had Carmichael made her suffer? Tears stung my eyes. That man was a monster, and I needed to make sure he didn't end up in control of the county. It was unlikely to help anyone if we stopped Hardshaw, only for *him* to step into the void.

Joe turned in his seat to glance back at me, compassion on his face. "You okay?" he asked quietly.

"I guess I have my answer for Randy," I said.

"You can't tell Deputy Miller that," Dermot said.

"I know," I said, my belly burning with rage. "But I intend to make Carmichael pay for what he's done."

"We will," Dermot said gruffly. "Don't you worry." He cast a glance at me in the mirror. "You told Carmichael he had two things that put him at an advantage but only named one before he tested you again. What's the second?"

"He doesn't actually have the second, just confirmation of where he can get it." My head began to pound, and I rubbed my temples. "I'd bet good money that Roberta Hanover knows what was in that safe. Rufus must have told Carmichael. He obviously also told him that Roberta has some kind of physical proof."

"But does he actually know what was on that flash drive?" Dermot asked.

"Yeah," I said. "I'm certain that he does. Maybe not the specifics, but enough to know he needs the proof." I pushed out a frustrated sigh. "Which means Carmichael is one step ahead of us."

Dermot's face hardened. "Well then, we'll make sure he doesn't get any farther. We need to find Roberta Hanover. Pronto."

Chapter Twenty-Three

"Let me have another vision to see if she still shows up at our house," I said. Since Joe lived in the same house, I reached over his seat and grabbed his shoulder, concentrating on when we would see Bobby. The vision popped into my head immediately. I was standing in the doorway from the living room to the kitchen, watching Vision Rose talk to Bobby at the kitchen table. Hope was in Vision Rose's arms. Two plates were on the table with the remains of sandwiches, but Bobby was sitting at a chair without a plate.

"I know what was in the safe," Bobby said, wiping tears from her face with the back of her hand. "Ruffie made a copy before he gave it to Skeeter."

"Can you get it?" Vision Rose asked.

Bobby hesitated, and then I was back in the car, staring at Joe's shoulder.

"She has a copy of what was in the safe," I said as the vision ended.

"You saw her?" Dermot asked.

"She was in our kitchen."

"Day or night?" he asked.

"Definitely day. It looked like she interrupted our lunch. I asked her if she could get the copy, but the vision ended before she answered."

"We need to get home," Joe said. "She could show up within a few hours."

Dermot was quiet for a moment, then said, "I guess it's as good a plan as any, but we really need the time and date of that meeting. Any ideas how to go about getting it?"

I hesitated, wondering if I was holding back to protect Joe, James, or myself. It didn't matter. I needed to come clean. "Yesterday, I had the same thought. I figured only one person would know for certain, so it would be best to go directly to the source."

Joe turned to look at me. "Did you go to see Skeeter Malcolm?"

"I didn't expect to be able to meet with him directly," I said, "so I went to Carter Hale's office to ask him to make the arrangements. But to my surprise, James was already there, takin' a meetin' with his attorney."

Joe turned to face the windshield.

Dermot shot him a glance, then looked up into the rearview mirror. "I take it you didn't get an opportunity to find out."

"No. He wasn't exactly thrilled to see me."

"It probably would have been risky if you'd tried to force a vision," Dermot said. "You didn't find out anything of use?"

I took a breath. There was no way I was going to tell them everything. Especially the parts about James shooting at me and threatening to kidnap me. "He was on edge and jumpy. I think he's nervous about this meetin'."

"That stands to reason," Dermot said. "He's got a lot ridin' on this."

"I don't know who else we can use to look for what we need," I said. "I guess I'll just keep forcin' visions of people until something shifts and I find what we need."

But both men were silent.

"That's not enough, is it?" I asked.

"We need at least a day to put something together," Dermot said. "Ideally, we'll be in place before they ever arrive. We're gonna be cordinatin' a bunch of hot-headed men, which means we'll need a plan, but to have a proper plan, we need a time and a location."

My heart sunk. "So I need to go see James again."

"No," Dermot said, sounding stern. "It's too risky. He's a smart man. He's going to wonder why you came to see him twice in a couple of days." He frowned. "What excuse did you use yesterday?"

"I told him I wanted to know his end game. I asked him if he was working with the Feds."

"You still think that's what he's doin'?" Dermot asked in surprise.

"I don't know," I said, resting my forehead in my hand. "I'm just tryin' to make sense of it all. This is not the man I knew."

"Rose," Dermot said, "there's a very good chance the man he encouraged you to see wasn't the man he truly is."

I had to accept that he might be right. Because Jed had known James for much longer than me, and he hadn't seen as much vulnerability in him as I had. "I think Jed might agree with that," I admitted.

"If anyone would know, he would."

"Did he tell you his end game?" Joe asked quietly.

"He didn't. The whole thing was a waste of time." And a wasted opportunity. Why hadn't I kept my head screwed on straight and forced a vision? That had been the sole purpose of seeing him.

But I'd struggled to remember that in that room with him. Because part of me still cared about James, and I was scared for him and the path he had chosen. He'd decided that if he couldn't have love, he'd take power and money. Yet he hadn't needed to choose. I'd offered him love—unconditional love—and he'd thrown it back in my face. Why wasn't I more furious? Why didn't I hate him?

I couldn't even let myself stop and think about how this had to be killing Joe. Emotions were complicated, and just because Joe was the man I loved, the man I wanted a life with, didn't mean my worry about James had died.

We were all quiet for nearly a minute, and I knew what had to be done. "I need to see him again," I insisted.

"Are you insane?" Dermot asked.

"No. He won't hurt me. I told him that one of my questions was whether he wanted me dead. He assured me if he had, I would have died a long time ago."

"Charming," Joe grunted.

"That may be true," Dermot said, "but his entire life is hangin' in the balance. If he figures out what you're attemptin', I wouldn't put it past him to see you as collateral damage. At the very least, he'll detain you until the meeting is over."

I suspected he was right. If it was just me, I might risk it, but James had already threatened to take me and leave Hope behind. Not to mention, Dermot had suggested he might try to kidnap her. I couldn't risk it.

I turned to Joe. "Now that you've left the sheriff's department and my vision changed, what if we give the sheriff department an anonymous head's up? Or maybe we can tip off the FBI."

"We need a location. A time. It could literally be anywhere in the county, and if both sides have the fire power we think they'll have, it could be a slaughter."

Dermot shot him a glare. "You said we."

Joe looked confused. "What?"

"You said *we* need a location. As though you're still with the sheriff's department."

Joe pushed out a frustrated sigh. "Habit. I quit the department, I swear."

"You say something like that around the wrong people, and it could get you killed," Dermot grunted.

But as Dermot was delivering his terse response, my phone began vibrating in my pocket. I pulled it out and gasped when I saw Levi Romano's name on the screen. My fingers fumbled to answer.

"Levi?" I asked. "Are you okay?"

Joe swung around to face me while Dermot sat upright and stared at me in the mirror.

"No, Rose," Levi said, his voice breaking. "I'm in trouble."

"Where are you?"

"They killed Margi, Rose," he choked out.

I leaned back in the seat. "I know, Levi. I'm *so* sorry, but right now we need to focus on *you*. Let me help you."

"Can you come get me? I had to run, and my truck broke down. I'm stuck out in the middle of nowhere."

"Just tell me where you are, and I'll come get you."

"Um…I'll send it to you," he said, sounding flustered.

A couple of seconds later, my phone dinged with the pin. He was in the southern part of the county, not too far from our current location. "I'm on the way, Levi. Stay hidden until I get there."

The call disconnected, and I glanced up at Joe. "We have to go get Levi." I pulled up the pin and handed Joe my phone. "Here's the location."

Joe took my phone and studied the screen, then looked up at Dermot. "Something's off here."

"Agreed," Dermot said. "Where the hell has he been for the last twenty-four hours?"

"My thoughts exactly," Joe agreed.

"What are you sayin?" I asked in disbelief. "He sounded desperate."

"It smells like a trap," Dermot said.

I shook my head. "No. You're wrong." I told him what Randy told me the night before about his recent talk with Levi after Margi broke up with him. "If Margi was doin' things for Hardshaw, Levi was clueless."

"Or so he told Randy," Dermot said.

"I know I'm the new guy," Joe said slowly, "so correct me if I'm wrong, but pickin' him up seems like an errand, and the Lady in Black is too important to be runnin' errands."

Dermot's eyes beamed. "Agreed." He adjusted his hands on the wheel. "I'm takin' you both back to the nursery. Simmons, your job is to watch over your family, and I'll take someone with me to pick up the vet. If he checks out, we'll take him to your place, and we can figure out where to go from there."

I started to protest, but it wasn't a bad plan. Besides, I wanted to get back to Hope. And I also wanted to be home in case today was the day Bobby showed up.

"Let me at least call Levi and warn him," I said.

"Okay," Dermot said, "but put him on speakerphone."

I tried calling him back, but it went straight to voicemail. "Maybe his phone's about to die," I suggested.

Joe gave me a pointed look.

"It's possible! He's been in the middle of nowhere for a day."

"Fine," Dermot grunted. "Text him and tell him I'll be comin' to get him."

"I'm not sure he'll trust a stranger if he's runnin' for his life, Dermot."

"Then make sure he knows *you* trust me," Dermot barked. "The rest is up to him."

The look on Joe's face suggested he one hundred percent agreed.

I sent Levi a text telling him that I was sending a trusted friend to bring him to my house. Levi didn't respond, but hopefully he'd check his phone sometime before they arrived.

Dermot dropped us off at the nursery, and Joe and I picked up Hope and Muffy. Maeve and Anna gushed that they'd loved every minute with her, and Witt had apparently watched her whenever they had a busy spell with customers.

As we were leaving, Joe asked Witt to come home with us in case he needed backup, and Witt didn't hesitate to agree. Turned out Jed and Joe had already had a conversation about it, and Witt's schedule had been cleared at the garage in case we needed him.

Hope started crying halfway home, so I brought her in to the sofa to nurse as soon as we got home. Joe headed to the kitchen to make us an early lunch, and Witt stayed outside with Muffy and let her get a good romp around the yard.

As I nursed my daughter, I studied every feature of her face, from her chubby cheeks to her small chin. Her slate-gray eyes stared up at me, and she clutched my finger in her hand. I cradled her tenderly and asked her about her morning and if Nana Maeve had spoiled her rotten and if Witt had gotten any better at holding her. She watched me intently as though listening to every word, occasionally stopping to just stare. I marveled once again that I had created this perfect, beautiful baby. That God had given me such a blessing.

When I studied her, I sometimes saw glimpses of James. Her eyes had already started changing color, and I suspected they'd turn dark brown like his, and her hair was closer in shade to his than mine. Still, it was more than her physical characteristics. The way she observed things with so much intensity reminded me of James when he was in a situation that made him uneasy. My baby was a combination of the two of us, and no matter how much I wanted her to be Joe's, she would always carry parts of James in her. He and I were forever linked because of her, and I couldn't help wondering if she was the reason I still cared about him.

After I finished nursing, I changed her diaper and then went to check on Joe in the kitchen. He was standing at the back window, typing on his phone. His gaze lifted to meet mine. "Dermot says Levi wasn't there."

My stomach lurched. "I knew I should have gone to meet him."

"Did Levi text you back?"

"No."

"It was a trap, Rose. Levi himself might not have set it up, but someone did. They were after you."

I wanted to argue with him, but I suspected he might be right. Still, I couldn't bring myself to believe that Levi would intentionally hurt me.

If he'd set up a trap, I suspected he'd done it unwillingly…and I hated to think what might have happened to him.

We sat down to eat, and Joe took Hope, telling her that when she got older and had teeth he'd make her grilled cheese sandwiches too.

I watched him, my heart overflowing with love. If we could survive the week and run Hardshaw out of town for good, I could have this all the time. I wanted that. I wanted it badly.

"Rose," Witt called out from the front door. "You've got company."

Chapter Twenty-Four

Joe was out of his seat in an instant, pulling his gun from its holster as he moved to the back door. He tested the deadbolt to be sure it was locked and glanced out the window. He strode through the living room toward the closed front door, with me and Hope trailing behind.

When he reached for the doorknob, he shot me a dark look. "Stay inside." But I saw Bobby through the crack as soon as he opened it. She stood on the front porch with Witt, and from her body language, she was just as likely to run as to come inside.

"Let her in, Joe."

"Not yet. Wait here."

He went out, shutting the door behind him, and I was tempted to open it. But if I wanted him to trust me, I needed to trust him too.

It was hard to wait, knowing that she might have the answers I'd desperately wanted for months—answers that might help me see Ashley and Mikey again and could give us the upper hand with James and Hardshaw. But I did it, and the door opened a few seconds later, Joe escorting Bobby inside. Muffy slipped through with them and stood by my legs, watching suspiciously.

Bobby was wearing what she had on the day before—a blue polo shirt with the Stop-N-Go logo and khaki pants. Her hair looked like it hadn't seen a hairbrush in a few days, and mascara was smeared under her eyes. She looked too bedraggled to be the answer to my prayers. I was more likely the answer to hers.

"Stay back, Rose," Joe said. "We checked her for weapons, but you still need to be careful."

I did as he said, because while I wanted to trust her, I had to protect Hope. We didn't know anything about this woman other than that she had the information we needed. It didn't mean she planned to share it or had anything but her own self-interest at heart.

"Bobby," I said, offering her a warm smile. "I'm so glad you came to see me. I'm sorry if you feel harassed, but I'm sure you understand."

"Yeah," she said, wrapping her arms around herself. "I get it." Her gaze landed on Hope. "You have your baby to protect."

She could just be a woman fascinated with babies, but the way she watched Hope unnerved me. Maybe I was being paranoid. "Are you hungry?" I asked. "Thirsty?"

She shook her head. "No. I'm too antsy to eat anything."

"We're gonna protect you, Bobby. You don't need to be worried."

"Sure," she sneered. "You'll protect me, but only if I help *you*."

"No," I said, shifting Hope up to my shoulder. "We'll help you either way, but if we protect you, I would hope you would want to help us too."

She gave me a haughty look. "I think you overestimate me bein' a nice person."

I shrugged. "I guess we'll find out. I was eatin' lunch when you showed up. You might not be hungry, but I am. Come with me. Let's have a chat." I turned and headed into the kitchen and sat down at the table. I considered putting Hope in her bouncy seat, but I wasn't sure if Bobby was here to stir up trouble. So I cradled Hope in one arm while I picked up my sandwich with the other.

Bobby walked over and sat at the end of the table while Joe stood in the doorway.

"Have you been hiding?" I asked.

She nodded. "I went to my granny's, but I worried they'd look for me there. So I drove her car to Shute Creek Park last night and stayed there overnight."

"In her car?"

"Yeah, with the windows rolled down. I stayed there until a sheriff cruiser pulled into the parking lot this morning."

I shot Joe a look. Was the sheriff's department looking for her too?

"Likely a routine check," Joe said. "Drug deals are known to go down there."

I nodded, then turned my attention back to Bobby. "If you had a car, why didn't you leave town?"

"That takes money," she said in disgust, her gaze taking in the room. "Money I don't have." Her tone insinuated that I did.

My kitchen didn't reek of money, but I supposed it was more than a lot of people had. She knew I was the Lady in Black, too, and probably had the misperception the role came with some money.

Still, I wondered why she was so broke. Sure, she didn't make much at the convenience store, but what about Rufus? How much did James pay his men? Funny, I'd never thought to ask. I decided to table that line of questioning for now.

I reached for my glass of water. "Do you know who was in the parking lot at the Stop-N-Go, watching you yesterday morning?" Although Jed had seemed fairly convinced her observer was from Hardshaw, I wanted to know her opinion on the matter.

She shook her head. "Coulda been Skeeter, worried about what I was gonna say. Coulda been Carmichael. I know that bastard was the one who killed Ruffie. His men snatched him from our front yard, threw him into a van, then hauled him away."

"What makes you think it was Carmichael?" Joe asked from the doorway.

She turned to look over her shoulder. "I recognized one of the guys. I went to high school with him, and I know he's makin' money workin' for Carmichael. Makin' more than my poor Ruffie was with Malcolm."

"So which one do you think was watchin' you?" I asked. "Skeeter or Carmichael?"

"Hard to say," she said, her gaze landing on Hope again. "Probably Carmichael, depending on what Ruffie told 'em. *Or* it coulda been Hardshaw."

"So you know about Hardshaw?"

She released a sharp laugh. "I thought you was supposed to be smart."

I gave her a pointed look. "Let me make something perfectly clear: you are welcome in my home, but only if you treat me and my people with respect. If you can't do that, you are more than welcome to leave." My brow rose. "After all, you're a guest here, not a prisoner."

It was a risk, but I had to take it. She knew three other groups were looking for her, and this was about the only potential safe space available to her. She needed me. I couldn't let her see how much I needed her.

She leaned her forearm on the table. "I thought you knew about Hardshaw."

"I do, but I have no idea what everyone else knows." I pushed my plate away, my appetite gone. "From what I know, Rufus was employed by Hardshaw and they sent him to work for Malcolm."

Wariness filled her eyes. "How'd you know that?"

"Maybe that reputation of me bein' smart has some truth to it," I said. "Did they send him here for a specific reason, or just because Hardshaw was lookin' to increase their numbers?"

She gave me a wary look.

"I know they've been slowly infiltration' the county. Heck, they're tied up with Sonder Tech. I also know that Denny Carmichael's been rootin' them out like a terrier after weasels," I said nonchalantly. "He killed one of their employees and her boyfriend. Did you know them? Calista Johnson and Patrick Nestle?"

She swallowed hard, staring at my glass of water.

"Would you like a drink, Bobby?" I asked.

She nodded.

"Joe." I leaned over to look at him. "Can you get our guest some ice water?"

"Yeah."

He headed to the cabinet, keeping an eye on her while he filled the glass.

I remained silent until he set it in front of her, keeping my gaze on her and letting her squirm.

She reached for the glass and took a couple of gulps before setting it down.

"What do you know about the safe break-in at the Gilliam law office last October?" I asked.

She stared at me with wide eyes.

"I know that Rufus was part of the break-in. He checked out the contents of the envelope he stole before he handed it over to Skeeter Malcolm."

A panicked look washed over her face.

I sat back and tilted my head. "I think you know what was in that envelope too, and what's more, so does Denny Carmichael. He is actively lookin' for you right now because he's pretty desperate to get his hands on that flash drive, or rather the knowledge of what was on it, because we both know Rufus would have been killed months ago if he didn't hand it over to Skeeter."

She lowered her gaze to the clasped hands in her lap.

"I'm not gonna lie to you, Bobby. I want to know what was on it too, but I have a more specific reason, which I suspect Rufus knew about. That envelope was bequeathed to me by my dead sister. I hear my name was even written on it. So I ask you, who do *you* think has more of a right to it? Me, Malcolm, or Denny Carmichael?"

"He was just doin' what he was told," she said, her gaze still lowered, but her hands shook and her voice trembled.

"I'm sure he was," I said evenly. "I'm not fool enough to think Rufus wouldn't have faced consequences had he dropped the contents off with me and told Skeeter he'd changed his mind and given the envelope to its rightful owner. But now you have to make a choice. Either me or Denny Carmichael."

Her head popped up, her eyes large with fear.

"Like I said, Carmichael's lookin' for you. He told me so face to face just a couple of hours ago." I leaned closer. "I can help you, Bobby, but that level of help will depend on how much you help me."

Her jaw tightened. "I knew you weren't gonna help me for nothin'."

"That's not true. We'll be more than happy to give you a room to stay in and three meals a day until this blows over, or you can tell me what I need to know, and we'll give you five hundred dollars so you can run hundreds of miles away. Or," I added, "you can always go to the sheriff's department and tell them you saw Carmichael's men take Rufus. If they know Carmichael's after you, surely they'll help you."

"Only if I cut a deal," she said with a sneer. "But they couldn't protect me. Just showin' up there would put me on two men's hit list."

"Why are you so convinced Skeeter Malcolm is after you?" I asked.

Her chin trembled. "He knows."

"He knows what?" I asked.

"That I have this." She reached into her purse, which made Joe tense and rest his hand on the butt of his gun. But then she pulled something small out and placed it on the table.

"Ruffie copied the flash drive onto one of his own."

Chapter Twenty-Five

I looked up at Joe, and he walked over and snatched it off the table. He glanced from me to Bobby, then back again. "Rose, come with me." He gave Bobby a direct look. "Stay at that table."

I got up and followed him into the living room. My hands shook with nerves, so I tightened my grip on Hope.

"I'll get the laptop," he said, ducking into his office. He came out with it a few seconds later and set it up on the coffee table. After booting it up, he inserted the flash drive into the USB port.

I stood in the doorway, staring at Bobby. "How do we know it's real?" After all, Joe had handed off fabricated evidence to Denny Carmichael just that morning.

"Look at it," she said, sounding exhausted. "See for yourself."

I glanced over at Joe as he typed on his keyboard. "It's an assortment of files...a *lot* of files. Some pdfs. Some audio clips." His gaze lifted to mine before dipping back to the screen. His eyes widened. "This is a floor plan of the courthouse."

A few seconds later, Mike's voice burst from the computer.

"Mike Beauregard," he said hesitantly.

"Just checkin' on your progress," a male voice said.

"This isn't something that can happen overnight," Mike said, sounding frustrated.

"Malcolm thinks you can manage it," the man said.

My eyes flew wide, but Joe kept his focus on his screen.

"If he thinks it's possible, then maybe *he* should do it," Mike grunted.

The recording ended, and Joe immediately tugged his phone out of his pocket and started tapping on the screen. He lifted it to his ear, waited a few seconds, then said, "You need to come over to our house. Rose found the missing flash drive, and it's gonna take more than just me to dig through what's on here." A pause. "Thanks."

He lowered his phone and looked up at me. "This appears to be real, and I suspect all these audio files are recordings from phone calls Mike made with Hardshaw."

"Why would he record his calls?" I asked.

"Insurance is my guess," Joe said, frowning as he cast a glance at the kitchen. "Maybe he got sucked further into this than he would have liked, and he wanted to make sure he had the leverage to work out a plea deal if he got caught, or if he decided he'd had enough."

"How did Violet get a hold of it?" I asked.

"I know for a fact that she used Mike's laptop," Joe said. "It was givin' her fits while she was in Houston. I sent her an iPad, but she told me she preferred a computer. So when she came home, I took her old one to the store and got it fixed."

I stared at him in disbelief. She'd told me about the iPad, but she'd never mentioned that Joe had given it to her. "You did? I didn't even know you two were talking."

"She was my friend," he said firmly. "I talked to her every week or so while she was gone."

I'd known that, to some extent. Joe had moved back into his old rental house for a while after returning to Henryetta, and Violet had been living next door at Momma's house. They'd hung out as neighbors and spent time together with the kids. But I hadn't realized their friendship had run so deep. "That was really sweet of you to do that for her," I said softly. "You should have told me."

"I think I'm gonna puke," Bobby called out from the kitchen. At first I thought she was being sarcastic about my conversation with Joe, but her face was pale and she was clutching her stomach.

"The powder room's over here." I pointed to the door on the other side of the kitchen.

She rushed for it, barely getting the door closed before we heard the sound of retching.

"I don't like the idea of her stayin' in our house," Joe said. "I don't trust her."

"I know," I said. "She brought us the flash drive, but something seems off. One minute she's belligerent, and the next she's handing us this evidence."

"You said you'd protect her. Are you really gonna kick her out?"

"No, I'm gonna stash her at Momma's house. I've used it as a safe house before." The idea had come to me from thinking about Joe and Violet, living next door to each other. Momma's house was empty now, and it had been for months.

He gave an astonished look, then shook his head. "No. Don't tell me. At least not right now. Who are we gonna get to take her over?"

"I'm presumin' you called Jed," I said.

"Yeah. He and Neely Kate are on their way over."

"We can ask him who we should get to take her." I moved to the living room window and glanced outside. "We'll also need to figure out what to do with her car."

He frowned. "One more issue I never had to consider before."

I walked over and sat on the sofa next to him. "I'm sure you're havin' second thoughts."

He stared at the computer screen, then looked up at me. "I will do whatever it takes to protect you and Hope. You need to know that."

"I do," I said with a soft smile.

"But this..." He gestured to his computer. "Rose, this is important evidence. It needs to be turned over to either the sheriff's department or the state police. And, depending what's on it, possibly the FBI."

"I know."

"But does Jed?" he asked. "Or Dermot?" He rubbed the back of his neck. "I'm strugglin' to believe they'll agree."

"I know that too," I said with a sigh. I leaned forward and took his hand. "This partnership only works if you're comfortable."

He released a short laugh. "Do you think I was comfortable this morning when you were a hair's breadth from gettin' shot and killed?"

My stomach fell. He already had regrets. "Joe..."

"Don't get me wrong, Rose," he said adamantly. "I wanted to be there. I *needed* to be there, and I went with no regrets, but comfortable isn't the word we're lookin' for."

"Okay," I conceded. "Then what is?"

"I don't know," he said in frustration. "Maybe it's not a word, but a line in the sand. You say you work in the criminal world, but you're not a criminal yourself. You're a mediator, someone who helps keep the peace."

I nodded.

"Don't you ever come across anything that you think should be handled by the authorities? Something that can't be glossed over or dealt with by vigilantism?"

"It's a fine line, Joe," I said. "And sometimes I'm not sure I'm makin' the right calls, but I'm tryin' to look at the end game and what is best for this county."

"When did law enforcement become the bad guy?" he pleaded. "Why can't you take everything to them? Why is there a decision at all?" His hand tightened around mine. "Let's take this to the sheriff's department. We'll tell them Bobby gave it to us and try to get her protection."

"She doesn't *want* protection, Joe," I argued. "At least not from the sheriff's department. She wants to hide, and how do you think it's gonna look if you bring them that flash drive the day after you quit? You wouldn't have a source for them either. I said I'd protect her, and I intend to keep my word."

"There's another reason she won't go to them," he said. "We must have some outstanding warrant on her or something."

"I wouldn't be so sure. Some people just flat out don't trust law enforcement," I said. "Especially when they've dallied on the wrong side of the law." Then I quietly added, "You said it again. You said *we* when you referenced the sheriff's department."

"What are you suggestin'?" he asked, his tone tense.

"I don't know that I'm suggestin' anything," I said, getting to my feet. "I know better than to ask you if you're undercover like you were when we met. You wouldn't do that to me, but someone else might be more suspicious. And as for your ethical concerns, don't you think I've wrestled with those same questions or versions of them myself? Some things might incriminate me or someone else I care about. Or sometimes I think a situation has been resolved and there's no reason to involve the law. And let's not forget I saw your death if we told them."

"And then you had"—he lowered his voice to an angry whisper—"*a vision* that showed I would be okay."

"If I told *you*, Joe. Not the sheriff's department. That was after you'd left."

"Why didn't you call the sheriff's department when you were kidnapped by Buck Reynolds?" he asked in frustration. "Who were you protectin' then?"

"You're bringin' this up *now*? Why not last night?"

Groaning, he got to his feet. "Because any minute now, Jed's goin' to show up, possibly with Dermot in tow, and they're gonna want to bury this like a squirrel hoardin' nuts." He took a breath. "If we find out where this meetin' is happening and when, we need to notify the Feds."

"Then let me look again," I said, reaching for him. Without waiting for his confirmation, I asked my question. *Will Joe be safe if we give this information to the sheriff's department?*

I was immediately enveloped in an icy cold darkness that had always signified one thing. I jerked myself out of the vision and said, "You're dead."

He started at me with pursed lips but didn't say anything.

I gasped. "You want to tell them anyway." When he didn't answer, my anger erupted. "You said you were on board with this. You quit your freakin' job, Joe!" I argued. "Why are you changin' your mind now?"

Surprisingly, Hope wasn't freaked out by our loud voices.

"Because I want them brought to justice, Rose," he said, his voice breaking. "Is that so wrong?"

I pushed out a breath. The thing was, we weren't as far apart on this as he might think. "No," I said, gently, moving closer to him. "It's not wrong at all, but not at the expense of your life." Even if it meant withholding information that could help me see Violet's kids again.

The front door opened, and Jed walked in with Neely Kate behind him. "Trouble in paradise already? I could hear you both shoutin' in the front yard." He glanced over at the laptop. "Is it on there?"

Joe hesitated. "Yeah..."

"Let him look at it, Joe," I said, standing in front of him. "We'll talk about what to do with it after you get a better sense of what's on it. Okay?"

He wrapped an arm around me, searching my face. "Do you mean that?" he whispered. "You'll consider handin' it over instead of actin' on it?"

"I promise, but only if I can find a way to do it that won't get you killed. But we need more information before we make that decision." I stretched up on tiptoes and gave him a kiss. "We'll talk more after you get a better look."

"Thank you." He gave me another kiss, then turned to Jed. "There must be over a hundred files in there, possibly more. I haven't had a chance to dig into all of it, but there are folders within folders. Violet was compiling a case against Mike, and that woman was very thorough."

"So you think this is what Skeeter had stolen from that safe?"

"Bobby said it was a copy." He glanced toward the kitchen. "Has she come out of the bathroom?"

I moved to the doorway and glanced at the door to the powder room. "The door's still closed."

"She's been in there an awfully long time. Maybe we should check on her."

"Good idea," I said, handing a drowsy looking Hope to Neely Kate. "Take care of her while I check."

Neely Kate scooped her up, and then I headed to the powder room door and knocked. "Bobby? You okay in there?"

"She just showed up at your door and handed you the flash drive?" Neely Kate asked in a whisper after she followed me into the kitchen.

"Not exactly like that, but yeah, I guess that's what it comes down to. She came on pretty strong, askin' for protection, and then she up and gave us the flash drive. Joe and I were discussin' it in the living room. She said she had to vomit, so I sent her in here." I knocked again. "Bobby? Are you okay? Do you need anything?"

I was met with silence.

"Are you sure she didn't come out already?" Neely Kate asked.

"No," I said. "I'm not." I tried the doorknob and it turned. Raising my brow, I gave Neely Kate a questioning look, then pushed it in. Sure enough, the room was empty, and there was no lingering stench of vomit.

Turning, I surveyed the kitchen and found the back door cracked. Bobby Hanover had chosen the only exit that could have gotten her out of the house unseen. If she'd gone out the front door or up the stairs, Joe and I would have noticed. "She's gone."

"I thought you said she wanted protection," Neely Kate said.

Joe filled the doorway. "She left? I knew there was something strange with her."

"Well maybe all that talk about turnin' her over to the sheriff sent her runnin'."

"Or maybe she was lyin' through her teeth," Neely Kate said, her face pale as she picked up a small, creased piece of paper off the table. She held it up. "Joe, it's for you."

He strode over and took it from her, while I looked over his shoulder. Sure enough, it was addressed to him.

Hey, Brother. I think it's time to mend some fences. Consider this gift a package full of nails. I'm about to bring the hammer.

Love, Kate

Chapter Twenty-Six

"Kate sent her," I said, looking up at Joe's horror-stricken face. "Kate sent that woman to our house."

Joe ran out the back door, and Jed followed. I hurried to the front door and found Witt lounging in a chair on the porch. Bobby's car was still parked in the drive.

"Did you see Bobby come out here? She's missin'."

He got to his feet. "No. Haven't seen her since she went inside."

"Kate sent her here to give Joe the flash drive," Neely Kate said while she clutched Hope to her chest. "Then she took off out the back door when they weren't lookin'."

"*What?*" Witt barked. "I thought you and Neely Kate went to see her the other day. She said you offered her protection. How did Kate get involved?"

"I don't know," I said, trying not to panic. While Kate had always seemed fond of Neely Kate (in her murderous sort of way), she barely tolerated her older brother and hated me.

"If Kate sent her," Witt said, "you need to assume everything she said came straight from her. She was a puppet."

He was right.

"But why send her at all?" I asked. "Why not leave the flash drive and note on the porch or give them to Neely Kate?"

Neely Kate shook her head. "You know how she likes to play games."

Guilt filled her eyes.

"This is not your fault," I said. "So wipe that look off your face right now. What is she up to?"

Neely Kate tightened her hold on Hope as Joe and Jed walked around the side of the house, both wearing grim looks.

"I take it you didn't find her," I said.

"Nothin'," Jed responded. "She must have run into the woods or along the path to Joe's old property."

"But she left her car." Neely Kate was bouncing Hope a little, and her eyes were nearly closed in contentment.

"I'll get Randy to run the tags," Joe said. "I wouldn't be surprised if it was stolen."

"So her story about camping out in her granny's car was a lie," I said.

Joe drew in a breath. "I don't know. Maybe. I guess it doesn't really matter. What we need to concern ourselves with is when she met with Kate and how Kate even knew who she was."

"Bobby's boyfriend was part of Hardshaw," I said. "I'm not surprised their paths crossed."

"Kate was the one who originally sent Hardshaw to Fenton County," Neely Kate said. "And she claimed she's tryin' to root them out to protect me, so yeah, I think she knows everyone involved with Hardshaw."

"We need to look at those files," Joe said, ushering us back into the house.

Hope was practically asleep, so I took her from Neely Kate and brought her upstairs to put her down for her nap. After I got her settled, I pocketed the monitor and headed into my room to send Mason a text.

Need to talk ASAP. Can't come to you.

Joe had gotten through to me more than he knew. He was right. We needed someone in a position of authority to know what was on that flash drive. And they needed to know about the meeting too, whether we had a time and location or not.

He texted back immediately. *Give me five minutes.*

I crept to the door to the hallway and listened. I could hear Joe and Jed discussing something about an audio file, and although I didn't hear Neely Kate, I was sure she was with them. But in case one of them came looking for me, I ducked into my bathroom and waited.

Several minutes later my phone rang with a call from an unknown number. "Hello?"

"I don't have long," Mason said in a hushed voice.

"Roberta Hanover came to my house a little while ago and asked me for her protection. Then she gave me a flash drive that contains a lot of files. I'm pretty sure it's a copy of what Violet had her attorney keep in his safe."

"When you say a lot of files, how many are we talkin'?"

"I don't know, at least a hundred. Some of them are audio, so we know they're not fakes."

"That's good," he said. "Have you had a chance to look them all over?"

"No," I said, "we're starting to do that now, but there's something else you should know." I took a breath. "Right after she gave me the flash drive, she took off and left a note."

"Why'd she leave?" he asked, confused. "I thought you said she wanted protection."

"It was all a ruse. Kate Simmons sent her to me, Mason, and she left a note from Kate to Joe, saying the flash drive was a gift."

"Well, shit."

"Joe thinks we should turn it in to the sheriff's department," I said.

Then, before I could tell him about my vision of Joe's death, he said, "Don't do that. They won't know what to do with it." His tone was surprisingly anxious.

"This is important evidence, Mason. From the looks of it, it definitively connects Mike to Hardshaw."

"I suspected," he said. "Mike brought evidence with him when he turned himself in to the state police."

"Wait...you knew what was on this?" I asked, my anger brewing.

"I didn't know it was on the drive, no. But I suspected some of it would be, and I'd heard rumors Bobby had a copy. I want you to hold onto it for now. Mike's using that information as a negotiating tool, and if we have the evidence, he no longer has leverage."

"I thought you worked for the state," I said, not quite trusting him. "It sounds like you're tryin' to help Mike."

"I'm trying to help *you*, Rose. But I'm asking you not to turn it over to the sheriff's department. If you want to turn it in to someone, I'm asking you to give it to me."

I wasn't sure what we were going to do with it yet—it wasn't just my call to make—so I didn't make any promises I might not be able to keep. "You know about Mike's plea deal? Do you know where he and the kids are?"

"I don't know where he is. I'm sorry."

I hadn't really expected him to tell me, but I wasn't entirely sure he was being truthful. "Was that why you told me about Bobby? Because you thought she might have it, and you were hoping I'd ultimately give it to you?"

He pushed out a sigh. "No. I told you yesterday that you weren't under any obligation to tell me anything."

"But you hoped I would," I said, unsure how to react.

"Let's put it this way," he said, sounding exhausted. "Out of everyone in the county who might get their hands on it, you're the only one I trust to handle it the right way."

I wasn't sure whether to take that as a compliment or a reason for suspicion. I needed to find out what all was on that drive before I made any decisions.

But there was one thing I suddenly felt ready to make a decision about. I didn't trust Denny Carmichael one iota, and the criminals in this county going up against Hardshaw and a South American drug cartel felt like cavemen with clubs going after a high-tech military force. It would be a slaughter. I couldn't just let it happen, so I'd tell Mason and then figure out how to save Joe if telling Mason endangered him. "Do you know anything about a big meetin' in Fenton County this week?"

He paused so long that I wondered whether he'd hung up. "Big meeting?" he finally said. "I'm sure there are plenty of meetings this week, some of which might be considered big."

My shoulders sank with relief. "I'm gonna take that as a yes. You know about it."

"You need to stay as far away from that mess as possible." Each word was enunciated carefully, his tone urgent.

"Is the state plannin' on getting' involved?"

"Rose, I can't talk about this, but for your own safety and well-being you need to let this go."

Did that mean that the state police knew about the meeting and planned to raid it? If so, why didn't the sheriff's office know anything?

"I find the timin' of Kate Simmons' reappearance in the county a bit suspicious given the meetin'," I said.

"Agreed." He was quiet for another long moment. "Will you promise me you'll stay away from that meeting?"

"Attend a meeting between Hardshaw and South American drug lords? No thanks," I said truthfully, because from where I stood, there was no reason for me to attend, and I was going to do everything in my power to avoid joining forces with Denny Carmichael. Still, I was well aware that he hadn't mentioned who was taking part in this meeting, and I wanted him to know that I wasn't bluffing. "I want no part of that, but I need more reassurance from you, Mason. Is this meeting being looked into?"

"I can assure you of that. It's the time and location that can't seem to be nailed down."

"Yeah," I said. "On our end too." I hesitated. "But if you got the time and location, and let's say there was a big bust, what exactly would come from this?"

"You mean in terms of Hardshaw's presence in the county?" he asked.

"And Hardshaw in general," I said, thinking of Carly. Because pushing them out of Fenton County wouldn't be good enough for her. She needed them gone. "Would they be weakened?"

He pushed out a breath. "Again, I could get in big trouble for saying this, but I suspect you have some pull in decidin' who shows up at this meetin', and you need to keep your friends away."

"That didn't answer my question about weakening Hardshaw."

He lowered his voice to a whisper. "Intel from Mike suggests that someone big in the Hardshaw organization will be attending."

"How high up?" I asked. And how was Mike privy to that information? I thought again about the contents of that flash drive, the hundred or more files it contained, and realized Mike was much more involved than I'd let myself think.

"The *very* top." Then he added, "I have to go, but if you need to contact me, use this phone, okay?"

"Yeah."

"Rose," he said in a worried tone, "I mean it. Stay away." Then he hung up.

I clutched the phone to my chest. What was I going to tell the group downstairs? How did I explain what I knew without implicating Mason?

I left my room to check on Hope. She was sleeping, her mouth slightly parted and her hands clenched next to her head. My heart filled with so much love for this tiny human I thought it would burst.

Muffy lay in her dog bed next to the crib, and I squatted in front of her, rubbing behind her ear. "You're a good girl, Muff," I whispered.

"You have no idea how much I appreciate you watchin' over our baby." I kissed the top of her head, and she licked my chin and cheek.

Sitting on the floor, I scooped her into my arms and held her close. She'd been my baby before Hope, and I didn't want her to think I'd forgotten her. "I will always, always love you," I whispered in her ear.

She responded with more doggie kisses on my chin and lips.

I placed another kiss on top of her head, then set her on the dog bed and got to my feet, surprised to see Neely Kate standing in the doorway, watching me with a worried look.

She backed up to let me out, and I followed her into the hallway, closing the door to a crack behind me.

"Are you okay?" she asked in a low voice.

"Knowing that woman came from Kate? No. I'm far from all right, but I'm not falling apart either."

She grabbed my arm and tugged me into my room, closing the door behind us. "I need you to back me up on something."

I crossed my arms over my chest. "What?"

"I want to call Kate. After I texted her yesterday, Jed told me to cut off all contact, but I don't agree with him. Sure, answering feeds her ego, but she doesn't like to be ignored. She tends to up her ante. Like sending Roberta Hanover here."

I wrapped my arms around myself tighter. "Do you think she's goin' to give you any information?"

"I don't know," she said, getting frustrated, "but I have to *try*. Maybe we can get enough information to at least figure out what she's up to."

I nodded. "For what it's worth, I'm not against it. It's obvious she thought you two bonded after she kidnapped you last fall. She may freak out if you ignore her."

She nodded. "I considered that too. And to be honest, while I love my husband to the moon and back, I don't want him hoverin' over me while I make the call." Tears filled her eyes. "Which makes me feel really, really guilty."

I pulled her to sit on the edge of the bed with me. "Neely Kate, I'm pretty sure I know why Kate's in town, but I'm not sure what to do with the information. Joe and Jed will want to know how I know, and I can't tell them. Yet I'm worried if just tellin' them what I know, they'll figure out my source. I can't put him at risk."

"I'll keep it secret, Rose," she said earnestly. "I won't tell Jed, I swear."

I swallowed, still uncertain I was doing the right thing, but I figured if anyone had the right to know, it was Neely Kate. Besides, I had to tell someone. Mason hadn't given me that information for no reason. "There's a reason everyone's being so cagey about this meetin'. It isn't just between Hardshaw representatives and a South American drug cartel. Someone high up in the Hardshaw organization is comin'. Someone from the very top."

"One of the *three?*"

I nodded. "My source didn't say which one, but it seems pretty obvious."

She gasped. "Carson Roberts. Kate's boyfriend."

"He knows her as a blonde, right?" I asked.

"And as Andrea Penske. She created an entire persona to seduce him."

"Neely Kate, what if she's using that name right now? What if she's stayin' in a hotel using that alias? If she's goin' around as a blonde, she can likely come and go as she pleases."

She stared at the bed as she considered it, then lifted her gaze. "Are you suggestin' *we* go to *her?*"

"I don't know," I said. "Maybe. You can ask her what she knows about the meeting and see if she knows the location and date."

"Slight problem with that thought," Neely Kate said. "She had brown hair when she went to see our birth mother."

Crappy doodles. She was right. "Neely Kate, even if we find out the time and date, we can't go to that meetin'. None of us."

She gave me a leery look. "I wasn't plannin' on it. It's gonna be nothin' but a gun fight, and Jed doesn't want to be anywhere near it. He was gonna try to talk you and Joe out of it."

"But Dermot still wants to go. He wants to try and stop it from happening."

"Do *you* want to go?" she asked.

I shook my head. "No. I want no part of it. Especially since some law enforcement agency is plannin' on goin'."

"What?" she whisper-shouted. "Who? The sheriff?"

"No. Joe said they don't know anything about it. I'm guessing state or federal, but they don't know when or where the meetin' is any better than we do."

"You can't tell Jed and Joe. They'll figure out the connection to Mason."

I narrowed my eyes. "I never told you it was Mason." Although I wasn't sure why I was surprised. She'd already figured out he was feeding me info.

She gave me an eye roll. "*Please*. But that's why you can't tell them. They'd figure it out."

"Especially since I told Joe that Mason is one of my sources." I pushed out a frustrated sigh. "I suck at this."

"No you don't," she said, reaching for my hand. She gave me a tentative smile. "Maybe Sparkle Investigations should look into finding the date and time of this meetin'."

My stomach twisted into a knot. "You're suggestin' we keep this from Jed and Joe?" I shook my head, my frustration growing. "Neely Kate, Joe quit his job to stop the secrets between us."

"Are you sure about that?" she asked, lifting her brow. "Because he told Jed he was quitting to protect you."

"The two go hand in hand," I said.

"Look," she said softly. "When Joe was with the sheriff and the state police, didn't he keep things from you?"

"Well yeah, but—"

"Rose, I know you're strivin' for one hundred precent honesty with him, but the fact is, that's never gonna happen."

"How can you say that?" I demanded. "I'm tryin' so hard, Neely Kate."

"Of course you are," she said with a warm smile. "And so is he, but you're always gonna have secrets. Like when he cooks his chicken cacciatore, and you pretend to like it."

I grimaced. "I don't want to hurt his feelings. He loves that dish, and it's not like it's inedible. It's just not my favorite."

"Exactly. So you pretend to like it to spare his feelings. Just like y'all spared mine when I was experimentin' in the kitchen."

I flushed with embarrassment. Neely Kate used to be known for her nearly inedible "gourmet" creations. Ultimately, Kate had been the one to tell her what none of us could bear to—that they were awful.

"That's not a secret," I said. "That's a white lie."

"But aren't secrets lies of omission?" she asked with a sad look in her eyes.

I turned away, my heart breaking.

Here I go again. Lying to the man I love.

She pulled her phone out of the pocket of her shorts. "I'm makin' a call, but you can only stay if you can keep this between us."

"Neely Kate…" I groaned.

She sat up straighter. "I'm doin' this, Rose, with or without you."

I shot a glance at the door, then back at my best friend. In the end, my loyalty and my curiosity won out. "Make the call."

She tapped on her screen, then gave me a long look and turned on the speaker button.

"Well, *hello*, sister mine," Kate said with a smile in her voice when she answered. "I wondered when you'd get around to calling. Is Joe there? I want to see if he got my gift."

"Oh, he got it all right," Neely Kate said. "Why couldn't you just give it to him like a normal person?"

"Where's the fun in that?" Kate asked. "Was Rose Petal there? Did she like it?"

Neely Kate released her annoyance. "She has a *baby*, Kate. That woman could have been dangerous!"

"Calm down," Kate said with a groan. "I made sure Bobby knew not to hurt little Hope. I threatened her life if she did."

I pushed out a sigh of relief. At least that suggested she didn't want to hurt my baby.

"Did Joe like his gift?" Kate asked in a smug tone.

"He's intrigued," Neely Kate said carefully. "He's lookin' at it now."

"With Mr. Sexy? I almost wish I was there to see him." She made a purring sound, and I was sure Neely Kate was going to reach through the phone and snatch her bald.

Instead, she took a deep breath and asked, "Why did you go see our birth mother?"

"I already told you. You deserve to be happy, NK. I'm gonna make sure all your dreams come true, but you need to let me handle things on my own."

"Why are you in town *now*?" Neely Kate asked.

"I got here a little early to prepare for tomorrow," she said. "I've got big plans, and it's all for you, little sis."

Our gazes met, Neely Kate's eyes as big as mine felt. "I want to see you, Kate. Let's meet up for coffee. That sounds fun, doesn't it?"

"Oh, I'd love to, but I'm afraid I have my hands full right now. We'll have to do a raincheck."

"Kate," Neely Kate said, her voice breaking. "I'm begging you, don't hurt our birth mother or our baby. *Please.*"

There was a moment of silence, and I worried that Kate had hung up. "I won't, NK," she finally said. "I promise. Don't you worry about that, okay?" Her smug tone was gone, and to my surprise, she sounded like she genuinely cared about her sister. "I wish I was with you right now so I could wipe those tears away and tell you everything's gonna be okay, but I can't. Just know that I'm doing this for you, baby sis. I'm doing this so you can be happy. At least one of us Simmons kids should be."

"Joe's happy," Neely Kate said. "He has Hope now, and he and Rose are gettin' married. He's happy, Kate."

She was quiet again. "Is he though?"

Neely Kate and I stared at each other.

"But *this* will make him happy," Kate said. "A clue. Tell him to look for the file labeled VAM4E. Oh, and Neely Kate?"

"Yeah?"

"I love you," Kate said, sounding more sincere than I'd ever heard her.

Then, to my utter surprise, Neely Kate said, "I love you too."

And from the look on her face she meant it.

Chapter Twenty-Seven

Kate hung up, and Neely Kate lowered the phone to her lap. "You love her?" I asked, trying to keep my judgment to myself.

Her gaze jerked up to mine. "We can't choose our family, Rose. You should know that first hand. Your momma was cruel to you, but you still loved her in some way. You've told me so yourself."

"Well, yeah, but…"

A fierce look filled her eyes. "I don't condone what she's done or what she is about to do, not for a hot second, but I can't deny that she's doin' it because she wants to help me. Before I met you, there weren't many people in my life outside of my Granny and Witt who'd lift their little finger to do that."

"That's messed up, Neely Kate."

"I know," she admitted. "I can't explain it, but something happened on our road trip, and I could see that she loves me in her messed-up Kate way. I can't help loving her a tiny bit too."

Only it seemed like more than a tiny bit.

She held my gaze. "Don't get me wrong. I'll do everything in my power to keep her from hurtin' people, but part of me loves her for wantin' to help me."

I nodded, trying to understand.

She ran a hand over her head. "I know what it sounds like. You're right. It's messed up."

I groaned. "I shouldn't have said that. That was mean and judgmental, and besides, you're right. We don't get to pick our birth family. And I think it's okay to love them even if they are…" I struggled to find a word to describe Kate that wouldn't offend my best friend.

"Monsters?" she supplied.

Like James. Did that explain why part of me still worried about him even though he'd turned into someone I barely recognized? Maybe the same part of me that had refused to give up on Momma was refusing to give up on him.

"I know she's a monster," Neely Kate said, "but she's *my* monster. Joe's too, and *he* still loves her. Even if she's crazier than a cuckoo clock that chimes at five minutes after the hour."

"And the bird comes out with a hatchet and starts choppin' up the clock," I added.

She grinned, but sadness filled her eyes. "Exactly."

"We're sisters too," I said, "and it'll be legal as soon as Joe and I get married."

"I know, and that means *so much* to me. I can never thank you enough for everything you've done for me."

I clasped her hand and squeezed. "I feel the exact same way about you. And together, we're going to go tell Joe and Jed about your call. Because we did what needed to be done, but they need to know what we found out. We'll have to look for that file."

She met my eyes and nodded, squeezing my hand back. "I'll take the heat for this one."

We headed downstairs and found Joe and Jed in the kitchen. They had identical setups, each with a laptop in front of him and a legal pad next to him, and their attention was squarely on their screens. Joe looked away to write something down.

"I did something you're not gonna like," Neely Kate announced as she walked into the room.

Jed sat up. "What?"

"I called my sister."

"You called Kate?" Jed demanded.

"She's the only one I've got that has my blood," she said, then reached for my hand. "This one's the sister of my heart."

"While I'm sure this would make a lovely greeting card," Joe said sarcastically as he turned in his chair to face us, "what possessed you to call her after Jed and I both expressly told you *not* to?"

Neely Kate had left that part out when pleading her case with me, but I wouldn't have tried to stop her.

Neely Kate dropped my hand and stared them down. "Because for one thing, neither one of you is the boss of me. Just because you put a ring on it, Jed Carlisle, doesn't mean you get to tell me what to do, and Joe, just because you're my older brother doesn't mean you always know best."

Jed stared up at her in surprise, which quickly morphed into anger. "I'm tryin' to protect you!"

"I don't always need protectin'!" she shouted. "I'm a grown woman who is perfectly capable of makin' my own decisions, thank you very much!"

Both men had the good sense to keep quiet.

"Look," she said with a sigh. "I know neither one of you understands, but the last thing we want is for Kate to get pissed or hurt. And if I'd ignored her, that's exactly what would have happened."

She made a convincing argument, but I'd heard the end of their call. It went deeper than that. Neely Kate had *wanted* to talk to her. Would it end up biting her in the butt?

"Okay," Joe said slowly. "What's done is done. What did she say? Did she give you anything?"

Neely Kate lifted her chin with a smug look in her eyes. "Whatever's happenin' is goin' down tomorrow."

Both men jolted in their chairs.

"When?" Joe asked.

"She just said tomorrow," Neely Kate said. "She asked if you liked your present and said to tell you to look at the file labeled VAM4E."

Joe turned to his laptop and scanned his screen. "I haven't seen anything like that."

"What else did she say?" Jed asked, his face expressionless.

Neely Kate walked over to the table and sat down at the far end, as though purposely placing distance between herself and her husband and brother. I hung back, moving to the sink to wash dishes.

Neely Kate held Jed's gaze. "The first thing she wanted to know was whether Joe got his gift. I laid into her for sending that woman here around Hope, but Kate assured me that she'd warned Bobby not to hurt Hope."

"Like we can trust that," Jed sniped.

"We can," Neely Kate said solemnly. "She was devastated to lose her baby. She would never take Joe's."

"Well, that's not exactly true, now is it?" Joe asked in a snide tone. "If Kate hadn't been so fixated on havin' her big showdown, my father wouldn't have shot Hilary." His face hardened. "Killed her while she was pregnant with *my baby*."

Neely Kate looked properly chastised. "I know, but Kate seemed adamant about not hurting Hope. She said she wants you to be happy too, Joe. That's why she gave you the flash drive and told me which file you should look for."

Joe's lips pressed into a line. "Forgive me if I'm not as accepting of Kate's sincerity as you seem to be."

I had to agree with Joe on that one, but I busied myself with filling the sink with sudsy water and kept my opinion to myself. Still, I couldn't deny that she'd sounded sincere about not hurting Hope. Losing her baby and her partner had driven her to seek revenge against her father. She was more likely to show a baby mercy than any adult, with the exception of Neely Kate and possibly Joe.

"What else did she say?" Jed asked, still looking pissed.

"I asked her to please stay away from our birth mother, and she said she would."

Joe's scowl suggested he wasn't convinced.

"She said she was doin' this for me. She's gonna make all my dreams come true, but I need to let her do it on her own."

"Wouldn't *that* make her life easier?" Jed said sarcastically.

"There's something else," Neely Kate said. She cast a quick glance at me, then turned to face Jed. "I think her big wig Hardshaw boyfriend's gonna be there."

"Carson Roberts?" Joe asked.

She nodded.

"She told you that?" Jed asked in shock.

"I can't remember how the conversation went exactly," Neely Kate said, "but I got the impression that she's here in town because he's gonna be there."

Neely Kate was covering for me.

The two men turned to each other with questioning looks.

"There's something else," Neely Kate said. "I think Kate is arrangin' for the FBI to bust it up."

"She said that?" Jed asked in disbelief.

"Not exactly…"

"Then what *did* she say, exactly?" Joe barked.

Neely Kate glanced at me, prompting him to swing his attention to me. "Were you privy to this conversation?"

I turned off the water and rested my back against the counter. "Look, it was Neely Kate's decision," I said to buy myself some time.

"I didn't ask if you approved of the call," Joe said, shifting in his seat to face me. "I asked if Kate told you the FBI would be there."

"Like Neely Kate, I don't remember exactly how the call went," I said, still stalling. "But she hinted that she was takin' care of everything and that Neely Kate didn't need to worry." Not a lie.

"That's not exactly the same as sayin' the FBI is gonna raid the meetin'," Joe said, crossing his arms over his chest. "Kate's way of 'handlin'' it could be showing up with a bazooka."

I shot a look at Neely Kate, trying to hide my desperation.

"She said the Feds were on it," Neely Kate said. "I just presumed it was the FBI. But she was adamant that we need to stay away."

Joe sat back in his chair, narrowing his eyes as he studied his sister. "What aren't you tellin' us?"

"Nothin'," Neely Kate said earnestly, "unless you want all the little details."

"Yeah," Jed said. "There might have been some hidden context."

"There wasn't," I said. "It was all very straightforward, with the exception of what she said about Carson and the authorities being there. She asked if you got your gift. She wanted to know if I was there. Neely Kate got pissed and suggested Bobby could have hurt Hope, but Kate insisted she'd threatened to kill Bobby if she hurt her. Neely Kate suggested that instead of scheming, Kate meet her for coffee like a normal sister, but Kate said she was too busy plannin' for tomorrow. She said someone from the very top would be there. See? No hidden context."

Both men were silent for a few seconds before Jed turned to Joe. "Do you think the Feds could be involved?"

"Maybe. The sheriff's department doesn't know anything about it, but we know the state's workin' on a case."

"We need to stay away," I said.

They gave me questioning looks.

"If some type of law enforcement is involved, then we need to steer clear and let them do their thing. I'll have another vision of Joe to make sure he's still safe, and if not, we'll keep changin' things until I see that he is, but as far as I'm concerned, we won't be anywhere near that meetin'."

Joe got up from his chair and crossed the room, wrapping his arms around and pulling me to his chest. "Thank God."

I hugged him back, burrowing into his shirt as I forced a vision.

Will Joe be killed if I tell Mason the time and location? The vision was slow to come, but when it finally appeared, I was looking down at toddling Hope. "There's Daddy's girl," I said in Joe's voice. "Are you ready to watch some fireworks?"

"You're gonna watch fireworks," I said.

Joe glanced down at me. "What?"

Relief coursed through me. "I had a vision asking if you'd be okay if we tell the Feds through Mason. You were with Hope, only she was a little bit bigger, and you asked her if she was ready to see fireworks."

"The Fourth of July?" Neely Kate asked.

"Probably," I agreed.

"You're really gonna trust the Feds to handle this?" Jed asked.

I pulled away from Joe to face him. "Yeah."

"What about Carmichael?" Joe said. "He wants the location and time of the meetin'."

"And I told him that I would only give it to him if he gave me something in return," I said. "And we don't even have it to give it to him."

"Maybe the answer's in those files," Neely Kate said. "Maybe that's why Kate told Joe to look at that particular one."

"Doubtful," Joe said. "I suspect the location has yet to be determined."

"But Skeeter's got to be the one who's pickin' it," Jed said. "And he's not goin' to pull it out of thin air. He'll have scouted locations, and maybe Mike was part of that."

"How so?" I asked.

"Skeeter's gonna be prepared for any kind of ambush or raid. He doesn't like goin' in without a way out."

"He's gonna build a trap door," Joe said in excitement. He gave me a hard kiss, then rushed over to his computer. "Just like the one you escaped from in the barn at the auction."

Jed's brow lifted. "You told him about that?"

"I told him a lot of things when he decided to quit his job."

"If Kate doesn't want us to go, then why are y'all chasin' this?" Neely Kate asked.

Joe glanced up. "Honestly, the thought of usin' a lead that Kate dangled doesn't sit well with me, but Denny Carmichael is goin' to want an answer."

"You actually want to give him the time and location?" I asked in disbelief.

"Seems to me it's a good way to kill two birds with one stone," Joe said. "If Carmichael's there, he gets swept up into the whole sting."

He had a point. But the sting would only happen if the Feds had the time and location. All the more reason for us to buckle down and find it.

I groaned. "What if he doesn't call with an offer? Do I lose face and just give the information to him anyway?"

"Let's not get ahead of ourselves," Joe said. "We don't have anything to give him yet."

And it might be a while before we did. "Maybe I can try another vision to see if anything's changed." I walked over to Joe and put my hand on his shoulder, forcing a vision to see the details of the meeting.

This one was less murky than the others had been, and I could see a brunette Kate with a man next to her. He wore a dark suit while she had on jeans and a flowy black tank top. I couldn't hear what they were saying, but Kate looked happy and he looked furious.

The vision vanished, and I was plunged back into my kitchen. "You're gonna see Kate."

He gave me a startled look. "You saw something this time?"

I nodded. "It wasn't clear, but I saw Kate with a man. I couldn't tell where you were or if it was day or night."

Worry filled his eyes, and Jed tapped on his keyboard before turning his screen around to face me.

"Him?"

There was a photo of a man in an expensive tailored black suit and red tie, posing in front of a stone wall. His dark hair was styled and his face was clean-shaven. His eyes were cold. He looked like he could be on the cover of *GQ*.

"I couldn't see him clearly," I said, my skin crawling. "But I'm pretty sure that was him."

"You saw Anthony Carson Roberts," Jed said. "Son of one of the original Hardshaw three."

"So Kate wasn't bluffin'," Neely Kate said.

"No," I said. "It was him." I turned to Joe. "But in my vision, you were *with* the both of them. Does that mean you're goin' to that meetin'?"

Joe shook his head. "I have no intention of goin' anywhere near it."

But he'd been there, nonetheless. Did that mean we were going to get roped into going anyway? I walked over to Neely Kate and put a hand on her arm.

Will Neely Kate be at the meeting with Joe and Kate?

The kitchen faded, and I found myself in a hospital waiting room with Jed, who was pacing with a worried look on his face.

"When are we gonna hear if she's okay?" I asked in Neely Kate's worried voice.

"I don't know," Jed said. "The doctor said he'd let us know as soon as he could."

"I can't lose her, Jed." I shook my head and started to sob. "I can't."

Then the vision faded, and I found myself staring into the worried face of my best friend. "You're scared you're gonna lose her."

Her eyes flew wide. "Lose who?" she asked in a panic.

"I don't know." I told them about my vision. "Who do you think it was?"

"It could have been the baby," Jed said. "Or Rose." He looked up at me. "What question did you ask?"

"Whether Neely Kate would be at the meeting with Kate and Joe."

"So that vision could have been of you and I waitin' at the hospital for the baby to be born," Jed said.

"It's more likely it's Rose," Neely Kate said. "The social worker is supposed to bring the baby to us at home. Her family doesn't want us at the hospital."

"But Rose asked if you were with me and Kate," Joe said. "Wouldn't the situation in the vision be happenin' *while* I'm seein' Kate?"

"Maybe, maybe not," I said. "My visions aren't always literal." I swallowed. "It could be the result of the meetin'."

"Then where the hell was I in Neely Kate's vision?" Joe asked. "Why wasn't *I* there?"

"Maybe you were in the room with Rose," Jed said.

Or he could have been dead. But I kept my thought to myself.

"Or the hospital scene could have been completely unrelated," Jed said. "For all we know it could be Neely Kate's granny. She's not in the best of health at the moment."

That suggestion sobered us. Neely Kate was already upset that her granny had missed her wedding. She'd be devastated if her granny died before meeting her baby.

"I want to have a vision of Jed," I said, marching around the table and putting my hand on his shoulder. I didn't waste any time asking my question.

Why will Jed and Neely Kate be in the hospital waiting room?

The vision slammed into me, and suddenly I was in Jed's head, running through the hospital emergency room sliding doors at night, trying not to panic. Then Neely Kate was in front of me, her face pale as a ghost's. "Have they told you anything?"

She shook her head. "Only that she's lost a lot of blood." She released a sob. "They're not sure if she's gonna make it."

Then I was back in the kitchen, saying, "She's lost a lot of blood."

Neely Kate gasped.

"What did you see, Rose?" Joe asked.

A dull ache sprang up behind my eyes, but I ignored it and told them everything I'd seen.

None of us spoke for several seconds.

Finally, Joe said, "We know that someone gets hurt enough to lose a lot of blood. And we know that I'll be meeting Kate and her boy toy." He turned to Jed. "Carmichael's expecting Rose to give him the time and location of the meeting. Does she have to do it in person?"

"He'll want an in-person exchange, especially since she wanted something in return."

Joe's jaw worked. "For all we know, Carmichael or one of his minions is the one to put her in the ER. That psychopath wouldn't blink an eye at shootin' her just because he feels like it...*after* she gives him what he wants."

Jed turned to look at me. "He has a point."

I rested my hand on Joe's shoulder and forced a vision, this time asking if I went to see Denny Carmichael.

I was plunged into a vision similar to the one I'd had of Carmichael last summer. We were in his front yard, surrounded by a crowd of rowdy men. Most of them were carrying torches. Fear and heat made me sweat.

Vision Rose was in front of me talking to Denny Carmichael.

"You holdin' out on me, Lady?" Carmichael spat out.

She stood her ground, sounding angry. "Why would I hold out on you?" she asked. "I want Hardshaw and Malcolm gone just as much, if not more, than you do. That's the place."

Carmichael studied her for a moment, then climbed up onto a four foot or so tall platform. Someone in the crowd handed him a torch, and he held high, waving it over his head.

The men quieted down.

"Are we gonna sit back and let Malcolm take what's rightfully ours?" he shouted.

"No!" they shouted back.

"Are we gonna go stop 'em?"

"Yes!" they shouted.

A maniacal grin spread across Carmichael's face. "Then *let's* go." He hopped off the platform and strode toward the trucks parked behind us, leaving me and Vision Rose in front of the platform.

The vision ended, and I said, "He's gonna go get James." The pounding in my head had turned to a sharp spike, and I felt like I was going to throw up, but I held it together and told them what I'd seen.

"It was similar to the vision I had last summer," I said, "but things were significantly different. For one, Joe was with me in this one, and for another, in the previous vision, Carmichael made me go with him. This time he left us behind."

"Did you see Dermot?" Jed asked.

I couldn't remember, so I forced another vision. It was identical to the first, but this time I purposely searched for Dermot. When the vision ended, I opened my eyes and winced from the light streaming in the back windows. A wave of nausea rolled through me. "Dermot wasn't there."

Jed nodded as concern filled his eyes. "Are you okay?"

"Fine," I said, placing a hand over my belly.

"Did you just have a vision?" Neely Kate asked.

"Yeah," I said, my head pounding as if a jackhammer was trying to split my skull.

She moved closer to me. "But Rose. You answered the question when you came out of it. You usually just blurt out something that you saw."

I turned to look at her in surprise, but the sudden movement made me dizzy, and I grabbed the back of the chair. "You're right. I was purposely looking for Dermot in the crowd. I wasn't just a casual observer in Joe's head."

"You took over my conscious thoughts and actively looked for him?" Joe asked in disbelief.

"Yeah," I said. "I guess I did."

"That means you can manipulate visions," Joe said, his voice filling with excitement. "You might have the ability to change things."

"Is that even ethical?" Jed asked. "That would mean takin' over someone's free will to change the outcome."

"Or maybe the things she's seein' are like holograms on that Star Trek show you like," Neely Kate said to Jed. "And they're only reflections of the real thing."

"Either way, I don't think I should be dabblin' in that," I said, feeling like I was about to throw up as the room spun. But I had serious doubts I could make it to the powder room.

"That's a topic for another time," Jed said. "At the moment we need to figure out when this thing is happenin' so we can get the information to Carmichael."

My vision was blurry, but I pulled out my phone to make sure I hadn't missed any messages, and my heart dropped when I saw Carmichael's initials on the screen with the message: *You've got your deal, come to my property at nine p.m.*

"Well," I said, trying to sound nonchalant. "Our time just ran out. He's offering me a deal, and he wants me at his property at nine."

Joe cursed under his breath.

"He's gonna expect an answer," Jed said, his face hard. "You're not gonna be able to bluff your way out of this."

I tried to swallow my panic. "I know." I only had myself to blame for this. Me and my stupid pride trying to one-up Denny Carmichael.

"So what are we gonna do if we don't have it by then?" Joe asked. "She can't go unless we pull something out of thin air."

"Not a good idea," Jed said. "They're not gonna take her at her word. They'll likely hold her until they get verification that she's right." He grimaced. "Or insist on takin' her with them. Besides, if Denny's not at that meetin', he won't get taken in with the rest of them. He'll stay a problem for us. And this county. We need him there."

"I don't think he intends to take me with them," I said. "Every vision I've had today shows them leaving us on Carmichael's property while they run off. Where to, I don't know, since the meeting's not until tomorrow. But if he intended to take me with him, I suspect he wouldn't have let us go." I paused, thinking, then added, "Last year he suspected there was something going on between me and James. He probably took me along to goad James. Now he knows there's nothin' between us. No point in havin' me slow them down."

"Maybe," Jed grunted. "But he's gonna hold you to whatever you tell him, and there will be retribution if you're wrong."

My heart hammered in my chest. "Do you think you can narrow down a location with the help of those files?"

"They're a mess," Joe said, his breath coming in short bursts. "It's gonna take some time." He glanced up at me, and I could see he didn't think they had enough time.

I nodded and nearly lost the contents of my lunch.

"Rose, honey," Neely Kate said. "You're not lookin' very good."

I closed my eyes and felt my body swaying. Suddenly, Joe's arms were around me, holding me upright.

"How many visions have you had today?" Jed asked.

"I dunno," I said, feeling like I was falling down a well.

"She's had a lot," Neely Kate said. "She had five or six just now. But that last one was what got to her."

"This happened to her before." Jed's voice sounded faint. "She got sick after questioning multiple men in a short period of time."

I felt Joe's hand brush hair from my cheek. "What does she need?"

"Sleep," I said. "I need sleep."

Joe scooped me up in his arms and headed for the living room and up the stairs. He didn't stop until he gently laid me down on our bed.

I cracked my eyelids enough to see the fear in his eyes, and I lifted my hand up to his cheek. "I'll be fine."

"Why did you push yourself so hard?"

"It had to be done."

"No," he said, "it didn't. We can get in the car right now—you, me, Hope, and Muffy—and we can leave Fenton County far behind us."

I gave him a soft smile. "We can't leave our friends. And what about the farm?"

"None of it means anything without you and Hope."

"What if I'm greedy?" I asked. "What if I want it all?"

He didn't respond.

"Find something for me to give to Carmichael," I said. "Even if I just send it to him in a text." I'd share it with Mason too, in the hopes that the Feds would successfully bust up the meeting. It was our best bet at stopping Hardshaw for good. And Denny, if he was there.

And James.

Joe's worry didn't ease, so I added, "But if you can't find anything, we'll discuss the runnin' part when I wake up, okay? It's not off the table."

"Okay." He pressed his lips to mine in a tender kiss. "I love you, Rose. You're my everything."

And then my consciousness faded.

Chapter Twenty-Eight

The room was darker when I woke up, but it wasn't night. I pushed myself to sitting and took a moment to gain my equilibrium. The clock next to the bed said it was nearly seven, which meant I'd slept almost five hours. It had been even longer since I'd nursed Hope, and my breasts were full.

I had two hours before I was supposed to face Denny Carmichael.

I headed downstairs and found Neely Kate in the living room with Hope. They were both on the floor, and Hope lay on her tummy on a thick quilt. She was making sweet little noises while Neely Kate talked to her.

"Oh, you're up," Neely Kate said when she saw me. "Feeling better?"

"Yeah. Still a bit groggy, but I think some water will help. What are you two up to?"

"We're havin' some tummy time. She seems to love it."

"She does." I sent Neely Kate a pleading look. "Please tell me she wants to nurse. Otherwise I have an immediate date with my breast pump."

She laughed. "It's been a few hours, so I bet she'll be ready soon. We used some of the frozen breast milk. Are you hungry? I made some spaghetti."

I gave her a stern look. "What did you put in the sauce?"

She laughed again. "Don't worry. Nothin' weird. By the way," she said, her eyes bright with excitement, "the guys have made some progress."

"Did they find something?"

"Go see for yourself."

They were still at the table, and when I walked in, Joe shot me a worried glance.

"Are you okay?" He hopped up and pulled out a chair next to his. "Sit. Let me get you something to eat."

I sat on the chair and hated that I kind of collapsed into it. This did not bode well for my meeting with Carmichael. I needed to be on top of my game. "I'm feeling better, but you shouldn't have let me sleep so long."

"There was nothing for you to do, and Neely Kate was loving every moment with Hope," Joe said as he grabbed a plate out of the cabinet and scooped some noodles and sauce onto it, then set it in front of me.

"Enough with the suspense," I said. "What have you found?"

Jed looked up from his legal pad. "We've decided there are three possible places. The first is the barn where they held the auction."

"You're kidding," I said as I stabbed some noodles with my fork and twisted them around the tines.

"As Joe pointed out, there's an escape hatch that very few people know about, and there are plenty of places for Hardshaw to hide men and weapons."

"Why would they hide men?"

"To ambush the drug cartel if things go sideways. So they don't realize they're outnumbered until it's too late," Jed said. "It's Skeeter's go-to defense." He hesitated, then added, "I was the one who originally implemented the plan years ago." He cleared his throat. "In any case, he's gonna know he's in a dicey situation. He'll want to plan for every contingency, especially savin' his own ass. The location will have to suit his needs."

"Okay," I said. "Where's the next place?"

Joe set a glass of ice water in front of me and lowered into his chair. "A vacant warehouse south of town in the Sugar Branch city limits. There's a file for it on the flash drive. Mike made note of doing work on it, but he's very vague about what he actually did."

"Does he normally go into detail in his records?" I asked.

Jed tapped the legal pad with his pen. "We still have a copy of his financial records and invoices from when we investigated him in April. We looked up those invoices, and they're different from the ones on the flash drive."

"How so?"

"There are invoices on the flash drive for work on the barn, the warehouse, and another location that we think would serve Skeeter's purposes. They're not itemized, and the descriptions are sparse. The one for the warehouse says it's for repairs made to weather-damaged surfaces. The files in Mike's personal records were much more detailed," Jed said.

"But why make the detailed ones public?" I asked. "Why make invoices at all rather than just do it under the table?"

"Mike needed something for his records," Jed said. "They're not made out to Skeeter, of course. They're made out to bogus names. The details on the publicly available ones are fake. We think the ones on the flash drive are real."

Which meant he'd been tied up with Hardshaw for a long time. When had this all started?

"But then we found the file VAM4E," Joe said. "He'd put an asterisk in the name and spelled out four, so we couldn't find it with a simple search. It was buried under multiple other folders, but it contains the full details of the work he did on the places in question."

"What exactly did he do?" I asked.

"Hidden panels. Electrical work to run cameras for surveillance."

"Which explains the electrician he used," I said. "The one who was killed. Mark Erickson."

Jed nodded. "According to the financials on the flash drive, Hardshaw paid Mike a lot of money to do the work and pay his contractors." Jed grimaced. "And he *did* compensate Erickson well."

"A fat lot of good that did him since he and his girlfriend are dead," I said, loading my fork with more spaghetti. Turned out I was hungrier than I'd thought. "You said there was a file for the barn?"

"Yeah. Mike had a work order for electrical and audio-video cables."

"So he installed security there too."

Jed nodded. "And he also did work on an old church outside of Pickle Junction."

"A *church*?" I asked in disbelief.

"It's abandoned," Joe said. "And it's out on a less frequently traveled county road. Secluded enough to help ensure privacy."

"But what about the courthouse?" I asked. "Vera said that Mike recruited Mark Erickson because he had access to restricted areas. Was there anything about that on the drive?"

"They installed cameras there too," Joe said.

"To spy on the DA's office?"

"That and Mason's office. They were installed around the same time Mason came back to town. He's investigating the corruption in the county, and Hardshaw is part of it. They aim to be an even bigger part. I suspect they were particularly interested in what was happening with his investigation."

"Someone has to tell Mason," I said, starting to panic. How much had Hardshaw learned?

"Already called him," Joe said. "I told him I came across the information and wanted to pass it along. He didn't even ask where it came from." He gave me a knowing look.

I nodded, taking a deep breath to help me settle down. "That's good. So we've narrowed it down to three possible locations?"

They exchanged an uncomfortable look.

"What?" I asked.

Joe leaned his forearm on the table and held my gaze. "This information is old, Rose. Violet must have gotten it last summer. The end of August at the latest, based on when she came to live with you. She wouldn't have had access to Mike's laptop after that."

And last August was nearly a year ago. "He could have scouted out entirely new locations." It meant something else too. James had been planning this for some time. He'd been planning it when we were together. I felt like a knife had been stabbed into my gut, and logical or not, I felt betrayed.

And if I felt betrayed, I couldn't imagine how Jed was feeling.

"Maybe," Jed said, his jaw tight, "*but* I think he planned on this happenin' a lot sooner. I think Hardshaw was lookin' to start the South American drug drops last spring, but then they had a long hiccup after Neely Kate sent that dirty money to the Secret Service and the FBI. Carson Roberts was never arrested, but there must have been some kind of investigation. It makes sense they would lie low."

"So you think James has had these three places ready for nearly a year, just waitin' for Hardshaw to resume with the original plan?"

Jed nodded. "Exactly. Why else would he do all the work last summer? Not to mention buyin' the police force down in Sugar Branch. He likes to plan ahead, but not *that* far ahead."

"So why did he buy the police force?" I asked. "To help cover for his meetings at the warehouse in Sugar Branch?"

"Likely," Jed said. "But things got out of hand, and he lost them. I suspect Hardshaw wasn't happy about that since they're likely the ones who were payin' for them."

I grimaced. "So the Sugar Branch location is out?"

"Not necessarily," Jed said. "But I suspect you're right. For one thing, it's not as secluded as the other two places."

"Hence purchasing his own police department, which had demanded total autonomy from the sheriff's department," Joe added. "They did whatever they wanted, as you know, but the sheriff's department definitely has a presence there now. They would pick up on any unusual activity. They routinely patrol that location and a dozen others."

"So that leaves two locations and a vague tomorrow meetin' time," I said. "I'm pretty sure Denny Carmichael's not gonna accept that. I have to give him something concrete."

"That's where Dermot comes in," Jed said. "I called him and brought him up to speed. He used a drone to investigate all three buildings. Turns out there's been activity at the church tonight but not those other places."

"So he thinks it's gonna take place at the church?"

"Yeah. Otherwise there'd be something going on. Even with all the previous plannin', Skeeter's got plenty of setup to do before he makes his last-minute announcement. But he wouldn't risk goin' out there until just before the meeting."

That made sense. He'd used a similar tactic prior to my meeting with J.R. Then the meaning of his words penetrated. "Wait," I said. "Does that mean what I think it does?"

Jed gave me a grim look. "The drone showed more activity than Dermot would anticipate if this was going down tomorrow night."

I shook my head. "What are you sayin'? It's happening *tonight*?"

"I'd bet good money on it."

"Joe and I are bettin' our lives on it, Jed."

He held my gaze. "Tonight."

"What time should I tell him?"

"Kate said tomorrow, right?" he asked.

"Yeah."

"Midnight is technically tomorrow."

"Well, crap." Was Carmichael going to be pissed at the late notice? I could technically blame it on him and his nine p.m. meeting time.

I glanced back at the clock on the oven. "I need to feed Hope before we go."

We were going to have to leave her with Neely Kate and Witt. Although it scared me spitless to think Kate might show up, after Neely Kate's conversation with her earlier, I had to believe she wouldn't harm my baby. And I knew that Neely Kate and Witt would do everything they could to protect her. Besides, based on what Kate had said, she was going to be busy.

"We don't have to go, Rose," Joe said. "You can just text him."

Could I get away with it? I'd look weak since he'd asked me to come in person, but if he got swept up in the raid, it would be a moot point. I picked up my phone from the table and pulled up his number.

"How long have you had Denny Carmichael's phone number on your phone?" Joe asked in a gruff voice.

I rolled my eyes. "Since he called me last October to threaten me if I exposed him during my grand jury testimony."

"How many times has he threatened you?"

Shaking my head, I pushed out a sigh. "Every single one of them has aimed a threat at me at one time or another." I waved my phone toward the man across from me. "Even Jed."

"*Jed* threatened you?" Joe asked.

"I never threatened you that way," Jed protested.

"Please. You did *not* appreciate havin' to deal with me. I was a wild card and a nuisance in the beginning." I grinned. "But I grew on you." I turned my attention to my phone. "I'm just gonna text him 'do you want the time and location sooner?' and see what he says."

"He may be so eager for the information that he won't want to waste time waiting for you to show up," Jed said.

"Let's hope." I sent another quick text to Mason on his throwaway phone. *Sweet Pickle Christian Church on County Rd 18, midnight tonight.* Once it was sent, I deleted the text.

Joe watched me but didn't say a word.

I finished my food over the next few minutes. Hope was starting to get fussy in the living room, and I still hadn't heard back from Carmichael.

"That's not good," Jed mumbled with a worried look.

"You think he's purposely ignoring me?"

"I don't know, but maybe you should try calling him."

"Let's hope this works." At this point, I didn't care about losing face, I just wanted to make sure he was at the church when the authorities showed up. Because despite my visions telling me otherwise, I had a terrible feeling things were going to go badly on the Carmichael property. I couldn't ignore my vision of Neely Kate in the hospital waiting room.

I placed the call, my heart beating as fast as a hummingbird's wings, but he didn't answer. I left him a voicemail suggesting we skip the theatrics and exchange the information over the phone.

"I don't know what to do," I said after I hung up.

"Text him the time and location," Joe said. "And hope he sees it."

Would that be enough?

"You were right. We need him at that meetin', Joe," I said, sending him a beseeching look. "We need him to be caught up in the raid. If they don't take him in with the rest, he'll never let us have any peace."

His jaw hardened. "It's not worth the risk of you gettin' killed."

Jed leaned back in his seat. "And that right there is why this whole setup was a bad idea."

We both turned to him.

"You wanted to be her bodyguard? Her backup? Do you even know what that entails?"

Joe's eyes flashed with anger. "Of course I know what that entails."

"No," Jed said through gritted teeth. "I don't think you do. It means you do what the person in charge tells you to do, and you do everything in your power to prepare for every contingency if things go bad."

Joe's face reddened, and a vein on his neck began to throb. "You expect me to let her just waltz up to that madman's front door while he's in the middle of stirrin' up a bunch of barely restrained criminals?"

"Yes," Jed said in a scarily calm voice. "If that's what Rose thinks needs to happen, that's exactly what I expect you to do. You can voice your opinion, but it's her call in the end."

"I can't accept that," Joe said.

Jed's words were ice cold. "Then you shouldn't have quit your job. You might as well be back at the sheriff's department."

They both glared at each other for a few seconds before Jed said, "Do you realize the message you're sendin' right now? You're sayin' you don't trust her judgment."

Joe started to protest, then glanced at me and closed his mouth.

"Look," Jed continued, his tone softening a bit. "She's been dealin' with people like Denny in one capacity or another for a year and a half, and she's been doin' just fine without any input from you."

"That's not entirely true," I interjected. "I've sought his advice from time to time."

Jed shot a glare in my direction. "You may seek counsel from other people, but your decisions are always your own. That's the way it has to be. I haven't liked a few of the choices you've made, but that didn't stop me from *doing my job.*"

I could think of a few instances when he'd put up more than a token resistance, but he'd always protected me. That much was true.

Jed's eyes darkened. "People come to Rose for advice, for mediation, because she has great instincts and doesn't put up with any bullshit. Your job is to state your piece, then accept her decision." He took a breath. "And if you're incapable of that, you need to step down."

Like he had done with James.

Turning to face me, Jed said, "Joe's incapable of doin' this job because he's too emotionally involved."

"Are you sayin' you didn't give a shit about her while *you* were her bodyguard?" Joe challenged.

"No," Jed said. "I would have given my life for her, just as I know you would. But here's the difference—you can't bring yourself to walk her into danger, even if that's exactly where she needs to be." He looked at me again. "Admit it, Rose. You're hesitatin' because you don't want to upset him."

I pushed out a weary sigh. "You're right, but—"

"Stop right there and leave off the but. You need to make this decision and everyone else be damned, Joe included."

"That's not how marriage works, Jed," I said softly. "We may not be married yet, but the rules don't start when the ring goes on my finger."

"Like it or not, this is your job," he said in a stern tone. "You took on this mantle the moment you set up that parley with Skeeter, Reynolds, and Wagner. And now here you are in a position to finally do something consequential with it." His glare softened. "You could run, that's what I intended to do with Neely Kate, but then I realized that would make me nothin' but a coward."

"Don't be puttin' that shit on her," Joe barked. "How is what you're doin' any different from what you're accusin' me of doin'? You're trying to influence her decision too, only you want her to make a different one. She's not a coward if she doesn't want to go to Denny. She has a baby now. Things have changed."

"I can't help thinkin' about Dora," Neely Kate said from the doorway, a fussy Hope in her arms. "You were around Hope's age when she died."

So I wasn't the only one who'd made the connection.

"Dora didn't *die*," Joe sneered. "She was *murdered*."

I gave Joe a sad smile. "I've been thinking about her lately too. How our lives are more similar than I thought."

"All the more reason to stay away from Denny Carmichael," Neely Kate said as she walked into the room and handed me Hope and a receiving blanket. "Joe's right," she said, shooting Jed a silencing look, "you don't need to go through with this."

I took Hope in my arms and adjusted the blanket over my shoulder before tugging down my dress. Hope latched on, and I turned to Neely Kate as she sat in the chair next to me. "If we don't make sure Carmichael is at that meetin', then he'll be a much bigger problem after Hardshaw and James are scooped up. He'll fill the vacuum, like he's been tryin' to do anyway. The county will be just as dangerous, if not more so, and none of us will ever be safe. Carmichael will just keep callin' on me for information."

"Fine," Joe said, "but you don't have to be the one to tell him. We'll send someone else."

"You'll likely be sendin' them to their death sentence," Jed said with an exhausted sigh. "He'll insist it has to be her and will kill anyone who tries to go in her place." He glanced up at me. "To send a message loud and clear."

Which was why it had to be me. Jed was right. I *knew* he was right. Heck. Joe probably knew it too.

"Dora gave her life to bring out the truth," I said softly. "To save lives."

"Fat lot of good that did," Joe said bitterly. "It got her killed, and you were raised by a monster. How much different would your life have been if Dora had raised you here out at the farm?"

Neely Kate reached out and squeezed my free hand. "He's right, Rose. You can't do this. If the vision you had of Jed and me in the hospital was about you, you might not make it. Think about Hope. Think about Joe and me and Jed and baby Daisy." Tears filled her eyes. "Don't you want to meet Daisy?"

It was the first time she'd let herself call her baby by name in weeks.

"Of course I want to be here for my baby and yours." I gave them all a bewildered look. "And everyone is gettin' worked up for nothing. I had two visions of Carmichael's compound. Everything's gonna be fine. He's not gonna make us go to the meeting. The scene at the hospital must have been about someone else."

But from the looks on their faces, they didn't quite buy it. I wasn't sure I did either.

I couldn't shake the heavy sense of dread that I was missing something important. That there was an angle to this mess that I'd missed.

Dora hadn't thought of everything either. Was that what had gotten her killed?

Would she have gone to see Carmichael too?

While I didn't remember my mother, I had been fortunate enough to meet her through her words. She'd written a journal while pregnant with me, something I'd since done for Hope because of how much it had meant to me. Because of that journal, I knew she had done what she thought was right to protect my future. To save innocent lives. She could have stopped her quest to expose the truth about the faulty airplane parts being made at her factory, and no one would have faulted her for it. Just like no one would fault me for leaving Carmichael's attendance at that meeting up to fate.

But would the woman I'd come to know in that journal be able to live with herself if she'd sat back and done nothing?

Could I?

"I would give anything to have my mother," I said. "And yes, my childhood was hell. But if my life had gone differently, I might be sittin' at this table right now, but you wouldn't be here, Joe. And neither would Neely Kate or Jed. I definitely wouldn't be holdin' our sweet baby. And while I would still have known Violet through Daddy, our relationship wouldn't have been the same."

"It probably would have been better," Joe argued. "Violet wouldn't have spent her entire life feeling like she had to protect you. She might have found her own happiness instead of obsessing over yours."

That stung, but he was right. Violet had spent her whole life hovering over me. Still, I wasn't convinced she would have had the picture-perfect life he was projecting.

"Not necessarily," I said, feeling an overwhelming sadness for my sister. "She would have lived alone with her momma, and she would have been miserable. She needed me just as much as I needed her when we were kids."

I was scared spitless because I knew what I had to do. I just needed to find the backbone to do it.

"I don't remember my mother," I said, opening my eyes. "I used to think I never had a hero when I was growin' up, but now I realize I did." My voice broke. "I just didn't know her yet."

Joe shook his head. "*Rose.*" He sounded anguished. "Why does it have to be *you?*"

"Because, just like Jed said, I've been buildin' up to this. I decided to be a neutral party to protect the county, and this is the biggest threat to our safety yet. We thought it was Hardshaw, but Denny's shown us he's as bad or worse. He's killed almost half a dozen people in the last three months, and those are just the ones we know about."

Dora had put everything on the line to protect innocent people from harm. On the surface, it didn't look like her meddling had done any good, but the contract to make the faulty airplane parts had been canceled. Dora had saved countless lives.

And now, so could I.

I could run, but we'd have to leave behind everything we loved. Jed was right. It would make me no better than a coward. How many innocent people would be hurt if Denny Carmichael was allowed to rule over the county?

I could be an example to my daughter. I wanted her to read my journal someday so she could see how I'd wrestled with the hard decisions in life and made mistakes, sometimes in the name of love. So she could see that women have more strength than the world gives them credit for, and anyone, even a friendless misfit like her momma had been, could find happiness. All it took was finding courage to face the world.

Maybe she would read Dora's journal too and see that we Middleton women were strong and fierce. And maybe Hope would find the courage to be fierce someday too.

I held my baby tighter, praying it wasn't one of the last times I would hold her, but if it was, I wanted to pour so much love into her it would make an imprint on her soul.

But before I walked into the void, into the unknown, I had to know one thing.

I closed my eyes and swallowed a sob as I asked, *Will Hope be happy?*

An image of Joe's smiling face filled my vision. He held a jar of baby food and a tiny spoon, saying, "Come on, Hope. I know you're gonna love carrots."

Then it morphed into another vision. This time, I was sitting in front of a mirror, the image in front of me a slightly older Hope with a mop of brown hair. Neely Kate sat behind her, holding a baby in her arms. "Who's that sweet baby in the mirror?" she sing-songed.

Both of the babies smiled and cooed.

Then the image changed again, and I was running toward the barn behind the house. Joe was rubbing the nose of a horse, and I was shouting excitedly in a sweet, tiny voice, "Daddy! Daddy! Can I ride Buttercup today?"

Then image after image shifted like a kaleidoscope, showing me scenes of my daughter's life as she grew. Jed pushing her and Daisy on swings. Elementary-aged Hope helping Maeve in the nursery. Hope riding horses on our farm, and then in competitions. Hope taking dance lessons. Winning the spelling bee. Becoming a cheerleader with Daisy. Graduating high school. The images dimmed as they got farther out, and a few things struck me. I wasn't in a single one. Hope was surrounded by our friends and family, but not once did I see myself. Or Ashley and Mikey. Or James. But I felt an overwhelming sense of happiness and love from my little girl.

Hope might lose me, but she'd still thrive. Joe and Neely Kate, and Jed and Maeve, and everyone else in her life would make sure of it.

I willed the vision to end and opened my eyes, her face blurry through my tears. "You're gonna have a happy life, my precious baby. Momma will make sure of it."

Only later did it hit me that I'd been in full control of what I'd said.

Chapter Twenty-Nine

"I'll brook no more arguments over this," I said as I switched Hope to my other breast. "I'm goin' to see Denny Carmichael."

"I'll be your second," Jed grunted in a tone that made it clear he wouldn't be talked out of it.

Joe looked devastated. "I want to go."

"No," I said, trying to be strong. "You have to stay with Hope."

He shook his head, the fear in his eyes replaced with determination. "I quit my job for a purpose, Rose. To protect you. Don't take that from me now."

I wasn't sure that bringing Joe was a good idea. If we were wrong about the location and time, anyone who showed up with the message would likely be a dead man walking. Still, I understood Joe's need to do this, and I took comfort in knowing he had been in my visions of Hope. I cast a questioning glance at Jed.

He studied Joe for a moment, his expression grim, then the corner of his mouth ticked up. "Welcome to the team."

"I already joined," Joe said in a tight voice. "You were just slow to notice."

"We need shirts," Neely Kate said, trying to sound cheery. "Team Lady in Black."

We all chuckled, but it was forced as we faced the reality of what we were about to do.

"There's one more thing," I said. "Have Dermot check the abandoned factory where we had our showdown with J.R."

"What?" Jed asked. "There was no record of that being an option."

"You yourself said that the flash drive was created late last summer or early fall. Many months ago. Mike's records are from April. See if you can find any record of him doin' any work out there."

"That doesn't make any sense, Rose," Jed protested. "Hell, I don't think there's even electricity out there."

"He won't need electricity," I said. "He can use generators. Send Dermot out there to get a look, but tell him not to get too close. If James is using it, the place is going to be crawling with Hardshaw henchmen." I got up, still nursing Hope. "I need to know by the time we leave in thirty minutes. Dermot has forty-five minutes to get back to us, tops."

"Rose," Jed said in confusion.

I understood why he was confused. This was coming out of nowhere, but everything with my mother seemed to be coming full circle. We had both been caught up in something dark and dangerous. We'd both had babies with a forbidden man. It made sense this would take place at the beginning of my mother's end, at the warehouse where she'd worked. "It's comin' from my gut. Trust me."

He gave me a blank look, then nodded and turned back to his computer.

Joe stared at me with a mixture of horror and dread.

I gave him a weak smile. "I'm gonna give Hope a bath."

He hesitated, then said, "I'm gonna keep diggin' and make sure we didn't miss anything."

"Good idea."

I carried Hope into the living room, and Neely Kate followed, sitting on the sofa next to me. "Neely Kate, will you stay here at the house and watch Hope while we're gone? I was hoping Witt would stay too."

"*Of course*," she said as though I'd asked the silliest question in the world. "But I can't help thinkin' I should go too."

"No," I said with a warm smile. "I need you to take care of my daughter. If anything happens to me—"

"You hush that mouth," she said, sounding pissed. "Nothin's gonna happen to you. Your visions of Carmichael's property said so."

"But if it *does*, I need you to promise me something."

"*Anything*."

I almost teased her about it being a bad idea to give a blanket promise like that, but it wasn't a time for teasing. "Make sure Joe and Hope are happy, okay? They're gonna need you."

"Of course," she said through her tears. "They'd get sick of seein' me."

"Not likely." Then I added, "And will you check on Ashley and Mikey? I feel like I've failed Vi. If Mike's not able to get a plea deal and he gets sent to prison, the kids will go to his parents and not with me like Vi had wanted."

"We'll check on them. I swear it."

"Thank you."

"But you're bein' morbid," she said. "Everything went just fine in your visions of Carmichael's compound, so stop talkin' like this. It's bad luck."

"Okay," I said. "Let's talk about happier things."

She and I took Hope upstairs to give her a bath, and I put her in her sleeper, talking to her nonstop about all the fun we were going to have once Neely Kate and Jed adopted Daisy. And I let myself believe that life was possible. That we'd all walk away from this unscathed. I put Hope to bed, and Neely Kate followed me into my room. She sat down on the bed and watched me in silence as I pulled out a pair of black jeans, a black tank top, and a pair of black ankle boots.

"You're not wearin' a dress?" she asked in surprise. "Where are you gonna hide your gun?"

"Everyone knows I have one by now, and if they don't, they're stupid. Might as well protect my legs." I secured my holster around my ankle, under my jeans, and put my small gun in it. Then I pulled a shoulder harness out of my dresser and slipped it over my head. Once it was in place, I grabbed a box from the top shelf of my closet, behind a box of photos, and set it on the bed.

"Another gun?" Neely Kate asked.

I didn't answer, just pulled it out and put a clip in the base, then loaded the chamber and put it in the harness. I grabbed a black lightweight jacket from my closet and put it on.

"You definitely look badass," she said approvingly.

"Time to play the part." I stared at myself in the mirror.

"You're not playin' a part anymore," she said in a somber tone. "This is you."

Was it? The woman who'd donned that hat and veil the first time had been trying to save her business. The woman staring at me in the mirror was driven to protect her child.

God help anyone who stood in my way.

I drew in a deep breath to steady my nerves. "I'm ready as I'll ever be." Then I spun on my heels and headed for the door. When I got downstairs, Joe and Jed were both still at their laptops.

"There's nothing in Mike's files to link him to the warehouse," Joe said, sneaking a glance at me, then doing a double take.

Jed wrote something on his notepad. "And Dermot reported back that it's completely silent over there. He also mentioned most of the other guys are stickin' with you."

"You mean Dermot," I said.

"No, *you*."

That was good news even if I found the part that they were following *me* more than a little worrisome.

"Okay," I said, slipping my phone into my pocket. "Then we pray we bet our lives on the right location."

Jed looked up, and his brow shot to his hairline.

"What?" I asked, propping my hands on my hips. "You don't approve?"

"It's not that, "Jed said. "It's just that I'm used to you wearin' a dress."

"No dress today," I said, flapping open my jacket to show him my gun. "And I've got one strapped to my ankle too."

"I thought we weren't expectin' trouble," Jed said carefully.

"My vision ends with them running off to the location. We both know if we got it wrong, they'll be on us like ticks on a coon dog," I countered. "It makes sense to be prepared. In the past, I only wore a dress because no one ever expected me to be armed. They all know I am now, so why hide it? It's smarter to wear jeans. How many times have my legs been scratched up from running through brush?"

"True." Jed got up from his seat and walked over to me, holding out his arm. "But a few key factors have changed now. Have another vision."

He was right. It had been just me and Joe in my last two visions, so I reached out for him.

"Do you think that's a good idea?" Joe asked, closing his laptop and standing. "She just slept for hours because she had too many visions in a row, and she's already had a couple since she got up. What if she weakens herself right before we show up at Carmichael's?"

"It's one vision," I said. "And Jed is right. We need to know what we might be dealin' with." Then, before he could protest, I forced the vision. It was similar to the previous one, with very few differences except for the fact Jed was now standing next to Joe. The vision ended when Carmichael and his associates headed to their vehicles.

"They're goin' to the meetin'," I said when I opened my eyes.

"Nobody hurt or threatened?" Jed asked, watching me intently.

"Nope," I said with a tight smile. "Practically identical to the one before."

Jed nodded, but he didn't look very relieved. I could tell I wasn't the only one waiting for the other shoe to drop. "Okay, then let's head out," Jed said. "We'll take my car."

Neely Kate was standing in the doorway with the baby monitor in her hand and tears in her eyes. She watched Jed with a mixture of pride and grief.

"Give us a moment," Jed said, his voice thick. "I'll meet you outside."

Joe grabbed my hand and led me outside to the front porch.

Witt was still sitting in a chair, reading a John Grisham book that had come from the shelves in Joe's office.

"Hey," Joe said. "Can you give us a moment?"

Witt glanced between the two of us and got to his feet, dropping the book on the table next to him. "I'll take a walk around the house and make sure everything looks okay."

"Thanks," Joe said, then pulled me into a hug.

I pressed my cheek to his chest and turned my gaze to the treeline that bordered the road. The sun was low in the sky, casting a golden glow. The trees obscured the horizon, but I loved watching sunsets color the sky from our front porch. I wanted to see thousands more, just like this. In Joe's arms.

"I'm scared," he whispered into my hair.

"Me too," I admitted. "But I know this is the right thing to do." Then I looked up at him and smiled. "I want you to give me the ring."

"What?" he asked in surprise. "*Now?*"

"Now."

Fear filled his eyes. "Let's wait until this is all settled. I'll even make it Instagram worthy. I'm sure Neely Kate can help me."

"Please," I whispered. "I don't want to wait."

"What aren't you tellin' me?" he asked, tilting his head to the side. "We're all nervous, but you're actin' like you're marchin' off to the guillotine. Did you see somethin' you didn't tell us about?"

"Nothin'," I assured him. "It's like I said. Carmichael and his men leave." I didn't have any doubts about that—it was the big stretch of unknown after they left that filled me with dread. Something was going to happen. I just didn't know what or when. "But I'm tired of hidin' and pretendin'. We're gonna get married, and to hell with what anyone thinks. Puttin' on your ring is the same as claimin' you, Joe. I'm telling the world that you're mine, and I won't tolerate anyone who messes with what is mine."

He grinned. "A less confident man might take offense to that."

I gave him a quick kiss. "Then it's a good thing you have confidence in spades." I turned serious. "Now will you get the ring?" I gave him a cheesy smile. "Please?"

He still looked uncertain, but he went inside the house and bounded up the stairs. Jed and Neely Kate were still in the kitchen, locked in a tight embrace, and I could hear Neely Kate crying. Obviously, I wasn't the only one who didn't totally trust we'd make it back from Denny's unscathed.

I turned away to give them privacy, my gaze landing on my truck, and it occurred to me that I had the perfect opportunity to go without them. I could grab the truck keys and go…maybe let the air out of Joe and Jed's tires so they couldn't follow right away. But I quickly realized it was a terrible idea. For one, I'd look weak if I showed up at Carmichael's without them. More importantly, I'd be taking their agency away if I left them behind. I'd just pleaded with them to understand why I had to go. Begged them to accept my decision. I'd be no better than a hypocrite if I didn't respect theirs. I'd just have to hold on to those sweet images I'd seen of that future.

Even if I hadn't been in any of them.

I heard Joe behind me before I saw him. He pressed his chest to my back, wrapping his arms around me. A ring box was in his hand.

"We can go find Carly," he said softly. "Start new lives."

I turned in his arms and gave him a sad smile.

He studied my face for several seconds, then dropped his arms and picked up my left hand. "You can only have this if you promise not to go dyin' on me tonight."

"And I'll only make that promise if you'll promise me the same," I said with a wobbly smile.

"That's the easiest promise I've ever made."

Maybe Neely Kate was right. Maybe a good relationship actually needed white lies. Neither of us could make such a promise, and we both knew it.

He opened the ring box and pulled the ring out too quickly for me to get a look at it, then gazed down into my eyes. "I know I'm supposed to get down one knee and make a pretty speech about how much you mean to me and how I can't live without you."

"Save the pretty speech for our wedding vows," I said, waggling my fingers. "Besides, I already know both of those things."

Laughing, he slipped it onto my ring finger.

When I saw it, my heart lit up with happiness. He'd given me a ring before, which I still had in my dresser drawer. I'd tried to give it back to him, but he'd refused. That one had a big solitaire diamond. It was the ring Joe had thought I wanted.

This one was nothing like the first. It had a larger diamond surrounded by smaller ones in an intricate white gold filigree. "Joe. It's beautiful," I gushed, then grinned up at him. "I now regret not letting you give it to me yesterday."

He laughed. "It's vintage, but it seemed more like you."

"Thank you," I said, wrapping my hand around the back of his neck. "I love it almost as much as I love you."

He kissed me and then smiled at me. "We're gonna have a long and happy life, Rose Gardner."

"Yeah." I smiled back like a fool. "We are."

"Congratulations," Jed grunted from the doorway. Neely Kate stood slightly behind him, beaming. "Now let's go." He stomped down the steps, mumbling something about bad timing.

"Don't mind him," Neely Kate said. "He's just nervous."

I gave her a quick hug and kissed her cheek. "You're the best best friend I could ever hope for." Then, before she could respond with something about me being morbid, I hurried down the steps and got into the back of Jed's car.

Joe hung back as Neely Kate hugged him and whispered something to him.

"Be honest with me," Jed said. "Why do I feel like you think you're marchin' off to your own funeral? Didn't your visions of Carmichael's compound suggest everything would turn out okay? We don't know what the ones at the hospital mean."

"I had another vision."

"You lied about it?"

"No, y'all just never realized I had it. I asked to see if Hope was happy in the future, and I saw a cascade of scenes through her eyes. She was happy. She was loved, and out of the countless images, I never once saw myself."

"Rose." His voice sounded strangled.

"If something happens, Joe and Neely Kate will fall to pieces. I need you to promise to be there for both of them."

"What makes you think I wouldn't fall to pieces too?"

Our eyes locked in the rearview mirror, but before I could answer, Joe opened the passenger door and got in.

"Let's go."

Chapter Thirty

Jed pulled out onto the county road and headed south. I checked my phone once again to see if Carmichael had texted in the last few minutes. Nothing, but Mason had texted back a simple thumbs up.

Did that mean the Feds would be there? Now we just had to get Carmichael and his men to show up.

I stared at my ring, smiling. Willing myself to believe it was still possible that we'd get our wedding. That we'd have some siblings for our baby girl. That there was a future waiting for me at the end of this.

Please God, let us all survive.

The sun had set by the time we reached Carmichael's property. Dread weighed down on me, heavier and heavier the closer we got. Where did this go wrong? The visions showed me that Carmichael and his men left without us. Maybe I had been asking the wrong question.

Two men stood at the entrance to Carmichael's property, blocking the entrance. They carried pistols at their hips and looked like the sort who would shoot first and ask questions later.

One of them approached Jed's window, and Jed lowered it halfway. "The Lady in Black is here to see Carmichael."

The man grinned, but it wasn't friendly. "He's been expectin' her. Fair warning, he's not happy she's late."

Jed rolled up his window as the guy motioned to his associate to move out of our way.

"It's just now nine," I protested as Jed started forward.

"It wouldn't have done any good to tell him that, and besides, it will be a minute or two after by the time you see him. You may have to address it with Carmichael."

"Great." I reached forward and placed my hand on Joe's shoulder, and he reached up and covered it with his own. Closing my eyes, I asked the cosmos if we would survive this visit to Carmichael and got the same vision I'd had with Jed back at the house.

"They're goin' to the meetin'," I said.

"You had another vision?" he asked in surprise.

"Just makin' sure nothing's changed."

What question could I ask to get a different answer?

We could see flames through the trees as we approached a corner in the lane. Enthusiastic cheering filled the air.

"This is not gonna be pretty," Jed grunted as the road opened to the compound. "I have a feelin' you're gonna have to stare that bastard down."

There had to be at least thirty men gathered on the compound. Half of them carried torches. I had no idea what they planned to do with them other than mimic the villagers in *Shrek* before they ran off to kill the ogre. It wasn't like they could take the torches in the trucks that were lined up and waiting for them. I suspected Carmichael cared more about stirring the crowd up than the practicality of it. Well, if they were working themselves into a frenzy to bust into an FBI raid, more power to them.

Jed parked at the edge of the trees surrounding the property, and our arrival drew the attention of the crowd. Or maybe just prompted them to look at us. I suspected the guards at the drive had already alerted Carmichael to our presence.

"Wait in the car until I open your door," Jed said. "Joe, when I open my door, get out and then come stand next to me."

"Got it," Joe grunted.

I took a breath and held it as they got out, hoping they didn't get shot. I took it as a good sign when Joe walked around, and Jed opened my door.

So far, so good.

I got out as the crowd parted like the Red Sea, revealing Carmichael at the end. He wore jeans and a button-down shirt, and his smile was downright macabre.

I was right to be worried.

I was sure the plan was for Jed and Joe to flank me, but Carmichael was looking for proof that I was weak. I refused to give him any ammunition.

With my face set in a hard expression, I marched between Joe and Jed, heading straight for Carmichael. I was pretty sure I heard Jed cursing me under his breath, but they followed close behind. Just like I'd known they would. Like he'd said earlier, Jed would always ultimately follow my lead.

Carmichael's legs were hip distance apart, his hands at his sides. He eyed me up and down as I approached, a sly grin lighting up his face. "I'd say I was missin' those sexy legs, but I love the way those jeans are huggin' your perky little ass."

He was obviously trying to rile up Joe, who thankfully remained silent. Maybe it helped that Carmichael hadn't once seen my butt since I'd gotten out of the car.

"I'm not here to discuss my fashion choices," I said dryly as I came to a stop about six feet in front of him.

"I'm not above it," he said with a hungry look in his eyes, but it quickly shifted to anger. "You're late. Given your messages, I was starting to wonder if you'd decided not to show. If you'd gone and chickened out."

I knew better than to try to reason with him or make an excuse. "Good things come to those who wait."

His eyes narrowed. "Do you have a time and location?"

"What do you have to offer me in return?" I countered with plenty of attitude.

"How do I know you're not bullshittin' me?" he asked in a teasing tone.

"And how do I know your offer is equal compensation?"

He hooked his thumbs in the waistband of his jeans. "Seems to me you'd want to just give the location to me. Last fall, you were all gung-ho to rid the county of foreign invaders," he said, making a big sweep with his hand. "What happened to your band of merry men? You were goin' to make a big stand."

Well, crap. In his mind, I'd been too weak to hold the group together. I needed to figure out a way to dig myself out of this hole. "Some men are too short-sighted."

He clapped his hands together and pointed at me. "That right there." His gaze swung around the crowd. "What'd I tell you, boys?" he asked gleefully. "I told you she was a visionary."

I didn't like the sound of that.

He shifted his attention back to me, taking a step forward. "You're right about the others bein' short-sighted. They can't see that we need to grow." His hands fisted at his sides, and his jaw clenched. "Without outside influence and definitely without those assholes from south of the border." He cocked an eyebrow. "Do you agree with that?"

What was he up to? "I'm not here to debate whether Hardshaw should stay. I definitely see all harm and no good from a foreign drug cartel movin' in."

He grinned. "Then we see eye to eye."

"What are you gettin' at, Mr. Carmichael?" I asked. "I came here for a business transaction, not to play games."

His eyes lit up, and he looked around at his men. "What'd I tell you?"

It would've been nice to get an answer. He was obviously building to something, and so far, I wasn't a fan of the framing.

It was time to nip this in the bud. "Do you have something for me or not?" I asked, sounding annoyed.

"I do," he said. Taking a step closer, he leaned in and lowered his face to mine. "An offer you can't refuse."

I had a feeling he meant that quite literally.

I pierced him with a steely gaze. "Go on."

His face lit up, and he took a step closer so that we were less than three feet apart. Jed and Joe tried to move closer to me, but two men blocked their path.

"Search them for weapons," Carmichael said.

His men took the guns in their holsters, plus one from the waist of Jed's jeans and one from Joe's ankle. They looked pissed, but they had to know resisting would get them hurt or dead.

I waited for Carmichael to use the opportunity to frisk me himself, but he seemed more interested in our conversation. He lowered his voice to a whisper. "I propose a working relationship. When I take over, I'm gonna need to unify the county just like Malcolm did in the beginnin' of his reign. You were the Wendy to his Peter Pan, and his men were the Lost Boys." His brow lifted. "They still need you, Wendy. They need you to come back to Neverland so we can defeat Captain Hook and the false Peter Pan."

He couldn't be serious, yet there was no doubt that he meant every word. "What would that look like?" I asked carefully.

Jed shifted his weight behind me. I suspected he hadn't heard Carmichael's proposal, but he'd heard my question.

Carmichael seemed elated. "A salary that will take care of your every need. Round the clock protection. The respect you insist upon."

With anyone else, that might have been a dream job, but with Carmichael, it was sure to be a nightmare. I suspected round the clock protection meant I'd have armed guards—guards who answered to *him*. "And what are your expectations?"

He licked his lips and shot a dark look to Joe before he turned back to me. "This is a working relationship. Completely aboveboard."

I had serious doubts about that. I gave him a wry smile. "Had I known this was a job interview, I would have come better prepared."

He laughed. "Not to worry, you're perfect just as you are."

"I'm still uncertain of your expectations, Mr. Carmichael."

"Why, you'll work for me, *Lady*." But the evil in his eyes suggested so much more.

He clasped his hands together and moved closer until we were less than a foot apart. "Now here's what we're gonna do. You're gonna tell me the time and place of Hardshaw's big meetin', and then you're gonna come with me. Your two bodyguards will be left behind, and if you're lyin' to me and Hardshaw and those south of the border boys don't show up, I'll have one of them shot. I'll even let you pick which one." His grin spread. "As for my offer, I *insist* that you accept it."

I tried to hide my horror.

"Time and place, please," he said in a mockingly sweet tone. "Or I might get trigger happy a little early."

I took a breath to keep my voice steady. "Sweet Pickle Christian Church. Midnight."

"See?" he said. "That wasn't so hard." Then he hopped up onto the stage and grabbed a torch. Waving it in the air, he shouted, "Are we gonna sit back and let Malcolm and those outsiders take what's rightfully ours?"

The crowd buzzed with excitement. "No!"

"What are we gonna do about it?" Carmichael called out.

"Stop 'em!"

Carmichael's face lit up with a wicked grin. "Then *let's* go."

He hopped off the platform and shot me a wink. "I'll let you say your goodbyes." Then he strode toward the vehicles.

I turned to Joe and Jed, who were still being held back by some of Carmichael's men. What had my hubris gotten them into? I should have come on my own. I shouldn't have insisted on a trade for the information. But I reassured myself that they would be fine if we got the location right.

I shoved the man in front of Joe to the side and took his face in my hands. "I need you to trust me, okay?"

"Why do I not like the sound of that?"

I pressed a kiss to his lips, then pulled back and forced a smile. "I'm going with Carmichael."

Joe's body shook. "*What? No!*"

I put my finger on his lips. "Shh." I threw my arms around his neck and turned my face into his ear, whispering, "That won't help anything right now. Listen. Carmichael's takin' me as insurance and plans to kill one of you if we were wrong. You two need to escape, okay? Because I don't trust him not to shoot you anyway."

He leaned back and searched my face. "What about you?"

I frowned. "He has big plans for me. He thinks I'm goin' to be the Wendy to his Peter Pan." I hugged him again. "I'm going to try to get away from him first chance I get, but I can't do that if you two are stuck here. Now, I need you to reach into my jacket and get my gun and hide it under your shirt."

"Rose. You need it."

"There's no time to argue, Joe. I have the other one, so just do it. That's an order."

He leaned back to stare down at me, then placed his hands at my waist, inside my jacket, and kissed me.

I kissed him back, trying to give him enough room to reach into my jacket without calling attention to it.

But Jed must have sensed that we were up to something because he shoved the guard in front of him. "We came here as a neutral party. What do you think you're doin'?"

"There is no neutral party," the guy said, giving Jed a shove of his own. "You're either for us or against us."

"Fuck you," Jed spat, then shoved the guy in our direction.

Joe swung me out of the way, and as the man got to his feet and lunged for Jed, Joe grabbed my gun and tucked into his front waistband under his shirt.

288

His eyes darkened. "We'll get away."

"Fair warning," I said. "Once you have the upper hand, Jed's liable to beat those assholes to death. Literally." Then I kissed him again and headed for the trucks.

I'd give them until we got to the church to get away, and then Denny Carmichael would rue the day he'd ever met me.

Chapter Thirty-One

Turned out that Denny Carmichael had a brand new Range Rover. He might not spend much of his drug fortune on his house, but he'd spent a chunk on his vehicle.

He was waiting by the open back door, wearing a smug smile as he motioned for me to climb inside.

Ignoring him, I got in and slid over to the far side, trying not to cringe as he got in behind me and shut the door. Two men sat in the front, Clyde in the driver's seat. The other men started piling into trucks.

Carmichael chuckled. "Get in a sexy goodbye with your boyfriend?"

The guy in the passenger seat turned around with a leering grin.

A non-response seemed like my best option, so I turned to stare out the side window, catching a glimpse of two men putting Joe and Jed's hands behind their backs as the vehicles turned around and pulled away. A chorus of cheers rang out, and I noticed that while most of the torches had been tossed into a pile on the ground, a few men lifted them into the air from the backs of the trucks.

The SUV drove at a speed that seemed unsafe given the condition of the crumbling asphalt drive. I considered putting on a seat belt, but it would get in the way if I found a chance to escape…although the risk of getting injured in a car accident seemed pretty high given Clyde's recklessness and the other trucks around us.

They reached the end of the drive, and the man in the passenger seat rolled down his window and waved a fist of solidarity at the two men standing guard. They shook their fists and let out whoops in response before Clyde whipped the SUV out onto the highway so quickly the back fishtailed.

The front passenger laughed, and Carmichael shot me a grin as I slid across the seat toward him.

"If you want to sit on my lap, Lady, you only have to ask," he said with a leer.

I considered telling him it would happen if hell froze over, but I didn't want him to take that as a personal invitation.

On the outside, I hoped I looked pissed and in control, but on the inside, I was struggling to hold myself together. Surely Jed and Joe could get the upper hand on the two men who'd been left behind. But what if there were more men than I'd seen?

I reminded myself that when Jed had followed me after I was kidnapped, he'd freed himself from the chair he'd been tied to, then taken three men down with his bare hands.

They'd get out of it.

But my nerves were humming. Joe and Jed aside, I had plenty of worries of my own. If I survived the car ride and actually showed up at this meeting as Carmichael's plus one, I had a good chance of either getting killed or arrested. Despite Carmichael's Peter Pan speech, I had a feeling I ranked high on the expendable list.

"You realize we're gonna be early," I said.

He laughed. "I know how to tell time."

"There's a good chance the meetup won't be takin' place when we get there, so I'm making sure you don't get trigger happy if you prematurely decide it's not happening."

A grin spread across his face. "Lady, I don't do anything *prematurely*."

The two men in front laughed.

I rolled my eyes. "What are you, thirteen?"

That just made him laugh more. When he settled down, he turned in his seat to face me. "So what did you find out from Wilson's girlfriend? Was she the one who told you the location?"

Narrowing my eyes, I shot him a glare. "I'd rather not give up my sources."

He grabbed my arm and squeezed tight, pulling me close enough I could smell his sour beer breath, which was stronger in the car. His fingers pinched my flesh through my lightweight jacket, and it took everything in me not to flinch. I could feel the anger thrumming through him in tight waves.

"Here's the thing, Lady," he said through gritted teeth. "You work for *me* now. Your sources are *mine*."

I reminded myself that this man was a time bomb. While James and most of the other men I'd dealt with in the criminal world had been somewhat predictable, this man was not. Still, I couldn't bring myself to cower before him.

I clenched my jaw. "I didn't even give Skeeter Malcolm my sources in the beginning. Why would I give them to *you*?"

"Let's make this perfectly clear, *Lady*. I am *not* Skeeter Malcolm."

"*That's* obvious," I said in disgust.

I wasn't surprised when he hit me, but I was surprised it was a slap across my cheek and not a punch.

"Let's set the ground rules and get that out of the way," he snarled, leaning into me. "You can take the way you've done things with everyone you've worked with in the past and shove them up your ass."

Everything in me wanted to curl up in a ball and protect myself, but I couldn't bring myself to give him the satisfaction, so I stared into his cold, dead eyes and shot him a look of challenge. It wasn't smart, but I couldn't hold back my fury. "Fuck you."

"Do you have a death wish?" he asked through gritted teeth. "Or maybe I should just kill your two men and use your baby as collateral for the meetin' instead."

The mention of Hope breached my steely resolve, and I let out a small gasp.

A grin slowly spread across his face, proving his threat had gotten exactly the reaction he'd hoped for. He pulled out his phone and placed a call. "Go ahead and take the baby. Let me know when you have it."

This disgusting man was sending even more disgusting men to take my child.

He ended the call and lifted his brow. "You heard of the five love languages?" He held up his hand, showing his extended fingers and thumb. "Well, I've got languages of my own. Threats." He tucked in his thumb. "Extortion." He folded in his pinky finger. "Murder. Torture." He lowered his index and ring fingers so his middle finger was standing tall. "There's *always* a way to make people talk. You just gotta know which language to speak."

My mind was whirling with panic, but I resisted the urge to break down. Hope needed me to keep my wits about me. If he was talking, then maybe I could get him to give me information that I could use later. If I didn't kill him first. "You couldn't get Rufus Wilson to talk."

He chuckled. "Oh, Wilson squealed all right. He just didn't know much. The only thing he had of use was that the meeting was happenin' tonight."

"Then what do you need me for?"

"We didn't know the location, *sweetheart*, and I know you specialized in gettin' information for Skeeter Malcolm. But I confess," he added nonchalantly, "I'm a little suspicious of your intel. Rufus said the meeting was happenin' between ten and eleven, and you claimed it was midnight." He paused. "Seems to me that if you got the easy part wrong, you coulda gotten the location wrong too." His eyes narrowed. "Which makes me think you're lyin'."

"I'm not," I said, my mind turning with the news. If he was right, that meant the Feds were going to be up to an hour late. They might get here after everything was said and done. They might be too late.

This might have all been for nothing.

"I can't abide by liars, Lady. If you're lyin', there will be consequences. *The Lord detests lying lips, but he delights in people who are trustworthy.* Proverbs 12:22."

I stared at him in disbelief. Did he consider himself trustworthy?

"I gave you the time and place I was given," I said, suddenly less confident now that Hope's life was on the line. The thought of Carmichael or his men anywhere near her made me nauseous. And then I realized that Witt and Neely Kate wouldn't just let his men take her. They'd fight to the death.

Don't panic. Don't panic. Don't panic.

How could my whole life have fallen apart in the matter of an hour?

I told myself that Joe and Jed wouldn't waste any time getting free and coming after me. But I didn't need them to come after me. I needed them to go find Hope. Yet they wouldn't find out she'd been taken until they got to the farm.

No, I told myself. *Neely Kate or Witt will call them.*

Sure, I argued with myself. *They will if they're not dead.*

The thought sent me into a spiral of panic that scattered my thoughts and ability to reason.

Get it together, Rose. You have to save Hope.

I took a deep breath and forced the chaos in my head to pause so I could figure out what to do.

One thing was clear: Every second my baby was with this madman's henchmen was a second too long. I had to find a way to tell Joe or Jed myself. But how? Then I realized that Carmichael's ego was so huge he still hadn't checked me for weapons or taken my phone. I had to figure out how to send Joe a text. The question was how to do it without Carmichael noticing.

"I'm gonna throw up," I blurted out.

"What?" Carmichael demanded, sitting upright.

It stood to reason he wouldn't want the smell of vomit to entwine with his new car smell, not to mention what it would do to the tan leather seat.

"I have to throw up," I said. It wasn't hard to conjure up a pukey look. "I get car sick, and after you hit me, I'm dizzy and my head's poundin' and—"

"You're lyin'," he snarled.

"I'm not." I made a retching sound to help sell it.

"She might have a concussion," the guy in the passenger seat said. "That might make her have to throw up."

"You're gonna wait," Carmichael said. "We're not pulling over now. And if you throw up in my car, I'll shoot you in the leg."

We were on the county road that led up to Pickle Junction, and I could understand why he didn't want to stop now. There was enough traffic that I could possibly get the attention of a passerby. Not that I would try. It would likely be a death sentence for them, and I'd already put enough people in danger.

How far away was the church? Ten minutes? Fifteen? We were bound to get there before Joe and Jed. I had to figure out a way to send him a message. Only…I had no idea where to tell him to go. Did I dare risk a vision of Carmichael? The thought of touching him was equally terrifying and revolting, plus he'd probably shake me off before I could see anything. Or, worse, take it as an invitation to do some touching of his own. Then there was the way I blurted out whatever I saw…I wasn't sure how he'd deal with that, presuming my new ability to control the visions didn't kick in.

But what if Joe and Jed hit a snag and couldn't escape? I squinched my eyes closed. I couldn't even let myself consider that possibility. They had the element of surprise on their side. They'd escape unscathed and then they'd save my baby.

While Carmichael leaned forward to talk to Clyde, discussing which country road to take, I felt my phone buzz in my pocket with a text. I prayed it was Joe telling me they'd gotten free. Thankfully, Carmichael was too busy to notice the sound.

Did I risk trying to get my phone out so I could read it? Carmichael and Clyde had shifted to discussing their best options for showing up at the church. Their plan was basic—they'd send scouts to watch the building and park far enough away to escape the notice of the various parties involved, then wait for the scouts' signal. Some of the men would approach on foot, and Carmichael and his men would show up in their vehicles. Carmichael would keep me by his side.

My despair began to grow. How was I going to save Hope? Getting her away from this lunatic and his men was my top priority. I didn't trust them with my child for one second, let alone hours.

Carmichael's phone rang, and he glanced at the screen before he answered, putting it on speaker. He shot me a dark grin. "You got the kid?"

"Uhhh," the guy on the other side stammered. "There's a problem."

My heart leapt into my throat. *Please, God, let my baby be okay.*

"What kind of problem?" Carmichael barked.

"The baby was already gone."

What?

"What do you mean the baby was gone?"

"When we got there, Carlisle's wife was a hysterical mess. She said the baby was already gone."

I tried not to panic. *Where was Hope?*

"You fool," Carmichael spat. "She was fakin' to throw you off."

"No," the man said, sounding nervous. "She was hysterical when we pulled up. We could hear her screamin' in the house. Her cousin had stayed to help guard the baby, and he was in the house tryin' to calm her down."

Carmichael did not look pleased. He grabbed my arm and gave me a hard shake. "Where is it?"

"I don't know," I shouted, jerking my arm away. "But thank God you didn't get your hands on her." But if he didn't have her, who did? For all I knew, she'd gone from a bad situation to a worse one.

Carmichael shoved me against the car door and wrapped his meaty hand around my neck, pressing into my windpipe.

I wrapped my hands around it, trying to pry his fingers off, but he had brute strength on his side.

"Where's your kid?" he asked, squeezing tighter.

"Go to hell," I wheezed out.

"We're gettin' close," Clyde said. "Whatdya you want to do?"

Carmichael looked like he was mad enough to beat me to a bloody pulp, but he gave my neck one last squeeze that had me seeing stars and then released me. "Stick to the goddamn plan!"

I coughed and wheezed as my airway opened, and I fell forward, nearly passing out.

"We tried to stick to the plan," the guy on the phone said in a pleading whine, "but I'm tellin' you, the woman swears the baby's gone. She said Wilson's woman hid in the basement and stole the baby. Keeps sayin' her car is gone."

I looked up at Carmichael in shock, sure I'd heard his man wrong. He was suggesting that Bobby Hanover had hidden in my basement, then snatched my baby when Neely Kate and Witt weren't looking, and left in her car.

Why would Bobby Hanover want my baby?

And then I knew.

Bobby had taken her for Kate.

Chapter Thirty-Two

A wave of dizziness hit me, and I was sure I was going to pass out this time. Kate was a lunatic who hated me. I didn't want to believe she'd hurt Hope, but why else would she have taken her? I couldn't help but worry her hatred for me might supersede her concern for my baby's safety.

My need to escape was more pressing than ever. I had no idea where Kate had gone, but I needed to find her. I needed to find my baby, and that meant I needed a car.

I drew in a sharp breath, and just like that I knew. The idea of the abandoned warehouse bringing things full circle didn't just fit Dora and me. For Kate, I was unfinished business. What better way to get me there than to use my baby as bait?

"You know who has her?"

"Malcolm," I blurted out, knowing he'd press me for a name, likely literally. If he thought James had her, it might give him more incentive to storm the church.

He grinned. "You don't say. What'd you do to piss him off?"

"The fact that I'm breathin' is enough," I bluffed in disgust.

"You don't look so scared anymore," Carmichael said. "You think your kid has a better chance with him than me? I plan on shootin' it first chance I get."

Carmichael had just won the title of worst possible villain. We'd been right about stopping him—he was as bad for this county as dark chocolate was for a dog. I only hoped the Feds would show up soon enough to snap him up.

"You'll have to kill me first," I said, only realizing after the words left my mouth that it was stupid to goad him. Sure, he claimed to have a use for me after this was all put to bed, but he had to know I'd never do anything for him if he hurt Hope.

Did that mean he'd planned on killing me all along?

They drove past the church, which looked abandoned from the front, but as soon as they drove past it, we could see cars and trucks gathered in the back.

"Hot damn," Carmichael said in awe. "She might have gotten the time wrong, but the location was spot on."

They drove another quarter mile, turning down a dirt side road before circling around and parking on the other side. A field of alfalfa was on one side of us, woods on the other.

I waited for the other cars and trucks to park with us, but no one else turned down the road. Clyde turned off the engine and killed the lights, plunging us into darkness, the only light from the glow of Carmichael's phone. It only took a couple of conversations between Carmichael and his man over the phone to establish that the others were scattered in a perimeter around the church.

The scouts moved into place, confirming this was the location. From the conversations they'd overheard between James' men, who were milling around outside, both groups were expected any time.

Hours seemed to crawl past, but in reality, it had only been ten minutes.

Ten minutes my baby had been with Kate.

I had to get away before the action started, otherwise I might never get to her in time. My only chance was to run through the woods and use my phone to call Joe or 911. The darkness and the trees would hide me, but first I had to get out of the car.

Releasing a moan, I clutched my stomach. "I'm gonna throw up."

"Swallow it," Carmichael grunted.

I'd make myself throw up if necessary. I leaned forward and made gagging sounds.

"Jesus, Carmichael," said the guy in the passenger seat—Austin, based on what had been said on those phone calls. "I can't handle that sound. She's gonna make *me* barf."

"*Fine*," Carmichael snapped. "Bring her to the side of the road, but make it quick. They're gonna show up at any minute, and we'll need to peel out."

The man grunted and the sound of the door unclicking nearly made me cry with relief. I quickly opened my door and practically fell out of the car, still playing my ruse to the hilt. While I'd gotten out of the SUV, I was well aware that I was still in Carmichael's clutches.

I stumbled to the other side of the road, near the trees, and bent over, making gagging noises. Cicadas croaked in the trees overhead.

The guy lumbered toward me. I could barely see his face, but he looked like he was going to be sick himself. "Can you throw up more quieter?" he grumbled.

"I'll try," I said sarcastically, casting a glance at the Range Rover. Carmichael was studying his phone, and Austin was so grossed out he wasn't even looking at me.

It was now or never.

Taking a deep breath, I reached down to my ankle and slipped out the small handgun. I could make a run for it and hope that Austin didn't catch up or shoot me in the back, or I could buy myself a short lead.

Hope's life was depending on me.

Without hesitation, I pointed the gun at his thigh and fired.

The gunshot cracked through the sounds of the cicadas, but I didn't pause to see if I'd made my mark or to look for Carmichael's reaction. I just ran, leaving Austin screaming behind me.

The trees and brush were dense, but I ran blindly, trying to put as much distance between me and Carmichael as possible.

He screamed my name from the road. "I'm gonna kill you, you stupid bitch!"

You'll have to catch me first.

I considered lying in wait to shoot them when they came after me, but I knew I'd have to shoot to kill, and even though Carmichael was pure evil, I wasn't prepared to do that. Not yet. Besides, for all I knew, his windows were bulletproof.

So I continued running, barely seeing where I was going, but thankful I was wearing jeans and a jacket to cover my limbs.

Carmichael was still shouting, but the sound became fainter beneath the din of Austin's screams. Enough so that I nearly missed him calling Clyde back for "show time."

A gunshot rang out, and then there was the sound of squealing tires. The screaming had stopped.

Had they just killed Austin to tie up loose ends?

I paused and dug out my phone, shocked to see a video text from Kate. "I have something you want, Rose Petal. I'll work out a trade, but you have to meet me at our old stomping grounds. Remember?" She shifted the camera so I could see the abandoned warehouse behind her, a low light glowing behind her. "But this deal is between *you* and *me*," she sing-songed. "You have to come alone. If I see a hint of anyone else, little baby Hope won't see the sunrise." The phone angled down to show my sleeping baby in her arms before drifting back up to her face. "Trust me on that, Rose Petal. No Joe. No Jed. Just you and me." Then she blew a kiss and the video ended.

I stared at my phone in shock. So much for Kate preferring babies to adults. She had my daughter, and she planned to kill her if I didn't do as she said.

There was a text from Joe that simply said *done*.

Done. Did that mean they were free? They would likely try to come to me at the church, so I sent a group text to Joe and Jed saying I'd gotten away. That I knew about Hope, and she should be their priority, not me.

My phone rang instantly, Joe's number on the screen, but I didn't dare talk to him or I knew I'd break down and spill everything. Kate had made it clear what would happen if anyone else showed up, and I didn't doubt her.

I turned my phone off and stuffed it into my pocket. Joe could find the location of my phone, and I couldn't risk him showing up at that warehouse.

Slipping my gun into the holster under my jacket, I headed toward the road, figuring Carmichael's men would be too preoccupied to deal with me if they saw me. Once I got to the shoulder of the country road, I ran my hand over my head, trying to figure out what to do. The warehouse was too far to walk, but I didn't dare ask someone to pick me up.

I headed west in search of houses with cars out front. Some people around these parts still left their keys in the ignition, especially if they had a connection to criminal activity themselves.

I took off running. I'd run nearly a quarter mile when I heard cars coming fast. I moved to the shadows of the trees on the side of the road, my side aching and chest heaving while I watched ten unmarked police cars whiz past.

They were early, which meant they'd make it.

I felt an immense satisfaction knowing they were going to bust Carmichael. Part of me hoped he lost his junk in a shootout. Only I couldn't help but think James would be in there too, a thought that filled me with sorrow. James had put himself in this position, but I still grieved for the man I'd fallen in love with. Even if he hadn't been real.

When the coast was clear, I took off running again. I'd sprinted several minutes before I reached a small house set back about twenty feet from the road. A small hatchback and a pickup truck were parked next to each other in the drive, and I prayed I'd find keys inside.

I bent over, taking a moment to catch my breath before I snuck up to the truck. It was old and rusted and looked like the last car any intelligent person would try to steal. Which meant I just might be able to do so. But the driver and passenger doors were both locked, so I crept over to the hatchback, testing its door. It was locked too.

Hot tears of frustration sprang to my eyes. How far would I have to run? How many cars would I have to try? I'd run all the way to the warehouse if I had to.

But then I spotted another car to the side of the property, next to a detached garage. It was an old Cadillac that looked like the engine wouldn't even turn over, but I had to try it. The door handle lifted, and I sucked in a breath as I carefully opened the door. It released a loud creak, and I froze, waiting to see if someone in the house heard and came out to investigate.

No one emerged, so I climbed into the front seat and nearly burst into tears when I felt the keys in the ignition. Now the stupid thing just needed to start. I knew the engine would be loud, and I wouldn't put it past the owners to chase me down once they realized I'd stolen their car out from under their noses.

I had to slow them down. I considered letting air out of the other cars' tires, but then I caught a glimpse of a utility knife on a cinder block next to the detached garage.

Guilt coursed through me, and I chanted, "I'm sorry. I'm sorry. I'm sorry," over and over as I punctured all eight tires. If I lived through this, I promised myself I'd compensate them. Then I hurried over to the Cadillac and shut the door. After saying a quick prayer full of begging, I cranked the engine.

It ground as though it was hung up on something. I eased off and turned it again, the engine giving a little sputter this time before dying.

A light turned on in the house.

Oh crappy doodles.

I cranked it again, knowing that I ran the risk of flooding the engine, but I was committed to this now. The engine roared to life just as the front door flung open, and a shirtless bearded man rushed out with a shotgun.

I shot the car in reverse, wrenching the wheel to turn it around, then shifted to drive, digging the wheels into the grass as I headed for the driveway that connected to the road.

"Stop!" the man shouted, running after me. "Stop or I'll shoot!"

I reached the driveway and made a hard left onto the county road, turning away from the big bust going down at the church.

"Stop!" he shouted again, and a gunshot rang out, blowing out the back passenger window and sending shattered glass all over the backseat.

I kept driving. Nothing was going to stand in the way of me and my baby.

That's exactly what Kate was counting on.

Chapter Thirty-Three

As I approached the warehouse in my stolen car, I started to pull into the parking lot, but then I realized that was what Kate wanted me to do—park next to the building so she would know that I was there, giving her plenty of time to set up for her big production. Because I had no doubt there would be a big production. Otherwise she would have just killed me and been done with it.

So I drove several hundred feet past the building, parking at the opening of a private dirt road with a No Trespassing sign on a chain at the entrance. I wasn't sure I'd come back to this car, but I left the keys in the ignition in case Kate searched me and took the contents of my pockets.

It had been nearly forty minutes since Kate had sent her video text, which was forty minutes too long for her to have my daughter. Everything in me screamed to rush inside, but I knew I had to be smart about this. I needed to sneak up on her.

I'd been in the building enough times to know the layout. She likely expected me to come through the unlocked door on the front of the building, but that would mean passing through a labyrinth of broken-down manufacturing equipment. She'd hear me coming.

Instead, I planned to move around the back of the building and climb through the broken massive picture window. I'd used it multiple times before. There was one problem: it led to a large open area, the place where our previous showdown had occurred, so there was a good chance she was sitting there, waiting. If she was by herself, I could potentially shoot her and save Hope, but if she was holding her, that option was out.

Then I realized what I was plotting—Kate Simmons' murder. Had I really sunk to this?

Yes. I would do whatever it took to save my daughter.

As I walked along the county road, it occurred to me that perhaps the reason I wasn't in any of Hope's visions wasn't because I was dead, but because I was in jail for Kate's murder.

The thought of spending years in a locked room still made me sweat, but I didn't let myself dwell on it. I cut into the edge of the field of tall grass that bordered the back of the warehouse, then approached the area across from the windows. Once there, I squatted in the field and studied the building. It occurred to me that there had been a light on inside the building in Kate's video, but now the building was completely dark. A dark sedan sat in the back lot.

Was Kate lying in wait? Was she watching for me out of the back window?

Just as I was about to slip out of the grass to dash over to the side of the building to peer in, I felt a presence behind me. A hand clamped over my mouth.

I started to fight like hell, clawing at the large hand, but instantly stopped when I heard a voice I recognized, even if it seemed out of place.

"Rose," James whisper-shouted. "Stop. It's me."

Dear God. Was he part of this? Did he hate his daughter's existence so much he'd helped Kate kidnap her?

I fought even harder.

He pulled my back against his chest hard, his hand putting more pressure on my already tender face as his other hand wrapped around my stomach, holding me in place. "*Rose.* I'm trying to help you."

I froze. Was he telling me the truth?

"I'm going to drop my hand, but you have to be quiet, okay?" he whispered in my ear.

Did I trust him? I knew I had to tell him yes regardless of the answer. What I needed to figure out was what to do after he let me go. I decided I could hear him out and go from there.

I nodded.

He kept me pressed to his firm body but slowly lowered his hand from my mouth.

"What are you doin' here?" I demanded in a hoarse whisper.

"Where's Joe?" he asked. "Where's Jed?"

I turned in his arms to look up at him but didn't answer. I didn't believe he would hurt me, but that didn't mean he wouldn't hurt the people I loved.

"Why are you here alone?" he asked, irritation flooding his eyes.

"That's none of your damn business," I snapped. "Why aren't you at the church?"

His brow lifted. "So you know about that."

"I would be dead right now if I didn't," I spat out, "and you didn't answer my question."

"I had a more urgent pressing matter. And why would you be dead?" Then he took a good look at my face, and his eyes turned deadly. "Who did this?"

I shook my head. "You lost the right to care about me months ago. Now you need to tell me why you're here. Are you helping Kate?" My voice cracked on her name.

He didn't answer right away, and my heart began to shatter when he finally said, "She sent me a message askin' to meet her here."

His story had all kind of holes. Why would he miss the meeting he'd gone to such pains to set up to go talk to Kate, of all people? He knew she was nuttier than a Snickers bar. But I settled for, "Then why are you skulkin' around in the weeds? Why aren't you in there?" I motioned to the building.

"Something's not right," he said, eyeing me carefully. "I decided to do a little recon first."

"Did you know I was comin'?" I asked.

He hesitated. "I suspected Kate might have contacted you, but I couldn't be sure."

"Why did you think she'd contact me?" I asked. Did he know about Hope?

"Gut feelin'," he said. "What did she say to lure you here alone?"

I was struggling with what to tell him, but my daughter made the decision for me. She belted out a wail that signaled pain or discomfort.

My heart jolted, and I instinctively tried to sprint toward the building, but James' arm was still around my back, and it clamped like a vise, holding my chest to his.

"Let me go," I snarled through gritted teeth, ready to fight to get away from him.

"Rose. That's what she wants you to do. Be smart."

Tears burned my eyes as I struggled to break free. "She's hurtin' my baby, James. To hell with smart."

"Rose Petal," Kate cried out from the darkness. "I thought you were a better mother than this. If you're not here yet, you don't deserve her, and if you are, well, shame on you. Babies' skin is so tender and easily torn."

Hope released a startled cry and wailed louder.

I fought James like a madwoman, but he tackled me to the ground, lying on top of me with his hand over my mouth again.

"Rose," he hissed. "*Listen to me*. If you go chargin' in there, what's to stop her from just killin' you outright? If you want to save your daughter, you can't run in there with no plan. It will just get you both killed."

I stared up at him in shock and pushed his hand away. "You're gonna help me?"

"That's why I'm really here. She sent me a text sayin' she had your baby, and unless I wanted her to die, I'd skip the big meetin' and come see her here."

"You came here for us?" I asked in shock. Had he really dropped everything to save Hope?

He gave a grim nod.

Another shriek echoed through the window, making me cringe.

"Any idea what Kate is up to?"

"This is all for Neely Kate."

"What?" he said in disbelief.

"Kate's takin' out all the people she thinks hurt Neely Kate. Last summer it was Stella and Branson. Pearce Manchester, the son of one Arthur Manchester, nearly killed Neely Kate, and Kate blames Hardshaw for it. She's been plotting revenge on them ever since. Carson Roberts is her in. She's been sleeping with him for two years to get intel and influence their operation." I paused. "She's the one who sent them to you, to get even with her dad but also to get back at you. I'm here because she meant for me to die the night J.R. was killed, and I suspect you were too." I looked him in the eye. "We're unfinished business."

He lifted his eyebrows. "She has her hooks in Carson, huh? That man's not a quarter as smart as he thinks he is. So the baby is to lure you here?"

"That, and I think she plans to give her to Neely Kate." At least I hoped so. She had to know that Neely Kate would never forgive her for killing my baby. But I suspected she'd deluded herself into believing Neely Kate would understand her reasons for killing me.

I shoved James' chest, trying to push him off me. *Get up.* I have to go to her."

He didn't budge. "Not yet. Let's think this through."

I knew he was right, but it was hard to concentrate while listening to my baby's hysterics. "Please," I begged. "Don't let Kate hurt her."

"I'm gonna help you save her," James said, his voice gruff. "But you need to do as I say, okay?"

"How am I supposed to believe you when just yesterday you threatened to kidnap me and take me from my baby?" I shot back.

He closed his eyes and pressed his forehead to mine. "I would never do that to you, Rose. I was just tryin' to hurt you."

"Well, you succeeded."

He lifted his head. "I'm sorry."

I stared at him in shock.

His face softened. "I'm sorry for a lot of things, but I deserve everything I have comin' to me and more, so just remember that if you ever feel guilty, okay?"

I shook my head. "What are you talkin' about?"

He pushed up onto his elbows and then his knees. He got to his feet, then pulled me to mine. "I'm gonna go around to the other side and go through the door in front. I need you to give me two minutes before you make yourself known to her."

Another shriek rent the air.

"I can't listen to Hope cry for two minutes," I said.

"Please, Rose. I know I haven't given you reason to trust me, but I'm askin' you to do it now. I'm gonna help you. We're gonna save her. Together."

I nodded but didn't trust myself to answer. I was barely holding myself together as it was.

"After two minutes, I want you to call out to Kate," he said. "Tell her you can't see and ask her to turn the lights on. Approach the window from the side and go in, but only if she's not holding a gun on the baby. If she is, keep her talking until I can make my move. Don't let her know I'm here. Let her know how much you hate me."

"I don't hate you."

"Then you're a fool," he grunted, and he took off through the field toward the front of the building.

Chapter Thirty-Four

Waiting two minutes was impossible. I didn't have a clock, and while I started to count, Hope's crying made me lose count. At least her high-pitched cries had eased a bit. She wasn't in pain. But this was the crying of a baby who wanted her parents, and it sliced into me almost as deeply.

Had I made a mistake not calling Joe? In my frantic need to save Hope, I'd taken Kate at her word. But Kate was so volatile I'd worried that doing anything else would set her off. Following her every direction had seemed like the best choice.

Kate called out, "Rose, if you're lyin' in wait out there, you're just prolonging your daughter's agony."

Hope released another startled cry, and panic washed over me, castigating me for letting my daughter endure pain at the hands of a madwoman while I placed my personal safety over hers.

A part of me knew James' plan made sense. I *knew* Kate was counting on me to react first and think later, but Hope's pathetic cries were wearing me down. I thought of what Joe had said a few days ago—that he always wanted Hope to know that her parents were there when she needed them.

The thought that my daughter might believe I'd abandoned her to her pain and fear pushed me out of the shadows.

"I'm here," I called out, still out of sight. "Give me back my baby, Kate."

"You don't deserve this baby, Rose," she snapped, her words laced with cold anger, the kind that had had plenty of time to brew.

"You're probably right about that," I said, shifting my weight from one foot to the other as my nervous energy begged for release, "but you can't hold Hope responsible for the wrongs you perceive I've done, so I'm beggin' you, Kate, stop hurtin' my baby."

"So you *have* been out there," she spat in disgust. "Listening to your baby cry and not doing a damn thing about it."

I didn't answer, because she was right. And while I knew I was running headlong into the trap she had laid out for me, I couldn't let that stop me. I'd already failed Hope by putting her in this situation in the first place. Still, something deep inside of me believed I'd been right about Kate's plans—that she intended to harm me but not Hope, because she wanted Neely Kate to have Hope. I took some manner of comfort from that.

"I suppose you want me to come in there," I said, still concealed in the tall grass. I watched the inside of the building, hoping for a glimpse of Kate or Hope, but all I saw was darkness. "Or do you plan on shooting me the moment you see me?"

"You think I plan to kill you?" she asked with a laugh.

"I know you plan to kill me," I said with a certainty that sank to my marrow. "So do us both a favor and tell me the truth."

"I'm not done with you yet," Kate said. "Like any clever cat, I like to play with my food."

I stepped out of the grass and moved a couple of feet closer to the busted-out window. "I'll come in, but I'm not walkin' into darkness. You need to turn on a light."

"You're not the one makin' the rules, Rose Petal."

I stood my ground.

"I'll hurt her again," Kate said.

My heart lurched. She would, I had no doubt about that, but I couldn't back down. I might be handing myself over, but I wasn't ready to give up just yet. James wouldn't have any hope of stopping her unless she turned a light on.

"She's scared of the dark," I called out in a pleading tone. It wasn't a total lie. For all I knew, that could be why she woke up so much at night. She woke up in a void without the love and warmth that surrounded her all day, and the contrast had to be startling.

"What?" Kate asked, but it wasn't in her typical sarcastic tone. It held a note of concern.

I took a step closer. "We moved her to her own room a few days ago, and she wakes up at night, terrified. She always stops cryin' the minute we go to her. We think she's scared of the dark." I took a breath and inched forward another step. "I know you hate my guts, Kate, but it's not Hope's fault that I'm her mother. Please, I'm *beggin'* you. Don't hurt her anymore, and turn on a light so she'll be less scared."

She didn't answer for several seconds, and I was terrified she'd hurt Hope again just to show me that she could. But then a small flame glowed in the darkness. A lighter.

Why did she have a lighter?

But then something caught fire—a torch from the look of it—and she tossed it into a pile of firewood on the concrete floor.

It lit up the space enough for me to see Kate, holding a bundle wrapped in Hope's receiving blanket.

I started to cry.

"You're gonna need to come inside," Kate said, taking a few steps backward, but she was bouncing the bundle in her arm as though trying to soothe my crying baby.

Relief poured through me. She might hurt Hope to rile me, but she'd wanted a baby of her own, once, and she still had a nurturing instinct buried under all that hate.

I closed the distance between me and the open window as the flames in the firewood took hold, going up in a blaze that released gasoline-tinged smoke.

"Climb inside," Kate said. Reaching behind her, she grabbed a handgun off an abandoned metal desk and pointed it toward me.

I climbed onto the three-foot-high window frame and then hopped the rest of the way in. Once landed, I held my hands out from my sides. She was about twenty feet away, the fire between us. "I'm here. Now what?"

"Where's Joe?"

"The last time I saw him he was being held captive with Jed on Carmichael's property."

She narrowed her eyes as she studied me. "You're lyin'. You wouldn't be this calm if he were being held prisoner."

"He texted me that he and Jed escaped," I admitted, seeing no reason to lie. "But he doesn't know where I am, and I turned off my phone so he can't track me."

"Let me see your phone," she said.

I took it out of my pocket and held it up. "See? It's turned off."

She moved closer to the fire, much too close for my comfort. All it would take was a tiny toss, and my daughter would be in that pile of burning wood. "Keep holding it up and turn it on."

I did as she asked. Was she wanting proof?

"Now find Joe's location."

She might be crazy, but no one had ever accused her of being stupid. I turned on my phone and pulled up the app. I wanted to know almost as much as she did, and I was equally relieved and distraught when I saw he was back at home.

I held it up for her. "He's at our farm."

"*Your* farm," she said in disgust. "He doesn't own it. Now toss the phone into the fire."

I wanted to argue, but I couldn't give her a reason to hurt Hope. It landed dead center and made popping and cracking sounds as it was consumed by fire.

Kate's gaze landed on my hand. "Is that a ring I see?" she asked in a fake squeal. "Who's the lucky man?"

"Who do you think?" I asked. "Joe."

"What about James Malcolm?"

She'd called him James, which caught me by surprise, but then again, Kate was full of surprises. "We haven't been together for nearly a year. He ended things with me last summer."

"So he doesn't care about your baby?" she asked, holding Hope up higher.

"He hates me, so why would he care about my baby?" I choked out.

Why *was* he here? He might not hate me, but he resented Hope and blamed her for ending our relationship. While I might not understand his motivations, he was out there somewhere, hiding behind twisted metal, looking for his chance to save us. But he wouldn't shoot Kate if she was holding Hope, and even if he tried it, Kate was standing too close to the fire. Hope could get burned.

God, I hoped he wouldn't try it.

I reached out my hands. "Just let me hold Hope. Please. She'll stop crying if she's with me."

She grinned, squeezing Hope tighter. "I like hearing you beg."

"Is that what you want? You want me to beg?" I asked. "Do you want me to get on my knees?"

"You want to know what I really want, Rose Petal?" Kate asked in a sneer. "I want James Malcolm to come out of the shadows."

"You think he's here?" I asked with a bitter laugh. "I came here alone. Just like you told me to."

She'd asked him to come, of course, so she knew he could be there. But I didn't want her to know that we'd seen each other.

"Oh, I *know* he's here," she said, turning to face the darkness. "Come out, come out wherever you are," she sang. Jostling Hope in her arms, she stuffed the gun into the waistband of her jeans and opened the blanket to reveal my daughter in the sleeper I'd put her in after her bath.

I released a sob.

"Every second it takes for you to come out is one step closer we get to this nice warm fire," Kate said, turning Hope so her feet were held out in front of her. Hope's hands were fisted, and her face scrunched up and red as she continued to cry. "Baby skin is so soft and tender, I suspect it wouldn't take much heat for it to burn."

It felt like all the air had been sucked out of my lungs.

"One." She took a step closer.

I watched in horror. "He's not here, Kate! Please don't do this!"

"Wrong answer," Kate said with a grin. "Two." Another step closer.

Hope screamed even louder.

Oh. God. Would James let her burn my baby?

I was about to call out to him, but he stepped into the light, his hands at his sides, palms up. He stood in an aisle between two large machines. "I'm here. Now give the baby to her mother."

But Kate stayed put by the fire, her face beaming with triumph. "I knew you'd come—if not for Rose Petal, then for your own kid."

"What do you want?" he asked, his hands clenched.

"I want you to answer a simple question. Yes or no."

"Go on," James grunted.

"When you were workin' for my father, you walked into his study one day when Daddy Dearest had his hand up my skirt." Her brow lifted. "Did you notice?"

He stared at her, his brow shooting up. "I saw you in his study many times."

"That doesn't answer my question, now does it?" she asked, moving closer to him.

"Did I see him stick his hand up your skirt? No."

"I don't believe you," she snapped. "He was molesting me. You stopped in the doorway, and your eyes went wide. You started to walk out, but my father called you back in and sent me away."

His face lost some of its hardness. "I didn't know, Kate, I swear it."

"But you surely suspected."

He drew in a breath, then said, "I sensed something, but when you walked past me on your way out of the room, you didn't seem upset. You seemed...happy. So I told myself I'd imagined it."

"You could have stopped him," she said, her voice breaking.

He looked bewildered as he shook his head. "I couldn't have stopped him, Kate. If I'd known, I would've beaten the shit out of him, but that wouldn't have stopped a man like that. The only difference it would have made is that I'd be dead."

"So you admit you knew and did nothing?" she demanded.

"I'll admit that I had my suspicions, but every time I looked to you for proof, I didn't see any signs."

"So you're blaming me?" she shrieked.

"No, Kate," he said. "I only blame myself."

She lifted her chin. "Well, I blame you too."

He nodded. "That's fair." Then his gaze zeroed in on Hope. "You blamin' that innocent baby too?"

"Sins of the father," Kate said, then her hate-filled eyes turned to me. "And the mother."

"I've wronged you," James said, taking a step closer. "But this has nothing to do with Rose."

"That's not true." She shifted Hope in her arms so that she was cradling her. Hope settled down and began to root for her breast. "She ripped my family apart. She's tried to turn my sister away from me. She hurt my brother."

James swallowed. "Seems to me she's makin' him happy now. That baby you're hurtin' is his. You're hurtin' your own niece."

She shook her head. "Now, now. We all know *you're* her father."

"So you're gonna hurt her for that?" James asked, taking another step closer. "If you're gonna go by that reasoning, then you should be payin' for your own father's crimes."

"I have," she said bitterly. "Trust me, I have."

Hope released a cry in frustration.

"She's hungry," I said. "Just let me have her," I pleaded, holding out my hands. "Please."

"Seems like this is between you and me," James said. "Hand the baby over to her mother, and we'll settle it. Just the two of us."

Kate laughed. "I'm not done with Rose Petal yet. I plan to right a few wrongs. It seems like poetic justice for me to deal with you together, wrapped up in a tight little ball." She cocked her head. "Our good friend Carson's on his way, you know, which means I have a little housekeeping to do before he arrives."

I turned to stare at James, terrified by what that might mean.

"Let them go," James pleaded. "You want me to beg you for it?"

She laughed again. "Look at the both of you with the begging."

Hope began to cry again, and irritation covered Kate's face. "Jesus, all this thing does is cry. Maybe it's better that I didn't have my baby. Maybe I wasn't cut out to be a mother."

"Neely Kate loves her," I said. If I couldn't save myself, I had to at least save Hope. I had to make sure she had that future I'd seen flickers of earlier. "That's your plan, right? That's why you went to see their birth mother. To test her. But you found her lacking, and you know how much Neely Kate wants to be a mother, so you plan to give her Hope."

"Her name is Daisy," Kate said, turning to face me.

"You plan to give her my baby and rename her Daisy," I said, tears streaming down my face.

Kate shifted Hope so that my daughter's head rested on her shoulder. "I plan to give Carson and Baby Daisy to Neely Kate at the same time. A gift to show her how much I love her."

I stared at her in disbelief, looking for even a hint of sarcasm, but she truly believed she was about to present Neely Kate with a gift that was better than every gift she'd ever received combined.

"Neely Kate doesn't want Rose's baby," James said in disgust. "If you knew anything about her, you'd know that."

"I *do* know her," Kate said, her face red with fury. "I know that if this baby doesn't have a mother, Neely Kate will love her with everything in her."

"And Carson?" James asked. "I assume you pulled him from the meeting tonight. What's his purpose?"

"Hardshaw tried to destroy her life," she said in a tone that suggested he was a fool. "I'll let her destroy his."

Kate had tried that with Stella and Branson last summer. She'd tried to force Neely Kate to murder Stella, but in the end, she'd done the deed herself. The whole episode had traumatized Neely Kate. I nearly pointed that out, but Kate wouldn't listen. Just like she wouldn't listen if I told her another deep truth—Neely Kate would write Kate off forever when she discovered Kate had killed me to give my baby to her.

Kate was past the point of reason.

She pulled out her gun and held it on James. "I'm gonna need you to remove your weapons and drop them onto the floor."

James' gaze dropped to Hope. "I'll do whatever you ask, but only if you swear you won't hurt another hair on her head."

I could tell from his tone, from the protective stance of his body, that he meant every word, and if our lives hadn't been in danger, the shock might have made my knees go out.

Kate laughed. "You're in no position to negotiate. And now that I know you care about her, your position is even weaker." She waved her gun. "Drop 'em. Now."

James reached behind his back and slowly pulled out his gun and tossed it to the floor. It skidded several feet away.

"Now your other one," Kate said.

James didn't hesitate as he squatted and unhooked the gun from his ankle. That went sliding across the floor too.

"Now your phone."

James tugged it out of his pocket and tossed it.

Kate pointed her gun at it and squeezed the trigger, sending pieces of the phone flying.

Hope began to scream again.

"You have my weapons and my phone," James said. "Now give the baby to Rose."

"I don't think so," Kate said. "Not *yet*." She turned to me. "Take off that coat."

I knew what she was after, so I opened up my jacket and slowly reached for the gun in my holster, gripping the end of the gun with my thumb and index finger, then threw it away from me. "I don't have any other weapons."

"Roll up your jeans."

I did as she asked, unstrapping the holster on my ankle and tossing it to the ground. "I gave my other gun to Joe when I left him at Carmichael's. That's all I have. I swear."

She studied me for a moment before motioning me toward the wall of offices. "Go over there if you want to hold Daisy."

I cast another glance toward James, then started to move toward the only open office door. I'd been in that room before, locked in with Kate's father.

I stopped in the opening and waited, my heart beating so fast I was surprised it didn't leap out of my chest.

Kate motioned with her gun for James to go around the other side of the fire toward me.

He slowly made his way around the flames, keeping his eyes on Kate until he reached the doorway.

"Stop right there," she said, then slowly dropped to a squat and laid Hope down on the filthy concrete floor. She got to her feet and began to back up, her gun trained on my daughter. "Okay, Skeeter Malcolm, come get your baby."

"What?" he asked in horror. It would have been comical if we weren't in mortal danger.

"You want to save her? *You* come get her. You. Not your whore."

Anger rippled through his body, but he slowly made his way to my screaming daughter.

Kate still kept her gun on Hope.

When James reached her, he squatted and carefully slid both hands under her, one under her butt and the other under her head, then slowly picked her up and held her awkwardly to his chest.

"Now back up," Kate said. "Slowly."

James closed the distance to the office.

"Now both of you go inside and shut the door," Kate said. "I'll let you out when it's time."

James backed into the room and pulled the door shut, plunging us into darkness.

Chapter Thirty-Five

James reached for me and awkwardly handed Hope to me. "Stay there. I'll look for someplace for you to sit."

My knees buckled slightly when he placed her in my arms, but I stayed upright. I knew what my frightened, sobbing daughter needed, and push come to shove, I didn't need a chair. Lifting the hem of my shirt, I tugged down my bra cup and guided Hope to my breast. Soon the soft sound of her suckling filled the room.

"There's only a desk," James called from the other side of the room.

"I can sit on the floor."

"Not there," he said. Seconds later, he was next to me, guiding me across the room and helping me lower to the floor. But he stepped away as soon as I was sitting, and my eyes adjusted to the darkness enough to see he'd moved over to the door. A small amount of light poured in through the crack. The rest came from a small window above the door that looked like it had been spray-painted white.

"What is she doin' with the fire?" he said, but it sounded like he was talking to himself. "She's goin' for a big show, so what's the purpose? Who's it for, besides her?"

"I don't know." I pressed my back into the hard wall.

"She means to kill us both," he said matter-of-factly.

"I know," I said with a heavy sigh.

"She removed the doorknob on the inside," he said. "I can't open the door." He moved around the room quietly, presumably looking for another escape. He wouldn't find one. Of that, I was sure.

Then he finally lowered himself to the ground, sitting against the wall next to me, our shoulders pressed together. He reached for my hand under Hope, covering it with his own and squeezing.

Tears streamed down my face. "You saved her."

"Not yet, I haven't," he grunted. I expected him to release my hand, but he held on.

"Why are you here?" I whispered. "Really."

"I'm here because you were in danger," he said, but then seconds later, he said gruffly, "And so was she."

More tears fell and I closed my eyes. "But tonight was your big meetin'."

"Bigger than you know," he said, sounding like he had the weight of the world on his shoulders.

"If you'd been there, you would have gotten caught up in a sting," I said dryly. "So maybe you owe Kate a favor."

He released a mirthless laugh. "Who do you think set it up?"

"*What?*"

"I've been working with the ATF and the DEA for nearly a year and a half."

I tried to pull my hand from his, but he held on tight.

"The ATF approached me first. Right before the auction. They knew Hardshaw was makin' a play for the county. They knew I'd supplied the Collards with firearms, and they suggested they could prove it if I proved unwilling to help them. I played it like I had no idea what they were talkin' about. But I put myself on their radar after we got J.R. Simmons busted, and they let me know I wasn't fallin' off. They'd come up with multiple charges, and they threatened to prosecute me to the fullest extent of the law if I didn't cooperate. They said all I had to do was be friendly when Hardshaw came knockin' at my door, because they knew they'd be comin'…and they were right. I was told to play along, because the more evidence they had, the more charges they could file. But then Hardshaw tried to kidnap Neely Kate, and I told my handler I was out. He threatened to slap more charges on me, ones so airtight I'd never see daylight again." He paused. "I almost decided to tell them off and let Carter Hale work his magic, but one thing stopped me."

"What?" I asked past the lump in my throat even though I already suspected the answer.

"You." He drew a deep breath. "You made me think that I could possibly have a future. That I could have a normal life. But it was a pipe dream," he said bitterly. "I realized they would never let me go."

"Which one?" I asked in a whisper. "Hardshaw or the ATF?"

"Both." He scoffed. "The DEA was involved by then. They were the hard sell at that point."

We sat in silence for several seconds, and I could tell that Hope was ready to switch sides, so I pulled my hand free and rearranged her. She latched on quickly.

I wanted to just forgive him, to view everything that had happened through this new lens, to let all of the hurt go, yet I couldn't wipe the slate clean. There were still too many dirty smudges. "I asked you point blank if you were working for the FBI and you denied it. Just yesterday you denied it."

There was silence, until he blithely said, "Technically, I haven't worked for the FBI."

That only pissed me off more. "You bought a police department, James," I hissed.

"There's no denyin' it."

"You sent Denny Carmichael to me when those men attacked me."

"One of the biggest regrets of my life, but he was closer to you, and I saw it as a way to earn his trust."

"Did it work?" I asked, my voice breaking.

"He saved you," he said, his voice gruff. "But he never trusted me."

"He shouldn't have trusted me," I muttered. "He threatened me if I couldn't get him the time and location of the meetin'. Little did he know I was leadin' him into a trap." I turned to face him. "He was there when the Feds showed up."

He grinned. "That's my girl." But then he sobered. "But the only reason he threatened you in the first place was because of your association with me. That night was when I realized you'd always be in danger if you were with me, so after the attack last August I had to distance myself from you. Still, I hoped it would be over soon, and we could have a life together. Hardshaw was gearing up for a big drug deal with the South Americans that was supposed to happen in the fall. But then the grand jury sprang up, makin' Hardshaw skittish. The ATF told me to tell the whole unvarnished truth if I was asked to testify. That they'd seal my testimony, and it would all come out anyway after they arrested everyone in the bust."

"Which is why you told me to tell the truth," I said.

"Yeah, but I realized something else around that time—the alphabet soup of law enforcement was never gonna let me go. They were gonna milk me for all I was worth. And then you said you were pregnant." He took a ragged breath. "I had representatives from Hardshaw in my office when you showed up that night, and even though they weren't privy to our conversation, I didn't want them to guess that we were together."

"So you lied about wanting me to get the abortion?"

"No," he said, his voice thick. "I meant it. I could only imagine what my enemies would do to you if they figured out you were pregnant with my baby. Havin' an abortion was the only way I knew how to keep you safe. If I could've, I'd've hauled you to Little Rock myself and dragged you into a doctor's office against your will, but then I realized that most people thought Simmons was the father. So I let it be, because I knew if I pushed you too hard, you'd never forgive me, and I'd be lyin' if I said that the hope of havin' you wasn't the light at the end of my very dark tunnel."

My heart broke. "James."

"But then Hardshaw came under investigation with the FBI and the Secret Service about some counterfeit money, and they decided to postpone future business with the South Americans for a while. I got stuck in a holding pattern, with Hardshaw takin' over more and more of my business, and me crossin' so many lines just to keep them on the hook. I wondered if it was ever going to end. And then they said they were finally ready to set up that meetin'. I'd already prepped three locations last summer for the DEA, but I'd told Hardshaw all the surveillance was for them. I just needed to figure out which location the day of the meetin'. But Hardshaw got jittery after Mike ran to the state police, and the South Americans were pissed about the delay and threatened to call it all off." He paused. "But everything got back on track, and better yet, Carson Roberts said he was comin' in person to smooth things over. All the alphabet agencies thought they'd hit the jackpot, and *everything* was riding on this meeting tonight. *Everything.*" He swiped a hand over his stubble. "They weren't offering full immunity. I'd have wound up with some minor weapons charges that would have gotten me a couple of years behind bars, but Carson Roberts would be arrested, and they were countin' on him to spill everything to cut a deal of his own. They'd also nip the pipeline from South America for a short bit and, most importantly, Fenton County would be free."

"But you didn't go."

He pushed out a breath. "I learned my lesson before," he said, his voice heavy. "I couldn't leave savin' you to anyone else."

My eyes burned and I swallowed. So much wasted time and tears. "Why didn't you tell me?" I pleaded again. I'd asked him point-blank multiple times if he was working with the Feds or the state, and he'd denied it every time. But then again, when I thought about his answers, he hadn't lied outright. Just dodged my questions. Still, they were lies of omission. He'd purposely cut me out of his life.

"I couldn't."

"That's *bullshit*," I said, getting pissed.

"Rose…"

"No. Don't you dare lie to me. You could have told me. You just *chose* not to."

He started to protest, then stopped. "I didn't want to drag you into it."

A fire burned in my gut. "I was already *there*, James!"

"I know, but I knew you'd stay. And if you did, you'd be in danger."

"It was *my* decision to make. You were the first man who'd ever treated me like I wasn't some clueless fool, and when it really mattered, you treated me like that too."

"I never treated you like a fool," he said, his voice faltering. "But I admit to not treatin' you with the respect you deserve."

"I waited for you," I said with a heaving sob. "I waited for you to come to your senses, but you only treated me with more anger and scorn. So I moved on, James. What else was I supposed to do?"

"I acted like that because I wanted you to move on," he said. "I knew Simmons would make a better father than I could ever dream of bein'."

"I'm engaged to be married."

And even though I was confused, even though James' words had split me down to my soul, I didn't regret it. Because, the thing was, Joe had been there for me through all of it. He'd become my partner, and I loved him with everything I was. I wanted the life we'd been building together.

Yet part of me still loved James too.

"I may be here right now," he said gruffly, "but nothin's changed. There is no you and me, especially now, and I sure as hell don't want anyone else to know Hope is mine. She belongs to Simmons, and it needs to stay that way."

My heart felt like it was being ripped in two. Joe was her father, but if James wanted to be part of her life too, I didn't feel right stopping him. And yet, if word got out that she was his biological daughter, she wouldn't be safe. "Maybe—"

"Rose," he said with a humorless laugh. "There is no future for me. Even if they busted the meeting, I didn't show. And judging from what Kate said, Carson Roberts wasn't there either. Seems like Kate always planned on bringing him here. My deal with the ATF and the DEA is null and void."

"How can that be?" I asked in shock. "After everything you did for them?"

"That's the way it works," he said, trying to sound nonchalant. "All that time and energy was gearin' up for this, and I blew it off."

"To come to me," I said, heartbroken.

"And to Hope. I may not claim her, but God help the fool who tries to hurt her."

"James."

"Hey," he said, slipping an arm around my back and tugging me to his side. Hope had stopped nursing, so I adjusted my shirt as she snuggled against my chest. "Remember outside when I said no guilt? I meant it."

I'd still feel guilt anyway.

"Why'd you name her Hope?" he asked softly.

"Because everything seemed so heavy. You may not have wanted her, and she was unexpected for me, but I decided to see her as a blessing. She gave me hope. Her middle name is Violet. After my sister."

"And her last name is Simmons." It was a statement, not a question.

"Joe wants to be her father in every way. He's been there for me since the beginning. And he's a great dad, James. The kind of father we all wished we had."

"He loves her?" he asked, his voice tight.

"So very much. He's likely out of his mind right now. Maybe I should have told him, but Kate said she'd hurt Hope…"

"I'll get you out of this, Rose. I'll get you both out."

I glanced up at him and gave him a soft smile. "Do you want to hold her?"

"*What?*"

I turned and held her out to him, placing her against his chest.

His arms wrapped around her tenderly, and he stared down at her sleeping face in awe. "She's so small. I was scared to death I was gonna hurt her picking her up. Scared Kate would hurt her."

The reminder of Kate made me shudder. "Me too."

"She's beautiful, Rose," he said softly.

"How can you tell?" I teased. "I can barely see your face."

"I've seen her," he said, and I wondered if he was talking about out in the warehouse or if he meant something else. "If anything happens to me," he said, hesitating, "she'll be taken care of."

"What?"

"You both will, but I know how stubborn you are, so even though there's money for you, I doubt you'll touch it. But I hope you'll use it for her. Carter Hale has the details."

"Don't talk like that," I said. "Nothin's gonna happen to you."

"No matter what happens, it won't end well for me." Then, before I could protest, he said, "I take it you found Violet's file. And that's how you figured out the location of the meeting."

"No thanks to you," I said, but I couldn't find it in me to dig up my anger. Not after everything he'd told me. Not while he held our daughter like she was the most precious thing in the world.

"I felt like an asshole takin' it, but I couldn't let that information get out. Still, I hoped Mike's involvement would come out after the deal was done. I planned on leakin' it myself if need be."

"Why didn't you tell me where Ashley and Mikey were? Why send Vera?"

"Another of the biggest mistakes of my life, and one of the reasons I'm here. It's like I said. I don't trust anyone else to protect you."

"You didn't need to kill her," I said softly. "I couldn't believe you did."

"I didn't. One of my men shot her. Thought he was doin' my biddin', but I showed him the door. How did you know?"

I was surprised by the relief I felt. I hadn't wanted another leaf added to that tattoo on his back, especially not on my account. I knew how those deaths weighed on him.

"A vision."

"Just like how this all started," he said.

Then he handed Hope back to me and got to his feet.

"What are you doin'?"

He started for the door. "Checkin' to see if the hinges are on the inside." A few seconds later, he shuffled over to the desk and rummaged around.

From Hope's steady breathing, I could tell she'd fallen asleep. She must have exhausted herself crying and from whatever torture Kate had put her through. I suddenly wished I had more light so I could examine every inch of her, but I took comfort knowing I hadn't seen any blood on her clothing after Kate had unbundled her.

"What are you lookin' for?"

"Something to help me get us out of here."

It looked like he had a metal ruler that he was using to scrape paint off the window. When he got a small patch off, he stepped onto a box and pressed his eye to the opening. "She's not out there."

He slid the ruler down the door, grunting as he presumably tried to pry up a hinge, but it didn't seem to be working well.

I got to my feet. "Give us more light," I said. "I'll look for something more substantial to use." Hope was sleeping, but this wouldn't be the first time I'd held her while working.

He cast a glance back at me and began scraping the rest of the paint off while I opened the desk drawers. There hadn't been much in here before, and no one had added anything since. Then a new thought hit me. "What about my boot? It's got a hard heel. You can use it as a hammer."

"I need something to actually hammer," he said in frustration. "Something hard."

The only place I hadn't really looked was the closet, so I opened it with one hand, Hope cradled against my chest. Metal brackets held up several empty shelves. "What about these brackets?"

He followed me inside and nudged me back into the room as he started to lift up a shelf. "Go look and see if she's comin' back. This is gonna make some noise."

I rushed over to the door, trying to keep Hope as motionless as possible, and looked out of the rectangle. Now that he'd cleared most of the paint, I didn't need to climb onto anything. "I don't see her."

"Good," he said, walking over with a four-foot-long piece of wood and two metal brackets. "There's no time to waste."

He made quick work of getting the hinges out with the bracket and a rock that looked like it had been a paperweight, stopping every five to ten seconds to see if Kate had returned.

I was feeling hopeful when he removed the first hinge and anxious when he removed the second. He'd been at work for less than five minutes, but she wouldn't be gone long, would she? Not to mention she'd hear the noise.

He removed the third hinge, fitting the ruler into the crack to try and pry the door open. He glanced through the window and instantly stopped what he was doing.

"She's back."

Chapter Thirty-Six

I heard the dull murmur of voices but couldn't make out any distinct words. Kate had brought someone with her. Not that that was surprising. She'd said Carson was coming, after all, and she'd always meant for this to be a show.

James turned to face me and whispered insistently, "Go hide in the closet. I'm going to jump her when she opens the door, but be prepared to run."

"Okay, but be careful," I pleaded.

He didn't respond, just shoved me into the closet and shut the door.

The voices were even more muffled now, but I could faintly hear Kate's coming out in a breathless, high-pitched rush. The man's voice was deeper and more audible.

"What the hell's goin' on, Andrea?" he grunted.

That had to be Carson Roberts. Neely Kate's other prize.

"I told you, it's a surprise, but if you want me to spoil it, fine," she huffed. "Skeeter Malcolm skipped out and double-crossed you, so I have him all packaged up for you. And you're lucky I told you not to go to that meeting. He'd set them all up to be arrested."

"*What?*"

"See? I told you that I have your back, so trust me. Use the keys and open the door."

I held my breath, turning my back to the closet door as I curled over Hope's sleeping body, praying my body would help protect her from any flying bullets.

I heard a screeching sound and then several bangs and grunts. Kate laughed with abandon before she stopped and shouted. "That's enough. Both of you stop, or I'll shoot you and be done with it."

"What the hell, Andrea?" Carson demanded.

She ignored him. "I need you to tie Skeeter Malcolm to a chair."

"To hell with that," Carson grunted. "Shoot the fucking traitor now."

"I have a surprise for you," she said. "But you need to tie him to a chair first. I suggest you cooperate, Skeeter Malcolm, or I'll put a bullet in your chest, and then I'll put one in Rose and your baby."

My heart skipped a beat.

"Baby?" Carson barked. "What the hell are you talking about?"

"Carson," she said, sounding bored. "Don't worry your pretty little head. Just do it. The rope's in my bag."

I clutched Hope tighter, my heart pounding so fast and hard I could hardly believe it didn't wake her up.

"I know you're in there, Rose Petal," Kate called out in a giddy tone. "Come on out and join us or I'll start shooting then look for you in there later."

If it were just me, I would have taken my chances, using the desk as a barrier, but I didn't dare risk Hope's life. I turned and slowly opened the closet door. "I'm comin' out."

She stood about six feet away from the office doorway. The door lay catawampus on the floor, blocking the exit.

A smug grin spread across her face. "I *knew* you'd see things my way."

"You can't blame me for tryin' to protect my baby."

"*Neely Kate's* baby. You're merely watching her until my sister shows up."

I considered arguing with her, but I didn't see the point. It seemed easier and safer for Hope if I went along with it. "I can live with that."

She smirked. "You won't be living with it much longer. Now come on out here."

I stopped at the door, trying to figure out the safest way to walk over it without dropping Hope.

"Carson," Kate said, sounding sweeter. "Come help Rose and the baby out of that room."

A few seconds later, a man in a gray suit appeared in the doorway. If he'd worn a tie, it was long gone, and the top buttons of his white shirt were undone. His eyes widened when he saw me and Hope.

"Andrea?" he called out, clearly wanting an explanation before he followed her orders.

"You want to salvage this mess, Carson? This is how. Trust me."

He hesitated, then reached in and grabbed my elbow, holding me steady as I walked over the door.

Once I reached the other side, he dropped my arm and turned to face her. "Enough of this bullshit," he snapped. "You've been draggin' me all over this God-forsaken hell hole all night. What the hell is going on?"

"I saved your ass from the raid, didn't I?" she demanded with one foot thrust out to the side. "You're gonna have to trust me, so take the other rope and tie her to that pillar over there." She motioned to a concrete post closer to the windows.

I considered trying to run, but Kate would just shoot me, and I'd drop Hope on the concrete floor. I cast a glance at James, who'd been tied to a metal office chair with nylon rope, his arms and legs secured. His face was expressionless as he tracked my movement across the room.

"This is never gonna work," I called out. "Neely Kate's never going to forgive you for this."

"Don't you worry about me."

Carson tied me with my back to the round pillar, the rope circling around my waist, holding me in place, but he'd been smart enough to put the knots in the back, not that I had two hands to untie it. Not with Hope in my arms. I prayed my arms didn't get tired.

While Carson was doing her bidding, he seemed reluctant about it. There was a bulge under his jacket, which I was sure was a gun. If he was starting to distrust Kate, he could turn out to be an ally, especially since he had no idea what role he was doomed to play in her little show tonight.

"Her name's not Andrea," I said.

He jerked his gaze to me. "What?"

"She's Kate Simmons, J.R. Simmons' daughter, and she's planning to kill you too. She holds you responsible for almost destroying her sister's life."

He shook his head as though he was trying to clear it. "*What?*"

Kate let out an exaggerated sigh. "Don't listen to her, Carson. She's a desperate woman, who will say anything to save herself."

He started to reach for his jacket, but something stopped him.

Kate smiled, then nodded her head toward James. "You need to trust me, Carson. That man is my gift to you. He's been setting you up since you first approached him over a year ago. You need to find out what he knows and what he's told the authorities if you have any chance of saving Hardshaw."

Carson shifted his attention to James, marching over to confront him. "Is that true?"

James gave him an evil grin. "Every word of it, and it doesn't matter what happens to me. You're still goin' down."

Carson punched James so hard the chair fell to the side.

James didn't move.

"Did you knock him out?" Kate asked, sounding baffled.

"Guess so." Carson turned back to Kate, cocking his head. He looked a lot less trustful than he had a few seconds ago. "What are we doin' here, Andrea? I could kill Malcolm anywhere."

"*Kate*," I said insistently. "Her name is Kate Simmons, and she's doin' this for revenge."

He shook his head in confusion. "Revenge? What the fuck does that mean?"

"I can tell you," Neely Kate called out of the darkness. "I'm the person she's tryin' to avenge."

"Neely Kate?" Kate called out in surprise. She looked downright giddy.

"It's me," Neely Kate said, still in the shadows.

"How did you find me?" Kate sounded like a proud parent whose toddler had put a round peg into the appropriate hole.

"It wasn't hard," Neely Kate said. "Something Rose mentioned earlier clued me in."

Kate's deadly glare shifted to me, but Neely Kate stepped out into the open and marched over to me, standing in front of me like a human shield. "If you're doin' what I think you're doin', then you have *truly* lost your ever-lovin' mind! Did you just think you could kill Rose and I'd be okay with it?"

"You weren't supposed to know," Kate said. "I was gonna let you think Skeeter Malcolm killed her in a fit of jealous rage and then killed himself. The poor baby would be an orphan and you could raise her."

"What about Joe?" Neely Kate cried out, her voice rising. "Hope wouldn't be an orphan. She'd still have Joe. Do you honestly think I'd take his baby from him? How is that any better than what J.R. did *to you*?" She took a deep breath. "I don't want this, Kate. Please, just let Rose and Hope go home."

Kate's expression softened. "I know you don't understand this, but I know what's best for you, little sis. As long as Rose is part of your life, you and I will never be close. Not like we're supposed to be. Once Rose is gone, you can finally have your baby."

Neely Kate shook her head. "No, Kate. Not like this. If you do this, I will never speak to you again. I will spend the rest of my life trying to make you pay for what you did."

Joe stepped out of the shadows in the middle aisle, about ten feet from Kate. His face was hard, and he had a gun aimed at his sister. "You're plannin' to give her *my* baby, Kate. You're talking about killin' the mother of my daughter. The woman I want to marry."

Kate turned to her brother. "That's not your baby, Joe. *Skeeter Malcolm* is her father."

Joe cast a dark glance at James, who was still lying on the ground, then turned back to Kate. "She *is* my child. I was there for almost every doctor's appointment before she was born and after. I was the one who put her crib together. I was there when she was born, terrified she and Rose would die in that damn field. Rose and I are the ones who get up with her every night. I change diapers. I walk with her when she's fussy. I cherish every smile that lights up her face and thank God for every moment I have with her. No one is pulling a fast one on me, Kate, and as we both know, DNA doesn't make a father. That is my little girl, and no one is takin' her from me. Not even you."

Kate stared at him in surprise, and a huge grin spread across her face. "Well, look at you." Then her smile faded. "But be that as it may, Neely Kate deserves this baby more."

Carson stared at Kate as though finally seeing the crazy he'd hooked his wagon to. "I have no idea why I'm here," he said, shaking his head. "This sounds like a family matter to me, *Andrea*."

"Don't you get all high and mighty," Kate said. "Your family is plenty messed up."

"Enough!" Joe shouted, then his shoulders sank, and he looked devastated. "Enough. You had your fun, but honestly, Kate, we're *done* with your drama. Your orchestrations are exhaustin'. The showdown you arranged with our father in which my fiancée was murdered, and I lost my baby. Last summer in the barn with Stella and Branson. Now this?" he shouted, his anger building. He gestured to the fire on the concrete floor. "What the hell is that? A damn fire in June? Are you plannin' on burning Rose at the stake? Because you're gonna have to go through me first. Neely Kate, take my wife and baby home."

"She's not your wife!" Kate shouted. "You're not married."

"It's a damn piece of paper," Joe said. Then he turned to Neely Kate. "Untie her and *go*."

Neely Kate scrambled behind me and started to work on the knots.

Kate swung her gun around to point at me. "Neely Kate, don't do it, or I'll shoot both Rose and the baby."

"Just get Hope," I whispered frantically. "Please, Neely Kate."

But then there was a thunk over by James. He hadn't been knocked out at all, of course. He'd gotten loose from his chair and tackled Carson.

"Get up!" Kate screamed at him, but it was James who got to his feet. When he did, he pointed his gun at...Joe. He stood about ten feet away, with Kate between them but off to the side. She stared at James in horror. "What do you think you're doing?"

James ignored her, hate radiating off his body. "You thought you could take what was mine, Simmons?"

"You could never deserve them, Malcolm," Joe countered, his body shaking.

Everything in me froze, my blood, my heart, my mind. This scene. I'd seen it again and again in my visions, but somehow I'd let myself believe it wouldn't happen. I didn't have time to react, I didn't have time to do anything but scream.

"Maybe not," James spat, "but neither do you."

A gunshot rang out, and then another, the second ringing in my ear. I turned to see Neely Kate standing next to me with tears streaming down her face, her arms extended and her pistol in hand.

It took me another half second to realize that Kate was lying on the ground.

But so was Joe.

"No!" I screamed, and Hope was screaming too. I frantically tore at the rope at my waist. *"No!"*

Jed emerged from the shadows, gently pushing Neely Kate's arms down and pulling her into his embrace. "It's okay," he murmured.

But it wasn't okay. James had shot Joe, just like in my vision, and Joe was now lying on the ground, and I was stuck, still tied to the pole.

"Let me go!" I shouted, hysterical. "Somebody *let me go!*"

Jed immediately cut me loose with his pocketknife, and I ran to Joe, dropping to my knees as I cried hysterically. He lay crumpled on his side, his eyes closed.

I jerked my gaze up to James, who was holding the gun on Carson. "How could you?" I screamed. *"How could you?"*

I got to my feet, sobbing. I started to advance on him, but Neely Kate grabbed my arm.

"Rose. *Stop.* You're scarin' Hope."

She was right. My poor daughter was flailing and screaming in my arms, and it hit me like a Mack truck that I was the one who was scaring her. I was the person she trusted, and not only had I terrified her, I'd let her father get killed. I handed her to Neely Kate and turned my wrath on James.

"What did you do?" I asked in a shockingly calm voice, but it was laced with hatred.

He gave me a defiant glare. "I did what I had to do to save you and Hope, and I refuse to apologize for it."

It was then I saw the blood on his shirt, just under his left shoulder.

I shook my head in confusion. Had Joe shot him before he'd been shot himself?

"Kate shot him," Neely Kate said, her entire body shaking so much I was scared she would drop my daughter, but Jed's arms were around her, holding them both. "When Kate realized Skeeter was goin' to shoot Joe, she turned her gun on him."

My mind spun out of control, trying to understand what had happened, and then Joe released a loud groan.

"Joe?" I ran back to him and dropped to his side as he rolled onto his back, grimacing.

"Lay still," I said, then searched his chest and abdomen, completely confused. "I don't see any blood."

"There damn well better not be," he grunted. "I'm wearin' a bulletproof vest."

"What?"

"After all those visions of Malcolm shootin' me in the chest, I'd be stupid not to wear one."

I looked up at James.

"I could see he was wearin' a vest under his shirt, so I was tryin' to draw her fire from you, hopin' Jed would take her out." He shot an appreciative glance at my best friend. "Looks like Neely Kate had it covered instead."

"How'd you know Jed was here?" Neely Kate asked.

"Please," he grunted. "That man is tied to you like a ball and chain. There's no way he'd let you come here on your own." Before, James would have said it as though it was a life sentence. Now, there was a wistfulness in his voice.

Sirens sounded in the distance, and I knew I should apologize to James for accusing him of trying to kill Joe, but the truth was he'd taken a huge gamble with Joe's life. I was furious with him, especially since he had no remorse whatsoever. But if I was being honest with myself, I was furious with him for everything he had done in the name of love. I'd expected him to treat me like a grown-ass woman, and in the end, he'd treated me like Joe had done in the beginning—like I was an inept child, incapable of making a rational decision. Maybe I would have stayed with him, or maybe I would have walked away, but now we'd never know.

Soon the building was swarming with sheriff deputies and EMTs. They arrested Carson and loaded up James and Joe onto stretchers, but Kate was declared dead on the scene. I could see that Neely Kate was upset by that, but I had a feeling it had as much to do with the fact she'd lost the sister who'd always wanted to please her as the fact that she'd been the one to kill her. I didn't pretend to understand, but sometimes you loved who you loved, no matter how awful they might be.

Just as they were loading Joe into his ambulance, Neely Kate got a call that made her as white as a sheet. I was terrified something had happened to her granny, but then she turned and looked up at Jed. "Claire was just rushed to the hospital, hemorrhaging. They're worried she's losing the baby."

She was still holding Hope, so I took my daughter and gave her a shove. "Go. We'll meet you there."

As she and Jed sprinted for his car, I prayed that Neely Kate wouldn't lose anyone else tonight.

Chapter Thirty-Seven

Thankfully, Joe had thought to bring Hope's car seat, so I was able to follow his ambulance directly to the hospital. I didn't plan on letting my baby out of my sight for a very long time.

The EMTs had checked Hope over in the ambulance that came for Joe, and they'd declared her relatively physically unscathed other than a few welts on her right arm and leg. The EMT had suggested with no small amount of disgust that Kate had pinched her to make her cry.

Joe was admitted right away, and after a quick examination that revealed he had deep bruising and possible broken ribs, they whisked him away to x-ray. Carrying a sleeping Hope in the baby wrap I'd found in Joe's car, I went off to look for Jed and Neely Kate and found them in the otherwise empty labor and delivery waiting room.

Neely Kate looked pale and scared, huddled in her chair. Jed sat next to her, his arm wrapped around her in consolation.

"Have you heard anything yet?" I asked as I approached.

Neely Kate shook her head. "No. They said she was hemorrhaging because her placenta tore. But we don't know if she's okay or if the baby..." Her voice trailed off and tears filled her eyes.

"We're going to think positive, okay?" I said, in a cheery voice. She nodded, but I could tell she couldn't quite let herself believe it yet.

"Before we left for Carmichael's, I had a vision of Hope. Several, actually. In one of them, Hope was sitting up and looking in a mirror. You were behind her, and you were holding a baby, Neely Kate. You were holding Daisy."

Her eyes widened, filling with hope, but then they glazed over. She was protecting herself in case I was wrong.

I understood. I wished I could do more for her, but the only thing I knew to do was to sit beside her and hold her hand. She sent a long look to Hope, and tears started coursing down her cheeks. "I'm so sorry I let Bobby take Hope. The monitor lost its signal, and when I went up to check on her, she wasn't there. So I screamed, and Witt came runnin', and as soon as he came inside, she must have rushed to her car and took off. She didn't even have Hope's car seat! Witt tried to chase her down, but by the time he left the property, she was out of sight. He called Deputy Miller, and while we were waiting for him to arrive, Witt searched the house. He found a blanket and some food in the basement. She'd holed up down there. Waiting."

I shuddered at the thought. Had she been down there before to scout the area? I'd noticed some moved boxes the other day, but I'd written it off. I wouldn't be surprised if Kate had. "You have nothing to apologize for. It's not your fault. It very well could have happened to me. What I don't understand is why Muffy didn't alert you. That dog is beyond devoted to Hope."

"We think she was drugged," Neely Kate said, wiping her face. "In any case, Randy showed up right after Carmichael's men, and he arrested them for attempted kidnapping since that's why they were there."

"They found Bobby dead in her car a few miles from your house," Jed added. "Looks like Kate convinced her to bring her Hope, probably for some sort of compensation, but then Kate killed her. Or at least that's our guess since both women are dead."

Neely Kate blinked hard and shivered. Jed tightened his grip on her.

"Sounds like Kate," I muttered, still horrified that that woman had touched my child. That she'd pinched her hard enough to leave marks. I turned a worried gaze to my best friend. "How are *you* doin'?"

"I don't deserve this baby," she said with fresh tears. "Maybe this is God's punishment for my past and for failin' Hope."

"You did *not* fail Hope," I said in a stern voice. "You saved her. No, you saved all three of us. I can never repay you, Neely Kate, but I'll spend the rest of my life tryin'. So no more guilt. It's time to focus on *your* baby now."

"I can't lose this baby too, Rose," Neely Kate said, her voice breaking. "I don't know what I'll do if she…"

"It's a good thing you don't have to consider it," I said in a stern voice. "She's going to be just fine. Let's trust my vision."

My eyes locked with Jed's, and for a man who so rarely advertised his emotions, he wasn't doing much to hide them now. They were full of naked fear.

"How's Joe?" Neely Kate asked. "Is he okay?"

"They think he has a few broken ribs and a lot of bruising, but he's going to be okay," I said reassuringly. "He's in x-ray now."

"And Kate?" she asked.

She already knew Kate was dead, but there were still plenty of unknowns. Like what would be done with the body. Like what, if anything, would happen to Neely Kate.

"The sheriff knows that you shot her in self-defense," I said. "Joe assured me that they're not going to press charges, if that's what you're worried about. He said they'd question you later."

They'd agreed to put it off as a courtesy due to the sensitive nature of the situation. Joe might not work for the department anymore, but there were plenty of people there who still accepted him as one of them.

"No," she said, sounding like she was lost. "That's not why I'm upset."

She'd killed someone, and there was nothing I could say or do that would make her feel better. I knew she'd killed a man before, but this was her sister. Kate had been a dangerous woman, and I had little doubt that she would have found a way to kill me if she'd survived, but I still felt the weight of what Neely Kate had done to protect me. Would she hate me for it later?

"How's Skeeter?" she asked, looking like she wasn't sure if she should broach the subject.

"I don't know," I said truthfully. "I haven't asked."

Jed's gaze lifted to mine again, and I could see his guilt. Did he feel guilty for not checking on James himself?

I cleared my throat. "I think he's goin' to jail for a long time, Jed. He made a deal with the ATF and the DEA a long time ago, but he was supposed to get Carson Roberts to that meetin' tonight to fulfill his end of the bargain. Instead, he ditched it. They got Roberts anyway, in the end, but he didn't do his part." Then I added, "Because of me."

Jed hung his head. "Shit…"

"Kate sent him a text that said she had Hope. He left to come save her…and me."

"He still loves you," Neely Kate said softly. My face flushed, and she added, "I'm not asking if you love him too. I'm just pointing out a fact."

"He may love me," I said, "but he doesn't *want* me. He told me so."

"If he's goin' away, he's tryin' to protect you," Jed said in a gruff tone.

I turned to him in surprise.

"We've known men who've been in prison for years. Their family comes to see them in that dark, grimy visitation room, but they can't touch each other. Can't really be a part of each other's lives. He doesn't want to trap you in a pointless relationship, and he doesn't want his daughter seein' him behind bars. He'd rather let Joe raise his child than for her to bear the pain of having a father in prison."

My throat was thick with emotion, but I managed a nod. I couldn't imagine trying to maintain a relationship under those conditions, and selfishly, I didn't want Hope to endure it either. She was so young, so innocent.

We stewed in silence for a few moments, and then a man walked out of a set of swinging double doors. He was wearing jeans and T-shirt, so it was obvious he wasn't hospital staff.

Jed jumped to his feet, and Neely Kate scrambled up after him while I anxiously watched.

"Brian," Jed said, his voice deep with emotion. "How's your sister?"

Brian scrubbed his hand over his head, looking like he was close to tears. "She's going to be okay. They saved her." He paused to gather himself, all of us hanging on his words, and then added, "And they saved the baby too."

Neely Kate burst into tears, then turned to me and threw her arms around my neck, squeezing me and Hope tight. I squeezed her right back.

Jed reached out and pumped Brian's hand. "That's great news."

"For all of us," Brian said. "Do you want to see the baby in the nursery?"

Neely Kate spun around to face him. "Yes. *Please.*" She gave me a questioning look.

"Go!" I said, giving her a little push. "Go meet your baby. Take lots of pictures."

Brian led them through the double doors, and I took Hope back to the ER.

Joe was back in his room, lying down on his propped-up bed, his eyes closed. I tried to be quiet as I slowly closed the door behind us, but his eyes opened, and he gave me a relieved smile. "I know this is irrational," he said with a grimace, "but I'm terrified every time either one of you leaves my sight. Scared I'll never see you again."

"I know the feeling." I held our sleeping daughter tighter.

It filled me with raw panic to think of what I'd seen earlier—my vision coming true. Watching Joe get shot in front of me...the memory filled me with panic, even knowing what I did. I couldn't imagine my life without Joe. I couldn't imagine Hope not having him for a father. My mind strayed to the visions I'd had of Hope. All those happy future memories. I still wanted them to come true, and Joe was very much a part of that.

I had no idea why I hadn't seen myself in those visions. Maybe I'd been thinking about Hope's relationships with other people, not just me, and so that's what I'd seen. Or maybe something would happen to me next week, and she'd still have to grow up without me. For now, I was ready to let the future unfold as a mystery.

"They said I have three broken ribs," Joe said with a grimace. "I'm not supposed to pick up Hope for several weeks." I knew that part was already killing him.

"We can prop her up on pillows," I said. "And you can hold her hand. She'll love that. She just wants to know you're there. She just wants to *feel* you there."

"I almost lost you tonight," he said, his voice tight. "I almost lost you several times. Why didn't you tell me about Kate?"

I let out a sigh as I lowered into the chair next to his bed. "She said that she would kill Hope. What else was I supposed to do?" I expected him to argue and tell me that I should've called him anyway, but he simply nodded. We both knew if the roles had been reversed, he would've done the same thing.

"How did Skeeter Malcolm get there?" he asked. The distant look in his eyes told me he was scared of the answer.

"Kate called him," I said. "She told him that she'd kidnapped Hope, and he came to save her."

He nodded again and then asked, "He said exactly what you saw in your vision. Has he decided to lay claim to her?"

I shook my head. "No. He thinks you're the better father, and he expects he's going to prison for a long time. He doesn't want her to know he exists."

Surprise filled his eyes, and he nodded, looking grateful. "How do you feel about all this?" He looked uncertain. And scared.

"I'm tired," I said with a sad smile. I knew it wasn't necessarily the answer he was looking for, but it was the best description I had. "And I just want to go home with you and Hope and Muffy, so we can all love on each other for the rest of our lives."

He smiled softly. "I want that too."

I gasped, feeling like a bad dog mother. "Where's Muffy? Neely Kate told me she was drugged."

"She's at home," he said, "and not at all happy about it. She was pretty groggy when I got there."

"Neely Kate and Jed told me what happened."

His eyes hardened. "I can't believe I didn't think to look for Bobby down there."

"Why would you?" I asked. "She left the back door open. We all thought she ran away."

"That's exactly what she wanted us to think," he said, "and I fell for it hook, line and sinker."

"It's okay," I said reassuringly, but he shook his head.

"No, it's not. But I promise you never to make that mistake again."

"I know," I said. He would probably beat himself up over that for a long time to come. "Will they let you come home tonight?"

He laughed. "Let them try to stop me."

"Neely Kate's baby is okay," I said, "and the mother is too. Jed and Neely Kate went to see her right before I came back to your room."

He looked relieved. "I don't think Neely Kate could have handled losing another baby."

"I know," I said.

Something shifted in his gaze, and he reached for me, flinching at the pain in his ribs. "I can't believe Kate thought that she could just kill you and hand our baby over to our sister," he said, his voice breaking.

"I can," I said, kissing his hand, then pressing it to my cheek. "She was insane."

"Still…" He pushed out a heavy sigh.

The door opened, and I turned, expecting a nurse or doctor to give us a report, but instead, it was Dermot wearing a sheepish look.

"I hope I'm not intrudin'."

The ER had strict visiting rules. It was surprising they'd let me bring Hope in, let alone allowed a visit from Dermot. But I had a feeling he hadn't asked. Or that he had some connection who'd allowed it.

"No," Joe said as he waved his hand, giving another pained grimace… "Come in."

"I thought you both might like an update."

"Yes," I said. "Please."

"We found Levi."

"Is he okay?" I asked.

"He's fine. Tired, hungry, and a bit dehydrated. We gave him some food and water. He ran when he saw my car this afternoon, but we decided to go back later, especially after I heard about Hope's abduction. We thought Hardshaw might be responsible, and if so, Romano might have some information, so we went back to the barn and snuck up on him. It didn't take long to realize he didn't know anything about anything. He was running scared because he knew Margi had been murdered. He figured Hardshaw had done it and worried they would come for him next because she'd been posing as his sister. Turns out Margi *was* involved with Hardshaw, but she was desperate to get out. She told Levi she had something of theirs, something she'd hidden and never intended to give back. Seems like a fit for the guns. Apparently, she hated Hardshaw bein' here too."

"She should have come to one of us," I said, shaking my head. "We could have helped her. Randy would have helped her."

"The representatives from Hardshaw were arrested in the raid at the church tonight. Skeeter and Carson Roberts might not have been there, but they were caught on camera workin' out the details of future shipments and payments." Then he winked at me. "Or so I hear from the rumor mill."

He wasn't fooling me. He had sources.

"But," he continued as a weary smile spread across his face. "Hardshaw is pretty much destroyed, and they'll never bother us again. Denny Carmichael and his men were caught up in the big sting, thanks to you, and they're currently in jail. Rumor has it a judge is issuing a search warrant to search his property even as we speak."

I sucked in a breath. "They'll find his meth lab."

"One can only hope," Dermot grunted. "And you and I both know he's killed plenty of people there, or had them killed. One more thing, the Collards were at the church, practically arm in arm with Hardshaw. Guess kidnapping your niece and nephew wasn't the only piece of business they did with them. Now they're behind bars too."

My heart lurched. "Was Brox with them?"

He shook his head. "Brox came to me today." He pulled a face. "Or I guess he came to me yesterday asking to be part of my group." He cast a glance at Joe. "You know...my group of fishing buddies."

Joe released a laugh and then a grunt of pain.

"Brox Collard is a good man," I said. "Treat him well."

"I intend to." He suddenly looked uncomfortable. "I know Joe has supposedly left the force—"

"No supposedly about it," Joe said in a deep voice. "I'm officially out."

"Nevertheless," Dermot said. "Rose, can I speak to you alone for a moment?"

"Yes," I said, getting to my feet and glancing back at Joe. "I'll be back in a few minutes." Then I teased, "Don't go home without us."

He grinned. "I don't intend to."

I gave him a quick kiss, then followed Dermot out into the hall and into an empty exam room.

"Rumors are flyin' that Skeeter Malcolm is about to be sent away to prison for a very long time."

"That's true," I said, feeling emotion wash through me again.

"Which means there's gonna be an empty leadership position."

I gave him a sad smile. "Just like we were workin' toward."

"I'm here to offer it to you."

My eyes flew wide. "What?"

"You're the one who brought Hardshaw down and ousted Malcolm. The conqueror takes the spoils."

I gaped at him in shock.

"No one would challenge you for it, plus you're a natural leader. You could unite them in way that hasn't happened since Prohibition."

I started shaking my head before he even finished. "I'm not interested. Besides, without an enemy knockin' at our door, I'd turn to the enemy within. I'm not sure what role Carmichael thought Wendy had in Peter Pan, but she civilized the Lost Boys."

He narrowed his eyes and shook his head. "I'm not gonna even pretend to understand what that meant, but you have to admit we could do with a lot of civilizin'."

I laughed. "There's plenty of truth to that, but I'm still not interested. I plan on hangin' up my hat and goin' into retirement."

The look he gave me suggested he didn't believe me, but he gave me a two-finger salute and said, "May you have a long and happy retirement."

"Amen." I gave him a smile. "The crown is yours, my friend. Do what James Malcolm wanted to achieve but couldn't. Make this county a better place."

He turned serious. "I intend to." He turned to walk out, then glanced back at me. "For what it's worth, you're makin' the right decision. I had the chance once, at the proverbial fork in the road, and I took the wrong turn. I paid for it with my family. With their murders." He swallowed and stared at the wall. "You're better off leavin' all of this behind." Then he walked out, leaving me and Hope alone.

I started to head back to Joe's room, but I realized I still had some unfinished business.

❧❦

It wasn't hard to find his room. He hadn't been charged with anything yet, so he didn't have a guard outside his door. But we all knew the charges were coming. It was just a matter of time.

His room was dark, and he lay back on his upright bed with his eyes closed. Gauze was taped to his left shoulder. He was shirtless, and I could see the tattoo on his chest, the one that used to fascinate me so.

He looked tired and defeated. I had never seen him that way before, but I wasn't surprised. He'd lost everything. His empire. His best friend. And me. I had to wonder if it was all worth it. Then again, I supposed he'd never had much of a choice, even before he joined J.R. Simmons.

He'd been born in poverty, grown up in violence. A hard life was all he'd ever known, and J.R. Simmons had given him the opportunity to have money and power.

Had that been the beginning of the end for him? Back when he was a kid? Or was it when he'd struck out on his own and decided to continue in a life of crime? Or maybe it had happened when he bought himself Daniel Crocker's crown.

I wasn't sure, and I doubted I'd ever know. I doubted he knew either. He never thought he'd find love, and then he'd found me and tried to make it all right.

But there were so many wrongs behind him, so many things stacked against him. I think we both knew that we could never truly be together. He'd given me such a beautiful gift in Hope, but she wasn't the only thing he'd given me. He'd helped me find the strength and the courage that had been buried within me for years, which had taken the form of the Lady in Black. He'd given me excitement and *power* and love. Now he was giving me another gift. He was setting us both free.

His eyes opened when he saw me, and he grimaced. "What are you doing here?" he asked. "You should be with Joe."

"I've already been with Joe," I said. "And I've checked on Neely Kate and Jed. Their baby's going to be okay."

"That's good," he said roughly with a sharp nod, and then he grimaced from pain.

I wasn't sure what to say to him. Part of me still loved him, and I knew I always would. But I knew the life he offered, even if he wasn't in prison, wasn't one I wanted. It certainly wasn't what I wanted for Hope.

My time with James had been a fantasy, but I needed real life. I needed Joe. "Thank you," I said. "Thank you for coming tonight and helping me save Hope."

He nodded again but didn't say anything as he stared at the ceiling.

"I'm not sure what you want," I said softly. "Do you want me to let you know how Hope is doing? I can send you letters and pictures."

He shook his head. "No. A clean break," he said. "That's what we all need."

I nodded, ashamed to find myself relieved. "Do you know when you'll be arrested?"

He lay there for a second before turning his head to face me. "Probably within a day or two. They know I'm not leaving town, so they won't arrest me tonight. Hale's already talking to the authorities, trying to make arrangements."

"Dermot's takin' over," I said.

He grunted. "That was a given. You're the one who encouraged most of the men in this county to follow him and not me. Why do you think I had so many Hardshaw men? All of my guys left. They followed you," he said. "They followed you to him."

"I'm sorry," I said, even though I wasn't sure I was.

"Nah," he said with a grunt. "It was for the best."

"You ended up alone," I said, my voice tight.

"That's exactly what I deserve," he said roughly. "Don't you feel sorry for me, Rose Gardner. I'm the one who put myself here. I'm the one who's paying the consequences."

"I wish things had been different," I said.

"I don't," he said. "Things worked out exactly the way they should've."

His gaze landed on Hope, and I took her out of her sling and placed her in his good arm. He stared down at her with a combination of awe and joy. "Is she okay?" he asked.

"Yeah," I said. "The EMTs looked her over earlier. They said Kate pinched her several times but didn't actually hurt her."

"That woman was capable of anything," James said.

"I know."

Tears filled his eyes, and he reached his finger down to her hand. She grasped it in her sleep and pulled it closer to her chest. His reaction caught me by surprise. He'd been so adamant that he didn't want her, and I suspected he truly thought that too…until he saw her. Until he held her.

He was just now understanding what I'd come to know months ago. Hope was a gift. I would have the rest of my life to love and cherish her, but he only had these few minutes until I took her away.

Seeing her in his arms stole my breath. How much had I longed for this last fall? It also brought their resemblance into sharper view. They had the same hairline. The same jaw. I had lost James, but I still had a part of him in our daughter.

"Promise me you won't tell her the truth," he said, his voice breaking. "Please don't saddle her with that. Let her think that Joe's her father."

"I will," I said. "But if you change your mind…"

"No," he barked. "I won't. That wouldn't be fair to her, and it wouldn't be fair to you and Joe. Just let her keep thinking he's her daddy." He studied her for another minute before he said, "She truly is a miracle, isn't she?"

"Yeah," I said, my heart bursting. "She is."

"Despite everything," he said, lifting his eyes to mine, "I'm not sorry. I'm not sorry for any of it, because without it, I never would've known you," he said. "I never would have had the chance to love you."

I didn't trust myself to answer, so I just nodded. But then a question sprang to my mind. "Why did you want me to spend forty-eight hours with you?"

His eyes widened slightly, and he swallowed as a dark look covered his face. "That was a whole lot of impulse and an equal part of delusion."

"What does that mean?"

"It means I still wanted somethin' I couldn't have." Then a look filled his eyes that told me he was never going to tell me.

He leaned over and kissed Hope's forehead, then lifted her up so I could take her. I scooped her up, but he grasped my hand, pulling me closer. "When you walk out of this room," he said, his voice breaking, "promise me you'll never look back. Promise me you'll forget me."

"I can't promise you that," I said, my heart breaking. "I can't promise that I'll forget you, when you helped make me who I am. But I promise to keep your memory alive in my heart and share it with no one else. What we had is between the two of us, and it will stay that way forever."

He nodded, his jaw working, and then he swallowed. "I suppose that's all I can ask," he said. He gave me a sad smile. "Have a good life, Rose. Give our daughter the life we both always wanted."

"I will," I said.

Then I turned around and walked away forever.

Epilogue

It was a beautiful day for a wedding.

Having an outdoor wedding in southern Arkansas at the end of June was a risk, even if it was scheduled for late morning. It could have been hot and humid, but God must've been smiling on us because it was cool and crisp, without a cloud in the sky.

Joe woke me up with a soft kiss on my neck. I was barely awake, but I quickly jumped on board as his mouth burned a line of kisses down my cleavage.

I grasped his head, about to guide him to my breast when the bedroom door burst open. "Aunt Rose!" Mikey shouted in excitement. "Uncle Joe! It's your weddin' day!"

Joe's face lifted to mine, and although I fully expected him to look irritated, he didn't—he was wearing a defeated grin. He sat up and held out his arms to our nephew. "Yes, it is."

Mikey jumped into his lap, and Joe grimaced when Mikey's knee landed in his crotch. "Do I still get to walk Muffy down the aisle?"

"You sure do, little man. What do you say we take her outside?"

"Okay!" Mikey hopped down and took Joe's hand, leading him out the bedroom door.

Joe glanced back at me, and mouthed, *I have naughty things planned for you later.*

"Promises, promises." Especially since we planned to spend our wedding night in our farmhouse with three kids.

He laughed and my heart filled with joy when I heard him and Mikey trying to be quiet as they convinced Muffy to leave her charge.

I still couldn't believe Violet's kids were living with us.

After I'd given Mason a copy of the flash drive, he'd passed it on to the FBI to handle however they saw fit. He told me they were throwing the book at Carson Roberts and Hardshaw had been cut off at the roots. The other two members of the Hardshaw Three—Carly's father, Robert Blakely, and Arthur Manchester—were still free men, but Mason was sure we wouldn't hear from them again in Fenton County. They were still digging into the Murray Portfolio, which they'd found on the hard drive. Mason was sure it would give them financial details about Hardshaw's offshore accounts. The file was password protected, however, and no one could seem to break it...until Mason got an anonymous tip, via Neely Kate and Jed. Apparently, Kate had given it to him when he'd gone to save Neely Kate in Oklahoma.

Would the information bring down the now Hardshaw Two? I couldn't help wondering what that meant for our friend. I'd sent her an email, but I had yet to hear back.

As for Mike, he'd worked out a deal, but he was still going to serve several years in prison. I felt guilty that I might have played a part in his sentencing, but Mason assured me that Mike had dug his own grave. The kids' grandparents wanted to keep them, but in the end, Mike had made the decision, saying it was in his children's best interest if they stayed with Joe and me, at least until he got out of prison. Violet's will stating that she wanted me to have her kids would have swayed the judge, but thankfully his parents had agreed not to fight us.

The Feds had filed a long list of charges against James, so many he'd spend the rest of his life in prison. Jed had gone to see him before his arrest. Neely Kate said he'd been gone for hours, but when he came back, he seemed to have found some peace.

The kids were devastated, of course. They'd lost their mother last October and now their father was going to prison, but they were surrounded by love, and I had to believe it would make a difference.

It had been an adjustment for Joe and me to go from a new family of three to a bursting house of five, but the kids adored Joe, and he adored them back. Other men might have resented the added burden and responsibility, but Joe welcomed them with open arms—literally—and it filled my heart with joy.

With our hands full of kids and Joe making the jump from law enforcement to working for the landscaping company, our wedding was going to be a simple affair. Neely Kate and Jed's ceremony had been simple too, and it was one of the most beautiful weddings I'd ever attended. That was exactly what I'd wanted for ours. Thankfully, Joe felt the same way.

Given my love of flowers, we'd decided on an outdoor wedding, despite the potential heat disaster. Neely Kate and Jed had spent a lot of time and effort making their backyard perfect for their own wedding, so she'd been thrilled by my request to have ours there too.

Her face had beamed with excitement. "We'd love for you two to get married here."

"I'll take care of everything," I assured her. "I know you've got your hands full with Daisy." She was only two weeks old, which meant they were sleeping even less than we were, but Neely Kate was loving every minute of it.

"Are you kiddin' me? I have scads of hours in the middle of the night. Just give me a job, because I can't wait for you to be my sister!"

She didn't say anything about her other sister, and I didn't ask. But I knew Neely Kate had kept Kate's ashes. They were in a simple urn over her fireplace.

Jed was Joe's best man, a testament to how far they'd come, and Neely Kate was of course my matron of honor. True to her word, she'd poured herself into the details, helping me select my dress—a long, sleeveless slip dress covered with lace—and the floral arrangements and bouquets. We'd decided I would carry Hope down the aisle. She had her own white dress, which had been my father's baptism gown. Aunt Bessie had brought it when she and Uncle Earl came for the wedding. Joe had insisted that Muffy be in the wedding too, not that I'd complained. She'd been a part of our shared lives from the beginning. Joe had taken her to the groomers the day before, and she was going to wear a rose-colored bow around her neck for the ceremony—a perfect match for Neely Kate's knee-length bridesmaid's dress.

Less than twenty people would attend, all of them close friends and family—Aunt Bessie and Uncle Earl, Bruce Wayne and Anna, Maeve, Witt, Marshall, and Dermot. Jonah was doing the ceremony, and his girlfriend, Jessica, would attend as a guest. Even Miss Mildred planned to come.

Ashley and Mikey were in the wedding as well. Ashley was our flower girl, and Mikey's job was to carry our rings on a satin pillow.

After Joe and Mikey took care of Muffy, we fed the kids breakfast. I left Hope with Joe and brought Ashley to Neely Kate's house early so we could get ready. She fussed over our hair and my makeup for the next hour while Jed took care of Daisy.

"I wish my momma was here," Ashley said while Neely Kate curled her hair with a curling iron.

Neely Kate stared at her in the mirror for a moment, then squatted behind her and pulled her into a tight hug. "So do we, Ashley. It's okay to miss her, because we all do."

"I miss your momma every day," I said past the lump in my throat. "It's not right that she's not here with me on my wedding day, and it won't be right when you get married either, but I believe she's with us all the same. Even if we can't see her. But I'm here, and while I'll never be able to replace your momma, I'll always be here for you."

Ashley got up and rushed over to me. I tugged her onto my lap and wrapped her up in my arms. Maybe I held her tighter than I needed to, but I'd been kept away from her for so long, it still felt like a miracle to have her back.

"I'll always be here for you too," Neely Kate said. "Daisy and Hope are lucky to have a cousin like you."

Ashley gave a small nod, her expression serious, and then Jed walked into the room with Daisy, who had just woken up from a nap. "Can I feed her, Aunt Neely Kate?" Ashley asked in a small voice.

"Why, you read my mind, Ashley Nicole, I was about to ask you to do just that," she said with a big smile. Ashley took Daisy in her arms, her expression brightening as if a lamp had been lit inside her, and Neely Kate hummed as she finished her hair.

As the time for the ceremony crept closer, Neely Kate became a bundle of nerves, worried we wouldn't be ready in time. Worried that everything wouldn't be perfect. I kept reassuring her that it would all be fine, that Joe and I would come out of it married regardless of anything that went wrong, and she finally put her hand on her hip and blurted out, "How can you be so calm?"

I smiled. "After everything we've been through, Neely Kate, this is nothing."

"This is your *wedding*, Rose," she said, with an exasperated look. "It's only the most important day of your life."

"No," I said, with a knowing smile, "the most important day of my life was the day I saw myself dead."

She shuddered. "Don't even say that."

But it was true. Everything had changed that day at the DMV. My life, which hadn't been much of a life back then, had expanded to include so much good and so much bad, it was busting at the seams with it. But it was like James had said. I wouldn't give it up for anything, because the journey here had brought so many people to me. It had brought me so much love.

Joe arrived with Hope, Mikey, and Muffy at around ten so I could nurse the baby and get her ready. He and Mikey changed and then took Muffy outside to welcome the guests.

And just like that, it was time. Neely Kate and I were gathered in the kitchen with the kids, looking out the window at the guests, seated in their white folding chairs, and Jonah, standing stood under the elegant wooden arch Joe had made for Neely Kate and Jed's wedding. Joe stood beside him, Jed a couple of steps to his left, holding Daisy.

Then the music began to play—our cue—and we sent Ashley and Mikey out the door, Mikey skipping a little with excitement as he held Muffy's leash.

Ashley scattered flower petals in the grass, and Mikey tried to keep up with Muffy as she ran straight to Joe.

It was Neely Kate's turn to enter the procession next, but she stopped short of opening the door. Looking deep into my eyes, she said, "You are a beautiful bride, Rose, and you deserve a beautiful life. Dora would be so proud of you."

I glanced down at Hope, who was cradled in my arms, before looking back up at her. "Thank you."

She kissed my cheek, then walked out the door, leaving me and Hope alone.

After Neely Kate joined Ashley in front of the arch, the music changed, and I carried Hope out the door, both of us moving toward our future.

It struck me that Neely Kate was right. Most brides were nervous, but I wasn't. Then again, Joe had proven himself to me time and time again. He'd been there in good times and bad. He was my partner in all ways, the kind of man who would change a diaper but also pin me to a wall to pleasure me. The kind of man who would always, always be there for me and for our children.

As I walked toward him, I did so with a full heart and a huge smile. My heart and my life were intertwined with Joe Simmons, and they always would be.

Joe watched me, beaming and with tears in his eyes. The sun hit his hair, his copper highlights glowing.

I handed Hope to Neely Kate, then turned to Joe.

He took my hands and pulled me to him, staring deeply into my eyes.

"You are the most beautiful woman in the world, Rose Gardner, and I'm so grateful you're about to be my wife."

I laughed with tears of my own. "And that will be the last time you ever call me that." Then I added, "Just to be clear, I meant my name, not wife."

Everyone laughed with us, and it felt so good to be surrounded by love and happiness. By this life we had built.

My mind and heart were so wrapped up in Joe, in the commitment we were making, that the ceremony itself passed in a blur. We'd written our own vows, but I completely forgot mine. All I could think about was that I couldn't wait to spend the rest of my life with him, so I told him so.

When the ceremony was over, Joe grabbed my face with both hands and kissed me with a tenderness and passion that stole my breath. Jonah laughed. "Um. I think we missed a step. I *now* pronounce you man and wife."

"That fits," Joe said with a grin. "We're used to doin' things backward."

Jonah graced us with a huge smile and held out his hands. "Now go and live a rich and joyful life."

This had all started when I'd had that vision and seen myself dead, and part of me was tempted to force one now, to make sure Joe and I had that rich and joyful life, but I stopped myself. Life was messy and chaotic and full of surprises, both the good and the bad. I wanted to experience it to its fullest, not sneak to the back of the book to see how it ended. Sometimes the uncertainty of life was what made it so beautiful.

So I smiled up at Joe, the adoration and love in his eyes stealing my breath away, and I took a leap of faith. It may have all started when I saw myself dead, but now it was time to live.

And what a beautiful life it would be.

The End

Acknowledgments

Wow. I can't believe we're here at the end.

Twenty-Eight and a Half Wishes was the first book I published, the third book I completed. While my beta readers LOVED Rose, agents did not, so I indie published it myself in July, 2011.

Rose has come a long way since that first book. In fact, I wrote it as a standalone. I had no intentions of making it a series until I pitched the book to an agent at a conference while it was still in revision. She liked my "elevator pitch" and told me to come up with plots for three more books. Then she asked me to send her the book.

I never heard from her again.

But that's okay, because I truly believe Rose wouldn't have been as successful if a publisher had bought it. And it wouldn't have two series, a companion series (Neely Kate), and a spin-off series (Carly Moore).

Rose Gardner has sixteen books, four novellas, several bonus/short pieces, eleven *USA Today*, six *New York Times*, and three *Wall Street Journal* titles. She's been translated into Turkish, Czechoslovakian, Croatian, German, and Lithuanian. I have given away over two million copies of *Twenty-Eight and Half Wishes*, and the Rose

Gardner Mystery and Investigations series have sold 1.8 million copies. *Twenty-Nine and a Half Reasons* has sold nearly three hundred thousand.

She's had a good run.

But all good things must come to an end.

I always said I'd write Rose until I got tired of writing her or she stopped growing, but the truth is I felt like it was time to let her have her happy ending.

They say you should always walk away leaving readers wanting more, and some would argue she went on too long. I think she's ended just right.

I know some of my readers only read Rose, and I've come to terms with that. If you're one of those readers, I hope you try one of my other series. Carly Moore is a good place to go next, especially since she was introduced in Rose's world. If you liked the humor of the first Rose books, then you might enjoy my Summer Butler Mystery series or one of my rom-com series, Asheville Brewing, Bachelor Brotherhood, or my Wedding Pact series.

Many people helped me bring this series to life, but Rose wouldn't have come this far without my developmental editor, Angela Polidoro. She came on board with *Thirty and a Half Excuses,* and she's edited almost every book I've written since. It helped that she became invested in Rose's world too. She's given me cherished advice. Shared my joy when *Thirty-Three and a Half Complications* hit the *New York Times* list. Comforted me when I was overwhelmed and upset by readers. And when I told her that *It All Falls Down* was the last Rose book, she assured me that it was a good time to end, and my career wouldn't be over.

I've said that Rose is over for now, and I *do* have plan for if I ever get the urge to revive her, but honestly, I doubt I will. I'd like to imagine Rose and Joe out on their farm with Hope, Ashley, and Mikey, and at least one more baby, possibly two. I might write some bonus content from time to time and include it in my newsletter, but we'll see about that too.

I hope Rose has given you as much joy as she's given me. Thank you for taking this journey with me.

Printed in Great Britain
by Amazon